I0772306

UNDISCOVERED

VELLORIA
CELESTARA MOUNTAINS
WHISPERING FOREST
FROZEN PLAINS
EMBERWYN
STYGIAN HOLLOWS

"To Olivia, for her unwavering friendship and support, and most of all, for her incredible perseverance through life's relentless pursuit to suffocate the human soul.

And to all the outcasts, misfits, and dreamers—may you never become what the world tells you to be, but instead, rediscover and embrace who you are."

(Book 1 of the "Eyeless Awakened" Series)

ECHOES OF VELLORIA

THE SOULWEAVER'S LEGACY

Robert King

CONTENTS

PROLOGUE

I move through the woods surrounding the village but my heart thunders in my chest, its sound amplified by the quiet of the night. Snowflakes drift lazily from the sky, laying their icy kisses upon my eyelashes, transforming the world into a monochrome tapestry of grays and whites, tinged with blue as dusk sets in. Shadows stretch long from the trees, draping my path in darkness, while their branches create unsettling sounds. The ground, hidden under a layer of leaves and twigs, renders each step uncertain as the cold wind lashes at my face, almost urging me to turn back. *I shouldn't be out here after nightfall*, I think. But the desire inside pushes me deeper into the forest's embrace.

The trees eventually give way to a massive, obsidian barrier standing thirty meters tall, topped with sharp metal spikes. The Rim marks the edge of our known world. Those who have lived in the village for the longest years sometimes speak of the mysteries beyond. They speak of dangers hidden on the other side, but mostly what they tell is lore.

I can see faint electricity snaking over the barrier's surface, and the air fills with the sharp smell of ozone mixed with my own fear. As I approach, the electricity on the wall becomes sharper but my curiosity about what lies beyond the Rim overpowers me. I can almost feel something beckoning me from the other side.

Inside me, an unusual and warm energy begins to awaken. It manifests as a bright orange light around my fingertips, resembling small, dancing flames. As I lift my hand in amazement, the Rim seems to react. The intimidating electric glow starts to fade, revealing a complex pattern that appears to synchronize with the energy emanating from my hand. It feels like I am deciphering runes of old. The energy meets the stone, and a light dazzles through the darkness. A pattern emerges, its lines forming a detailed mosaic of light and dark. There is silence around me as the last line of the pattern completes this intricate design.

Then, with a sound as gentle as a whisper, a section of the wall vanishes, opening a gateway. Beyond it stretches a terrain dominated by lifeless trees. The Stygian Hollows. A world of twilight and mysteries, illuminated by the orange glow, that now beckons me. In this mist-covered, forbidding territory, I witness the Eyeless. Creatures that seem to emerge from the darkest corners of nightmares. They stand taller than any human; their shapes are distorted, swathed in layers of black, sinewy flesh that absorbs the light around them. Gaping voids fill the spaces where their eyes should be, and their movements are smooth and unsettling, reminiscent of ghosts gliding under the moonlight. Their long limbs brush against the ground as they draw nearer. One of them moves toward the opening, head tilted curiously. Its eyeless voids seem to bore into me, suffocating my soul in an icy grip that leaves me gasping for air.

Suddenly, the world erupts in violent tremors. The earth beneath me convulses with powerful quakes that slice through the base of the Rim. It splits open, unleashing deep fissures that sprawl across the terrain.

Panic engulfs me. The structure that had long served as a bastion for our land is falling. A primal urge to flee clouds my thoughts. I turn and run. Each step forward feels as though I am battling against a force determined to pull me back into the unfolding turmoil. The Rim succumbs to ruin around me. The formidable stones that had fortified the barrier plummet in a perilous cascade, threatening all in their path.

Amidst this havoc, a new terror strikes when one of the Eyeless latches onto my shoulder from behind. Its touch, icy and solid, extinguishes any flicker of hope.

I suddenly wake up, struggling to breathe in the safety of my own bed. My heart beats rapidly, still affected by the intensity of the nightmare. The gentle light of dawn has come in through the window. But it does little to ease the memory of the dream lingering in my mind. I lie back, allowing myself to recover from the night's scare. I can't shake the feeling that something has changed.

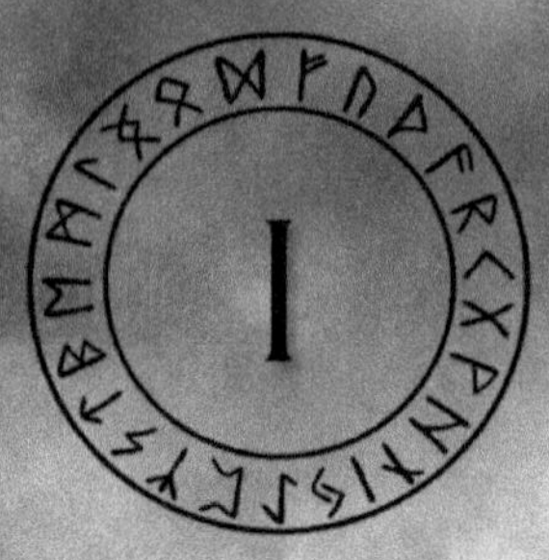

THE SHADOW'S HEART

Emberwyn awakens with a chorus of sounds that greet the dawn. Voices of birds perched in the ancient oaks weave through the cool, misty air. Their calls are a comforting reminder of another day in our village as I step out of my thatched-roof cottage. The damp earth under my bare feet carries the promise of a new day, and the scent of dew-kissed grass hangs in the air, mingling with the earthy aroma of the nearby forest. It's a fragrance that fills my senses, grounding me in the familiar.

Around me, the villagers bustle with the energy of daily life. The blacksmith's hammer rings out in a rhythmic cadence, forging steel with an artistry born of generations. The clucking of hens echoes from the nearby coop, punctuated by the occasional crow of a rooster announcing the hour. The tantalizing scent of freshly baked bread wafts from the baker's shop and mingles with the smoky aroma of a wood fire burning steadily in the communal hearth, where villagers gather to share stories, laughter, and the warmth of companionship.

Taking in all the comforting sounds and scents of Emberwyn, I pause for a moment. My gaze is drawn to the imposing wall that protrudes above the distant trees. Even in the light of day, its surface is veiled in darkness as it isolates our land from the rest of the world. I can feel the low, ominous thrumming that comes from that wall. It tells me the story of my father Easton's disappearance. As the commander of the Great Battalion of Emberwyn, he was leading a small patrol through the eastern forest near the base of the rim.

The screams of villagers still echo in my head. My sister Lili grabbed my shawl with her small iron fists. She had just turned six, and that day we were supposed to celebrate her name day. Instead, I quickly ushered her into the cottage and told her to stay there until I returned.

I ran into the forest to find my father. The images of what I found near the eastern rim still haunt me. My father's soldiers, mutilated. Their bodies were scattered in pieces across the open snow.

I searched for hours looking for my father without any luck. He wasn't there. I would have believed he had just left for the forbidden lands if I hadn't found the hilt of his ancient blade protruding from the snow. The subtle glint from the sun on the steel blade reinforced a truth that he would never have left his blade willingly.

The blade was a study in contrasts: one half impeccably smooth, honed to a deadly sharpness, while the other half was broken and jagged, as if it had been shattered in a fierce battle. It spoke of violence and history, a remnant of a past that whispered of great turmoil. Strips of worn leather wrapped around the hilt felt smooth and familiar under my fingers. Burned into the leather was a strange symbol, intricate and mysterious. Holding the blade in that moment, I had felt a connection to my father, to his unspoken stories. It was a gift passed down from his father, and his father's father before him. A blade that I now kept locked away in a chest of his belongings. I never understood why he had brought the blade with him that day, or why he left it alone in the snow.

"Asha!" The sudden call of my name jolts me back to the present, and I turn to see Lili bounding towards me, her hair a wild cascade of brown waves dancing in the wind's playful embrace. Her youthful charm is infectious, and a smile instinctively spreads across my face. "Look what I found," she exclaims, her voice bubbling with excitement as she opens her small hands to reveal her treasures.

Kneeling down to her level, I brush my white braids back over my shoulder and take her hands gently in mine, examining her find. Nestled in her palms are several smooth, perfectly-sized stones. "These are impressive, Lili," I say, my eyes meeting hers. "What will you use them for?"

Her face lights up with the kind of pure joy only a child could possess. "They're perfect for my sling," she declares proudly. I had crafted the sling for her after weeks of her persistent pleading. Despite her young age, she has shown an unexpected aptitude with it, her aim growing more accurate each day.

I smile, my heart swelling with pride and a touch of amusement. "You're becoming quite the marksman," I tease gently. Then, struck with an idea, I reach into my leather pouch and pull out a small rabbit pelt, soft and well-cured. "How about we ask Amara to craft a pouch for them?"

Lili's eyes, so much like our mother's—deep and brown as the forest floor—widen in delight. The thought of having her own customized pouch for her sling stones seems to thrill her. "Really?" she gasps, her excitement overflowing.

"Yes, really," I chuckle. "Go on, take it to Amara. Tell her I'll come by later with her payment." Amara is the best seamstress in Emberwyn and a good friend of the family. She rarely accepts coin payment for anything but will accept food and materials, and I have both for her today. Her husband was a loyal soldier under my father's command. He, too, fell at the eastern rim, leaving her to shutter her shop in the wake of his death. Those were somber days that cast a shadow over us all, yet amidst the gloom, my mother, sister, and I dedicated ourselves to the task of delivering food and medicine to each family.

Amara has never spoken of the tragedy of that day. Nevertheless, I saw the gratitude in her eyes, a silent acknowledgment of the solace my family brought to her in her darkest hours. The act of kindness was a beacon in her storm and she eventually began sewing and telling stories again.

With a squeal of delight and a quick, affectionate hug that squeezes the breath from me, Lili dashes off, her unruly brown hair trailing behind her like a banner in the wind. I watch her go, a fond smile on my lips, thinking how I need to braid that wild mane before it becomes a tangled mess. In that moment, with Lili's laughter echoing in the air, the burdens of my own world seem to lift, replaced by the simple, infectious joy of my little sister's happiness.

As Lili vanishes into the distance, her excitement still echoing around me, I rise and dust off my knees. My mother must be waiting for me at the Obsidian Monolith. I sigh to myself heavily. The morning is too nice to spend inside a musky monolith. I don't want to go, but if I don't, my mother would have my hide. Reluctantly I turn to walk towards the village's core.

The comforting sounds and aromas of Emberwyn wrap around me as I draw near to the monolith. It stands not merely as a marker but as a sanctum.

Touching the obsidian wall, I feel its smooth, cold surface under my fingers. It is adorned with ancient symbols that tell the story of our village and the natural laws that govern it. This is where the village elders gather for vital decisions and the preservation of ancient rites.

Having spent my life in the shadow of the monolith, its presence has always been a profound force in my life. Though I've only caught snippets of the assemblies within.

"There you are, Asha," calls out my mother, drawing my gaze and prompting a smile from me. The aura of serene authority she embodies never fails to impress me. Her brown hair cascades in soft waves, adorned with metal pendants. Her eyes appear to carry the secrets of our ancestors, but what captivates me most are the ancient tribal tattoos etched into her skin. These markings are more than mere adornments; they represent the journey of her soul. Each design tells stories of challenges faced and the wisdom acquired. With every change in her expression, the tattoos seem to dance, as though alive, manifesting her profound bond with the spiritual realm. These are the markings I am destined to receive, signifying the onset of my reign over Emberwyn. "Come, darling. There's much we need to discuss before your initiation tomorrow."

As we proceed, her presence merges authority with care. The pendant around her neck symbolizes her role in the high council, and mirrors the complexity of the traditions she upholds. To me, she transcends her title of High Priestess; she is my mentor, my mother. In her, I witness the balance and harmony I aspire to achieve. She stands as the custodian of our history and the guiding light for our future, and within her steady gaze, I catch a glimpse of the path that lies before me. Then my thoughts begin to drift elsewhere.

"Mother, may I... ask you something?" My voice carries a blend of hope and nervousness. A part of me harbors a slender hope for a different outcome this time, while another, more resigned part of me, prepares me to face the usual answer I get every time I've asked the question.

My mother stops and sighs heavily before facing me. Her ring-adorned hands reach out to hold mine, and her deep, probing eyes search mine for the hidden turmoil behind my question. A spark of frustration ignites within me; she must know the reason this question plagues me.

"I know, Mother, we've discussed this," I persist, the words laden with gravity. "But I must know the truth about Father. He wasn't found with his men at the east rim." Memories whirl within me, and I scour them for any overlooked detail.

Her face tightens, her gaze fixing on mine with unwavering intensity. "Asha, your father was the most courageous man I knew," she starts, her voice is solid but laced with sorrow. "When his body remained undiscovered, I dispatched search parties into the forest, yet they returned empty-handed. There was no sign of him." I steel myself against the direction of her words. "The Eyeless took him to the Hollows. He won't return. You need to come to terms with this, for your own sanity."

"Mother, I..." I begin, but she interrupts, her voice now imbued with an unyielding firmness.

"No, Asha. You must cease this fixation on what has passed." Her gaze, forceful and commanding, demands my attention. "Tomorrow, you ascend as High Priestess, with me at your side as counselor. You need to exhibit strength and clarity. How can you guide our people if you remain ensnared by your personal struggles?" To challenge her is to tread into the treacherous unknown, akin to venturing deep into the Stygian Hollows. That temperament is not my most favorite to take with her so I withdraw.

"I understand, Mother." The admission leaves a bitter taste in my mouth. "I won't ask again." She puts her arms around me, but her embrace only amplifies the frustration in me. How can she dismiss the memory of my father, her partner, with such ease? Within her hold, I yearn to flee her blatant disregard for my feelings.

"Good. Come, there is something I wish to show you." Mixed feelings of respect and irritation towards her stir within me. Her commitment to our people is undeniable, yet her refusal to confront the mystery of my father's fate irks me.

"Asha," she whispers, her voice soft yet carrying a weight of authority, "you are about to experience a privilege reserved for the High Priestess, a secret kept from the many and revealed to only a chosen few." With a measured movement, she reaches out, her palm making contact with the monolith's cool exterior. In response, the stone surface subtly shifts, greeting her touch with a slight shimmer, as if recognizing her right to unveil its secrets.

The ground beneath us trembles softly, and in utter silence, a section of the Monolith moves, revealing a hidden entrance.

My mother's voice, tender yet solemn, guides me forward into the dimly lit recess. "This is the heart of our heritage, Asha."

The walls of the chamber leading away from the entrance are adorned with symbols that speak of the secrets of Emberwyn's past. Accessible only to the High Priestess and her intimate circle, the space I am stepping into is distinct from the ordinary world. I can feel the air, cool and motionless, suspending time. Staring further into the dimness of the chamber, I realize that once inside the monolith, you might even lose your way navigating the labyrinth of chambers that burrow away into the earth.

Mother continues to speak, her gaze reflecting the chamber's subtle glow. "To assume the mantle of High Priestess is to weave yourself into a legacy that spans centuries." I think about the gravity of the role I am about to undertake. "You must be prepared to embrace the entirety of this responsibility—the visible and the invisible, the revelations and the mysteries." I nod, my mind swirling with a mix of emotions.

As the heavy door seals us within, she guides me deeper into the chamber, leading me to a smaller room concealed behind a closed stone door. There, on a pedestal, lies an object that immediately captures my attention.

"Is that…?" I stare at the gold surface of the object, its brilliance contrasted by the intricate network of black veins that appear to pulse with life. At its center, a red symbol is emblazoned—a mark that awakens within me memories of bedtime stories filled with valor, sacrifice, and the perennial struggle between light and shadow. Awe and apprehension fill me. "This is the actual Shadow's Heart? I always thought it was just a tale."

"It is real," my mother confirms, her eyes mirroring a trace of sorrow. "Our ancestors crafted the Shadow's Heart deep within the Whispering Forest, imbuing it with the forest's protective essence to serve as a bastion against peril." She explains, picking up the artifact and rotating it in her hands.

She recounts the epic battle against the Legion of the Embers and their army of Eyeless warriors. "During that battle, the Shadow's Heart cast a protective shroud over Velloria. It summoned a veil that repelled the encroaching evil, though only for a time." She pauses, and her usually steady hands tremble slightly. Her gaze is distant as if entranced by it.

"Mother?" I whisper. She snaps back to her thoughts, looking at me with a smile.

"I…" Her voice quivers slightly, then she continues. "The Heart bore the brunt of the conflict, its surface fracturing under the strain of combating such potent evil. This dispersion of its power not only forced the Eyeless to retreat into the shadows but also cemented the Heart as a symbol of Velloria's enduring spirit. The Heart was lost to the annals of time following the battle, though, the fates intervened many years later. A refugee from Velloria, a young woman, unearthed the fragmented relic within the Stygian Hollows. Though, with Velloria now in ruin, she sought to build a new land. That land is Emberwyn. Despite the Heart's compromised state, it held enough power to construct the Rim and this monolith." Her touch is gentle on the artifact, tracing lines of history with her fingertips before she hands it to me.

As I hold the Shadow's Heart, experiencing its cool, vibrant energy, I struggle to grasp the full scale of my inheritance. The Heart extends beyond a mere object; it embodies a piece of our history, a chapter of conflict and resilience that has defined our village's core. Now, it rests in my grasp, a beacon that has endured the darkest of wars. My thoughts wander to her difficulty in telling the story. Her distant gaze and quivering lips. Was she the young woman she was referring to? I open my mouth to ask, but my words are interrupted by hers.

"I know that this is a considerable amount to absorb all at once," my mother's voice flows softly, her words threading through the cold, spectral halls of the Monolith as we make our way toward the exit. "But remember, Asha, I stand by to aid you, to guide you along the right path." The warmth of her support is tangible, but it bears the weight of the complex challenges that lie ahead. The right path, I ponder, seems like an intricate labyrinth, where simple guidance may prove hard to untangle my looming future of High Priestess.

"Thank you, Mother," I say. I lean in, pressing a soft kiss to her cheek, even as a whirlpool of questions swirls inside me.

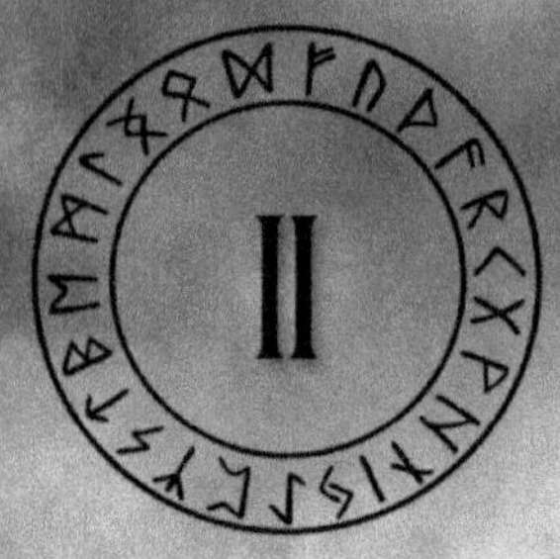

ORDER OF VELLORIA

Exiting the shadowed confines of the Monolith, I step into the blinding sunlight. I shield my eyes until they adjust. Even with the sights and sounds of daily life enveloping me, a gnawing sense of unrest settles within me. The lore of the Shadow's Heart clings to my thoughts. It is a mystery that my mother, for reasons unspoken, seemed hesitant to fully unravel.

The smell of fresh loaves from the bakery calls my name as I navigate through the village, compelling me to quench the devilish cries of my stomach. As I move toward the warm, welcoming glow of the bakery, a familiar voice calls out from behind.

"Asha! Wait up!" Nico's voice slices through the tranquil morning, stopping me in my tracks. I turn around, my lips already curving into a smile at the sight of him bounding toward me. His approach is as spirited as the first rays of dawn filtering through the dense foliage above a forest, casting a dappled dance of light across the trails. His hair, as untamed and jet black as a raven's wing, seems to bristle with his boundless energy, each strand defying gravity in a declaration of his inherent wildness. And his eyes, those eyes—they sparkle with a mischievous gleam that has been their hallmark since our younger days.

I am instantly transported back to a cherished memory, one that has nestled itself deep within the recesses of my heart. We were children then, no taller than the waist-high grass swaying in the meadows surrounding our village. It was a day much like today, with the sun playing hide and seek among the clouds, casting shadows that danced upon the ground like spirited phantoms. Nico had concocted one of his infamous plans, a treasure hunt of sorts, with a map crudely drawn in charcoal on a scrap of parchment. With the seriousness of seasoned adventurers, we set out, our laughter echoing through the air as we navigated our imagined dangers. The "treasure" we sought was nothing more than an old, weathered stone, but to us, it was as precious as any jewel. When we finally discovered it, hidden beneath the twisted roots of an ancient oak, Nico's eyes had lit up with triumph, that same spark that I see in him now.

His laughter, as open and sincere as the daylight itself, is soothing and joyful all at once.

"Figured you'd be heading this way," he says, closing the distance between us. "The allure of Mrs. Dahlia's pastries is too much for you, isn't it?"

A chuckle breaks from me. "You've got me figured out," I admit. "Though, by the look of anticipation on your face, I'd say the bakery's charms have ensnared you just as much."

"Absolutely. Who could resist the simple pleasure of a fresh honey loaf?" he says, his smile growing. "But honestly, I was really just hoping to run into you. It feels like forever since we've had the chance to sit and catch up." His words are a gentle nudge about the swift passage of days that often leave little room for leisurely chats.

Nico's words touch me. Time indeed slips away from us, especially with his days packed, splitting time between assisting his father with the horses and aiding the Outhwaites in rebuilding their lives after a sudden lightning calamity devastated their home last month.

"It really has been too long." I feel a mix of gratitude and comfort at the idea of pausing life's relentless pace, if only for a while, to reconnect with my best friend.

Crossing the threshold of the bakery, we step into a world filled with the rich aromas of baking dough and sweet confections, a sensory welcome that instantly lifts my spirits. Amidst the rush of daily life and the looming shadows of duties, I realize just how deeply I've missed sharing these simple pleasures with Nico. His presence always reminds me of more carefree times.

I can't help but smile at the sight of Ms. Dahlia, bustling around her kitchen with a wooden spoon in hand.

"Good morning, Ms. Dahlia," I greet her, leaning against the counter. "How's the bakery faring these days?" She looks up from her dough with a sprinkle of flour dusting her cheeks.

"I was wondering when you would happen by," she smiles, "Business is steady, although there's been a bit of trouble getting enough ingredients from trade this month. Nothing to worry yourself over. The honey loaves will always be here." She smiles and uncovers two loaves, glazed in dripping honey. I set a silver shilling on the counter and watch her brows furrow slightly.

"Now, child. You know I won't take your coin," she laughs, turning back to kneed dough. I leave it there anyways.

With a honey loaf each in hand, we find ourselves a quiet corner. The warmth of the bread as we tear into it brings a momentary sense of normalcy. Here, in the company of my oldest friend, my fellow adventurer, the complexities of life beyond the bakery's embrace recede. Nico's laughter momentarily eases the weight of the foreboding future.

"So, Asha, how are the preparations for your initiation going?" Nico leans in, his voice dropping to a conspiratorial whisper and eyes alight with the thrill of shared secrets. "You know, there are whispers about the Monolith—that it transforms people into monsters." I can't help but let a small smile break through, but I respond with an exaggerated roll of my eyes.

"Actually, you're onto something. I've already been inside," I say, now keeping my expression neutral as I observe his shift from amusement to astonishment. "This morning, my mother revealed the chamber where they keep all the monster parts." For a moment, he stares at me, his eyes narrowing as he tries to sift through my words for truth. Finally we both break into laughter over the sheer ridiculousness of it all.

Just as our laughter hits its crescendo, a voice, both familiar and unwelcome to my ears, slices the air. "I doubt anything is that funny," Elias chimes in from behind me, prompting a simultaneous eye roll from Nico and me. Elias, always a thorn in my side, has this uncanny ability to appear at just the wrong times. He advances, his tall, lanky figure moving with a clunky elegance that somehow contributes to his distinct allure. His short, wavy white hair almost sparkles in the subdued light, contrasting sharply with his deep brown eyes, which flicker with amusement and a hint of challenge. Those eyes, ever probing, seem to capture the essence of any situation with unsettling precision.

"I've heard that for tomorrow's ritual, they'll have to slice open your arm and let the blood fill a goblet." He is unable to resist contributing his own twist to the village gossip.

"Enough, Elias," I shoot back, my voice echoing my annoyance. He casually takes a seat next to us, unbothered. His ghostly white hair and pale complexion catches the sunlight streaming through the bakery window, casting him in an almost otherworldly light. "All these stories are complete fabrications. Nobody is cutting my arm open tomorrow," I say, aiming to dispel the latest rumor before it spirals further. Yet, despite the outlandishness of these tales, a part of me enjoys the attention.

"Believe what you wish, Asha," he retorts as he nonchalantly snags a piece of my honey loaf, lifting it in a mock toast to an invisible audience. "But we both sense there's more hidden within those walls than we see. Consider me your lookout."

"My lookout?" I scoff. "Since when did you do that without wanting some sort of reward?" His face briefly adopts a look of mock hurt, showcasing his flair for drama.

"Tough words, Asha. Though, there is a bit of truth in them, isn't there? So, what's the prize for me this time?" He casually takes a bite of the pilfered bread.

"Nothing at all," Nico and I say together, our shared laughter nearly spilling over as we exchange glances, fighting to keep our composure.

"Fine," Elias gives in with an exaggerated sigh of defeat. "I'll just have to satisfy myself with the excitement of your grand initiation and the bloodletting." His words, laced with humor, aim to stir a reaction, and he gets it.

"Enough," I declare, causing him to halt momentarily. I've reached my limit with his interruptions disturbing mine and Nico's peaceful moment.

"Anyway, I'm off to find Skylar. Thinking of seeing if she's down for some archery practice," he says.

"Have you managed to finally hit a target? You should trade it for stitching or something," I retort. Instead of being bothered by my prodding, he laughs.

"Might as well be shooting with my eyes closed! But hey, maybe it'll improve by the time I find her." He gestures towards my loaf of bread, now notably diminished, and I wave my hand in assent, my shoulders lifting in a shrug. It's not as if he hasn't already claimed half of it. With a broad smile, he grabs the loaf and offers a mock bow before exiting the bakery.

"You know, I kind of worry about him," Nico comments. Elias, a longtime friend to both of us, hails from a humble background. Orphaned young, he was raised by his grandmother Amara, the storyteller and seamstress residing in a modest cottage at the town's edge. I can't help but think he's yet to come to terms with his parents' death, masking his sorrow with that obnoxious demeanor.

"He's always alright in the end," I respond. "He manages."

"Alright, spill it. I demand knowledge of the Monolith. Don't skip anything," Nico leans in, his eagerness sparking my own. With a gesture both generous and enticing, he offers up half of his honey loaf, silently forging a pact of full disclosure. I hesitate, considering the depth of what I should tell him. But, as I ponder my hesitations, I acknowledge that if there's anyone I can trust fully, it's Nico. So, I begin to share everything about the Monolith's interior, the ambiance that surrounds it, and the enchanting but ominous aura of the Shadow's Heart.

"The Shadow's Heart is inside the monolith?" he whispers, a mix of awe. His fascination with ancient legends is evident. "Just imagining it... I must see it." His large, brown eyes gaze at me with longing, and I return his look with my best 'not a chance' expression.

"Perhaps..." The word escapes me, teetering on the edge of caution and impulse. No, it's far too risky. I couldn't put him in that position.

"Come on, Ash," he urges, his excitement igniting the air.

My determination wavers, and in a surge of bold recklessness, I whisper, "Maybe I can arrange for you to see it, just a quick glimpse, before my initiation tomorrow night." His face transforms, lit by a thrilling mix of joy and astonishment, as though he's been offered a key to a hidden realm.

"However, we absolutely can't be seen," I warn, the weight of our potential venture pressing heavily upon me. "If we are discovered—"

"We'll be fine," he interjects with confidence. "A quick look and I'll disappear, as if I were never there. No one will know." His look, burning with the excitement of forbidden ventures, tempts me into the realm of the unthinkable.

"Alright," I say, my voice carrying a trace of reluctance, "during the preparations tomorrow, I'll find you." Excitement dances in his eyes at my consent while a tangle of emotions tightens within me. What am I thinking? This isn't just any secret to be casually revealed to anyone. But he's not just anyone; he's my best friend. Nevertheless, the burden of my choice weighs on me, dimming the sweetness of the honey loaf we're sharing. After a few more laughs and light conversation, Nico departs for his home to attend to his father's horses and I'm left in solitude, haunted by the precarious journey I've agreed to embark upon.

Navigating the well-trodden paths of our village, guilt nibbles at my conscience for entangling him in the dense mesh of ancient mysteries. The thought of subjecting him to potential dangers tightens a vice around my heart. Although, Nico's insight and viewpoint are exactly what I need as I navigate the storm of duties threatening to engulf me.

My feet, moving of their own accord, bring me to the threshold of Amara's cottage. A wave of serenity sweeps over me, momentarily displacing my internal strife. Amara's dwelling is cradled by wildflowers and ivy, seamlessly integrated into the embrace of the wilderness. The door emits a gentle creak as I step inside, and I'm immediately cocooned in the soothing aromas of herbs and ancient timber. Her home unfolds like a treasury of marvels; shelves brimming with age-old scrolls and enigmatic relics, walls draped with tapestries narrating ancient epics, and a hearth alive with welcoming flames. Sunbeams pierce through stained-glass windows, scattering a dance of colors throughout the space, while the soft drone of a spinning wheel intertwines with the delicate strains of a flute from afar. The atmosphere is laden with the enchantment of myriad legends, each nook of the cottage whispering echoes of forgotten eras. In the sanctuary of Amara's abode, the world outside fades, beckoning me to lose myself in the seduction of history and myth.

"Welcome, child." Amara's voice, soothing and gentle, fills the room as she emerges from her bedroom, her hand sweeping aside the large bear skin that serves as a door. My father's gift to her from one of his hunting expeditions. It brings a surge of warmth to my heart each time I lay eyes on it. "I've just completed Lili's pouch. See for yourself," she says, her smile radiant across her time-softened features as she places the small pouch on the table before settling into her rocking chair by the fire. I pick it up, my smile mirroring hers.

"It's absolutely perfect," I say with a smile. "Lili will love it." After a brief pause, I reach into my bag, pulling out a small token of appreciation. "And for you, I've brought these as a thank you." I carefully unveil a modest sack, its contents— a rabbit caught last evening and a collection of herbs from the forest's edge—wrapped in paper and tied with twine. I set them on the table.

Her smile doesn't waver as her attention drifts back to the fire's mesmerizing dance. The essence of my gifts seems irrelevant to her. In the twilight of her years, she finds joy not in material offerings but in the mere company of someone.

"Amara, may I ask a question?" I find a spot on the rug, embracing the warmth of the fire in a cross-legged seat. "Do you know of the Shadow's Heart?" Her eyes light up in the fire's glow, turning to me with a look of deep anticipation, as if my question has unlocked an archive of cherished memories.

As I settle into the cozy embrace of Amara's home, engulfed by the scent of sage and the venerable aroma of old parchment, she leans in. It's evident she's on the cusp of divulging a tale, one unraveled from the fabrics of ancient history.

"As it happens," she begins, her voice soft yet carrying, reminiscent of a song borne upon the breeze.

"Many centuries past, during a night cloaked in shadows, the heavens wept with stars, and the earth murmured of an impending strife. It was this very night, under the tapestry of the cosmos, that Master Eolan commenced a hallowed odyssey. Guided by visions granted by the Spirits of ancient Gods, he set forth from Velloria into the untouched depths of the Celestara mountains, home to Astralith, the noble white dragon reputed to reign over the realms of land and sky.

"With a heart filled with reverence and a purpose firm in mind, Eolan journeyed to the mountains' core to create a blade of unmatched power and elegance, the Blade of Velloria. The components he carried were not merely of this earth but were celestial gifts—a sliver of star-metal, aglow with the essence of the cosmos, and the heartwood from the eldest tree in the Whispering Forest, a vigilant guardian that had overseen the land through millennia.

"His pilgrimage persisted for two moons, until at last, he arrived at the pinnacle where the terrestrial and the celestial converge, and there he stood before Astralith. This white dragon, a being of legend, gazed upon him with eyes brimming with the wisdom of millennia. From the dragon's breath emerged a flame of celestial light and supreme might, a blaze that surpassed mortal comprehension.

"With hands both steady and filled with reverence, Eolan brought the celestial components into the embrace of Astralith's ethereal flame. Instead of consuming them, the dragon's breath wove enchantments into the metal and wood, imbuing them with a formidable magic. The metal gleamed with the radiance of myriad stars, the wood vibrated with the ancient forest's life force, and together, they gave birth to a blade that struck a perfect balance between the heavens and the earth. Crafted in this hallowed forge, atop peaks that grazed the skies, the Blade of Velloria came into being, a melding of power and wisdom, destined to echo through time." Amara's voice, now a whisper imbued with deep respect, draws me closer.

"The Blade of Velloria was a spectacle of wonder, possessed of powers both grand and gentle. It could cut through the deepest shadows, mend the most grievous wounds, and despite its formidable power, it was as light as if it had a spirit of its own. Yet, its might was so vast that only those of pure heart and clear intent, untouched by greed or spite, could wield it without being overwhelmed." She pauses, her hands coming together as though cradling an unseen treasure from an age long past.

"The Order of Velloria, a cadre of the most enlightened and skilled from the ancient city, were the blade's stewards and the keepers of equilibrium, ensuring the sacred weapon was never wielded for dark purposes. They were wise counselors to Velloria's rulers, steering the city through times of peace and turmoil with sagacity and clairvoyance. However," Amara's tone grows softer, venturing further into the narrative that defined Velloria's fate, "the tale of the Blade of Velloria and the Order is intertwined with the recounting of the darkest battle ever waged—the struggle against the dark Legion of Embers and their Eyeless army, a pivotal moment marked by the Shadow's Heart." I lean in, spellbound as she continues, "The Eyeless are not mere legends. They are real, conjured from the abyss by one who wielded the dark power of the Shadow's Heart."

"Wait a moment," I find myself cutting in. "Are you suggesting the Eyeless were called forth by the Shadow's Heart?" Suddenly, my mind buzzes with fresh inquiries.

"That's the tale," she confirms with a nod. "These beings are believed to be incarnations of fear, twisting minds and plunging individuals into despair. This occurred under the Order of Velloria's rule, a period marked by tranquility and abundance. However, peace often becomes a magnet for jealousy and wickedness." As she recounts the ominous day, her hands quiver slightly, her gaze lost to memory.

"It was a confrontation that pushed the Order to their limits, testing both their resilience and the blade's might. The Order, at the helm of a valiant force, met the Eyeless in battle beneath a sky fractured by sorcery and wrath. Amidst the turmoil, the Blade of Velloria emerged as a beacon of hope, its light empowering Velloria's warriors to pierce the darkness unleashed by the Eyeless. Yet," her voice drops to a hush, "in a dire move to sway the battle's course, the Eyeless' commander, Bhailer, harnessed the Shadow's Heart with a malevolent force. At the apex of their confrontation, the Blade of Velloria collided with the

Heart's dark energies. The impact was devastating." My thoughts whirl in confusion. This account diverges sharply from the version my mother shared about the Heart. Yet, my eagerness to learn more overrides my immediate need for clarity.

"What became of the Blade?" I inquire, wrapped in a growing sense of unease.

"The Blade of Velloria, overwhelmed by the Shadow's Heart's corrupting energy, fractured into three pieces. The cataclysmic release of power dispelled the Eyeless, yet it came with dire consequences. The Order of Velloria lay in ruins. The final guardian, in a last-ditch effort to keep the blade from falling into the wrong hands, hid its fragments in secret locations throughout the realm, known only to him and the ancient spirits of the woods." Amara's gaze returns to mine, her eyes shimmering with a depth of wisdom and secrets untold. "A piece of this storied blade, it is whispered, journeyed from Velloria to Emberwyn. Though many dismiss it as mere legend, a tale to stir the imaginations of the young," she says, her laughter light.

A lump forms in my throat. "But what's your belief? Could it be real?" I whisper, my question hanging in the air like a fragile thread.

With a gentle smile, she offers her final thoughts, "Within the venerable scrolls of Velloria, a prophecy is recorded, timeless and softly spoken across generations. It foretells of an heir from Velloria's blood, pure of heart and courageous as the fiercest gales. This chosen one is destined to gather the scattered shards of the blade and mend our fractured realm. Rising from the remnants of long-forgotten stories, wielding Velloria's enduring legacy, they will confront the encroaching shadows and reclaim the light."

My gaze falls to the firelight dancing on the rug beneath me, wrestling with the discrepancies between the tales. "Amara, this morning, my mother revealed the Shadow's Heart to me," I share. Her rocking halts abruptly, her gaze fixed on the flames as though my words have rooted her to the spot. "She mentioned—," I begin again, but Amara interrupts.

"Yes, child, I'm aware of what she shared with you." She faces me with a gentle smile and resumes her rocking. "Over the years, many tales have transformed, some twisted to conceal truths, casting others into shadows." Is she saying my mother lied to me? A swell of defensive disbelief rises within me. Impossible. My mother would never mislead me, least of all about this.

"My mother wouldn't deceive me," I blurt out, a flush of embarrassment coloring my cheeks, yet I stand by my conviction. She wouldn't. Amara's smile turns tender.

"There exist countless tales, Asha. The choice of which to believe rests with you." Her gaze drifts back to the fire, leaving me enveloped in a deepening unease, compelling me towards departure.

"Thank you for sharing your story," I murmur, rising. Approaching her, I clasp her hand, its coolness and the network of veins beneath her wrinkled skin reminiscent of winter's barren branches. She lifts her eyes to mine, offering a smile illuminated by the fire's glow. Her eyes, weary with age and drawing near to their journey's end, reflect back at me. I return her smile. Regardless of her story's factual accuracy, I understand the significance of cherishing it, as time will inevitably transform her presence into mere memories soon.

THE INITIATION

As the morning's gray and somber light seeps through my curtains, I instinctively pull the covers over my head, yearning for just a few more moments of sleep. Maybe sleep will oust the thoughts invading my head, but it doesn't do much good. What Amara told me the evening prior prompts a sigh from deep within me. Soon sleep eludes me, forcing me to rise with the rigidity of a marionette. I must prepare for the day ahead. Under the whirling thoughts, a significant yet understated duty calls—I have to deliver the pouch Amara crafted for my sister. After I'm dressed, I find Lili dancing near the garden outside, surrounded by the fresh snow of the season's first snowfall.

"Lili," I call. My voice is softer than I mean for it to be. She spins around, her face lighting up. Snowflakes that sparkle like tiny jewels cling to her hair. I pull Amara's exquisite handiwork from my bag.

"This is for you." I offer the pouch to her. Excitement leaps from her eyes as she takes it. She turns it over in her hands with the pure wonder of a child.

"It's so pretty, Asha," she bubbles over with enthusiasm. She dives into her pocket and pulls out her collection of smooth, round stones she found yesterday. Holding her face serious, she fills the pouch with the tiny treasures. She clutches the pouch to her chest and the brilliant smile on her face reflects the glow of the whiteness around us.

"Thank you, thank you, thank you!" She wraps me in a tight hug. A sense of calm sweeps through me as I'm filled with her warmth and innocence.

"Just make sure you keep it safe, okay?" I advise her. "Now, let's tackle your hair before it's too late."

"Do we have to?" She releases a dramatic sigh. "I'd rather practice with my sling."

"Yes, let's get your hair done quickly then you can return to your fun," I coax her. Reluctantly, she follows me into the kitchen and settles into a chair. Her attention never leaves the pouch as her little brown eyes scrutinize every detail.

"Are you looking forward to tonight's celebration?" I ask, gently untangling her hair. She nods. Tonight's rare event will be a celebration that occurs once every twenty years to honor the ascension of a new High Priestess and ruler of Emberwyn. The weight of becoming the land's ruler presses heavily on me. Am I even prepared for such a role? Is it something I even desire? This will be Lili's first experience of the celebration, and technically my second, though I was merely a newborn during my mother's initiation. It hardly counts if I cannot remember it. So I suppose it's my first as well.

"Will you always be at the Monolith like mom?" Lili's question pierces me. My mother's responsibilities have indeed kept her distant. Until now, the full impact of her absence hadn't struck me, but Lili's query lays bare the extent of that distance and its effect on her. I pause, turning her chair to face me, and kneel to meet her gaze.

"No, I won't be away all the time," I assure her. "Tonight, I may step into the role of High Priestess, but more importantly, I am your sister. You are more important to me than any duty." Her gaze searches mine, vigilant for any hint of insincerity, but she won't find it. I'm determined not to let the same responsibilities that alienated mother from her take hold of our relationship.

"Plus," I add with a light tone, "it's too dark and chilly in there, and they don't serve honey bread." A smile breaks across my face, prompting a giggle and an eager nod from her. I finish smoothing out her hair before braiding it neatly. Once done, she hops from the chair, clutching her new pouch, and dashes outside.

Lili's carefree laughter trails a melody in the air as I watch her skipping away. As soon as I turn to head back,

Skylar materializes beside me with her usual dramatic flair.

Her long, wavy brown hair whips around in the wind. Her constant, bubbling personality always seems to drown out stories of her childhood, but I can't help thinking about them every time I see her.

She had been taken gravely ill when she was three, and no healer within our walls could cure her mysterious ailment. Desperation drove her parents to venture beyond the safety of the Rim, into the unknown, in search of a legendary healer rumored to possess knowledge and abilities beyond our understanding. They left under the cover of night, and the village had woken to their absence. In their absence, Elder Lysa, who had long been a friend of their family, took it upon herself to care for her. Days turned to weeks, then months, and finally years, with no word of their fate. Skylar miraculously began to recover over time, but she was shadowed by the loss of her parents for many years, until eventually she found new life in the poetry book her mother had left her.

"Asha! You won't believe what happened," she says. Even though her smile radiates enthusiasm, I doubt if I'm going to believe what she has to say. And yet, I cannot deny that Skylar's energy could make any tale captivating.

"What's the latest news?" I inquire, offering a polite smile. Skylar, always at the heart of village whispers, has a talent for uncovering tales that range from the mildly plausible to the wildly fantastical.

She leans in with a clever curl to her mouth. "Last night, near the forest's edge, I saw a hooded figure moving through the shadows," she confides. "It was chilling."

There goes my initial resistance to what she has to share. The narrative is inviting despite my skepticism. Skylar paints a picture of the shadowy figure, and embroiders it with mystery and intrigue. "Could he be part of a secret group? Or perhaps a spy from beyond our borders?" she ponders. Her speculation ignites possibilities in my own imagination.

My usual reservation against gossip fades for a moment. Butted up against the often predictable rhythm of village life, her knack for storytelling proves once again that however far-fetched, her narratives break the captivity of the mundane.

"That's quite the story, Skylar," I respond with a laugh, finding myself unexpectedly entertained. "But I find it hard to believe that a spy could simply waltz through the rim without a scratch. Still, the mystery of it all is intriguing."

Her smile widens, "Who knows? With the world as strange as it is, anything's possible. By the way, how are you feeling about tonight's initiation?"

Her inquiry snaps me back to the present. "It's a lot to take in. But I suppose I'm as prepared as I'll ever be," I reply, infusing my voice with a semblance of assurance. Skylar offers a knowing nod.

"Are you coming with Elias?" I ask.

"Fate's no," she declares, her cheeks coloring. She then dives into a rant about Elias. "He's just... so irritating and immature. Honestly, being around him is like trying to navigate a storm without a compass. You never know what you're going to get, but you can bet it'll be a headache." I can't help but laugh, aware of their history of flipping between close friends and arch enemies from one moment to the next. I know her frustration is temporary; they'll reconcile by tomorrow. "Anyway," she swiftly changes the subject, "you're going to be amazing. The whole village is buzzing about it." Her comment takes me aback. The entire village discussing my initiation? While I doubt I share her level of confidence, her encouragement is unexpectedly comforting. I offer her a grateful smile. Our conversation meanders from mysterious figures to more everyday village topics until Skylar eventually bids farewell and departs.

Left alone, I appreciate the brief diversion from my pre-initiation nerves. Soon the unavoidable reality beckons—I must meet with my mother to begin the preparations. I cast a hopeful glance around, half-wishing for an unexpected interruption to delay the inevitable. Alas, no such diversion appears. With a resigned sigh, I step indoors to retrieve my fur skin cloak. This cloak is my father's craftsmanship. It was meticulously assembled from the pelts of majestic gray wolves that hunt in the forests encircling our village.

The cloak's clasp, simple in design yet elegant, is wrought from iron and bears the emblem of a dragon. Could it be Astralith, the legendary white dragon? My thoughts wander as my fingers gently explore the emblem's detailed craftsmanship. My father's tales often danced with dragons, mythical beings that vanished long before his time, creatures he never laid eyes upon. Draping the cloak over my shoulders, I am enveloped in a sense of my father's strength and bravery, and also a deep longing. Perhaps, he's still out there, somewhere in the vast unknown.

By the time I reach the Monolith, the sun marks noon. The thought of spending this moment preparing for tonight's initiation with my mother isn't exactly appealing. I'd far prefer to be out in the forest, checking traps under the freshly fallen snow. Just as I'm about to delay our meeting by another hour, my mother's determined approach catches my eye, effectively anchoring me in place.

"Ah, there you are, darling," she greets, her voice effortlessly calm and soothing—the opposite of my nerves. Why would she be nervous, after all? It's not her facing the ceremonial blade. Elias's wild speculation about the initiation ritual crosses my mind, and I can't help but laugh, earning a look of bewilderment from my mother.

"I haven't lost my mind, mother," I assure her with a grin. "Shall we begin?" Her look quickly shifts from confusion to a stern seriousness that could unsettle even the most formidable adversary.

"Asha, you must understand the gravity of this moment. This is your destiny—leading this land as I have," she reminds me, guiding me inside. The massive obsidian door swings shut behind us, sealing off the crisp winter air and immersing us in the Monolith's ancient, musty atmosphere. The interior's polished obsidian walls gleam in the subdued light, mimicking a starry night sky.

We walk in silence down the corridor that leads to another door. As it opens I see massive stone pillars lining the pathway. Carved with intricate runes and symbols of our ancestors, the pillars lead to the heart of the Monolith. Each step echoes softly. The faint glow of torches mounted on the walls casts dancing shadows. The shadows give life to the ancient tapestries and murals that depict the history and legends of our people.

We move deeper until the corridor opens into a vast chamber at the center of the Monolith. Here, the ceiling arches high above. One look up and a grand mosaic telling the story of the creation of Emberwyn looks back at me. In the middle of the chamber stands the ceremonial dais, a stone slab worn smooth by time. It is surrounded by a circle of old yet vibrant crystals that hum with a barely perceptible energy.

This place, a sanctuary of our heritage, feels like a bridge between the past and the future, between the earthly realm and something far more ancient and mystical. Here, in the heart of the monolith, I am acutely aware of the weight of my destiny as High Priestess. The room resonates with echoes of past rituals and the whispers of ancestors, bearing witness to the responsibility I stand on the brink of accepting. I'm not ready for this. Anxiety begins to set in.

My mother faces me, and I detect a touch of pride in her eye. Her voice is a somber echo through the sacred expanse. "Asha, this day is significant not only because it's going to be your initiation. A lot more is going to change for you, because once you accept the honor, it will challenge the core of your being."

Her statement only adds to my already smothered nerves. "I understand, Mother. But, the thought of filling your shoes and guiding our people, feels overwhelming. I have no clue where to even start."

Her hand rests reassuringly on my shoulder. "You have been preparing for this time your entire life. It unfolded in ways that might not have always been apparent to you. Leadership is about more than just making decisions. One has to know empathy and there are times when you must accept being alone."

She studies the slight frown that shows on my face. "Solitude comes with the mantle of power," she says. "You have to be ready for that kind of solitude."

Looking into her eyes, I search for the strength to overcome my fears. "I'm scared of making mistakes, of letting down people who look to me for guidance. I don't think I'm ready for this." My nerves are now surging.

"Asha, error is a facet of leadership, an unavoidable one. What distinguishes a true leader isn't the absence of error, but the capacity to learn from these mistakes and to prioritize the well-being of our people." The assurance does not help as much as I would have liked.

"Remain faithful to what your heart tells you, Asha. Heed its guidance, for it will steer you. Always bear in mind that you won't be performing tasks in isolation, even when you feel alone. You will have ancestral wisdom at your side, the support of the community, and above all, the vigor of your own spirit. I have no doubt, my daughter, that you are ready for this. Trust in yourself, just as I trust in you."

Her words reassure me, suggesting that perhaps the journey ahead might not be as daunting as I currently fear. Hopefully, and it's a big hope, with my mother's wisdom to guide me, I might be able to face the new challenge of becoming High Priestess.

The hours unfold swiftly as my mother leads me through the Monolith's intricate network. The grand tour reveals secluded nooks and hidden chambers. Some of the lore that I hear during my instruction I had only ever heard of in whispered legends before.

In the midst of this exploration, the Monolith buzzes with preparations for the anointing ceremony—sacred spaces are meticulously arranged with ritualistic items; ancient incense is burned to cleanse the atmosphere, and elaborate tapestries showcasing our lineage are carefully hung. The Monolith, typically a place of silence, now thrums with activity, as though the very foundation is stirring in anticipation of what is to come. Amid the flurry of preparations and revelations, I am acutely aware of the evening's significance. Each moment draws me closer to a destiny filled with privilege and burden. I find myself becoming overwhelmed again and need to get some fresh air.

Stepping into the Monolith's threshold, the day has already dwindled into night. The village, ordinarily calm, teems with an infectious vibrancy as residents converge around the Monolith. The air is electric with a blend of excitement and solemnity. This evening, a tradition that spans decades, the Monolith's doors have opened wide, inviting all to partake in the festivities and witness the anointing in the grand hall.

People flow towards the Monolith in a gentle tide of anticipation. Their murmurs and laughter weave a tapestry of joy and expectation. Children dart around with uninhibited glee, while the elders move with deliberate grace. The soft glow of torches and lanterns punctuate the dusk, bathing the gathering in a cozy luminescence.

From the Monolith's threshold, I absorb the scene, enveloped in the collective embrace of my community. This sense of connection and shared anticipation underscores the enormity of the role I am about to assume. I glance around, hoping to find Nico amongst the bustling villagers, but he's not there. He should be here already, I think. It's not like him to be late. I find myself fighting the urge to run back to my home and hide.

At that instant, Nico emerges from the assembling crowd, his presence acting as a lighthouse amidst the sea of faces, momentarily diverting me from my urge to run and hide. Our eyes lock from afar, and within his look, I find a solace so deeply familiar. A smile, unbidden, softens my previously stern expression.

"Well, well, well..." he murmurs, almost inaudibly, as he draws near. For a brief pause, he simply stands there, his eyes lit with wonder. It seems as though he perceives me as not merely Asha, his lifelong companion, but as the forthcoming guardian of Emberwyn. Or perhaps, his awe is rooted in something deeper. I muse to myself for a moment as his eyes drift to the dress my mother has made me wear.

The dress seems to weave the spirit of our land and its heritage around me. Its fabric is dyed in rich, earthy tones that echo the depths of the forest. The material drapes elegantly around me, its design flowing gracefully to the ground, while its hem and sleeves are embellished with elaborate embroidery.

"You're late," I say, half smiling but half serious. "A moment later and I would be hiding under my bed and you would have had to drag me out." He laughs, but I mean every word of it.

"I'm sorry, Asha. I meant to be here sooner, but my father needed help checking traps." I notice a small spot of blood on his shirt. I suppose I can't blame him. I would rather be checking traps myself.

"What did you catch?"

"A wolf," he replies. "Big one, too. We took it down to the butcher."

He offers me his arm with a smile and I can't suppress a grin as I feel the warmth spread across my cheeks. Our arms entwined, we venture inside together.

Nico had only once before entered the chamber at the age of three. In this moment, with Nico by my side, I feel a sense of completeness and security unlike any I have known before.

"Asha!" The festive air is pierced by Lili's exuberant voice as she wraps me in a jubilant hug.

"Hey there, my little star. Are you enjoying the celebration?" I smile at her enthusiasm. "Have you stumbled upon the chocolate truffles yet?" One mention of the coveted treats launches her into a flurry of excitement. With an eager shake of her head and a smile that rivals the luminance of the moon, she scampers off to explore the banquet's delights.

Nico's voice draws my attention away from Lili's departing joy. "Feeling nervous?" he asks, his voice solid yet laced with a layer of concern. In his company, the apprehensions that had shadowed my thoughts begin to dissolve.

"Yes, I guess you could say I'm a bit nervous," I confess, allowing myself a moment to take in the splendor that surrounds us. "However, there's something I have to show you, remember? Let's go." His eyes widen as we venture through the Monolith's shadowed hallways, away from the lively ambiance of the ceremony. When we arrive at the specific chamber, I ease the massive stone door open. The Shadow's Heart is solemnly stationed on its pedestal inside. The flickering torchlight casts unsettling shadows over it, imbuing the relic with an illusion of pulsating vitality. Nico's expression shifts to one of awe as he gawks at it.

"This... is it?" he murmurs.

"Yes," I reply, as something about his reaction catches my attention. I observe him take another step closer to the artifact. I can see he wants to reach for it but he doesn't lift a hand. A subtle shiver touches his shoulders and it betrays his attempt to mask his fear. I place my hand on his arm. "Nico, are you alright?"

He offers me a tentative smile. "Yes, I'm fine. It's just... overwhelming, to stand so close to something that once held such ancient power." He has not completely regained his composure. The fear lingering in his eyes tells me there's more he's holding back. "Nico, if there's something troubling you..."

He interrupts with a shake of his head. "No, it's nothing. Just nerves about the ceremony." He sneaks a gaze at the Shadow's Heart before looking at me. "Listen, Asha..." However, the sound of distant footsteps halts our conversation. "I'll explain everything later, after the ceremony. I shouldn't be seen here. Meet me in the chamber hall later?"

I nod, though worry gnaws at me. Nico's usual composure seems unsettled by the Shadow's Heart, indicating fears that run deeper than he admits. "Alright, after the ceremony," I agree, my mind already swirling with questions. He quickly blends into the shadows outside the chamber as he heads back to the celebration.

Alone in the dim light of the obsidian chamber, I linger with the Heart in my grasp. What is it about this ancient stone that seems to fill my friend with fear? Standing near the Heart, he certainly didn't seem like himself. Why should such a source of unfaltering protection cause apprehension in someone? I try to gauge my own emotions, running my fingers over its surface. Then Amara's story comes back to me and I begin to wrestle with the sharp contrast between what she said and that which mother told me. Regardless of which story is more real, the secrets of the Heart are locked within its fractured, dormant core. One thought towers above the others as I hear my own breathing in the flickering torchlight: No matter how staunchly I may try to tell myself otherwise, I am not ready for whatever it means to become the High Priestess of Emberwyn. I place the Heart back in its place and leave the chamber.

The crowd's whispers quiet down as I enter the room, and the ceremony starts. Torches cast a warm, otherworldly light over the black obsidian walls as I take my seat. At the center, before the raised dais, stands my mother. She lifts her hands to begin the ancient rites.

"As we gather in Emberwyn's heart," my mother's voice rings clear and strong, "let's honor the journey of our ancestors, the obstacles they conquered, and the heritage they passed down to us." Her gaze sweeps across the audience as every villager clings to her words. "In our ancestors' era, our realm was wild. The forests were dense and unclear, the rivers broad and untamed. Yet, this freedom brought challenges, for our domain was a land of perils and mysteries." She pauses.

"Yet, our forebears, undaunted and courageous, did not waver. They attuned to the forest whispers, deciphered the rivers' language, and the wind's melodies. They formed a bond with the land, a covenant of respect and balance." I am captivated by the story of Emberwyn's emergence as a sanctuary amidst the wild.

"Tonight," my mother continues, "we gather to honor that heritage. We come together to witness the appointment of a new leader, one who will uphold the sacred bond between our people and the earth." Her eyes meet mine and she signals me to approach. I hesitate and she has to signal me again.

Slowly rising, I move to stand beside her. The villagers are gathered around the stone table with their gaze fixed on the ceremonial pedestal where the ritual is about to occur. Standing next to this pedestal, my mother holds a small, intricately designed tool.

"Asha," she says, "you are now to receive the Mark of the Spirit, a symbol of your connection to the ancient spirits of our land and to our ancestors." With solemn grace, she touches the tool to the center of my forehead, just above the space between my eyebrows. The contact is light, yet the sensation that follows is profound. A warm, tingling energy radiates from the touch point, spreading across my skin. The villagers watch in silent wonder as the mark starts to form—a single, subtle dot that gradually, almost imperceptibly, begins to expand.

The dot unfolds and spirals outward into a pattern of intricate lines and curves. As each stroke of the magical pattern swirls, I feel the Mark of the Spirit being etched onto my skin. The sensation is almost like meditation. The gentle energy pulsing through me is unmistakable as the designs spread down my temples, glide along my neck, and touch my skin as softly as a breeze. Soon they flow down to my breastbone and along my arms to create an arabesque drawn by unseen hands.

The hall fills with murmurs of wonder and awe as the tattoo completes its sprawl on my hands and fingers. But then, I catch a fleeting glimpse of an emotion on my mother's face, usually a picture of composed serenity, that looks a lot like fear. She quickly hides it behind a practiced smile, but I've already caught the fleeting moment of vulnerability.

With the final design imprinted on my skin, my mother hands me a mirror. The reflection staring back at me is both familiar and transformed. The tattoo is stunning. Yet, my gaze shifts from its beauty to the small symbol on my forehead. A chill runs through me as questions start to flood my mind. It's the symbol that's burned into the leather of my father's blade.

My eyes lock with my mother's. Her gaze holds a depth of unspoken truths—a hint that the path ahead will be more complex than I ever imagined. But, for now, the ceremony continues uninterrupted as villagers come forward to offer their blessings, oblivious to the storm of questions raging inside me.

As the ceremony's festivities envelop me in the great chamber hall, a blend of music, laughter, and celebratory chants fills the air. I find myself lost in thought amidst the revelry. This shift from simply being Asha to now leading Emberwyn seems almost dreamlike. Observing my people celebrate with such unbridled joy, a part of me remains tethered to the reality of the duties that now rest on my shoulders.

My eyes find Nico, standing out in the crowd. He's comfortably seated next to Lili, with our friends Elias and Skylar flanking them. Our gaze connects, and he raises his glass in a silent toast. It's a gesture so appropriately him that it automatically elicits an eye roll and a smile from me. His simple act, though playful, is laden with genuine respect.

That moment triggers a whirlwind of emotions inside me. The warmth of our friendship, shaped by laughter and challenges, brings a bittersweet feeling. As I brace myself to step into this leadership role, a shade of worry crosses my mind—I silently pray that the bond we share remains unchanged by the weight of my responsibilities and the potential distance they might bring. Amidst the festivities and the sparkle of toasting glasses, there's a part of me that quietly yearns, deeply hopes, that the core of our friendship endures through the shifts of time and circumstance.

Just as I am moving to join them, the grand chamber doors burst open, their booming sound echoing against the stone walls. The music stops and a chilling silence takes over. All eyes turn toward the cause of the interruption.

A villager stands in the doorway, his breathing heavy. His eyes seem filled with panic, as sweat beads on his forehead. "Forgive me, your highness," he says in a trembling voice. "There's been a disturbing occurrence in the eastern forest, near the rim."

Worry sweeps through the hall and I can feel a flush of anxiety. My mother steps forward, her composure unshaken, though her eyes narrow with concern. "What has happened?" she demands, her voice cutting through the growing whispers sharply.

The villager gulps, his eyes meet mine in a brief, ominous exchange. "We've found a body," he announces. "It's... it's Amara."

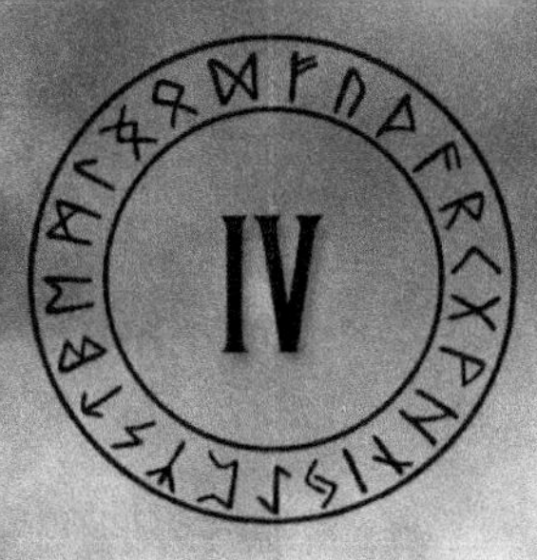

PREMONITION

*A*mara? My heart plummets at the villager's words.

Urgency surges through the crowd in the grand chamber. The atmosphere, previously aglow with celebration, now vibrates with tension. Villagers, propelled by alarm and fear, start a hasty retreat. I'm swept up in the flow of bodies moving toward the exit, carried by their wave of anxious energy. Whispers and speculations ripple through them.

Looking around for Lili, I find comfort in the sight of her leaning into Nico. His arm wraps around her securely like a silent vow of protection in the middle of the turmoil. His gaze finds mine across the room, his nod offering silent reassurance.

Amid the stream of people pulling toward the fresh air outside, my focus sharpens on finding Elias, who has just lost his grandmother. The urgency propels me through the crowd, the need to locate him straining each second.

Outside, villagers form small, tight-knit circles under the moon's glow, their murmurs creating a subdued backdrop to the night's tension. Amidst them, Elias appears. His presence, usually vibrant, is now overshadowed by sorrow. I thread my way to him.

"Elias," I say softly, my approach careful. He was poking fun at me just this morning and now the same face is a canvas of grief. Before I can say more, a stir breaks through the quiet. A group, including several elders, starts to form a search party for the shadowed forest near the east rim. That is where Elias's grandmother was discovered, and the need to shed light on this calamity is urgent.

Elias turns away to go join the group, whereas I am caught in the conflict between the necessity for action and another fear. The east rim is the place of my father's vanishing.

Startled by an unexpected touch, I spin around. My mother is standing beside me. Instantly, the commotion of the crowd gives way to a quiet filled only by her intense gaze.

"Asha," she says, "this is your first challenge and it will test both your leadership and your bond with our community."

"Mother, I... I'm feeling overwhelmed. It feels like too much," I confess.

She squeezes my shoulder, a simple gesture meant to bring peace but doesn't. Turmoil has been filling me since the news broke. "It's in moments of crisis that your people will seek your guidance. Now is when they rely on your strength to weather the storm."

"I can't. I'm scared." The murmur that comes out of me is a search for some piece of clarity. Why do I have to face this?

"Showing them that even in fear we stand united will bring them solace. They need their High Priestess now, Asha, but they also need you." The spark the words kindle is almost too small to notice. As the crowd moves toward the east rim, she clasps my hand. "We will face this together, Asha." I nod without a sound as we move to join our people.

We walk through the forest, leaving the village's familiar warmth behind. Moonlight seeps through the dense foliage above, and the trees quietly guard over our grave procession. Their branches form a solemn but natural cathedral over our heads.

Here again is the path I've avoided fervently since my father vanished. It snakes through the woods before me. The trees flank it with roots sprawling into hurdles I carefully step over. The scent in the air carries a crisp edge, hinting at the coming of a harsh winter. A faint mist wraps its ghostly fingers around our feet as we press on. The only sounds to break the otherworldly silence are the crunching of leaves and the occasional crack of a twig underfoot.

As we approach the East Rim, the forest thins out. The trees spread farther apart, letting moonlight and the fresh snow covering the ground brighten our way. This region on the east rim, has rarely been crossed since the tragic loss of my father's men.

The looming silhouette of this wall makes my heart beat faster. There, under the eerie quiet of the moonlight, the sight of Amara's body against the blood-stained snow chills me to the core. Grief and disbelief fill the faces quietly surrounding her.

Accepting the death of our village's lively storyteller feels like an abrupt violation of reality. All eyes turn to me, seeking reassurance, direction. Yet, at that moment, words escape me. *This is too much pressure.* The weight of their expectation is daunting. *I need to speak to them*, my thoughts insist, but a counter impulse holds me back. *What can I say that would matter?* Doubt consumes me. *I can't. I can't...*

My mother moves to the forefront with her characteristic grace. Her aura is always a pillar of strength. "We're all one people," she begins, her voice soft yet filled with a richness that fills the night, "the stars watch us and the forest stands by as we come together. Not to mourn a loss, but to celebrate the passing of a cherished soul into the spirit realm."

Her gaze tenderly sweeps over each person. "Amara's spirit was woven from strands of love and wisdom. In her, we found not just a storyteller but a mother, a guide, and a dear friend. Though she no longer walks with us, her passage to the afterlife is now beginning."

The words of my mother act as a salve. I can already feel them working on the sting of our loss. "Let us find solace in the knowledge that Amara now journeys to a place beyond our understanding. The spirits of our ancestors light her path while her laughter and stories will eternally echo in the world around us."

With a deep breath she continues, "Be assured, together we will unveil the truth behind tonight's events. Her dear soul warrants this pursuit, and in our quest for clarity, we pay tribute to her legacy."

Her speech, rich with a natural grasp of life's fleeting essence, instills tranquility among the crowd. Slowly, with great respect, they begin the process of returning Amara to our village.

As the assembly disperses, my eyes find Elias. Our glances communicate a shared loss. Once the crowd has carried away Amara, I join him in silence. This shared grief seems to bridge any previous rifts between us. In this moment, the magnitude of his current loss overshadows my past disagreements with him.

After sitting silently for a while, Elias rises, and his thank you is barely audible. Soon he is gone and I am alone at the East Rim's edge. I, too, need to get away from this suffocating place.

Just as I am rising to leave, a fleeting glow on the rim's stone face captures my attention. Intrigue momentarily displaces grief. With measured steps, I move towards the location of the mysterious light. But when I get close to the wall all I encounter is the stone's cold presence and the soft hum of its electricity. The light has disappeared. I wonder if it was just an illusion cast by the moon.

As I stand scanning the wall one last time, I experience something unexpected — a light tingling sensation on my forehead, exactly where the symbol from my father's blade had been marked. Initially faint, the sensation grows stronger, spreading like a whisper of wind over my skin.

With a curious feeling I raise my hand to my forehead and that is when I witness a transformation on the wall before me. To my amazement, the detailed pattern of the tattoo imprinted on my skin starts to materialize on the stone. It seems as though the symbol on my forehead is in harmony with the ancient stone.

A soft shimmer runs through the lines of the delicate pattern. Awe and fear engulf me. But the sensation of a deep connection to something far greater than anything I have ever imagined is stronger than the two. This couldn't be happening by pure chance. What I see is the unlocking of some dormant magic in the wall. The conforming symbol on the old stone face must be a bridge to mysteries left unresolved by my father. .,

And then I remember the vision I saw in my dream. It was a doorway that had given way in the wall. In a flashing instant, the vision clashes with reality… *Eyeless!* Panic strikes me, and I step back. The tingling ceases at once, and the glowing seal on the wall disappears as the electricity resumes its ethereal dance.

There, in the silence, with the pattern's image lingering in my thoughts, a cold shiver whips through me. How is this symbol connected with the mystery of my father? Is it even connected? It must be. Haunted by the vision of the Eyeless specters beyond the rim, a fear stirs deep inside me as I turn my back toward the wall. It is now returned to its normal state. I must go. Perhaps I will come back tomorrow with Nico.

The time returning to the Monolith stretches longer than ever before. The night seems to weigh down my footsteps, despite the earlier thrill of becoming High Priestess. I know I was not ready to accept the initiation and now the forest feels like a corridor leading to a reality I'm hesitant to confront. This same forest used to be a sanctuary, but now the night's chill offers little solace against the storm of emotions within me.

Breaking free from the forest's shadowy grasp, I approach the Monolith's dim clearing and see Nico waiting by the entrance. Lili is there beside him and as my eyes meet his, I see my own turmoil mirrored in his gaze. But his voice is soft when he speaks to me. "She's been brave, but she's worried about you."

As Lili moves to embrace me, I manage a weary smile of gratitude for Nico's presence on this distressing night. The fire from the torches around the village dances a slow dance in his eyes as I step closer to hug him. I hold back the sudden urge for tears because I don't want my sister to see me cry. This day was supposed to be a day of celebration, but, just like Lili's name day last year, it has become a day of death. With a sigh I push away from Nico's scent of forest and earth.

"Thank you, Nico. It means more than I can express," I say.

Before I can respond further, my mother walks out from the Monolith. "Asha, you've done all you could tonight," she says. "Now, take Lili home. Rest. We face much contemplation, and the morrow will challenge us anew. A meeting is set for tomorrow morning in the chamber, and your presence as the new High Priestess is imperative."

Her words bounce around in my fogged mind. She's right; the night has left me drained, I need to rest. "Yes, Mother," I answer. The thought of sleep welcomes me. "I will not be late." I take Lili's hand and offer Nico a nod of silent thank you and goodbye.

Emberwyn's streets are tranquil as the village is slowly recovering from the edge's turmoil. Lili's firm hold on my hand is comforting, and I squeeze some back for her. When we reach our small cottage, the house greets us in silence, save for the hearth's softly crackling embers. As we enter, Lili's hold relaxes, her earlier courage fading to reveal the fatigue in her eyes.

Lili's bedroom is surrounded by modest tapestries and her collection of small toys and trinkets. It is a child's refuge from the world's complexities. She changes into her nightgown and scrambles into bed.

"Time for sleep," I tell her, tucking the covers up to her chin and smoothing the hair away from her forehead.

With a tired nod, she looks at me with a glimmer of hope. "Asha, could you tell me a story? Like Amara used to tell?"

Her request pierces through me reminding me of Amara's absence. "Of course, Lili," I say, the ache evident in my tone. I settle by her side. Feeling the covers snug around her, I search my mind for a story to ease her into dreams.

"In a land where the forests whispered and rivers gleamed under the sun," I begin, "there lived a girl named Lili, renowned for her compassion and valor."

Lili's interest shines, and I weave a narrative of adventure and enchantment. Her eyelids flutter as my tale progresses, my voice's cadence coaxing her towards sleep.

"This courageous girl pledged to guard the forest and its inhabitants, who, in turn, promised to always be her best friends. Together, they shared a wonderful life, making the forest a sanctuary of peace and magic…"

By the end of the tale, Lili is sound asleep, her breath deep and steady. I watch over her for a brief moment before I adjust the blankets and kiss her forehead.

"Goodnight, Lili," I whisper, my heart brimming with affection. Casting one final glance at her serene face, I switch off the light and quietly exit the room.

The comfort of my own bed is heavenly after the evening's turmoil. Yet, sleep remains just beyond grasp as my mind refuses to rest its thoughts. Finally, exhaustion plunges me into the splendor of an age-old city, its majestic structures casting deep shadows over stone-laid paths.

A profound silence envelops the city, devoid of any life, yet it throbs with an unseen vitality. Before me, a colossal gate looms, its ironwork elaborate and foreboding, twisted with symbols that feel both ancient and eerily animate. Whispers fill the air around me, propelling me forward. My hand, moving with a will of its own, presses against the gate's cold surface. With a mournful creak, it swings open, unveiling a world shrouded in dense fog that lies beyond the city's embrace.

From this misty void, the Eyeless emerge, their forms a dark maelstrom of shadow and malevolence. They move toward the gate, toward me, their presence unleashing a torrent of fear. My feet refuse to flee, held fast by a terror that devours all semblance of reason. Nearing...nearing... their faceless visages become chasms of despair, blurring the line between the dream and waking world. I feel my very essence teetering on the brink of oblivion, my soul wrenched from me in an agony of fear unlike any I have known.

Jolting awake, my heart pounds furiously. Gasps escape my mouth in rapid succession. The dream lingers for a moment, its memory vividly haunting and ominously prophetic.

The Eyeless, the gate, and the path that fate seems to be drawing me toward… What am I meant to do? My night has veered into realms where myth and reality intertwine. I sigh heavily and lie back down. The moonlight washes over me through the window. Despite the overwhelming sense of foreboding, I know that this path is mine alone to tread. But fear and doubt cloud my understanding as to the true nature of this path.

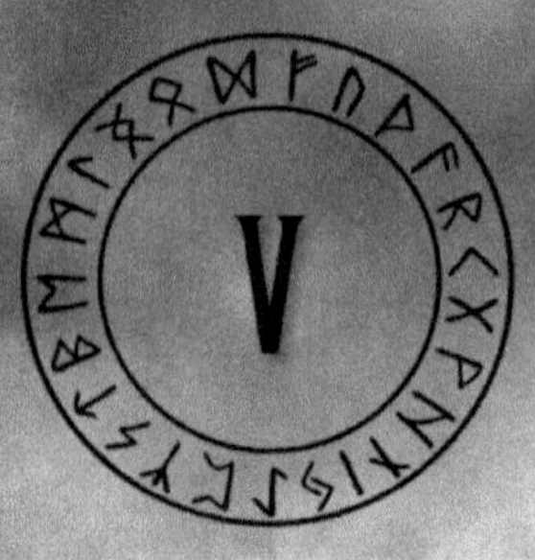

SECRETS OF AMARA

As I wake up to the dawn softly illuminating my room, my thoughts are entangled with the occurrences of the night before. The morning air is fresh and calm. I lie there on the comforting warmth of the bed for a while, then sit up and reach under it for an old, dusty wooden box. It contains the last of my father's belongings.

I dust off the lid with the corner of my blanket and open it. Inside, less dusty, are an old pocket watch that doesn't work, an old leather pouch he used for hunting bait, and some old buckles and straps. Digging beneath it all, I pull out his blade that had been left in the forest at the east rim. Its leather-wrapped hilt is burned with the mark that is on my forehead.

"What is this mark?" I whisper to myself as I run my fingers across it. The symbol is the same that had appeared on the rim, and feels too significant to be mere chance.

There must be a link to the puzzle of my dad's vanishing and the odd happenings at the rim. I need to understand what it means.

Determined, I quickly get dressed in my snug black leather outfit, designed for movement but also warm for winter. I don my fur-lined hood and tuck my father's blade into my boot before hurrying out to meet Nico. Discussing the previous night's events with him might help me figure things out.

In the crisp winter air of the morning the village is already awake and stirring to life. Wisps of smoke curl skyward from the hearths, and the muffled sounds of the day's early starters fill the air. My steps carry an urgency but it isn't long before a known voice slices through the morning's calm.

"Asha!"

Glancing back, I see my mother advancing towards me with a brisk and determined pace. I sigh inside but hold my composure.

"Asha, why the rush this morning?" she says.

"I was on my way to…" The words dwindle into silence as it dawns on me. Amidst my morning desire to find Nico, the meeting in the Monolith has entirely escaped my mind.

"You've forgotten, haven't you?" A mild, knowing smile plays on her lips. "Remember, we're due at the

Monolith. The council members are expecting our arrival."
I can only nod in response as annoyance washes over me.

"Right, the meeting. I was just—"

With a comforting hand on my shoulder, she cuts me off. "Given recent events, it's understandable. Yet, we cannot delay any further." I allow myself a brief look towards the path I had initially intended to take. Finding Nico will have to wait. Reluctantly I turn and follow her.

We walk toward our village's center where the dark, smooth surface of the Obsidian Monolith sparkles in the morning sun. The weight of the day's plans settles on my shoulders. This meeting is about our village's future, and about Amara's death. I need to focus, but the mysteries beyond our borders linger in my thoughts.

My mother stops just outside of the entrance. "I almost forgot," she says, turning to me with a smile. She unclasps the pendant from around her neck and places it around mine. My hand finds it, the heavy metal cold in my grasp. It is the signet of the High Priestess, making my role feel even more real. "There, come along now."

Inside the Monolith, seriousness and worry fill the air. The winding halls echo the sound of our steps as we navigate to the High Chamber. This space, where the village council makes decisions, is vast, with towering ceilings, and walls adorned with torches. In the center of the room is a large stone table that wraps around in a circle. On the other end of the table is the elegantly carved, obsidian throne. My throne. Around the table, the members of the council, dressed in ceremonial clothes, look concerned. *Am I late?* My nerves are all over the place today.

The council is made up of respected elders representing different parts of village life. Elder Orin, the sage, knows a lot about our history and lore. Next to him is Elder Brann, a warrior from past battles and my father's former lieutenant, now our defense leader. Elder Lysa, who oversees our traditions and rituals, is known for her deep spiritual insight. And there's Elder Tarn, Nico's father and Emberwyn's best blacksmith. I never did like him. He is an excellent craftsman, but he can be a bit arrogant and rude. I don't think he likes me. Nico told me once that his father forbade him from spending time with me because I distracted him from his work. However, he soon found out that keeping us apart was impossible and he's learned to accept it.

Through an air filled with a quiet respect I make my way to the throne and take my seat. The stone is cold, even through my warm clothes. They all look at me with waiting eyes. Nervousness twists in my belly but I know I have to speak to them.

"Our meeting today is about Amara's death." The slight shaking in my voice shows my lack of experience. I meet the eyes that are watching me and the chill in the room seems to deepen. "Her loss..." I pause, her image, lifeless in the snow, flashing in my mind.

"Is a tragedy," Elder Lysa cuts in, and I sink back into my seat, grateful for the break from the spotlight. "We need to understand what occurred."

"We do understand," Elder Tarn interrupts firmly. "She left at night, on her own, and was attacked. The wall doesn't keep out the eyeless anymore. They've breached it!" His declaration sends a ripple of concern through the room, and I feel a shiver of fear within me.

Elder Brann's voice is full of decisive action. "We must increase our patrols. Understanding the Eyeless's movements and finding where they break through is vital. High Priestess Asha, I ask for your permission to start non-stop patrols along the east rim." He looks at me, his eyes asking quietly for my agreement. My mind races to my father's last patrol and the danger of sending others to face the same fate. I look to my mother for reassurance, and her gentle smile and slight nod give me the courage I need. I turn back to Elder Brann and nod slowly. Instantly I am plagued with regret. Have I just signed off on more deaths?

Then Elder Tarn, known for his straightforward talk, breaks the quiet. "We shouldn't let the same haste that ended Amara lead us astray. She made the same mistake Easton did by visiting the east rim at night, and it cost her life." His blunt words hang heavy in the air.

A wave of anger and hurt crashes over me and I can't control it. "How dare you!" I roar, my voice echoing through the hall. My fist slams down on the throne's armrest hard enough to make a sound that silences any murmurs. The force of my anger makes the elders startle. My eyes lock on Elder Tarn with a chilling intensity. "My father gave everything for Emberwyn and its people, including you. And you dare tarnish his name with your baseless accusations?" My words reel with the power of my station, but it's a power I'm only just beginning to understand. The council members are clearly shaken.

He quickly avoids my stare, looking down at the table, and speaks in a soft, sincere voice, "I'm sorry, Your Highness. I meant no disrespect."

My mother steps in quietly, "Let's focus on the matters at hand." Her calm words cut through the tension, guiding us back to the pressing issue of Amara and the Eyeless.

As I sit back in my throne, I'm hit with a wave of insight. Seeing a grown man shrink back from my words brings a mix of regret and unease. Though a small part of me subtly enjoys the power I wield as High Priestess.

An hour of intense discussions blurs by, and as the meeting ends, I'm left with a storm of thoughts. Elder Tarn's words had cut deep, and my heated reaction left me feeling uneasy. I decide to approach him, ready to apologize for my outburst.

But before I get the chance, my mother's firm hand is on my arm. She pulls me aside. "Asha, stand firm in what you said. You need not apologize to Elder Tarn." Her gaze pierces into mine.

I look at her surprised. "But Mother, I lost my temper. It wasn't the right way to respond." She waves away my worries with a simple gesture.

"Stepping into the role of High Priestess means holding fast to your beliefs, especially in matters of honor. Sometimes, showing your strength is necessary, even if it appears harsh. To back down now would only undermine your authority." Her words sink deep.

"I… I just don't want to lead with fear or anger," I say. With a softening smile she places her hand on mine.

"And you won't. There's a difference between displaying strength and breeding fear. Today, you stood firm, upholding your convictions and honoring your father's legacy. That's not fear; that's courage." Her words offer a comfort I hadn't realized I needed.

"Thank you, Mother. I will try to remember that." I return her smile.

"Your path is filled with responsibilities, Asha, but remember, as High Priestess, your actions and words carry great weight. Use your influence wisely." Her hand gently catches a braid, and her fingers trace the gray and blue yarn interwoven through my hair. Her touch, feather light, carries an understanding. She smiles a tender knowing expression that speaks louder than words. The yarn is a silent tribute. It is my reminder of overcast skies, the silence of snow underfoot; of laughter in the cold air, and my father's reassuring presence. Each strand of yarn is a link to those treasured moments. With one last, caring touch, she lets go of the braid, her action a clear signal – the past has shaped me, but the future calls, and it's time I embrace what comes next.

The village, bathed in the soft, golden light of the morning is a relief from the musky gloom of the monolith. A gentle breeze kisses my skin as my eyes sweep over the peaceful vista of cobblestone paths snaking through snug cottages with thatched roofs. The gentle rustle of leaves in the nearby woods, and the distant, joyful laughter of children pry me away from the ancient, shadowy grip of the monolith.

My mind wanders back to the council's discussions and my outburst. I'm so buried in my thoughts that I almost don't notice Skylar hurrying my way. Her pace is quick, her demeanor charged with an urgency that's foreign to her usual calm.

"Skylar?" I call, piqued by her rush. As she closes the distance, I brace for more on the mysterious tale of the cloaked figure she witnessed the other evening.

"Asha!" Her tone carries a sense of urgency.

"What's wrong, Skylar?" I ask.

She glances around warily, confirming we are alone, before whispering, "Keep this just between us." Intrigued, I nodded, urging her to continue.

"It's about Amara," she says in a hushed tone. "There's talk among the villagers. They doubt she was taken by the eyeless. The rumors... they're hinting at murder." Her eyes are not reflecting the forest's peace, but are glowing with intensity. I feel a shiver at the introduction of such dark thoughts.

"Murdered? But why? Amara had no enemies in Emberwyn, or anywhere for that matter."

Skylar looks even more troubled now. "That's the strange thing. Whispers are she stumbled upon a secret, something dangerous." The gravity of her words hangs heavily between us.

"Thanks for telling me, Skylar," I say, my mind racing with this alarming insight. "But let's keep this conversation confidential. Not a word to anyone else."

Skylar's response is a grave nod. "Of course, Asha. I just thought you needed to know this." The thought of Amara, dearly held in Emberwyn's heart, fallen to foul play was almost too much to bear. Yet, the village's recent atmosphere of dread and suspicion make the rumor all too believable.

After she has departed, I stand absorbed by the intimidating responsibilities of my role. If there is even a hint of truth in these rumors, Emberwyn might be entangled in dangers far darker and more intricate than I'd dared to imagine. How would I even begin unraveling the truth? Pushing aside these concerns for the moment, my thoughts shift to finding Nico.

Away from the lively buzz, Nico is with the horses, where nature's tranquil murmur surrounds his father's stables on the outskirts of Emberwyn. It's his favorite place to be under the weathered wood and thatch. After I watch him delicately brushing the horses' manes for several seconds, my voice is cautious not to disturb the animals. "Nico." He turns and his expression brightens as he brushes his hands on his apron.

"Hey, Asha. Didn't expect to see you here," he greets. "Oh, I almost forgot. Have a look." He strides over to a saddle hanging on the stall door and reaches for something hidden within its folds—a newly crafted sword, its sheath clinging to the saddle as if it were part of it. With a careful, almost reverent touch, he draws the blade, revealing its gleaming surface to the dim light of the stable. He holds it out to me and I take it. It's heavy for me but the craftsmanship is exquisite, every inch of the metal worked with precision and care. The hilt is wrapped in dark leather that compliments the iron blade.

"My father made it for me," Nico explains, "An early name day gift. He's desperately trying to get me to join Brann's detachment." Fates be damned, I forgot his birthday is tomorrow.

"It's beautiful," I say, handing it back to him while taking mental note to get him a gift.

"So, what brings you this way?"

"Nico, there's something I need to share with you."

Noticing the seriousness in my voice, his demeanor shifts to one of alertness and interest. He gestures to a hay bale nearby. *Away from eavesdropping animals?* I think to myself. "What's going on, Asha?" His tone is earnest.

Taking a deep breath, the events of the previous night replay vividly in my mind. "Last night, at the east rim, I saw something..." I start, my voice pricked by hesitation. "It was after everyone left. There was a symbol that started glowing on the wall. It's the same one, Nico— the same as the one on my father's blade. And now, it's here." I touched my forehead lightly, indicating the mark.

Nico's expression subtly shifts, his eyes widen slightly, caught between disbelief and concern. "The same symbol?"

I confirm with a decisive nod. "Yes, see for yourself." Gently, I pull the blade from its concealment in my boot and hand it to him. He carefully inspects it and his eyes dart between the blade and my forehead. With every glance, his surprise grows.

"There's more," I say. "Amara told me of a Blade of Velloria, tied to a prophecy. It foretells a descendant of Velloria, chosen by the spirits, destined to gather the blade's pieces and bring balance." As I recount Amara's story, Nico's initial skepticism shifts to intrigue.

"And you think this prophecy is about you? The mark on the blade and your forehead?" he asks, leaning in.

Looking away, I feel the weight of uncertainty enveloping me. "I don't know. My father's vanishing, the symbol, the prophecy... they're connected somehow. I can feel it."

Nico reaches out, his hand clasping mine, offering a solid, comforting presence. My heart flutters slightly at his touch. "That's quite a theory," he whispers. "It seems you are destined for greatness." His attempt at humor isn't amusing. His supportive words lack the full conviction I was hoping for. I pull my hand away, annoyed with him. He returns the blade to me and resumes his work with the horse.

"You don't have to believe it," I say sharply.

He stops but doesn't turn to face me. "It's not about belief, Asha. You say you saw the same symbol appear on the rim wall? Is it still there?"

"It was there for some time before it disappeared. I think I had a vision, it hardly lasted a few moments. I can't remember it clearly now but by the time it had passed the wall got back to normal, just the way it was before."

"It's just a lot to wrap my head around," he responds, his hand moving over the back of the horse.

His response does little to dampen my frustration. "So, what? It's just a story to you, isn't it? I'm making it up, is what you think?" I feel even more frustrated now than before. He should take this seriously, but instead he's just brushing it off like I'm telling tall tales. I wanted his support. I wanted him to believe me.

"Alright, Nico," my tone comes out sharper than I mean for it to. "I get it, it's a lot to swallow. It overwhelms me too." I return the blade to its place in my boot.

Nico faces me, concern etched across his features. "Asha, you know I'm here for you, don't you? It's just... all of this is quite a lot to take in."

"Yes, you told me that. Unfortunately I didn't have the luxury of taking anything in. It all was just dumped on me." His lips move, perhaps to bridge the distance growing between us, but I turn away before he can speak and walk out of the stable.

With each step, I feel the divide between us deepen. Angrily I kick at the gravel as I walk back into town. Why doesn't he take me seriously? I thought that showing him the symbol on the blade and my forehead would at least be enough for him to… to what? Stand by my side? Hold me and tell me it was going to be okay? At least enough not to make it into a joke.

My steps aimlessly carry me through the village lanes, drawing me towards the home of Elias—Amara's former sanctuary. The house stands ivy-clad at the edge of the forest. Pausing at the doorstep, I'm mindful of the raw grief that Amara's passing has inflicted on both Elias and myself, and I proceed with caution.

Bracing for the encounter, I knock gently, ready to extend whatever comfort I can muster.

"Come in," Elias calls from within.

The door opens to the push of my hand to reveal Elias, slouched in the very chair from which Amara had shared her tales with me only yesterday. His eyes, once vibrant, now cast shadows that seem to dim the surrounding light.

"Elias, I came to see how you're managing," my voice is a soft intrusion in the somber quietude. The presence of grief is thick and suffocating inside. Elias rises, his rigid posture a silent scream of his inner turmoil. His eyes mirror a loss so profound, it eludes expression.

"I'm so sorry, Elias," I murmur. He acknowledges with a small nod. His gaze seems to stare through me.

"Thanks, Asha. It's... I will be fine," he manages to say.

I linger awkwardly wanting to bridge the chasm of his mourning with more than just words of sympathy. His attention shifts momentarily to the kitchen table.

"She left something for you…" his voice trails off. "Nothing for me, though," he adds, almost to himself.

Curiosity draws me to the table. There, an aged package lies, secured with simple twine, accompanied by a note penned in Amara's distinctive handwriting. With reverence, I loosen the twine and unfold the note and read it silently.

My Dearest Asha,

In these darkening times, I write to you with a heart full of hope. Lately, I've felt the shadows closing in. A figure cloaked in darkness, watches me from the edge of the forest every night. I feel it is only a matter of time before someone finds out what I am planning.

Time is a luxury I fear we no longer possess. I cannot delay any further; the ritual to announce the heir of Velloria's return must be completed tonight. The signs are clear, and the spirits are restless. You, my dear, are entwined deeply in this ancient prophecy, a truth I've sensed since you were but a child. The legacy of Velloria beckons to you, its rightful heir. Trust in the mark bestowed upon you, for it is a sign of your destiny.

I must go now. They are near. Take the scroll. Keep it safe, Asha, and trust in the light of your spirit to guide you through the darkness.

With the fullness of my heart, Amara

Tears obscure the lines as I read, making each sentence a throb within my chest. Amara's message, laden with urgency, is beckoning me toward a fate entangled with Velloria's ancient secrets. Holding the note close, I am filled with a void left by her absence. I miss her. Setting the message aside, I clear my vision and focus on the ancient scroll inside the package. Its parchment smells of dust. Gently, I unfurl it. Amidst the scroll, I discover another note, this one for Elias. With a heavy heart, I pass it to him. His hands shake as he unfolds the note.

The room falls into a profound silence as he reads. His expression transitions from shock to anger, then a semblance of understanding, as if Amara's message has bridged a gap in his heart.

"Elias?" I break the silence, hoping he might share the essence of Amara's message. A spark of his former self flickers in his eyes as they meet my gaze. There is a long pause, as if he's struggling to process the note before he finally speaks.

"She knew," he says. "Knew what was coming..." His laughter breaks through the somberness and I stare at him confused. "I always thought her stories were just that—stories," he admits, looking at me. "It appears I was mistaken. It seems, Asha, you're not merely Emberwyn's Priestess but also the rightful heir to Velloria."

His words linger in the silence. The tension is so thick it feels as if the room is holding its breath for what comes next.

"How could she have possibly known?" My question is barely above a breath, yet it fills the room, making the shadows seem to lean in closer.

Elias's gaze, which had been clouded with grief, now shines with a hint of awe. "Amara had a gift for seeing beyond the veil. She trusted in the old prophecies, the ancient wisdom," he says in a low voice. Feeling myself on the brink of an immense revelation, I stand there overwhelmed by everything.

"I need to figure all of this out," I say, pinching the bridge of my nose. First I'm the High Priestess, and now I'm an heir to the ancient city of Velloria from Amara's tales? It's too much.

Elias offers a nod. "It is a lot to take in. However," he adds, lifting the note from Amara with a wry smile, "it seems we are in this together. Amara's last wish was for me to protect you. And frankly, I'd rather not have her spirit chasing me for eternity if I fail."

A small smile breaks through my lips. It's comforting to be believed and taken seriously, even if it isn't Nico.

"Thank you, Elias." Gratitude mingles with deep thought in me. "I need some time to process this." He acknowledges me with a nod of understanding. I quietly excuse myself and move towards the door, but pause at the threshold and glance back. From the doorway, he feels both close and worlds apart. A sudden urge catches me, and I close the gap between us with a quick, firm hug. His warmth wraps around me, offering a small relief from the looming solitude of my future. For a moment, I want to stay, to soak in the comfort of his presence and postpone facing a future I'm terrified to face alone.

Stepping back, I catch his eye again. "Let's get Nico and Skylar and we'll meet here in a few hours," I propose. He agrees with calm, assuring nod. I turn back to the chill of the evening, the ancient scroll clutched in my grasp.

VI

Burning Embers

The snowflakes dance lightly in the evening before they come to rest on the cobblestones while Amara's message swirls in my mind. The serene twilight taking over the village feels distant as I walk, buried in thoughts about my uncertain destiny. The village's daytime bustle is subsiding behind the sound of a blacksmith's hammer striking metal, but the normalcy feels almost alien. Scents fresh from the oven drift out from the bakery and tempt me to anchor my wandering mind.

In the midst of my strolling, Nico steps out of the bakery and almost collides with me. His expression bears a look of genuine concern.

"Asha," he says softly, "I've been thinking about what you said. I'm sorry for not being there when you needed me."

His apology, so genuine, seems to clear the mist in my thoughts for a moment. I look at his eyes as they shift back and forth, waiting for me to acknowledge his apology. For a moment, I don't want to. I am still a bit upset at him. But those eyes… they melt me.

"Nico, it's okay," I finally whisper back. "I know it was a lot to take in all at once. I might have overwhelmed you."

He shakes his head in a gentle dismissal. "No, it's fine, really. I was just surprised, that's all."

For a brief instant, the world seems to still around us. I surrender my flimsy grudge and embrace him. The warmth of his sturdy frame is a reminder of the ties that anchor me amidst turmoil.

And then the solace of his arms is washed away as I glance over his shoulder. In the day's fading hustle, I spot a figure and unease settles over me like the approaching dusk. The figure is hooded and standing unnaturally still. Fear tremors in my chest as I cling tighter to Nico's frame.

"Asha, I need to breathe," Nico says in a half-joking tone, pulling me back to reality. I release him, and step back with an apologetic glance.

"Sorry." My gaze darts back to where the figure had stood, only to find it vanished. I search the crowd to no avail; the figure is gone. Had my mind played tricks on me? No. I know what I saw. It was the same figure Skylar had seen going into the forest, and the one Amara mentioned in her message. It must be the same figure who had watched her and now it had found me.

I force a smile, trying to dispel the tension. "I thought I saw something. It's probably nothing." I play it off, remembering his disregard for my earlier conversation. Nico looks at me with concern and curiosity, but I quickly change the subject.

"Let's head to Amara's place. Elias and Skylar are waiting. There's something important we need to discuss."

His curiosity is piqued and he nods. "Actually, that reminds me, I have something to tell you. But later, at Amara's. Too many curious ears around." He then breaks off a piece of the honey loaf he bought and hands it to me. I gratefully accept, linking arms with him as we make our way to meet the others. The sweetness of the honey briefly distracts me from the shadows that seem to linger just out of sight.

As we approach Amara's house, the sound of laughter from Elias and Skylar cut through the evening air, easing the heavy cloak of my thoughts. Skylar is sitting on the floor next to Elias, completely mesmerized by his witty charm. She has never told me, but I can tell she has a crush on him. I think Elias knows it too, but refuses to acknowledge it. They greet us with smiles that seem to light up the dim room as we walk through the door.

"You know what, Asha," Elias begins, his eyes gleaming with mischief, "it's a real letdown that granny didn't leave us a hidden collection of cloaks and daggers from her secret society." Skylar's laughter fills the room, growing louder as she moves to join us. Her adoration for

Elias is unmistakable. I chuckle then place the scroll down under the dim light on the dining table.

Skylar leaps towards the table, her eyes alight with excitement. "This is wild! Mysterious symbols, hidden messages, and witches!" Her excitement is so extravagant that even Elias raises an eyebrow.

"Witches?" I repeat, looking at Elias, who just shrugs in confusion. What did he tell her before we arrived?

"If there are witches involved, I might just reconsider my disappointment about the missing cloaks and daggers," he quips with a grin playing at the corners of his mouth.

"Imagine the possibilities, Elias!" Skylar exclaims, lightly grasping the material of his shirt at the shoulder. He tries to pry her fingers away, looking at me as if asking me to save him. I won't.

"It's a map," I say, my fingers gently exploring its surface. It details areas both known to us and those beyond our understanding, with the famed city of Velloria taking a central, though slightly off-center, position at the top. The city is intricately drawn, showcasing grand buildings and structures, all surrounded by a dark, thick wall. To the East of Velloria, the Celestara Mountains rise, marked by the depiction of Astralith, the legendary white dragon perched on the snowy peaks overlooking the land.

Beneath the city and the mountains lies the Whispering Forest, and a river runs beneath the forest, dividing these lands from the territories we know well. Emberwyn is shown at the map's lower left edge, encircled by a wall that mirrors Velloria's own defenses. To the east of Emberwyn, the vast Stygian Hollows is depicted. Tracing my finger from the forest, across the river, to Velloria and up to the dragon in the mountains, it becomes evident that the world beyond Emberwyn is vast and filled with mysteries yet to be uncovered.

Flipping the map, my attention is captured by a small, detailed symbol at its base, mirroring the mark upon my forehead. A thrill of connection electrifies me, binding me to the map's ancient lore. Beneath this symbol, the words "To the Order of Velloria" are etched in ink. The words are followed by a riddle that seems to echo across ages: "Seek ye, where the dark devours the day."

The words send chills through me. "What could this possibly mean?" I whisper to myself.

Elias leans closer, his eyes scrutinizing the cryptic message. "Does this mean we're supposed to head towards the horizon looking for the sunset?"

"I don't believe that's it," I counter. "The journey of the sun is perpetually circling our world. This riddle hints at something deeper." The challenges of recent days loom over me, obscuring the answer even further. Skylar's gaze lights up with excitement.

"This feels like something out of a legend! A concealed gateway, mysteries shrouded in darkness... What an adventure!" Her overboard enthusiasm is eating at my nerves now.

Nico, silent until now, voices his concerns with a hint of caution. "Let's not forget the dangers. This isn't just a story. After what happened to Amara..." He trails off, and my gaze flicks towards Elias to catch a glimpse of sorrow in his eyes.

"What do we do now?" he asks, eager to lighten the mood.

"I don't know," I murmur. "It is a lot to think about right now. I'm also the High Priestess. I can't just neglect my responsibilities and go on a wild chase for a city we don't even know exists anymore." Gently, I roll up the map and tuck it into my pouch. Then I lean on the table and seek some sign of what to do next from my companions.

"Of course, you can," Elias teases with a light chuckle. "I manage to shirk my duties all the time. It's easy."

"If only it were that simple," I exhale. "I need to talk to my mother about this."

Suddenly, Nico interjects with surprising intensity. "No!" he says then quickly lowers his tone. "Asha, this is what I wanted to tell you at the initiation. It's the Shadow's Heart." He draws out a bundle of ancient, creased papers from his pocket and hands them to me. With a mix of anticipation and apprehension, I unfold them.

"Read it out," Skylar encourages me.

"It's an Official Order of Preservation," I say, starting to read it aloud. "By this decree, let it be known that the artifact known as the Shadow's Heart shall henceforth be secured and its truth obscured from the world at large to safeguard its dawn."

Pausing, I glance at Nico, before proceeding. "Henceforth, the following measures are to be strictly adhered to: The Shadow's Heart shall remain under the guardianship of the High Council of Emberwyn. All knowledge pertaining to the true nature and origin of the Shadow's Heart shall be restricted to members of the High Council and select advisors. Any and all lore, legends, or documentation related to the Shadow's Heart shall be altered or obfuscated to prevent its truth from being known. The punishment for those who seek to divulge the hidden knowledge of the Shadow's Heart is death. By the power vested in us, we, the undersigned members of the High Council, affirm this order to be in effect immediately and indefinitely."

Turning the document, I am met with numerous signatures. The earliest dates back to the Darkest Battle. Pages and pages of names. But the last page stops me cold. Everything comes to a standstill.

"Look," I say, placing the last sheet before them. "These are the signatures of our present council members." My finger slides over the names until it halts at one shockingly familiar. Kimora. My mother's name stands there, underlining the gravity of it all. Beneath the names is the seal of the Legion of Embers. The profound silence that envelopes us is thick with implications. Lifting my gaze, I whisper, "Nico, where did you come across this?" He pauses, and his gaze flickers towards the door then back at me. His nervous look makes me worry.

"I found it in my father's desk drawer." His voice is firm yet quiet.

"Your father?" I feel a heavy realization draping around me. His father, Elder Tarn, the man I lashed out at in the meeting, had this document? My dislike for the man grows even more now.

"Yes. He's been acting more secretive, more... distracted. I tried talking to him. Asking what was bothering him." His gaze falls down to the table as he continues, "But he kept telling me not to worry. Everything was fine." As each piece of this dark puzzle falls into place, the room seems to grow heavier with the silence of our thoughts.

"This isn't simply a secret; it's a generation-spanning conspiracy," I say. I can feel the oppressive truth of our discovery.

Skylar's voice pierces the silence, filled with incredulity. "And your mother, Asha... Kimora. She's implicated as well."

As the statement lingers in the air, a cold suspicion worms its way into my consciousness. My mother, a pillar of virtue, involved in this scheme? The space around us seems to be shrinking as disbelief grips me. The implications of the Order of Preservation bear down on me. What can this mean but painful betrayal? Might the shadowed figure be an assassin, possibly under Kimora's command?

The notion leaves a sour trace in my thoughts. The specter of treachery within our circle acts like a venom spreading through my veins. How long before we're the ones found lifeless in the woods, silenced for our knowledge? Here we were, at the edge of a chasm of doubts while the Legion of Ember looms over us.

Then, a new thought ignites a fury within me. The document trembles in my grip. Each endorsement is a testament to deceit and lies. I turn to Nico, my voice laced with anger. "How could you keep this from me? Knowing my mother, my own blood, is a part of this madness?"

He shrinks from my look, his eyes dodging mine. "Asha, I... I didn't know how to break it to you. I feared how you might react."

My heart pounds with rage and shock. "You feared how I would react? You feared how I... so you thought leaving me alone in the shadows would be better?" I fling the papers onto the table. "You should have had faith in me!" The need to escape a room dense with secrets overwhelms me, and I storm out, letting the door slam shut behind me.

The chill of the night fails to soothe the fire inside me as I sink onto the porch. Disappointment simmers through my veins at the realization that Nico, my closest friend, kept such a secret from me. The trust I had placed in him shatters like delicate glass. But beyond the sting of deceit, a profound sadness settles heavily in my heart. Why didn't he trust me? What have I ever done to make him not to? Then the knowledge of my mother's involvement is more painful than any wound from Nico. Amidst the conflicting emotions, each vying for control, I feel exposed and defenseless.

The door creaks open, and Skylar's cautious voice reaches out to me. "Asha, are you okay?"

Burying my head in my knees, the anger seeps away, replaced by a deep, echoing emptiness. Tears begin to spill. "No, Skylar, I'm far from okay. Everything I believed in... it's all just been one great lie. Everyone is keeping secrets and no one is telling the truth." I sob, my voice breaking under the strain of this harrowing truth. Skylar sits down and places an arm around me. Her presence is a gentle comfort in the madness of my emotions.

"When I was young," she says, "I played in the fields by my house. There was this solitary tall tree in the midst of it all. Come nightfall, it became my fear; it was like a malevolent giant watching over the darkness." I look up at her. A brief smile plays on her lips as she halts. Though her story's connection to my current despair is lost on me, her calm voice is oddly consoling. "One night, braving my fears, I approached the tree. Shadows around me morphed into beasts. Yet, nearing it, I uncovered something enchanting." Her gaze finds mine, glowing with the warmth of that recollection. "The tree was alive with fireflies, countless of them. What I feared veiled the most stunning spectacle I'd ever witnessed. That experience showed me that our fears can sometimes hide the most wondrous secrets, revealing their beauty only within the cloak of night."

Her story, as out of place as it is, lingers between us. What is she even talking about? Though, I suppose much like Amara, perhaps the content doesn't matter. The fact that she has come out here to comfort me is enough. Suddenly, clarity is a puzzle piece precisely clicking into its destined slot.

"Skylar," I burst out, gripping her arm with an urgency that makes her start. "The riddle on the map, 'seek where dark devours the day'. It's the fireflies!" Her reaction is a mix of shock and confusion.

"What? Asha, that doesn't make any sense," she protests, clearly puzzled. But, to me, the meaning is crystal clear. The map's secrets were hidden not despite the darkness but within it. Darkness isn't just a cover but a key to unveiling secrets. Looking at Skylar, my eyes spark with fresh determination.

"Thank you, Skylar." I grab her face and kiss her cheek before standing up quickly. Dragging Skylar along, I rush back into the room, driven by the adrenaline of our discovery. Without a word, I begin to cover the windows, dimming the room into shades of twilight. The abrupt shift from light to semi-darkness stirs a wave of bewilderment in everyone. As the last light flicks off, a suspenseful quiet cloaks us in anticipation.

"What in the hollows are you doing, Asha?" Elias's voice cuts through the suspense. "If you were going for dramatic effect, you're succeeding." His jest barely touches me; my focus is riveted on the map laying on the table, now enveloped in mystery.

"Let's just hope any spirits we call upon are in a good mood," Elias jokes, trying to lighten the mood again. Then, as if by magic, a gentle, ancient blue light begins to emanate from the map, transforming the darkness around us. The symbol, invisible in light, now glows with a soft, magical luminescence, its intricate designs alive with an otherworldly energy, bathing our faces in a surreal light.

Silence envelopes the room. The glowing symbol infuses the paper with a semblance of life, captivating us as we watch in awe. It is as if the map has been roused from a long sleep, now divulging its mysteries through the veil of ancient enchantments. Drawing in closer, I observe as the map discloses further secrets—a legend with two icons: the emblem of Velloria and a depiction of a sword.

"Wow," Skylar's voice, barely above a whisper, pierces the quiet. "What do they mean?"

I turned the map over, marveling at the discovery. These symbols are being replicated in various locations. "Look!" I can't contain my enthusiasm, pointing towards Emberwyn's eastern rim where the Velloria emblem now shines. "This is where I saw the symbol on the rim." My gaze follows the recurring symbols across the map: one on the walls surrounding Velloria, and another nestled in the Celestara mountains.

"Here," Nico adds, his finger hovering over the sword symbols. "There are only three. Maybe these mark where the shards of the sword are hidden?" Our collective excitement grows as we peer closer. The map suggests one piece lay in Velloria, another amidst the Celestara mountains, and the final one within Emberwyn itself.

"This matches perfectly," I say. "Amara had mentioned a shard being in Emberwyn." My scrutiny of the map intensifies, leading to a striking realization.

"Guys... This sword symbol is directly above us, over this house." I quickly switch on the light.

"Asha, that's bright," Elias winces, his hand covering his eyes from the glare.

"Elias, did Amara ever speak to you about the shard?" I probe, hopeful for any clue. He shakes his head in denial. "Or possibly something she concealed, like a cellar or spare room?"

After a brief pause, he responds with a hint of sarcasm, "If she hid it, how would I know?" His logic momentarily dampens my spirits. Yet, I can't shake the conviction that there is something more here, perhaps a secret chamber or an unseen nook.

"Okay," I announce, "we need to search the house. She must have hidden it here somewhere. This is why the hooded figure came after her." My eyes rove across the room, delving into the familiar yet now mysterious nooks of Elias's home, on the lookout for any hint or clue Amara might have left.

A sudden burst of crimson light outside the window paints the walls of Amara's house with an ominous glow. We all stop and stare mesmerized at the intensifying light. Resembling the eye of an angered god, the malevolent red orb speeds towards the window, all the while throbbing larger with a sinister force. In that moment, panic seizes me.

"Get down," I shout. Time suddenly dilates. The window shatters with a sound both instantaneous and drawn out across time. As I leap towards the ground, my friends echo my motion in a surreal choreography with the room setting the stage for impending doom.

A wave of heat follows the fiery blaze of the explosion. Everything moves as though ensnared in molasses. As glass shards spin all around, a piece drifts so close that I can see my reflection in it. Smoke fills the air and burns my eyes. My skin prickles at the invasive heat, the safety of our refuge converted into an all-consuming blaze. Time instantly resumes its natural pace as we collapse on the ground in a heap amidst the shattered glass. Each breath rebels against the smoke that blinds us.

"I need to find Lili," I cough out. "Nico. Get horses and meet us at the rim. We need to leave, now!"

The air is thick with the acrid bite of smoke. We crawl towards the back door, our only escape from the fiery nightmare. My thoughts are scattered and frantic as we maneuver through the chaos. I don't have time to contemplate how or why time had slowed to a crawl a moment ago, but I am glad it did because it gave me time to react.

Outside, the serene night in Emberwyn has erupted into a spectacle of flames and pandemonium. Fires, as ferocious as dragon's breath, consume dwellings and storefronts with a relentless appetite. The heavens, usually speckled with stars, now bear the grim colors of calamity through the smoky air.

I race through the village. Each stride echoes my escalating fear as I traverse familiar paths now eerily transformed. The central village square, once the heart of camaraderie and laughter, has turned into a scene of chaos.

Villagers are fleeing the inferno, their forms casting bizarre shadows amidst the blaze. The air is filled with their screams in a harrowing cacophony of terror mingled with the incessant hiss and bellow of the fire. A woman stumbles from a shop, her body flailing around, screaming in agony from the flames claiming her.

In this whirlwind of fear and loss, my eyes find my mother. She is standing in the midst of the chaos. Her eyes sweep over the havoc, finally fixing upon me. "Asha!" Her call slices through the turmoil with a strange intensity.

Our gazes lock, and in that brief exchange, a storm of feelings surge in me. Her eyes reflect worry and bewilderment, maybe even a trace of fear. But, for me, it is overshadowed by an irrevocable sense of betrayal. Nico's revelation and her signature on that secretive order. It looms between us like a chasm of lies without a bridge.

Her hand stretches towards me, but my heart, burdened by Emberwyn's ruin, aches with a deeper sorrow. A sorrow born not of fire, but of deep-seated treachery. Overwhelmed, I recoil, expanding the gap between us. Her expression mirrors my anguish, reflects the internal chaos I feel. Our confrontation is impossible against the backdrop of our burning village.

Unwilling to reconcile with the tarnished image of a woman I once revered, I turn my back. Her calls fade into the obscurity of the night. Each step is a blend of flight and avoidance; a desperate bid to escape the harsh reality of her deceit. I run towards what remains of my home.

unwilling to reconcile with the tarnished image of a woman I once revered.

Upon entering our cottage, now crackling in flames, I discover Lili hiding beneath her bed in her nightgown. Her small form is quivering in fear. "Lili, we need to go, now," I urge, my voice laden with urgency and muffled by the dense smoke. Draping her in her cloak, a frail barrier against the blistering heat, I lift her and plunge into the cold clasp of the night air.

Nico is waiting for us at the east rim, his face smeared with ash. He has readied four horses. The eyes of the steeds are wide with the night's terror.

"Asha! Lili!" he calls. The atmosphere here at the rim lies oppressively quiet. Elias and Skylar are close by, lost in their own maelstrom of thoughts and emotions. Lili, amidst it all, is a portrait of anguish, her cries slicing the silence.

Nico, with a look of deep concern, gently hoists Lili onto one of the horses and wraps his coat around her. Her tiny fingers clutch the reins, her tears carving paths down her face. Breaking the hush, Nico's voice carries our collective anxiety, "We need to move quickly. We can't stay here. Where can we head?"

A spark of recollection ignites within me - the cryptic symbol on the map, the mysterious phrase, and tales of hidden passages. I face the imposing boundary of the rim, leading my horse forward. My companions watch, puzzled, as I approach the barrier.

Tentatively, I extend my hand towards the charged obsidian wall. It begins to pulse with a gentle, ancient orange glow. Then the emblem of the Order of Velloria begins to sketch on its surface, mirroring the vision from my dream. The once impenetrable wall shifts, and an entrance aglow with ethereal light is unveiled. Our earlier fears are momentarily displaced by awe as we stand before the revealed gateway. Lili's tearful eyes are now alight with amazement.

Yet, as we face the open threshold, a tremor of recollection runs down my spine – I recall the eyeless beings from my nightmare with chilling vividness. I pause, my eyes scanning the dark, dense and dead forest that lies beyond. The trees stand like silent guardians with limbs interlocked against the backdrop of the sky. A premonition of an unseen menace dwelling in the shadows envelopes me.

Nico's voice, hushed yet laden with urgency, implores, "Asha, it's time to move." With a heavy yet hopeful heart, I climb atop my steed.

Just as my thoughts bid the village a haunting farewell the earth trembles. As I turn my head back, an immense blaze erupts from the village center, annihilating any remnants of what once was. The horses neigh in terror as the blinding light surges through the night.

Just then, a chilling vision seizes my attention. There, through the trees and amidst the roaring flames of the village, stands the hooded figure, calmly surveying the collapse. Suddenly, its gaze snaps up to look at me. An icy chill crawls up my spine and I quickly turn away, spurring my horse to move faster through the glowing door, with the others tailing close behind.

As we venture into the shadowy unknown, the opening closes with a silent finality, severing our ties to the chaos that Emberwyn has become. Ahead, an unfamiliar trail stretches out, winding through the vast land filled with barren trees. Our horses surge forward, their hooves thundering against the ground. Emberwyn, our once peaceful hamlet, is now a nightmare in the background.

With our homeland receding, we press deeper into the shadowy path that lies before us. The east rim, now a mere memory behind us, marks the threshold between the world we knew and the uncertain future that awaits us ahead.

THE STYGIAN HOLLOWS

Beneath the ghostly glow of the opal moon, our small convoy moves through the silence of the Stygian Hollows. Everything around us is quiet as death. As we delve deeper into the clutches of this strange new realm, the feeling that it is tightening around us grows. The thick blanket of snow softens the horses' steps so they tread carefully, as if they too are wary of the forest's grim reputation. Overhead, like the withered hands of long-forgotten spirits, the bare branches of ancient trees interlace into a canopy that seems to stretch infinitely into the darkened sky.

The air is dense, pierced occasionally by the rustle of a startled bird or the distant snap of a twig. Each sound revives the images from my dreams to send a shiver through me. The dark voids between the trees…the eyeless specters wandering through the voids…

My unease seems to call forth a change in the weather, as snowflakes begin to fall from the sky. The gentle flurry quickly escalates, erasing the forest from view beneath a sea of violent white. In this blizzard, nothing is visible but shadows and vague outlines. The horses, their coats now frosted, battle against the deepening snow. I pull my cloak tighter around me. The Stygian Hollows, once only the subject of whispered tales and nightmares, now surrounds me with an all-too-real sense of dread.

I maneuver my horse closer to Nico's.

"Hey, Lili," I say. The frigid air wants to steal my words as the cold cuts through my clothing. Lili, huddled on Nico's horse and wrapped in his coat, trembles in clear discomfort. Hidden beneath the hood, her face is marked by fear and exhaustion.

"She's tough, but this cold is overwhelming," Nico says, looking at me as if to ask what the plan is. I don't know what the plan is. We need shelter from the storm, that's all I know. All of a sudden a soft light breaks through the oppressive darkness like a manifested beacon.

"Over there." I point towards the glow. With a shared nod, Nico and I dismount, ready to head off the trail and into the forest. My feet batter the snow as I make my way towards the source of the light. The horses follow with lowered heads, braving the storm's assault.

As we draw closer, the shape of a quaint, secluded cabin appears through the flurry. It's an old, sturdy construction. A warm light spills from a window. The door is battered by the elements and stands slightly open as we approach. I knock with urgency and the sound echoes in the silence within.

"Hello! Is anyone there?" I shout, yet only the wind's mournful cry answers back. I push the door wider and step into the warmth. The cabin's interior is simple and the embers in the fireplace are dying. It appears the inhabitants have just left the warmth of this place, or perhaps they're merely absent for some time.

Lili is the first we guide to the warmth inside, wrapping her in blankets we see stacked on a chair. The gentle heat of the fire begins to gradually restore color to her pale face.

"I'll tie up the horses," Nico says, his tone betraying none of the weariness that shadows his movements. He steps back into the storm, leaving me to care for Lili and the rest.

Skylar joins us by the fire. A fierce shivering has overtaken her and her teeth click together from the cold. Now closer to the strengthening flames, her eyes reflect gratitude amidst the discomfort for a moment before sleep quickly overtakes her. Lili curls up next to Skylar and her heavy breathing signals that sleep has taken her as well. I smile, drying my braids from the melted snow. A blast of icy air rushes in as Nico is briefly framed by the snowy backdrop. He shuts the door, shaking the chill from his coat as he joins me by the fire's warmth.

Elias is already rummaging through the cabinets in the kitchen. He comes back victorious with a modest collection of provisions — dried fruits, nuts, and some pieces of hard cheese.

"Behold our banquet," he declares with a flourish. He holds up a piece of cheese. "And the fabled 'Cheese of Comfort.' It's said one bite can erase all your troubles!"

I can't help but laugh, yet Nico's response is unexpectedly sharp. "Do you always have to make a joke about everything, Elias?" he snaps. Elias's smile disappears and a hint of sadness etches his features as the light-hearted mood vanishes.

"I just was..." he starts, his voice tinged with disappointment.

"Nico, that's enough," I quickly speak up. Elias stands, his usual vibrancy dimmed.

"I'm going to head to bed," he says softly and retreats to a small room off the main space. In the ensuing silence, I face Nico.

"You shouldn't lash out at him like that," I whisper sternly, cautious not to disturb the rest. "He's coping in his own way."

Nico exhales, staring into the fire's fading light. "I get it. But his endless jests... It feels like he doesn't grasp the gravity of our situation. And truthfully," he adds, "I'm not sure I can fully trust him." His admission lingers between us. Not trust him?

"What has he ever done to make you not trust him?" I ask, slightly annoyed at his behavior. Where is this coming from?

"I don't know. Do you trust him, Asha?" Nico locks eyes with me. I shift my gaze to the open bedroom door through which Elias has vanished. A complex web of emotions envelops me—trust, doubt, hope.

"I have no reason not to trust him. He's stood by us through everything. But Nico, what's really bothering you? What's all this about?"

The comforting glow of the fire seems to diminish as the weight of our predicament settles over us. Nico's eyes are searching for an answer. He lets out a deep sigh.

"I'm just worried, Asha," he confesses. "About my father, about everything. Events are unfolding so fast, and I... what if... what if he didn't make it out of Emberwyn?" His voice trails off. Drawing nearer, I envelop him in a reassuring hug. The tension in his body is evident, like a manifestation of his inner turmoil.

"Nico, you're not alone," I murmur, aiming to instill a sense of comfort amidst his swirling uncertainty. "I am here. We will figure it out together. Your father is resilient. He will be okay." His gaze lingers on the dancing fire before he leans into my embrace. The silence is heavy with my own unspoken worries. The concern for his father is clear, but I can sense deeper, unshared troubles beneath his surface. My thoughts drift to Elias, now probably asleep, and the tension that flared between him and Nico. There's a comfortable silence between us, filled only by the occasional pop of burning wood. As I watch the fire dance, a realization dawns on me.

"I almost forgot, happy name day," I say. "I wanted to get you something but…" My voice fades into the crackling noise of the fire. He turns to me, a faint smile touching his lips, but there's a shadow in his eyes that wasn't there before.

"Thanks, Asha. But let's not make a big deal out of it, okay?" His response, gentle yet dismissive, sends a pang through my chest.

"Is something wrong?" The question slips out, laced with concern. I notice his shoulders tense ever so slightly before he relaxes again.

"No. It's just everything," he murmurs, his attention shifting to the flames, as if seeking answers in their chaotic swirl. "Let's just focus on making it through tonight. We'll tackle everything else come morning." His voice is soft, almost resigned.

I'm torn between pressing him for more and respecting his wish to leave the conversation for another day. The urge to understand what he's going through is overwhelming. Instead, I scoot closer, hoping my proximity offers some comfort. We remain there, side by side, enveloped by the warmth of the fire until sleep's gentle embrace leads me into a night filled with restless dreams.

⸻ ⁂ ⸻

Dawn seeps through the cabin's modest windows, casting a soft, blue glow across the room. My limbs are stiff from a night spent pressed against Nico. While hardly comfortable, the makeshift bed by the hearth offered a measure of peace to the two of us. Nico's head is slightly tilted and he murmurs something indistinct in his sleep. With only a handful of hardly breathing embers in the fireplace, a creeping chill has now replaced the warmth. I nudge Nico gently, rousing him from his disturbed rest.

"Nico," I say softly, "You should check on the horses." He opens his eyes slowly, squinting as he adjusts to the morning. With a muted groan, he rises, wiping away the remnants of sleep.

"Alright, I'll take care of them," he murmurs, pushing himself to his feet. As he makes his way to the door, his movements weary, I can't help but feel guilt for bringing him into this. The enormity of everything weighs visibly on him. The door shuts behind him, leaving a tangible silence. I set about reigniting the fire, methodically arranging the charred pieces of wood and kindling. The initial spark against the chill is a small triumph and the newly kindled flames begin to flicker and grow.

In the corner, Lili and Skylar lie huddled together. Their peaceful slumber brings a smile to my lips. Lili's small hand clutches Skylar's shirt, her face deep in sleep. It's a moment of innocence amidst the chaos, and it melts my heart. It also makes me sad. Lili is only seven, and seven-year-old little girls shouldn't have to endure all this. She's supposed to be playing in the snow, letting the wind tangle her hair. Not here. Not like this.

As the fire fills the room with its glow, I settle back, absorbed in the dance of the flames. The heat penetrates deep, dispelling the chill of the thoughts that have plagued me. In that brief moment, tranquility reigns. Yet, even as I bask in the fire's warmth, my thoughts inevitably drift towards the future. The road ahead is full of uncertainty. My confidence in my leadership seems so distant. How can I lead anyone? I'm not a leader. I'm just…me.

It is during this contemplation that a stirring from the next room draws my attention. Elias appears, his usually neat white hair now a disheveled mess as he makes his way to the kitchen and begins searching through a cupboard. A faint smile creeps onto my lips.

"Good morning, Elias. Seeking out the legendary cheese, are you?" I attempt to lighten the air after last night, but he simply responds with a subdued and flat: "Just looking for something to eat." The change in his demeanor is disheartening. I observe him for a moment as he continues his search, then redirect my focus to the fire. Nico's earlier outburst towards him seems even more unjustified now.

Just then, Nico enters, brushing off the morning's chill. He joins me by the fire.

"We need to decide on our next steps," he says. "This refuge is temporary at best. The Legion could already be on our trail, and our proximity to Emberwyn poses a risk."

"You're right. We obviously can't go back to Emberwyn, not after last night. We need to keep moving." Elias now joins us at the fire and the air becomes thick with an unspoken tension until he breaks the silence.

"So, what's the strategy? Are we planning to become part of the furniture here, or is there an actual plan?" I smile, happy to hear his humor coming back.

Nico, staring into the fire, raises his eyes. "He's right. We can't afford to stay put. The longer we remain, the higher the risk becomes. The Legion is likely scouring the area as we speak."

A wave of apprehension washes over me. "Moving on is our only choice. Velloria lies at the heart of all this mystery. It's our most plausible destination. I need answers."

Skylar is now awake and she looks over, her curiosity piqued. "Where are we, exactly?" she asks.

Chuckling lightly, Elias turns toward her with dramatic flair. "In a strange cabin in the woods, obviously."

"But where is 'here' in relation to the map?" Skylar insists, her voice carrying a decisive edge. Elias draws a deep breath and prepares to reply, but I intervene. I unfold the map on the floor before us and they gather around. I point out our position—or rather, the lack thereof. The cabin isn't on the map anywhere.

"Our safest route is northward, towards the river," I say. It should offer a crossing point. From there, Velloria is straight ahead. Going back isn't an option."

Elias's playful demeanor gives way to intense concentration as he peers closely at the map. "But what about food? We can't head off into the unknown without food."

"I'll search the cabin for anything we can use. Food, blankets, whatever might help us," Nico says.

"I'm in," Skylar adds, standing up eagerly.

"Me too." Lili's voice joins in. She sits up, rubbing her eyes. Her brown braids are a mess. I can't remember the last time I had freely sat down to braid my sister's hair.

Our temporary shelter hums with activity as each of us spreads out within its confines to scour every possible hiding spot—drawers, cupboards, and shelves—in search of anything that might aid our journey. Watching the determination on Lili's face stirs emotions in me. Her youthful optimism seems almost out of place against the reality we are facing. I turn my attention to gathering our essential supplies, pulling blankets from a concealed chest, collecting dried food, and filling a sturdy leather canteen. Elias, who has been quietly observing from the sidelines, stands up.

"I'll take a look in the back room," he announces. Shortly afterward, Nico returns, laden with a sack brimming with additional blankets. Skylar follows, her hands clutching a box of matches and a handful of candles. Lili, clutching a quaint, rusted lantern and balancing some garments under her other arm, is clearly proud of her contributions.

"What have you found?" I ask, reaching out to relieve Lili of the garments.

"Some warm clothes for me," she replies with a wide smile. Holding the garments, I inspect the modest woolen tunic, sturdy trousers, and a pair of slightly worn boots. They all seem tailored to fit her. The discovery seems like a stroke of luck. Yet, the thought that these items had once belonged to another child, perhaps one still facing the harshness of the world, fills me with a sense of unease. As I weigh our needs against those of the unknown child, Elias notices my hesitation.

"Asha," he says gently, "if they've left these behind, it's likely they have others. The previous occupants don't need them now. Lili does." His straightforward perspective slices through my moral dilemma. Looking into Lili's expectant eyes, I am reminded of the reality we are navigating. My primary concern has to be the well-being of ourselves; ensuring our warmth and comfort is an obligation I can't ignore.

"Well, it looks like you have some new clothes now." I smile, assisting her into the new layers. With each piece of clothing, she seems to regain a bit more vitality, the garments fitting her as if they were made with her in mind.

The air outside the cabin is brisk, carrying the bite of early morning frost. The horses' breaths are visible in the cold air as they await us patiently. Lili, now comfortably dressed, walks with her hand in mine.

"Asha, may I ride with you?" she asks eagerly.

"Of course," I assure her, squeezing her hand slightly. Nico observes our exchange and lifts Lili onto the horse, where she settles into the saddle with a brave smile lighting up her face. Just as we are loading our supplies, an unexpected stillness falls upon the forest. The horses become restless. I reach out, whispering calming words to my steed, trying to soothe its growing anxiety, but it's too agitated. Without warning, the horse rears, its hooves slashing the air. I step back just in time to avoid its flailing limbs, but my heart sinks as I see Lili's stability falter and her small hands losing their hold.

I scream her name as she slips from the saddle and her small form lands softly in the thick snow below. The very same instant, the ground beneath the horse erupts, revealing a creature that defies explanation—a grotesque fusion of worm and insect, propelling soil and snow into the air with violent force. It's the size of a large dog but possesses a terror beyond any natural beast. Its multiple segments are armed with sharp, barbed appendages. Its skin is a disturbing shade of gray, slick with a sinister sheen that makes it seem as if it had slithered straight out of a nightmare.

The horse, caught in the grip of terror, thrashes wildly, its hooves churning up clouds of snow that swirl around us, casting everything into a disorienting white chaos. The creature's gaping maw fastens onto the horse's thigh, its form writhing from the horse's agony like a hellish parasite.

Acting on sheer impulse, I cover Lili with my own body, forming a human shield as snow and debris burst into the air around us. The air fills with the horse's petrified screams and the vile, slurping sounds of the creature.

"Nico," I scream.

He swiftly moves to his horse and grabs his sword and strikes the creature with immense force. The creature lets out a hiss and releases its grip on the horse's thigh, its body contorting in a chaotic blend of rage and agony. As it recoils, a deep, hissing growl escapes its tooth-filled maw. Nico stumbles backward but finds his footing. I sense a whipping motion somewhere near my feet but I am transfixed by the sight of the menace looming large in front of us.

Elias tosses his bow on the ground and dashes to the horse. He struggles with the reins before successfully releasing the terrified animal. Seizing the chance to flee, the horse kicks frantically. Its hooves knock the creature back, disorienting it as the horse vanishes into the forest's dense underbrush, leaving a trail of blood behind. The creature regains its bearings and shifts its menacing gaze to Nico. Its body moves with the sinuous grace of a snake poised to attack. Nico positions himself protectively in front of me, raising the sword with a threatening glare.

"Kill it," Skylar screams.

Lili's small body is shaking with fear as I clutch her close. Our short, rapid breaths spurt white into the cold air. For a long moment the only sounds are heavy breathing and the guttural hissing of the creature. Then, as if deciding it has had enough, the enormous entomic creature quickly burrows into the earth and disappears. Nico hovers over the hole it has left behind, his eyes feverishly scanning the ground, as if expecting the insectoid thing to reemerge any moment. His stance is tense, the sword gripped tightly in his hand.

Elias moves swiftly to my side. "Asha, are you okay?" he asks, grabbing my arm to help me to my feet. Lili clings to me trembling. I glance down beside me to find an arrow stuck in the snow only a few inches from where I lay. I look at Elias.

"I'm sorry. I was trying to shoot that thing, but I… I missed," he says.

"You nearly shot me, Elias," I say and take a deep breath. "It's fine. I'm fine, really. We should focus on getting out of here." I kneel down beside Lili, my hands sweeping over her small frame to check for any signs of injury. Her wide eyes are still reflecting the fright of the ordeal.

"Lili, sweetheart, are you hurt anywhere?" I ask. She shakes her head, her braids swaying slightly. I can tell she's still shaken. Gently, I turn her around, inspecting her back and limbs, ensuring the creature hasn't hurt her. Relief washes over me as I only find the cold dampness of the snow on her clothes. I wrap my arms around her. Her small arms encircle me in return.

"We need to move," Elias says as he loosens the reins of his horse from the tree. "Whatever that was, encountering another is not on my list of things to do before I die."

"Is there any chance the horse will be okay?" Skylar asks. Nico somberly shakes his head in response.

"Not with injuries that severe," he says quietly, eying the trail of blood left by the steed. A deep quiet settles among us, punctuated by Lili's muted sobs. Turning to her, I offer a comforting smile.

"Lili, why don't you go with Skylar?" I suggest softly. She nods her head and I lift her up to the saddle in front of Skylar. She quickly settles in with a firm grip on Skylar's hand. I turn to Nico. "We should go." He quickly assists me with getting on to his horse before climbing on behind me. Even though the horse is still anxious, it seems stable enough to carry us.

As the cabin shrinks into the silence of the woods behind us, a vivid memory of the nerve-wracking ordeal clings to me. It is a brutal reminder of why this place is called the Stygian Hollows.

VIII

CRIMSON THUNDER

Elias's persistent inquiries, "Are you sure we're heading in the right direction?" echo the uncertainties that plague me. Our convoy seems to weave through the vast, snow-draped wilderness with no clear direction.

Nico responds with unwavering certainty, not once glancing back. "We're headed north. You can tell by the sun's position," he says. His voice is steady but tinged with a hint of irritation. Lili, nestled in front of Skylar, lets out a soft sigh of discomfort.

"I'm tired of the trees," she murmurs. Her fatigue is evident in her longing for a break from the ceaseless view of dead, icy branches. The best I can do is to offer her a smile.

"We'll find something different soon, Lili," I promise, more out of hope than certainty. My eyes roam the horizon, searching for any sign of change in the monotonous terrain, a hint that our path is leading us to… anywhere.

"Who knew the Stygian Hollows were such a treat," Elias quips. His attempt at humor barely makes a dent in the dense silence enveloping us. The bare trees throw long, ghostly shadows across the snow, adding to the eerie atmosphere. Our horses move steadily. Their breath forms misty clouds in the frigid air while the sound of their footsteps crunching the snow fills the quiet.

Elias shatters the contemplative quiet again. "Why would the Legion of Embers attack Emberwyn? It was their home as well."

"The Legion... they're like shadows," Nico responds. "Everywhere and nowhere. Their ties to the Eyeless are strong, rooted deep in dark magic. We've barely begun to uncover the extent of it."

"But why choose now to show themselves? What changed?" Skylar chimes in. Her gaze flits about in apprehension as though just discussing the Legion could conjure them forth from the forest.

"It's us," I say, though I lean more heavily on the 'me' side of 'us'. "We stumbled upon secrets meant to remain secret. We know too much." A shiver unrelated to the cold trails down my spine as I recall the vision of the hooded figure. "In Emberwyn... in the fire, there was a hooded figure," I share, "it seemed to be directing the havoc. I saw it watching us as we escaped."

A heavy silence settles around us, each of us lost in thought. It's Lili who voices a different fear that has been silently preying on my mind.

"Are the Eyeless in these woods?" Her question seems to resonate through the trees. The heavy silence around us almost becomes audible for a few moments. It has a crisp, sizzling sound, as if it were only a veil through which something imperceptibly hideous was trying to get through.

Elias, attempting to dispel the tension with laughter, responds, "There are no Eyeless here because they're all haunting Emberwyn." His words, meant to reassure, instead trigger a flood of tears from Lili.

"I miss my mother." With a trembling voice she buries her face in Skylar's coat.

"Nico, stop for a moment," I say sharply. He pulls on the reins to slow our progress and brings the horse near Skylar and Lili. I glance at Elias with a frown of frustration for his careless remark.

"Lili, listen to me," I urge. "The Eyeless aren't in Emberwyn. Our mother is strong and safe. She's looking after everyone in the village." Gradually, Lili's sobs quiet as she raises her eyes to meet mine.

"Really?" she whispers.

"Yes, absolutely," I assure her with a gentle smile, softly wiping away her tears. "I saw her as we were leaving. She is safe." The memory of seeing mother standing in the chaos flickers through my mind. I quickly push away the anger that starts to boil. Nico, who has been watching silently, offers his support, placing a comforting hand on Lili's shoulder.

"It's true, Lili. Your mother is strong," he says. A brave little smile flickers on her face as Lili wipes her tears on her sleeve. I sit back upright and give Elias another stern look. He meets it with a sheepish and apologetic shrug as I shake my head.

"Asha, look!" Skylar stretches her hand out towards the horizon.

I shift my gaze in the direction she's pointing. As we approach the forest's edge, I can't help but pause to take in the scene unfolding in front of us. The cold air bites at my cheek as my heart skips a beat. The interminable rows of trees are almost behind us, and the world ahead is opening up dramatically. The snow-covered field stretches out as far as the eye can see. The openness of its surface glistens under the pale winter sun. This sudden boundless expanse feels both liberating and daunting. Without the trees' shelter, we are exposed, vulnerable to both the elements and any lurking eyes. The cold air bites at my cheeks as I pause to take in the scene.

"If this is the edge of the forest," I say, pulling the map from my coat, "then the river is out there, and after that we should find the Whispering Forest."

Lili groans. "I don't want more forests. I'm sick of them." Ironically, Lili's statement sounds fetching in front of my misgiving about traveling in such an exposed environment.

"Either way, we need to keep heading north," I say, tracing the route with my finger. "The river will be our next landmark."

Nico, squinting at the map and then surveying the horizon, nods in agreement. "We won't make it across by nightfall," he says, "It's better to rest here and build a fire. We don't want to be caught in the middle of that field, especially if another blizzard hits." I fold the map, tucking it away securely. As much as I want to get to the city, he's right.

We choose a small clearing just within the edge of the forest, where the trees can offer some shelter against the wind. Lili, wrapped tightly in her cloak, huddles close to Skylar on a fallen log as Elias and Nico begin gathering wood. I brush away snow to clear a space for our fire.

As the twilight deepens, the fire is now crackling with life. We sit close to it, the flames warming my body and illuminating everyone's tired faces.

"I never imagine we'd be doing this," Skylar murmurs, staring into the fire. "You know… journeying through unknown lands, fleeing... whatever we're fleeing from."

"It's like we're part of a fairytale story, but without fairies," Lili adds wearily through her droopy eyes.

Nico leans back, his eyes reflecting the flames. "If this is a fairytale, it's one with too many twists," he remarks.

Elias pokes at the fire with a stick and lets out a small chuckle. "Well, every good story needs a bit of suspense, doesn't it? Keeps our hearts pumping."

I smooth Lili's hair back as she nestles closer, her eyelids closing towards sleep. "Not every tale is suited for bedtime," I say as my mind ponders the shadowed path this unpredictable adventure has brought us down so far. The gaze of the others settles on me, silently urging me for a story.

"I'm not really in a story kind of mood tonight," I murmur, drawing my coat tighter around me. The day's journey through the snow-laden forest has left me craving silence and the simple comfort of the flames.

"Perhaps some poetry then?" Skylar suggests. From her satchel, she pulls out a small, well-worn book with a cover barely visible under the firelight. "It's my mother's old poetry book. I always keep it with me." I hear Elias grumble something, but a quick glare from Skylar silences him. He shifts, resigned, and settles back against the log, the fire casting shadows across his face.

Skylar opens the book with reverence and flips through the pages until she finds what she's looking for.

Clearing her throat softly, she begins to read, her voice carrying over the fire:

"In a realm of frost and shadow,

Two hearts kindled a flame,

A love whispered by the meadow,

Bearing neither wealth nor fame.

He, a wanderer of the snowy plains,

She, a spirit of the forest's heart,

Their meeting foretold by ancient chains,

In the winter's chill, they'd never part.

Through the snow, they danced, carefree,

Beneath the moon's watchful eye,

Promises made under the canopy,

Underneath the starlit sky.

But as seasons change, so too fate,

A test of time and tide,

Their bond, strong, would not abate,

Together, side by side.

For in the end, it's love that wins,

A story old as time,

Through every loss and all our sins,

In every mountain we climb."

The poetry weaves through the air a tale of enduring love against the backdrop of an unforgiving winter. It feels almost as if it is our story, here by this fire, as the endless snow surrounds us. She closes the book and holds it to her chest for a moment with a smile before placing it back in her satchel.

The soft crackling of the fire lends a moment of silence. Lili nestles close to me. "Asha, will we be okay?" she whispers. The firelight reflected in her eyes does not hide the shadows of doubt that are haunting her. I pull her closer and look into her eyes.

"Yes, Lili, we will be okay," I whisper back with confidence. Confidence that I don't really feel, but I hope she will. The worry slowly pries from her expression and she lays her head against my chest, falling fast asleep. Elias, Nico, and Skylar sit around the gently flickering fire, quietly fiddling with their own thoughts.

"So," Elias's voice breaks the quiet, "what exactly is your plan, Asha? I mean, I know we're heading to Velloria. But, I feel like we're just traveling with no solid goal in sight."

I contemplate his question for a moment before answering.

"When my father disappeared at the east rim a year ago," I begin, "he left his blade. The blade that has the same seal as my tattoo, and the same as the one on the map for Velloria." I pause, then continue, "I need answers, and if the lore your grandmother told me is true, then we need the shard of the sword."

"But, why do we need it? What's the point? We can't put it back together."

"I don't know, Elias," I say.

"It's okay, Asha. We will figure it out," Skylar says softly. I glance up at her from across the fire. "If my father was missing, I would want to know what happened. We can figure out all the blade stuff later."

"Thank you," I smile. "You guys didn't have to come with me. You could have stayed back at the village."

"Yes, but if we hadn't come then you and Lili would have been eaten by that monster already." Elias chuckles.

"He does have a point," Nico says, grinning.

"You're probably right," I say with a laugh.

As the night deepens, fatigue begins to claim us. Elias leans back contentedly and Skylar finds her place beside him, her form molding to his. Nico, after a final contemplative glance at the dying fire, succumbs to sleep as well. I linger awake a while longer, comforted by the rhythm of Lili's breathing in the stillness. Watching my friends and my sister, I let the fire's residual warmth and soft sound of the embers coax me towards sleep. My eyelids are heavy with the weight of the day's memories floating through my mind like shadows.

Instantly, like a snap of a twig, the fire dims to mere embers as if snuffed out. Darkness and silence flood the forest. Shadows like specters filigree the snow as the moonlight weaves through the border of the trees. Confusion washes over me until I realize I had drifted off and woken without meaning to. The others lie in peaceful slumber, their outlines faint in the dim light. Lili is a curled treasure in my lap.

As I try to come to terms with my sleep-addled haze, something splits from the shadows and moves swiftly between the trees. My heart jumps into my throat. It's too far to discern any details, but its presence sends a jolt of fear through me. It was large, whatever it was. My entire body tingles with alarm. I want to scream, to wake the others, but the lump in my throat seems to choke me. The forest air thickens with tension as the shadowy figure quickly emerges from the line of trees. My breath catches in my throat and wedges itself tightly against my heart. The moonlight reveals the form of… an Eyeless.

Its humanoid shape is hunched and unnatural and moves with a jerky, almost insect-like motion. Its skin is a black sheen. Even in the dimness the thick, pulsing veins are visible beneath the surface. Its arms, long and slender, drag hands laden with sharp claws through the snow. It slinks toward me… I want to scream, to run, but my body refuses to obey. I am paralyzed, my grip on Lili my only connection to reality.

As it draws nearer, deep terror takes hold of me. Its presence is suffocating, like an oppressive force that seems to weigh down on my very soul. I feel like I am being crushed into the earth. I can feel its gaze, though it has no eyes, peering into me, probing the depths of my deepest fears. Then, its attention shifts. It turns its head to where

Skylar lies sleeping, oblivious to the nightmare unfolding mere feet away.

A guttural clicking emanates from its throat with a sound so alien and disturbing it makes my skin crawl. For a moment, the Eyeless stands there, its head cocked in Skylar's direction. Its body contracts and expands as its heavy breath sends bellows of fog into the air through its razor-sharp teeth. The frigid night air holds me in a suffocating grip as the creature begins to creep closer to her. *Skylar! Run!* My mind screams. Its hideous form moves with sinister fluidity, eerily silent under the mutely watching moon. My heart thunders against my chest, yet I am paralyzed by the invisible force that continues to press on top of me.

The ghostly silhouette of one clawed hand reaches out towards Skylar. Panic screams within my mind, but my body remains a captive to an unseen terror, and my voice remains a prisoner in my throat. In an instant, as its black claws gently touch Skylar's skin, the world erupts in a blinding light, shattering the night's oppressive hold. My paralysis splinters and I release a raw scream that pierces the silence of the morning.

I am madly gasping for air when Nico gets up with a jolt, his eyes wide with confusion and fear, followed by Elias and Skylar, roused by the raw urgency of my cry.

"What? What is it?" Elias shouts in blind fear as he looks around in a panic. Lili is squirming in frenzy in my lap, trying to make sense of what's going on. I shush her and hold her tightly as I look this way and that. The morning light bathes the open field in a golden hue, prompting me to question if I had fallen asleep once more. Was the terror of the night just another nightmare? My heart races as I touch my chest. Skylar's gaze, filled with worry, meets mine.

"I... I'm sorry. It was just a nightmare," I manage to say, my voice quivering. But my doubts remain. The experience felt too real to be just a dream. Elias's initial alarm has now morphed into a look of concern.

"Well," he declares, as he surveys our surroundings, "I've had enough of this forest. Let's leave and never come back."

"I think we can all agree to that," Skylar says, her eyes cautiously sweeping the forest perimeter. "This place unnerves me."

I press a reassuring kiss atop Lili's head, exhaling a deep sigh of relief, before assisting her to stand. We quickly pack up and extinguish the fire's last embers as the sun ascends. As Skylar mounts her horse, a faint cough pierces the quiet. "This cold is relentless. Let's go. Velloria promises warmth and refuge. Well, maybe not a promise, but I hope it's better than this."

With that, we mount our horses. The forest, with all its secrets, watches in silence as we depart from its hold and begin our trek across the snowy plane.

The snowfield stretches endlessly before us and it begins to weigh heavily on my spirit. After hours of travel, with nothing but the shifting snowdrifts to mark our journey, Elias breaks the silence. His usual charm is replaced by a hint of despair.

"It feels like we're trapped in an infinite loop. Are we even sure this is the way? It's just endless snow everywhere."

"Better endless snow than endless trees," Lili chimes in from within her cocoon of blankets, eliciting a light laugh from Skylar.

"All I'm asking for is a bit of variety in the landscape," Elias adds. "You know. Something more… appealing."

No sooner have his words faded than a thunderous roar reverberates from behind, halting us in our tracks. The sky, previously clear, now roils with a menacing storm heading our way. Crimson lightning tears through the gathering clouds, illuminating the snow in a red glow.

"Was that the change of scenery you were hoping for?" Nico quips. But the brewing storm quickly squashes any semblance of humor among us. The wind, growing increasingly violent, begins whipping the snow around us into a blinding chaos. Another bolt of scarlet lightning strikes the ground. The thunderous echo rattles me to my core. We quickly spur our horses into a desperate gallop, trying to outpace the rapidly approaching storm. Skylar's face is pale as Lili clings to her, trembling uncontrollably.

Above us, the sky transforms into a theater of apocalypse, lit sporadically by the violent dance of red lightning. The ground beneath us shakes with the impact of each bolt, hurling shards of ice and snow into the air, enveloping us in pure chaos. The constant barrage of thunder seems to fracture the very air around us.

Abruptly, our horses come to a stop, their bodies pitching upwards in panic. Both Nico and I fight to regain control, our hands clenching the reins with desperate strength. Before us yawns a vast chasm, its jagged edges cutting into the landscape, plunging into a seemingly bottomless icy void.

In that moment, a bolt of scarlet lightning cleaves the stormy heavens, heading straight for us. Time slows to a crawl as the lightning falls like a divine weapon cast down by an invisible hand in slow motion. Its red glare pierces the gloom, bathing the swirling snow in an eerie, blood-red light. The air around it vibrates with its power, outlining the chaos of the storm in a grotesque palette of reds and shadows. Our horse, driven by a primal urge to flee the lethal threat, executes a sharp turn. The maneuver, executed with a desperate elegance, diverts us from the lightning's path, but just barely. The earth shakes as the lightning explodes the ground where we had just been, sending a jarring tremor through the earth.

"We're cornered!" Nico's voice rises above the roar of the wind as time resumes its natural pace. "The storm—"

His yell is abruptly interrupted as the ground at the chasm's edge crumbles beneath us, throwing us into a harrowing descent down the steep incline. Our cries merge with the howl of the storm as we scrabble for a hold on the slick, unyielding surface, but to no avail. The force of our fall, accompanied by the sinister glow of red lightning, makes it a nightmarish descent.

"Lili!" I scream, my hands frantically reaching out for something. Anything. The horses' distressed cries pierce the air as their hooves lose traction on the icy slope. Our efforts to halt the slide are futile. We are at the mercy of the chasm's pull. The landscape blurs into a chaotic whirl of white and gray, punctuated by the sinister flickers of red lightning. We slide off the end of the slope into the chasm's open maw eager for its feast.

Hovering momentarily in the heart of the storm, we are bathed in an eerie red glow from the lightning. Each of us is outlined in a spectral light that seems to freeze us in a scene of horror. Then, as if released by an unseen force, we are pulled downward into the void.

The air fills with Nico's cry and Lili's piercing scream but their voices are woven into the howling din of the storm. Darkness envelops me completely, transforming the descent into a journey through the pitch black. A sudden luminescent green light engulfs me. This sudden illumination seems to bring with it a fleeting sense of calm, but, this illusion shatters as cold water devours me in a shock of clarity that robs me of my breath. We have plunged into a concealed body of water, its unforgiving abyss threatening to drag us further into its icy bosom.

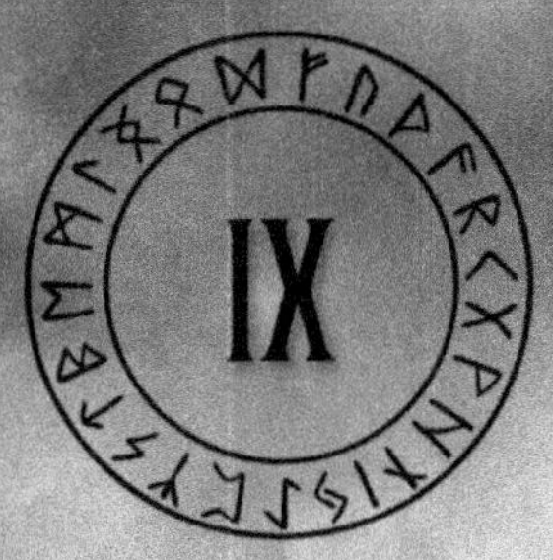

ANYTHING & EVERYTHING DOOR

Gasping for air, I break the surface, my limbs flailing in the icy shock of the water. The sound of splashing and coughing from the others echoes in the strange green glow.

Nico's voice cuts through the darkness. "Asha! Where are you?"

"Over here." My voice is a raw scrape. My hands find something solid. A ledge. I grip it and feel grass under my fingers; it's instantly confusing but I can't think about it now. "Lili, where are you?" My voice is pure panic as I call out. Soon I see her silhouette; she is safe in Skylar's arms. My arms plow the cold water in circles as I feel the warmth of relief.

We help each other onto the ledge. Skylar trembles uncontrollably as she climbs out of the water, and Elias follows with an expression of sheer exhaustion. Lili clings to me sobbing as her small body shivers. Nico makes his way to us, his body wracked with coughs as he spits out water. The horses, it seems, are lost to the river's currents.

As we lie there trying to collect ourselves, the darkness begins to fade around us, pushed back by the soft, phosphorescent green light. It emanates from the cavern walls, casting eerie shadows and giving the stone a ghostly luminescence. Underneath me, the ground is a surprising grassy softness. Grass in an underground cave? It's a foreign yet slightly comforting sensation feeling it between my fingers.

"Oh no," Skylar exclaims.

"What is it?" I ask quickly.

"My poetry book. It's gone…" She lets out a small coughing sob. I sigh thinking it was something else but I'm also sad for her. It was the only piece of her mother she had left, and it is gone now.

"I'm so sorry," I say softly.

A small movement against my hand startles me and I recoil. I look down expecting to find a snake or a rat, but instead of a creature, I find a flower. It is opening its petals slowly, releasing a soft green light that slices through the dark with its tender beams. My chilled body starts to warm, energized by the peculiar warmth coming from this flower. The oppressive dark retreats further, as more flowers bloom in a silent explosion of light.

Looking around, I find myself in a mystical intersection, where summer blends with autumn's deep colors, all inside an underground cavern. A whole forest is revealing itself around us, its trees a mix of vibrant green and the rich gold and red of fall. A breeze carrying the scent of moss and ancient earth flutters through the leaves.

"Wow..." Lili says. "It's so magical. Could there be fairies? *Real* fairies?" As I'm staring absentmindedly at the transformation around us, a woman's voice, as melodious as flowing water, echoes softly from nearby.

"Of course, my child." We all turn toward the sound. From the shadows steps a figure that appears to be born from the forest itself. She stands before us like a vision, her clothes fluttering as though caught in a gentle breeze like leaves dancing in the autumn air. Her skin emits a gentle glow that merges perfectly with the forest's ambient light. Her hair flows in waves, adorned with the hues of green and gold that echo the overhead canopy. Her eyes are deep pools of vibrant green that glance over us as she speaks.

"This forest is home to marvels that extend beyond simple fairy tales," she says with a smile. Her voice is as soothing as a lullaby. She extends her hand, and from it, a glowing flower spirals into being. It floats from her hand and drifts towards Lili, who watches in awe. I lower my head, pulling my cloak over my face to hide the mark on my forehead. Her demeanor hints at her being a possible friend. But until I understand who she is and where we are, I decide it best not to unveil too much just yet.

"So... who are you, and what do you want?" Elias's tone is too impolite for the situation and I quickly speak up.

"Don't be rude, Elias," I say sternly. The woman responds with a calm smile. Then, moving with a grace that seems as natural as the wind, she begins walking toward the edge of the forest.

"Well done," I grumble, annoyed. "There was no need for that rudeness, Elias. We need to follow her." I receive Lili's agreement with an enthusiastic nod, as her small hand squeezes mine.

"Fine, but if we end up as monster food, I'm blaming you, Asha." Elias tries to lighten the mood with a joke, but I am already irritated. Since our escape from the village and after the ordeal we've just survived, this woman represents the first real encounter. I'm not about to let Elias's lack of manners drive her away before I have a chance to know who she is. I walk towards the woman with Lili's hand in mine. Nico and Skylar follow, and after a moment's hesitation, Elias joins us.

"My name is Lavinia," she says as we approach. "I serve as the overseer of the Whispering Forest. My life is committed to protecting these ancient woods and all its inhabitants. This sanctuary represents a fragment of the world in its primal magic, teeming with wonders and enchantments."

"The Whispering Forest," I repeat softly. We made it. Not just, but Velloria is much closer than I had thought.

"Are you a fairy?" Lili's small voice asks.

"No, my dear. I am a Meliae. An ash tree nymph. I am a part of this forest, just as the leaves are a part of the trees." She smiles gently, then as she gives a wave of her hand, small lights emerge along a path. Housed inside little orbs of glass, the lights create a path leading deeper into the forest. Hanging from a branch and nestled at the foot of the tree, they run in pairs. Lavinia's gait displays a grace as integral to the forest as the ancient trees themselves.

"I protect every creature here. I give a voice to the voiceless; strength to those who weaken," she says. Her words seem to resonate with the forest, making it feel alive as we follow her down the path.

"Long ago," she continues, "this forest thrived in the daylight. It was a haven of magic and beauty on the surface of the earth. But during the Darkest Battle, our enemies tried to destroy it, attacking with a relentless fury of black magic." Her gaze turns somber as she looks around at the thriving greenery.

"In that darkest hour, The Sylvan Circle—ancient mages of deep magic—cast a powerful spell that hid what remained of our beloved forest underground, protecting it from those who wished its end. Thus, the Whispering Forest was preserved in this secluded sanctuary." She gestures broadly, drawing attention to the vibrant life around us. The glowing flowers and the rich canopy seem to listen to her tale.

"This is the last remnant of a once vast, enchanted land. Hidden and sustained by the sacrifices of our ancestors and our diligent protection. We guard it until the darkness over Velloria clears, and the world is ready to embrace its magic once more."

A weight presses on my chest. "What darkness looms over Velloria?" I ask. Her eyes soften as she faces me.

"Velloria fell during the Darkest Battle. The forces of the Legion of Embers aimed not only to annihilate this forest but every haven of hope on earth. Velloria's defenders became overwhelmed and could not withstand the dark onslaught that followed." Her eyes wander to the glowing autumn leaves around us.

"Velloria now shadows its former self. Its once vibrant streets and grand edifices now lie in ruin, home to creatures of the dark. The vilest beings claim it, staining its legacy." Her words linger like a veil over the forest's enchantment. "This is why we safeguard the forest. We hope that Velloria will one day emerge from the darkness."

"So, I take it we're not heading to Velloria, are we?" Elias's eyes meet mine. The thought of going to a city that's home to dark creatures scares him. It scares me too, honestly, but I need answers, and I want to find the missing shard.

"I don't have a choice, Elias," I whisper back. "I have to go."

His shoulders sag. I told him he didn't have to come, but I also know that if Skylar is staying for the journey then he would too.

The orb lanterns lead us down a path that opens into a beautiful clearing. At its center stands a breathtaking tree. Its bark gleams white like ash and its Amaranth leaves cast a soft, twinkling glow over the ground.

"This," Lavinia announces with pride, "is the forest's heart." She gestures to the majestic tree. "Its roots are deeply entwined with the earth's essence, tapping into the ley lines of magic that flow beneath us."

Drawn by the tree's majesty, I step closer, and am surrounded by a warmth that pulses with energy. The Amaranth leaves whisper with a breeze that seems to breathe the world into existence, pulling me nearer. I pause to touch the enormous, sprawling roots at the tree's base. As my skin meets the ashen bark, a burst of golden light spreads from my touch, tracing the intricate patterns of veins under its surface. This energy climbs the tree, infusing the Amaranth leaves with vibrant life, and causes them to glow more intensely. Lavinia watches with a gentle smile.

"Ah. The tree senses you. This exchange, your touch, is a rare sight. You have a deep connection with nature's core, Asha." Her eyes study me and I lower my head slightly, making sure not to let her see my forehead.

"How do you know my name?" I ask.

"I know all of your names." She smiles. "This is the Whispering Forest, and the trees whisper to me." The idea of trees actually whispering secrets to her is not something I expected. I suppose, given the impossible nature of this place, anything could be possible. I turn back to the tree. The golden light dances through the leaves. I feel a subtle, but profound sense of oneness with the surrounding life. This ancient tree seems to lure my mind away from the moment.

In the engulfing silence, a loud noise fractures the peace and I pull my hand back. A small, moss-clad cabin I hadn't noticed before expels a figure both amusing and startling. A tiny old man, his beard wild like the underbrush, comes toward us wielding a small walking stick.

"Stop this racket!" he shouts. His voice sends birds flying from their perches. I move back from the tree as he plants himself defiantly between us and the tree. His clothes tell tales of numerous adventures from all the patched holes with different colored fabrics. Cinched at his waist is a leather belt laden with pouches and vials. Over his shoulder… oh my… a small leather bag holds a remarkably calm frog, whose large eyes protrude just above the opening. Lavinia raises an eyebrow at his frosty welcome.

"Such welcome hardly befits visitors," she says sternly. The old man snorts, shaking his stick even more aggressively. "Outsiders aren't welcome here," he mutters, glancing over his spectacles with a cautious look.

Lili, unfazed by his gruffness, chuckles. "You're funny," she declares. Despite himself, he emits a reluctant snort, and a brief smile crosses his face as he looks at her.

"Haven't you got anything better to do than to disturb the peace?" he questions. Clearly, he's the only one causing a fuss here.

Elias steps forward. "Well, I'm sure we do have better things than to make friends with an angry little dwarf," he retorts. But his confidence disappears instantly as the old man brandishes his stick more fiercely.

"Dwarf! How dare you… you… giant of a boy!"

"We're on our way to Velloria." Elias quickly recovers, taking a step back. His response causes a burst of scoffing laughter from the man.

"I suppose you just happened to stop by to disturb me on your way, huh?" he mocks. His laughter fades as his gaze sharpens upon me.

"He's out of his mind, clearly," Nico whispers to me. I nod. He is right. This little man has clearly lost his mind.

"Why do you have a frog?" Lili's voice interrupts the tension as she fixates on his peculiar companion. The man's stern look softens momentarily before he adopts a threatening pose, waving his stick.

"A warning for the nosy! This frog was the last curious little girl," he says. My patience snaps, and I snatch the stick from him. He tumbles back, shocked and furious, his anger now directed at me. But I have had enough of his attitude, and I definitely won't tolerate him threatening to turn Lili into a frog. Before I can say a word, Lavinia steps in and her voice brings calm to the escalating situation.

"That's enough, Thaddeus," she says. "Can you not extend the hospitality of the Whispering Forest to these young ones?" Her gaze holds Thaddeus in place and I get the feeling that her authority is not one to be challenged. His hostility slackens as he reluctantly heeds her. Standing tall, as tall as a tiny man can stand, he extends his hand to me. With some hesitation, I return the stick to him.

"Good," Lavinia says giving him a nod, then turns to us with a proposal. "You must be starving. Thaddeus will lead you to the dining hall."

"Dining hall?" Skylar repeats. We all look at each other with wide grins spreading across our faces. Lavinia gives a knowing smile with a twinkle of mischief in her eye before disappearing into the underbrush. Thaddeus is now less irate and somewhat appeased.

"This way," he mutters, shuffling out of the clearing. As we trail behind, Elias seizes the moment for a jest, patting my back.

"Lucky for us you're so good at making friends, or we'd surely be in trouble," he quips, then rushes to keep pace with Thaddeus. Somehow, I get the feeling that Elias seems to be enjoying my irritation with Thaddeus a little too much. With a sigh, I clasp Lili's hand.

"Come on, Lili. Let's go get some food."

As we venture into the forest, each step draws us into a fantastical domain. The essence of the place hums with the melodious calls of unseen creatures. The ground beneath us is a lush tapestry of moss and vibrant flora. It's like a living mosaic, I think to myself. Lili, enthralled by the magic around us, tugs on my hand at every marvel she notices.

"Asha, look!" she exclaims as she points to a squirrel with iridescent blue fur, or to mushrooms that cast a gentle pink glow in the dim light. Her joy is contagious, and slowly, a sense of peace washes over my tired spirit.

Once again the forest clears ahead of us and this time reveals a solitary door. Standing all on its own, the door is a spectacle. Its frame is decked with intricate symbols that shimmer with a gentle, colorful light.

"Well, this ought to be interesting." Elias makes the statement a little too loudly, only to emit a soft *oof* as Skylar promptly silences him with a playful smack to his stomach. Thaddeus stops before the door and turns to us with a smirk.

"Here we are," he declares, gesturing at the door dramatically. We all stand in silence. Upon noticing our lack of enthusiasm for the seemingly misplaced door, his smile shifts to a puzzled look.

He eyes the door and, with a sheepish laugh, admits, "Ah! How could I forget?" A swift tap of his stick against the frame, and the words Anything and Everything Door materialize above it. His smile returns, now even wider, as he showcases the door once more with far too much flare.

Elias draws out a long, mocking sigh, gesturing toward the door, "Now I see. It's a door." I snort trying to hold in a laugh.

"Mock all you wish, Beanpole," Thaddeus shoots back, "but even a cynic of your stature will soon be begging to go through it again." Laughter from Lili fills the clearing. Nico, too, tries to stifle his chuckles.

"Beanpole? Really?" Elias asks, almost to himself. "Am I really that tall?"

"Of course you are," Thaddeus retorts. "If you were any taller I'd have to get a ladder to speak to you. Now come along." I can't help but join in the laughter, catching Elias's bewildered expression.

"So," I interject, "what is this door's purpose?" Thaddeus's eyes gleam with eagerness as his lips curve into a sly grin.

"In response to your query," he flourishes his hand toward the door, "yes, I forgive you for taking my stick. And secondly, this door currently leads to the dining hall."

I narrow my eyes at him. "Firstly…" I am ready to argue about the apology I never made.

"Bear in mind," he cuts me off, "the Door's destinations vary with necessity. Today, it's the dining hall, given your collective appearance of starvation and this young one's fixation on my amphibious friend." His glance shifts to Lili as he tosses the frog pouch over his shoulder, concealing it from view. A whimsical croak from the hidden frog punctuates his words.

"Ew, yuck," Lili's mock gag sound echoes in the clearing.

"Alright then," he nods, "enter. But remember your manners." He then approaches the door, swinging it open with grandeur. The view beyond leaves me dumbstruck. It is far more than I had anticipated. In our shared astonishment, we gaze upon an ancient dining hall of mythic proportions, its splendor eclipsing any feast hall in my wildest dreams.

Majestic columns of aged stone uphold a mosaic ceiling where crystal chandeliers dangle. Semi-circular tables surrounding a central fireplace are filled with elegant dishes and food. A real meal. My stomach starts to grumble and I step through the door. As I enter a wave of warmth envelops me. The air, thick with magic, transforms our soaked and worn clothes into dry and refurbished garments.

"What is this sorcery?" Skylar asks in astonishment.

"Not sorcery, my dear. Magic!" Thaddeus exclaims. My boots, previously stained by my travels, now shine as if freshly polished. Lili's cloak, faded from our adventures, now bursts with life, its colors gleaming in the hall's gentle light. She twirls around. Her laughter of happiness reverberates against the stone walls. Skylar strokes her hair, now lustrous and untangled. Thaddeus observes us with a mischievous glint in his eye, delighted by the transformation.

"The Whispering Forest outdoes itself for its visitors," he comments, the edge in his voice seemingly softened by the enchantment surrounding us. "Now, let's not delay the banquet. Come. Come." He guides us towards the feast. The smell of it all is overwhelming. I glance over at Elias, who looks like he's about to cry with joy. Juicy meats, fresh vegetables, and radiant fruits decorate the tables, while freshly baked bread warms the air. Crystal pitchers filled with water and exquisite wine stand ready to satisfy our thirst.

As we quickly settle into our seats, dying to fill our grumbling stomachs, the chairs mold to our forms, offering comfort as if tailored for each of us. Lili claps her hands in delight at the sight of the food. Her earlier encounter with Thaddeus's pouch-friend is now a distant memory.

"This," Thaddeus announces with a flourish toward the lavish spread, "is just a glimpse of the forest's generosity to those who venture into its secret heart. Feast, savor, and let its enchantment rejuvenate you! Once you've had your fill, simply pass back through the door." With that, he exits through the door, back into the forest.

This banquet isn't just a meal; it's an entire event conjured by the forest. Lili's giggles fill the room as she discovers a cake slice that changes flavors with each bite. Elias observes a goblet before him fill up with sparkling water at his touch. His initial skepticism melts into a satisfied smile as he samples it.

"I can die happy now," he says. I laugh, looking around, unsure of what food I want to try first.

"This is unlike anything I've ever experienced," Nico says in awe. Caught in the spell of our surroundings, I find myself speechless. The table offers an endless parade of culinary wonders, each dish unveiling its own magic.

Our laughter and shared astonishment fill the hall as we eat until at last, we can't eat another bite.

"Despite his rough exterior, Thaddeus sure knows his way around a feast," Elias comments, leaning back with a satisfied sigh. Lili, now quiet and content, snuggles into her chair's plush embrace.

"Can we just live here?" she whispers, her voice heavy with drowsiness.

"I second that," Skylar says, then turns to Elias. "It's pretty impressive for just a door, wouldn't you say, beanpole?" She jests, her eyelids starting to droop. Elias, overwhelmed by the feast and joy, simply stares at his emptied goblet with a contented smile.

Nico stands to stretch. "Let's see if Thaddeus can whip up some beds," he suggests, moving toward the door, only to halt abruptly after opening it. "You all need to see this."

We gather at the door. Rather than the forest, a cozy room greets us, and in it, five beds await us. Elias immediately jumps into the nearest one with a satisfied sigh.

"This is the greatest door. Ever," Skylar says with enthusiasm. "When I have my own home, I need to get one like it."

"You don't even need a home. Just the door. Then you can simply open it to a home," Elias replies. Skylar's eyes light up at the thought as she reaches her bed. She instantly falls asleep, her breathing growing deep and steady. I guide Lili to a bed, tucking her in with the softest blankets. Her eyes flutter shut almost instantly. I climb into a bed next to Nico's. The room is now filled with everyone's deep breathing. I wish it was that easy to fall asleep for me. But, in the quiet, my mind wanders.

"Nico," I murmur quietly, eyeing his bed near mine, "is taking Lili to Velloria the right move?" My question hangs in the air. Nico rolls over to face me.

"I'm not sure, honestly," he replies. "Velloria doesn't sound like a dreamland. That's certain. But, Lili… she has more resilience than a lot of children her age. It's hard to say."

I feel the deep burden of my worry. "But…" I hesitate, "Lavinia said it's swarming with dark creatures, Nico. I can't bear the thought of losing her." Nico extends his hand across the gap between our beds. His fingers intertwine with mine. My heart flutters at his touch, and I feel an urge to pull my hand away.

"We'll protect her," he asserts with conviction. "You and I, we've faced a lot already. Lili has her own kind of strength. We'll get through this together."

"Maybe it's best to leave her here." Elias's voice pierces the quiet, startling me. He's been awake, listening. He props himself up. "Look. Lili's strong, sure, but this place... it's safe and has everything she could need." A tense silence ensues until Nico sits up.

"Just abandon her in this unknown place, with strangers?" His voice carries a sharpness. "How can you even suggest that?"

Elias meets his stare, unwavering. "It's about safety, Nico. Velloria's dangers are not safe. This place is safe. It's really that simple." Their debate leaves me torn. The forest could offer Lili a sanctuary, yet the thought of abandoning her stirs a deep unease within me.

"Lili is my responsibility," I finally say. My tone is surprisingly steady despite my inner struggle. "I promised her we would be okay, and that I would look after her. I can't just leave her here and go without her."

Elias sighs, lying back down. The air seems thick with unresolved tensions. "Just consider it, Asha. That's all I'm saying."

The discussion fades, leaving me lost in thought. The room grows cold. The sense of unity we had is now strained as I glance at Lili, peaceful in her sleep. Skylar lets out a small coughing fit before rolling over to resume her deep breathing. Nico's hand finds mine again, but this time I pull away gently and roll over ready to let sleep take me. The gap between our beds feels wider than it had a moment ago.

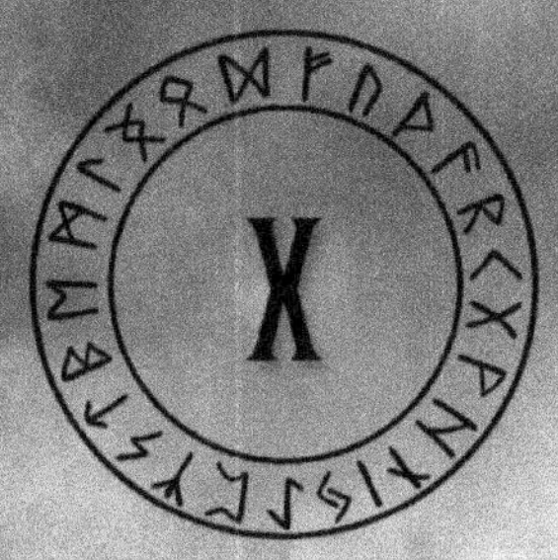

Ripple Sprite & Potions

"Rise and shine." Thaddeus bursts into the bedroom like a thunderclap. "The sun's up and here you are, sleeping like Manticores in winter," he exclaims. Elias, visibly annoyed, buries a complaint in his pillow.

"Manticores don't exist... and it's too soon for this. Is turning you into a toad an option?" His mumbled protest barely makes it through the fabric.

"Ridiculous," Thaddeus retorts with a smile so wide, it nearly splits his face. "You wouldn't dare, Beanpole. Plus, I've got backup." On cue, the large frog on his shoulder makes itself known with a loud croak. Lili sits up with interest.

"Is that frog the same one? Was it really a girl once?" she asks.

"Ah, Geraldine here chose the frog life—wanted a break from the chaos of the shark life. Thought it was all too... ribbiting." His quip draws an exasperated sigh from Elias and giggles from Lili.

"Make it stop," Elias whines from under the pillow clamped down on his face.

"Fine. Let's get to the point," Thaddeus shifts his tone to serious but it is still brimming with an infectious enthusiasm that is a bit overboard for this hour. "Time is of the essence. The Whispering Forest is about to unveil a spectacle, and you, my intrepid adventurers, are invited to partake." With a flourish of his stick, Geraldine showcases her prowess by vaulting onto his head.

Elias unfolds himself with a lengthy yawn. "A party, you mention? Is there more magical food? Because, frankly, after yesterday's feast, I might just turn into an enchanted dessert myself."

"Fear not," Thaddeus proclaims, striding toward the exit with purpose. "Today's revelry demands less feasting and more engagement. Expect to engage in song, dance, and bear witness to the truly extraordinary. And you," he throws a teasing look at Elias, "well, we might just stumble upon a potion to stretch you out a bit. How about reaching for the stars, Beanpole?"

Elias, flashing a jesting grin, shoots back, "I'm in, provided that potion doesn't include more of your sarcasm."

"Be careful. You might find yourself shorter than when you began," Thaddeus says. I can't help grinning at their exchange of quips. Elias's humor, which had often been a source of annoyance for me, has finally found a worthy counterpart.

"Are there going to be actual fairies? Can I hold one?" Lili asks. The mere possibility of encountering fairies seems to drown out the banter.

Thaddeus leans closer, whispering as if confiding a great secret. "There might be. But fairies are delicate, tiny beings. If you touch them they might lose their magic." Straightening, he jests, "Perhaps Elias was a fairy himself before opting for his current towering stature." I let out a laugh at Elias's expression of mock hurt. Skylar buckles over laughing.

"Skylar, you're supposed to be on my side," Elias says.

"I am, but—" Her words are cut off by another fit of laughter.

Elias sags his shoulders in defeat and turns to Thaddeus. "Okay, you've got our attention. Tell us about this party."

"Ah, yes! Today we find ourselves on the eve of the Midnight Concord."

"A what?"

"It is a rare sight! A moment of magic. A—"

"Get to the point, Thaddeus."

"Shush, Beanpole. I'm the one telling the story," he shoots back, then continues, "it is a celebration of the thinning of the veil. It is a rare time when the veil between many realms thins, and beings from all over come to visit."

"Sounds somewhat dangerous, doesn't it?" Nico says.

Thaddeus disregards the concern with a wave of his stick. "Perilous? Far from it. The Midnight Concord is a homage to equilibrium and the splendor of the invisible. True, mythical beings wander more freely, yet they adhere to the ancient covenant safeguarding this forest and its inhabitants. They couldn't hurt you even if you wanted it."

Lili's eyes widen. "What kinds of beings?"

Pausing, as if savoring the moment, Thaddeus replies, "Throughout the Concord, I've met many beings. The Will-o'-the-Wisps, Naiads, Dryads." His excitement is overflowing as he rambles on. "Not to forget the Phoenixes!" Then his voice softens: "And if fortune favors us, we might witness the Faerie Folk's ethereal dance."

"This Concord... it seems like a gathering of the most magical beings one could ever hope to see," Skylar marvels.

"Indeed, tonight, you all are granted the rare chance to see these marvels with your own eyes." He wraps himself in his cloak, signaling a shift in focus. "But, before tonight's celebration, we have an essential task. We need to gather Celestial Dewdrops. Not ordinary droplets but enchanted ones. Vital for casting protective spells."

"But if it's a celebration, why do we need protection spells?" Nico asks.

"Because the Concord can also draw in creatures with… darker intentions. Come, come." Waving his stick, he rushes out the door.

As we follow him through the forest, golden rays of sunlight dapple the path. We are walking through a luminous corridor.

"Our adventure begins at my cottage," Thaddeus announces. "I must fetch a few essentials for our quest." The entrance to the dwelling, though charmingly quaint, proves to be an obstacle for Elias as his head runs into the doorjamb.

"Ow," he says. "Exclusive entry for the vertically challenged, I see." he rubs his head, wryly hooking his mouth to one side.

The interior of the cottage is a delightful contradiction to its small exterior. High ceilings supported by beams wrapped with glowing vines, giving the space an enchanted feel. Shelves on the wall are brimming with books, potions, and curious artifacts.

"Be careful where you step and what you touch," Thaddeus cautions, leading us through the marvels crowding his home. "Everything here is either extraordinarily delicate, perilously potent, or has the ability to alter your form." Lili approaches a curious invention that looks like a timepiece, except it also looks like a birdcage. Held close, the device suddenly animates, producing a melody that fills the room with chirping, then ceases as quickly as it had begun.

Elias examines a crystal orb shrouded in mist. "Is this supposed to reveal the future?" he asks, only to jump back as a sudden spark nips at his touch. "Just for zapping nosy guests, I see."

Reappearing from behind a pile of scrolls and tomes, Thaddeus sniggers. "That is merely my weathervane. Apparently, it's forecasting a high probability of 'beanpole storms' today." Lili's laughter fills the room, while Elias, less entertained, continues to nurse his startled finger.

Skylar makes her way over to a shelf, drawn by a display of bottles shimmering in an array of changing colors. She reaches out but is abruptly stopped by Thaddeus's sharp warning.

"Don't touch that," he shouts. Skylar withdraws her hand as if stung. "Those are for viewing, not for handling. They could turn you into a spectrum of colors if you're not careful."

Meanwhile, Nico has found himself ensnared by what appears to be a coat rack that has wrapped a wooden limb around him in a surprisingly affectionate gesture.

"It's just being hospitable," Thaddeus explains, stepping in to free Nico by hitting the rack with his cane a few times until it finally lets go. "I crafted it for the odd moment of loneliness when I need a hug. However, it does tend to show a bit too much enthusiasm at times." Nico rolls his eyes at me and I stifle a chuckle. This place is incredible. Wild, but incredible with its many contraptions. I suppose I shouldn't expect less from Thaddeus.

"He's a strange little man, isn't he?" Nico whispers. I nod with a smile, delighted at the audacity of it all.

Amidst the curiosities, Thaddeus's voice rings out with a victorious "Aha" as he retrieves a small, ornately carved wooden box from beneath a pile of magical attire. With a flourish, he opens it, revealing a tiny outfit made of purple velvet, designed for a frog. It leaves everyone in a momentary state of bewildered silence.

"For Geraldine, naturally," Thaddeus exclaims, presenting the frog-sized garment as if it were the most natural thing in the world. "One must look their best for the Midnight Concord." The notion of dressing a frog for such an occasion is as perplexing as it is charmingly quirky.

Elias, unable to resist, quips softly, "Of course, we can't have a poorly dressed frog at a magical concord. That would be the real tragedy here."

"Better a well-dressed frog than a beanpole with no sense of occasion," Thaddeus says. "Now, if everyone is quite finished terrorizing my possessions, we shall head out. The dewdrops won't wait all day, and neither will the Midnight Concord."

We leave his contraptions and follow Thaddeus down a narrow path that leads us to a clearing. Flanked on all sides by age-old trees, it cradles a peaceful pond in the middle, whose surface mirrors the vibrant canopy above. The air, fresh with the scent of earth and the subtle fragrance of concealed flowers, fills my senses.

"This is the place," Thaddeus says. "We will need the dew from those leaves." He points at the reeds surrounding the pond with their large leaves before producing several delicate glass vials.

"It is very important you do not disturb the water," he says, and begins showing us how to collect the dew.

"Why don't we want to disturb it?" Skylar asks. He grins and turns to Elias, handing him a vial.

"Your turn. Try not to cause a stir. The pond must remain still."

Elias gives him a skeptical glance, then attempts to replicate his method. It's nearly perfect, but he accidentally lets a droplet fall into the stillness of the pond. This minor disturbance causes a peculiar creature to emerge from the pond. It's a tiny creature shimmering with colors yet looks distinctly like an angry cat. It fixes Elias with a stern look, freezing him in place, the vial trembling in his hand.

"Behold, the Ripple Sprite!" Thaddeus exclaims, unable to hide his delight. "A guardian of tranquil waters. They take a dim view of disturbances. Best to remain motionless and avoid eye contact." Before Elias can take the advice into consideration, the sprite springs into action, darting towards him with surprising agility. Elias's startled yelp is met with the sprite's playful antics as it tugs at his hair, hops onto his shoulders, and nimbly ties his shoelaces together. The scene unfolds with such ferocity that everyone erupts with laughter.

"Just stay still, Beanpole! It'll soon find something else to pique its interest." But the sprite finds Elias very amusing. It buzzes around him with dramatic flair, and vocalizes its displeasure whenever Elias makes a move to shoo it away. Eventually, with an air of exaggerated huff that seems too large for its tiny body, it dives back into the pond, leaving us in a brief silence before we start laughing again.

Elias is now seated on the ground with his hair in a complete mess, and his pride keeping the sprite company underwater. "Guess there's a first time for everything," he says, "including encounters with a peacock-cat-toad with a love for drama. Was that creature Geraldine's boyfriend?"

Thaddeus replies with a laugh, "Geraldine prefers companions of a less... animated nature. That Ripple Sprite is merely one of the many guardians here. A bit more mischievous than most, I'd wager." Once untangled and back on his feet, Elias dusts himself off.

"Mischievous? That thing was a full-blown menace."

"Can we meet more animals like that one?" Lili asks excitedly.

"The forest might share more of its secrets if we move quietly. Its creatures tend to avoid the loud and the boisterous," Thaddeus replies. "If Elias can steer clear of any more babbling and chaos, we might indeed see more."

"That was hardly my fault," Elias says.

"Naturally," Thaddeus smiles, "but for now, let's focus on gathering the dew. The Midnight Concord doesn't wait, and we've preparations to attend to."

With the dew collected and safely stored, and no further run-ins with the Ripple Sprite, we trek back to Thaddeus's house of contraptions.

He navigates his crowded space with ease, retrieving various jars and pouches from shelves laden with arcane materials while we all watch. His dexterity is amazing for such a small man.

"Observe closely," Thaddeus finally begins, setting a small cauldron on his workbench. "Crafting potions is an art of precision. It's not mere mixology but a game of balance, purpose, and a dash of whatever you fancy to dash." Lili chuckles as he proceeds with his carefully selected ingredients. Geraldine the frog nestles beside Lili, who is visibly charmed by its presence.

Then Thaddeus, reaching for a vial labeled 'Stardust' mistakenly grabs the Moonbeam Essence instead. I'm slightly confused about how I know he grabbed the wrong one, but my instinct to correct him is too slow. The vial's contents are already merging with the cauldron's brew. The reaction is instant and chaotic—a robust explosion of colors and sounds. The cauldron reacts to the unintended mix, overflows in a spectacle of magic. The cabin comes alive. Inanimate objects embark on a spontaneous dance, and the frog, now temporarily winged, ascends with a perplexed croak.

"This can't be good," Elias says, dodging a lively quill that tries to write on his forehead. This results in him tripping over a chair and tumbling into Nico. They both crash into a bookshelf. The books fall around them and begin chomping like animals as they hop across the floor. Skylar, torn between amusement and shock, skillfully sidesteps some marching footwear with a nervous laugh.

Lavinia's entrance marks a return to order. Her mere presence halts the unbridled enchantment instantly. The cabin's objects, including the bemused frog, are now grounded, ceasing their unexpected activities. Her eyes slowly glance around the room. Thaddeus, with a look of embarrassment, and perhaps a little pride, meets Lavinia's gaze.

"A minor misjudgment," he confesses with a chuckle but his smile fades under her composed look.

"Maybe, Thaddeus, we should keep our potion experiments to more... predictable projects," she says. The cabin, still resonating with the echoes of magical mayhem, seems to sigh in relief. With the commotion settled, she turns to me with a smile. "Asha, could I have a word?"

Stepping outside with Lavinia, the crisp air of the Whispering Forest washes over me, offering a breather from the chaos in the cabin.

"Asha," she begins, "I sense your quest is bound to the fragments of the Blade of Velloria." My surprise at her knowledge is evident, but she simply smiles. "The forest has its ways of communicating, Asha. Velloria is a realm overshadowed by darkness, haunted by the echoes of ancient conflicts. The shadows there are thick with the debris of bygone battles, and the creatures who reside in those shadows can often not be seen from this realm." Her eyes meet mine as she continues.

"The journey you contemplate is dangerous, not just because of the creatures of the netherworld, but because of the remnants of a dark history that refuse to lie dormant. However, your determination resonates with a purpose I cannot deny." With a gentle gesture, she reaches toward my hood that is still covering my tattoo. I pull back slightly, but I know the trees have probably already told her about it. I let her remove my hood to reveal the mark of Velloria on my forehead. I search her eyes, wondering what is going through her mind. She seems to view it not with fear, as my mother had seemed to, but with a mixture of respect and awe.

"Asha, you are the one foretold, that we have awaited for centuries," she continues in a mild voice. "The ancient tree's response to your presence was no accident. It recognized the echo of a lineage long thought extinct."

I don't know what to say to her. Only days ago I was made the High Priestess of Emberwyn, and I had thought that it was my only future. Now, the ancient lore Amara had told me is becoming more and more real and I'm unsure what to do with all the information. I feel myself becoming overwhelmed. She brushes her fingers against the symbol on my forehead, sending a shiver down my spine. Her smile is warm and comforting. I have so many questions I want to ask. I open my mouth to speak, but the opportunity is suddenly shattered by the cabin door swinging open. The laughter and chatter spill out to pierce the quiet. I sigh. My questions will have to wait.

Nico makes his way over to us. "Is everything alright?" he inquires, his gaze probing mine for any hint of unease.

I offer a reassuring smile, "Yes, just absorbing the essence of this place." I keep the details of my conversation with Lavinia to myself for now. Lili's earlier question about living here and Elias's suggestion about leaving her behind edge into my thoughts. Before I can dwell further, Lili rushes over.

"Asha, see what I made you." She presents to me a beautifully crafted necklace with its pendant softly glowing. "It's to scare off monsters tonight. We each made one." I'm touched by the gesture, and impressed by her handiwork.

"Did you make this all by yourself? That was fast," I say.

"Well, Thaddeus helped me a little with magic." She gives him a smile. "He said it'd keep you safe." I thank Thaddeus and clasp the necklace around my neck. No doubt I can feel a surge of protective warmth wearing it. Then I crouch down to give Lili a tight squeeze. The wild little hairs from her braids tickle my nose.

"Thank you, Lili. You are truly incredible," I say softly.

"Ugh. I know, I know," she says as she pushes away. She's growing up far too fast, I think to myself.

Nico's presence feels slightly distant when I stand. Maybe he's upset because I pulled my hand away last night? But we're only friends, so that's ridiculous. Regardless, something is troubling him. I don't know what, but I also don't want to inquire if it really is about last night. If he says yes, it would make things awkward. Then he speaks, and I am relieved I did not have to ask him.

"Seems we're all prepared for tonight," he comments, noting the protective talismans each one of us is now wearing.

"I just hope this Midnight Concord comes with fewer surprises than your potion mix-ups," Elias says to Thaddeus with a playful edge to his voice. From the corner of my eye, I catch Lavinia's smile broadening in amusement.

Thaddeus instantly shoots back, "No need for concern, Beanpole. The real surprise will be seeing you try to keep up on the dance floor. I bet a broomstick could outdance you."

The Midnight Concord

The evening air buzzes with the quiet thrill of the soon-to-begin Midnight Concord. While Thaddeus treats our group with tales inside his cabin, I step outside, craving the forest's calm.

Drawn to the Anything and Everything Door, I take a moment to breathe. The ethereal mist weaves through the trees and my thoughts are as tangled as the underbrush. Touching the door, I can feel it humming with a subtle magic, as if it were inviting me in. I don't want to just go in and spend time in the bedroom, or the dining hall. I want to escape to a place that will help me unwind my thoughts.

I push the door open and it lets out a subtle creak. Going through, I find myself in a surprisingly cozy room. Maybe it is crafted by the forest itself for moments like these. Bookshelves line the walls, and lanterns bathe the room in a gentle warmth. In the center of this sanctuary is a pond with a small waterfall cascading serenely from the surrounding rocks.

My own reflection meets my gaze when I approach the pond. As the door closes softly behind me, the daunting shadows of Velloria feel miles away. But only for a moment. The thoughts of Velloria return even in this secluded spot. The enormity of my quest to retrieve a fragment of the Blade of Velloria, and find answers about my father weighs on me heavily.

My thoughts drift to Lili. The idea of taking her into that darkness tears at me. Can I, in good conscience, expose her to such danger? I already have done so by taking her out of the village with me, but this… Velloria… is not the same. Leaving her behind in the safety of the Whispering Forest also fills me with an unbearable sense of separation. I can't leave her. She needs me. I need her. Besides, she has become more than just a companion for everyone; she is a part of the fragile family we have formed. She is my favorite soul in the whole world.

Leave her here, Elias's words echo in my mind and irritation festers in me. He was so quick to want to abandon her here. But why? Why does he want to leave her? To protect her from Velloria? It is the answer I know is true, but I can't shake my irritation at the quickness of his suggestion.

As I sit in the stillness, a new doubt begins to weave through my thoughts—not about our quest, but about Nico. The question of whether my feelings for him are real quietly bubbles to the surface in this secluded space. Why am I even thinking about this? Do I have feelings for him? The questions I've been sidelining during our adventure now demand attention. There is an undeniable connection between the two of us that has become a comfort. His presence, his unwavering support, and those moments when our eyes meet and seem to echo with a deeper, perhaps mutual longing, have now left me questioning the nature of our friendship.

Admitting to these emotions feels like stepping into uncharted waters, and I don't want to complicate things. So I don't really want to admit anything. I can't. The fear of harboring distraction, for either of us, is too much. Why should these feelings have to surface now? Is it genuine affection, or just a byproduct of our shared adventures? Do I like him more than I thought I did? It's all so confusing. I don't want to think about it anymore.

This room was supposed to offer clarity. Instead it is plunging me into more questions. Frustrated, I get up and leave.

As I emerge from the room, the forest seems to reflect the turmoil within me. Down the path, Nico is waiting. His eyes are clouded with concern despite his attempt at a reassuring smile.

"Nico, what's wrong?" My voice sounds slightly harsh to me from the frustration of the room. He hesitates, obviously wrestling with something.

"It's Elias," he finally shares. "I saw him take a potion from Thaddeus's collection tonight. Earlier, when we were asking about the different potions, Thaddeus had mentioned it's used for summoning dark spirits." Great. Just when I thought things were already complicated enough.

"Nico, what are you talking about? Are you serious?" I hope he has made a mistake. Instead, he nods gravely.

"Yes, I'm sure, Asha. I wouldn't bring it up if I wasn't. With the Midnight Concord nearing, we can't overlook this." His words send a shiver through me, introducing a new mistrust to my already large pile of doubts.

"There must a good explanation," I say. Though I can't shake off the feeling that Elias is involved in something darker than I want to admit. *No. Don't jump to conclusions.* But, if Nico is right…

"I hope so," Nico interrupts my thoughts. "But we should keep an eye on him, especially for Lili's safety." His mention of Lili in the midst of this makes me uneasy.

"Nico, we can't just jump to conclusions," I say. "He's our friend." He scoffs slightly at this, but I'm not shocked. He's never liked Elias much. He pulls me in close, but his embrace is anything but comforting.

"Let's just head back. They're waiting for us." I break away gently and make my way back to Thaddeus's cabin, not really bothering to see if he's following.

The memory of Elias's earlier arguments about Lili's safety now lingers with a darker tone in my mind as I approach the cabin. Nico's words have definitely planted doubts, but the idea of Elias summoning dark spirits is very hard for me to believe.

Caught between trust and suspicion, I enter the laughter and light-hearted exchanges between Thaddeus and Elias inside the cabin.

"Ah, Beanpole, challenging an old sorcerer like myself? I've concocted brews that could very well turn you inside out."

"Yet, you've still to brew something that might shrink that insanely large ego of yours, Thad," Elias quickly counters. Skylar lets out a coughing laugh at that but covers her mouth quickly. My smile is a forced one as I attempt to align the image of my friend Elias with Nico's concerning revelation. It's impossible.

"I once crafted a potion so strong, it convinced a man he was a chicken for an entire week," Thaddeus continues. Lili's patience is clearly wearing thin and she interrupts them.

"Are we going yet?"

Caught off guard, Thaddeus dramatically slaps his forehead. "By the heavens, the Midnight Concord," he exclaims. "The night calls to us. The Concord awaits!" Geraldine, in her elegant velvet attire, hops into her pouch on Thaddeus's shoulder with a dignified croak.

"Oh yes, as we head out," Thaddeus's voice adopts a note of caution at the door, "remember, the Concord is bustling with life. Beware not to wander too far amidst the celebration. There are a myriad of splendid entities, some of whom have traversed great distances to come here. Be nice." His glance fleetingly rests on Elias, who responds with a puzzled shrug. "Then forward we go," he says.

Swinging the door wide into the night's cool air, we follow Thaddeus deep into the forest through a trail lit by glowing orbs.

The trail opens into a large clearing. The air vibrates with anticipation, mingled with the heavy scent of nocturnal blooms. Glowing orbs float above, bathing the clearing in a soft ethereal light that mirrors the stars to cast an enchanted glow on every face.

Tables draped in cloths of midnight blue and emerald green line the perimeter, offering an array of delicacies. Foods both familiar and exotic call to my stomach, while pitchers filled with luminescent liquids promise tastes of otherworldly delight.

At the clearing's center, elven musicians cradle their instruments, beginning a melody that resonates with the ancient spirit of the Whispering Forest. The music weaves through the bustle of people. Listening to the complex harmonies seems to dissolve my worries.

Standing on a chair, Lavinia announces, "Welcome to the Midnight Concord!" Her voice is full of warmth and joy as it carries across the crowd. "Tonight, we celebrate the harmony of all realms, a time when barriers dissolve and the wonders of our worlds unite. Embrace the joy, the camaraderie, and the thrill of discovery that this night offers."

Elias and Skylar, overtaken by excitement, dash towards the tables in laughter. Lili tugs at my sleeve.

"Asha, can I go with them?" she asks with sparkling eyes. Nico's words of caution echo in my mind briefly, but the idea of dampening her excitement is unthinkable.

"Go on," I smile. "But please, stay close to Skylar, will you?"

Her agreement is swift as she turns to follow them. "I promise! Thank you, Asha." Her figure quickly blends into the festivities, leaving Nico and me alone. It is slightly awkward. I am still a little frustrated at his wanting me to instantly condemn Elias.

"Let us acquaint you with some of our distinguished attendees," Lavinia's words bring me back to the moment as she approaches us.

"I'm going to go grab some food," Nico says. I give him a quick smile and nod before he leaves, then follow behind Lavinia as she creates a path for us through the revelers. Her mere presence seems to command attention, drawing looks of admiration and reverence from the crowd. She reminds me so much of my mother with her confident stride.

Our introduction begins with a figure whose robes seem to embody the night sky, adorned with luminous constellations that echo the heavens.

"Meet Elenor, the starweaver," Lavinia announces warmly. Elenor's eyes seem to hold an endless mystery of the cosmos. "Elenor weaves tales of the stars into her tapestries, her threads are made from moonlight and kissed by stardust. Her masterpieces grace the halls of our grand library."

"A library?"

"Indeed, we have a library that rivals any imagination. It houses wonders and knowledge from every corner of our world."

Our path then leads us to a group of short, stout men clad in leather armor. They seem quite out of place in their attire.

"These esteemed men are the Guardians, the stewards of our revered woodlands," Lavinia explains. The Guardians offer me a gesture of recognition. "They are also the ones who set up our battle defenses, if ever there is a need."

"Has there ever been a need?" I ask cautiously.

"Not since the Darkest Battle, my dear." Her smile is reassuring.

As we weave through the crowd, we come upon two elegantly clad figures in long robes.

"Ah, Seraphina and Alaric," she says, greeting them with a warm hug each. "Asha, Seraphina and Alaric are adept mages of the Sylvian Circle and distinguished keepers of the Arcane Archives." With a smile Seraphina gives me a welcoming hug, while Alaric, seemingly engaged with invisible scrolls, acknowledges us with a subtle nod.

"Is this the girl?" inquires Seraphina.

"Indeed, this is she," Lavinia replies. Their eyes fix on me, stirring a flicker of unease.

"Give them no heed," Alaric says with a chuckle. "They indulge in their flights of fancy with great frequency. Verily whimsical, these two, when they are in company together." His words seem to jumble around in my head as I try to understand what he was trying to say. His way of speaking sounds so ancient.

"Oh, hush now," Lavinia chides, then shifts her focus to me. "Their mission involves decoding the mysteries of both ancient and contemporary lore, gathering wisdom that stretches across dimensions and eras. And, just between you and I, their command of magic is without equal."

As she continues to introduce me to the guests, each new encounter seems to pull me deeper into a realm of wonders. Eventually, I am drawn by the aromatic scents of the feast and soon find myself near Thaddeus, who is entertaining a captivated audience with his tales.

"It was larger than life, I say! Yet, there we were, Geraldine and I. Standing like a couple of tiny ants. Could have been squashed! Yet, we battled until we couldn't battle more, and finally captured the menace and locked it away for good, didn't we?" Geraldine lets out a croak, either to agree with him or confirm that the tale was outrageously exaggerated.

"Ah, Asha, come to hear the famous tale of the dragon slayer have you?" he asks. I laugh. The thought of this small man being a slayer of dragons is not something my mind can comprehend. He offers me a luminous fruit with a playful warning.

"This one might lull you into dreams with its melody, so proceed with caution."

"I think I'll have to pass on that one, Thaddeus." I certainly don't want to accidentally find myself asleep on the ground. My attention, however, is quickly diverted by Elias from the corner of my eye, who is moving discreetly behind a tent with a vial firmly in his grasp. My heart lurches as Nico's words jump back into the foreground of my mind. *We should keep an eye on him.* Just as I start moving to follow him, Skylar and Lili approach, brimming with happiness.

"Asha, come dance with us," Skylar's voice breaks through a mean cough, her excitement briefly dimmed as she leans on the table for support. Her hand, in a shaky attempt to steady herself, grazes a goblet, threatening to tip it over. I reach out to steady both Skylar and the goblet.

"Skylar, are you okay?"

She manages a frail smile, still struggling for breath.

"Just a bit of a cold from our travels. It's nothing serious." Lili, undeterred by the momentary pause, pulls at me with enthusiasm. "The musicians are amazing. You must see."

I find myself being drawn away by their excitement into the swirl of dancers. The melody, crafted by the skilled hands of elven musicians, envelops us. Its enchanting rhythm seems to seep into my bones. Even as I surrender to the dance, Elias and the mysterious vial haunt the edges of my thoughts. What was he doing?

Just then, the music is suddenly interrupted by the sound of a commanding horn, turning everyone's attention to Lavinia. Her voice cuts through the silence.

"The time draws near." Her gaze, luminous under the moonlight, captures me in a sparking wave of anticipation. "We are at the threshold of the thinning of the veil."

The atmosphere is charged with excitement. Nico and Elias rejoin me. I shoot a quick glance at Elias, the thought of the vial lingering. He shoots me back a glance before diverting his attention to the unfolding event. I can sense something is wrong. I can sense it in his heavy demeanor. Then, Lavinia's voice breaks my thoughts and I turn to watch, telling myself to talk to him after the event.

"Let us welcome those who journey through the veil with open hearts." Lavinia's voice deepens. "Tonight's conclave serves as a reminder of the friendships that weave together the fabric of our magical communities. In this realm and all others."

Her declaration sets the stage for the extraordinary display that begins to materialize. The floating orb lanterns begin to dim. The earth trembles slightly under our feet as two pillars of dark obsidian rise from the ground in the open field. Between them, a slender beam of pure white light cuts through the night, its brilliance growing into a vast portal framed by the pillars, its surface alive with a dance of energies. As the portal widens, a mist spills forth from it, blanketing the ground and weaving its cool touch around our ankles.

"I can't see," Lili's voice cuts through the wonder, her small hands clutching at my cloak in frustration.

Without missing a beat, Nico lifts her onto his shoulders, granting her a clear view of the spectacle. Her frustration dissolves into excitement.

Thaddeus seizes the moment, playfully eyeing Elias.

"Don't even think about it," Elias quickly retorts.

"But, Beanpole! I can't see either!" he protests, tugging at Elias's cloak with a grin. Then, he stops tugging to lift his frog with both hands. "Or perhaps Geraldine would appreciate a perch atop your head for a better view?"

A collective gasp draws my attention upward to the stunning entrance of a phoenix. Its feathers, ablaze with vibrant hues of fire, streak the sky in a dazzling display, leaving behind a trail of softly glowing embers. Lili, perched on Nico's shoulders, shouts joyously, reaching toward the sky as if to catch the fleeting sparks that dance like stars against the night.

Then, a unicorn, glowing in soft, pearlescent light, steps gracefully through the portal, its mane flowing in ethereal waves. It pauses to bow respectfully to us, enchanting everyone with its serene beauty before it moves deeper into the celebration. Suddenly, the powerful beat of wings fill the air as a griffin enters, landing with a dignified poise. Its keen eyes survey the crowd, and with a solemn bow, it honors the Midnight Concord's age-old tradition, adding its presence to the night's wonders.

The procession of mythical creatures continues to captivate me, but it's the entrance of a particularly mesmerizing assembly that sends ripples of delight through the onlookers.

A swarm of pixies, their wings catching the moonlight and breaking it into kaleidoscopic shards, flits above us, accompanied by a procession of very small beings no taller than rabbits. The small beings wear clothes spun from leaves. Their caps are petals topped with dewdrops. As they march forward, the pixies dip and twirl around them, performing aerial salutes to Lavinia. The small beings on the ground offer their own respects with meaningful bows. Their leader, distinguishable by a crown of interwoven wildflowers, approaches Lavinia and hands her a flower.

As magical as the moment is, Lili's reaction to the pixies is the height of the evening's wonder for me. Perched high on Nico's shoulders, she's a picture of pure astonishment and delight as she attempts to grasp the elusive fairies flitting about.

"Fairies," she cries out, "Asha, they're real!" Seeing her so happy fills my heart with unparalleled warmth. But this moment is short-lived.

Suddenly, the atmosphere shifts dramatically as the portal's serene glow turns volatile, spitting out embers into the evening. These embers unravel into tendrils of smoke that slither downwards like snakes. Silence falls over the murmuring crowd. Sparks of electricity sizzle and snap where the portal meets the pillars.

From the midst of the new, angry portal, an enormous figure emerges. Its immense shadow looms over the festivities. Its presence evokes in me a fear more profound than any inspired by the legendary eyeless. This entity, hulking and misshapen, stands as an aberration against the diminishing light of the celebration, its form shrouded in shadows so thick they seem to swallow light around it. Many tendrils dangle beneath it in a writhing blackness that mimics legs.

Grasping one of the obsidian pillars for support with long, slender claws, the figure firmly plants itself in our realm. Shadowy spikes adorn its back, each one pulsating with every breath. The mist at its feet swirls in angry spirals. Its eyes, if they can be called eyes, are abysses of despair that seem to suck in all semblance of hope. Those hollow gazes fix upon the crowd. Shifting back and forth as if searching for something. The air around me thickens making it hard to breathe.

"Stand back!" Lavinia commands, cutting through the tension as she, along with Alaric and Seraphina, steps forward. A flash of light from a cast spell nearly halts in midair, frozen in time, when the creature's gaze captures mine. A small scratching click sounds inside my head as if my mind had been stretched, and broken.

The sun has been pounding me relentlessly for hours. I shield my eyes until they adjust. The earth beneath my feet is cracked and desolate. Its surface is littered with bones. Tattered remnants of clothes whip about in the wind with clouds of fine sandy grit. My mouth, nose and eyes are dry. How long have I been here? How long have I been wandering this desert, aimlessly searching for… searching for… I stop walking, confused. What was I searching for?

Looking around at the bones that stretch across the surface like a layer of death, I can sense a great battle has been fought and lost here. Somehow, inside, I know this battle hasn't yet happened. A raven's caw echoes across the scorched earth. Its black and brown feathers reflect the sun as it hops from one dry skull to the next, searching for food in the empty eye sockets. An unsettling energy pulses through the air. I turn around.

Before me stands an enormous structure, a monolith carved into a perfect cube, its surface so smooth it seems to drink the light. Grand stairs lead to a yawning doorway. It is calling me into its depths. I can hear it. Deep inside me. *Asha… Asha…* My feet shuffle, running into bones that clatter as they break away from their resting place on skeletons. I walk up the steps and into the doorway. Stretching into the depths is a corridor. Dust swirls in from the desert as I enter, and the light becomes dimmer the deeper I go. A thick, black fog begins to ooze across the floor, swirling around my feet as I reach a chamber. Shadows cling to every corner of the room.

In the heart of this chamber sits a figure on a throne of black stone, obscured by the dark atmosphere in the room. A chill runs down my spine. Is this what I have been searching for? I venture closer. The atmosphere thickens, and a heavy, looming dread begins to settle over me like a cloak. It's deathly silent. I can hear my heartbeat in my chest.

Suddenly the eerie silence is shattered when the shadows in the corner begin to morph into two large entities, unlike any recorded in the annals of the known or the imagined. These beings resemble neither beast nor specter. Their bodies are composed of swirling, dark mists, coalescing into forms that hint at something that was once human but is now twisted beyond recognition. Eyes like molten gold pierce the darkness, then fix upon me. Each step they take is a soundless ballet as they flow across the chamber floor to flank the throne on either side.

I soon become aware of a soft red glow starting to emanate from the ground. The light slices through the swirling ooze and illuminates the seal of the Legion of Embers embedded in the floor. My hairs stand on end. Why was I searching for this? Was I even? The emblem bathes the chamber in a bright, blood-red light. I shield my eyes.

"Who are you?" I ask. "Why am I here?" I can't remember why I'm here, or where I came from. I had wandered for hours to get here. Where? Why was I searching? What was I trying to find? As my eyes adjust, the figure on the throne comes into view, and my heart freezes.

"Elias?" My voice is raspy and my throat itches from the dry desert air.

He's not the Elias I know. Clad in black robes, wearing a black crown, this version of him is consumed by power and darkness. His gaze pierces through the room at me. A slow, unnaturally wide grin starts to spread across his face. I want to scream, to run, but my body is paralyzed.

A flash of white light rips me from the room, and I find myself lying on the grass at the conclave. Violent shards of energy erupt all around me as I struggle to catch my bearings. What just happened? My mind is spinning.

Lavinia stands before me with her hands lifted skyward as if summoning the very essence of the forest. Next to her, Alaric, Seraphina, and the Guardians have formed a half-circle and their voices are melding in an arcane dialect. A vibrant aura envelops them, breaking the line of sight between the creature and me. The dark creature seems to falter momentarily under the influence of the magical barrage. Lavinia and her companions are unyielding, and their powers erupt in an explosion of light that dazzles the darkness. The creature, overwhelmed, emits a despairing cry and soon it is repelled through the portal back to its own abominable domain. The portal instantly returns to its tranquil glow. No evidence of the hideous intrusion remains.

Lavinia's arms finally fall to her sides in exhaustion, and she surveys the aftermath. Her eyes meet mine. The immediate danger has passed, yet the shadow of the intrusion lingers.

She offers me her hand and gently pulls me to my feet. My body feels drained. My mind reels from the vision I was thrown into. Was it a vision? I can still taste the sand on my tongue and my eyes are dry. It must have been real.

"Where's Lili?" My voice is barely above a hoarse whisper as I scan the clearing for any sign of her. Lavinia places a comforting hand on my shoulder.

"Thaddeus has taken her and the others to his cabin for safety," she says. "As soon as the demon appeared, he knew to get them out of harm's way." Even though I am relieved at her words, they don't quench the turmoil inside me. Why did I see Elias sitting on that grotesque throne? I need to go get Lili.

"Are they all okay?" I find myself asking.

"Yes, Asha, they're safe," she assures me. "Thaddeus may be many things, but above all, he's protective of those he looks after. They couldn't be in better hands." Her reassurance helps to loosen the knot of fear in my chest, but only slightly. Taking a deep breath, I draw in the forest's refreshing air.

"Thank you," I say. "What was that thing?"

Lavinia looks towards the horizon, where the portal is now quietly radiating its serene light.

"That was a Valthorix," she explains. "It's a demon capable of transporting a human consciousness into another time and place, ensnaring its victims in experiences that merge the boundaries of reality and illusion."

"So… like the eyeless?" I am trying to understand the magnitude of what I've just faced.

"No," she replies, "the Eyeless can only implant illusions, making you believe you see something that isn't there, and they usually do so while you are alone. Valthorix, on the other hand, are much more powerful and can take your consciousness to real places that have existed or exist in the future." My heart drops.

"In the future? I saw… something," I admit. The unsettling image of a throne inside a dark room and the room's hellish occupants rushes back to me. "Elias was there, on a throne, surrounded by monstrous figures." Lavinia's face turns serious, shadowed with concern, yet she remains composed in her reply.

"Valthorix can craft complex illusions, Asha. Their visions might mingle falsehoods meant to sow fear and doubt, with strands of possible futures, weaving truth into their deceptions. This dual nature makes them particularly dangerous." The idea that what I saw might have been a real future sends a shiver through me.

"How can I know if what I saw is a lie or a reality?" I am caught between fear and a defiant need to know. The weight of this uncertainty is pressing down on me.

"Discerning that truth is a path you must navigate on your own. Trust in your own inner strength. Reality may not always be what it appears, and sometimes, the heart perceives more clearly than the eyes."

Her words, intended to comfort, stir more turmoil within me. The vivid image of Elias, crowned in darkness amid vile creatures, echoes in my thoughts.

"Thank you," is all I can manage to say. She doesn't press more, but instead gives my hand a gentle squeeze and ushers me off to Thaddeus's cabin to join the others.

As I walk to Thaddeus's cabin, Nico's warning about Elias holds new weight. The possibility that my friend Elias might not be who I thought he was gnaws at me relentlessly. My fists clench as a simmering anger takes root. If he had indeed summoned the Valthorix or aligned with malevolent forces, particularly any that might endanger Lili, I would never forgive him. I would confront him, and it wouldn't be pretty. I refuse to allow my mission and our group's safety to be compromised by betrayal.

As Thaddeus's cabin comes into view, Elias's carefree laughter from inside the dwelling violently clashes with the turmoil within me. How can he seem so carefree when such dark forces could be at play, potentially the result of his own doing? My hand grips the door, poised to confront him, yet hesitation washes over me.

The sound of Lili's laughter, mingling with Elias's, reminds me of the bond they've formed over the last few days. Could he really have summoned the Valthorix? Put Lili at risk? My thoughts are a whirlwind and my resolve wavers. I step back, fighting to calm my racing heart. Anger, confusion, and doubt threaten to engulf me. What if I'm wrong? I can't risk it. I need undeniable proof of Elias's motives with the vial, before I can make any move. Yes, that's what I need—clarity. But I'm simply too worn out tonight. I gently push the door open and step in. But the warmth of the room and the echoing laughter do little to dispel the thoughts storming my mind.

"Lili," I call out. Her face seems a world away from the shadows plaguing my thoughts. "It's time for bed," I say. She nods eagerly and rushes towards me. Her world is still a place of magic and wonder. To her, the evening's enchantments remain untarnished by the complexities and betrayals that loom in the shadows of adulthood.

I wrap her in a hug, finding a moment of peace in her innocent joy. Then we leave the room without looking back. As Lili shares her excitement over the night's wonders, my mind is ensnared. I can only respond with subdued nods and weak smiles as we make our way to our bedroom. I just need to sleep. Tomorrow I will face reality.

GIFTS FOR A THOUSAND JOURNEYS

The first light of dawn creeps into the dining hall, painting everything in a warm, golden glow. But, my night has been far from peaceful. My thoughts have been a battleground, replaying the events of the Midnight Concord over and over, each memory weaving a tangled mesh of confusion and worry. The unnerving vision, Elias's carefree laughter amidst turmoil, and the sinister shadow of the Valthorix meld into a daunting tapestry that is fogging up my mind.

Elias's voice cuts through the fog in my head. "Asha, you okay?" His expression softly reveals his concern. I'm about to reply because I still need to have the talk with him, but Thaddeus bursts into the room with his usual vibrancy. *Later,* I tell myself.

"Good morning, my fearless explorers," he announces. How does he always have this much energy in the morning? "A grand adventure awaits us today, to seek out a creature of legend, a being so wondrous it scarcely seems real. Who's with me?" The room is instantly charged with a buzz of anticipation. Well, everyone's anticipation but mine.

"I'll be staying back today," I tell everyone in the room. "I want to talk with Lavinia about Velloria."

"I'll stay as well," Nico says. My eyes meet his, but their usual charming allure seems to be absent. I give him a smile so subtle that I wonder if it was even a smile. Thaddeus nods at us.

"Wise, indeed. Lavinia knows much about Velloria. But worry not," he assures us with a twinkle in his eye, "we'll tell you all about it when we return."

As the group readies to leave, I call after them, "Lili, stay close to Skylar, please." Her little nod is barely noticeable under the hood of her cloak as she skips away. I watch them set off and a complex mix of relief and solitude wraps around me.

"You didn't have to stay," I say to Nico. I don't know why I'm annoyed by him staying, but I am.

"It's fine, Asha," he replies. "Besides, we should be on the same page with whatever information Lavina has. Two heads are usually better than one." He moves in closer and asks, "Have you talked to Elias yet?"

"No," is all I can say. I look at Nico and can sense his frustration. I exhale deeply, the weight of decisions pressing on my mind.

"Nico, I know you're concerned, but we can't cast judgment on Elias without solid evidence."

His expression tightens. "Asha, considering the events of last night, that creature, it can't just be coincidence. He—"

"I'm aware, painfully aware," I cut him off. "But I need proof. I'm sorry. I can't just assume he's responsible for that. He is still my friend, much as that may irritate you. I don't need you pressuring me to get rid of him." The words slip out of my mouth much harsher than I mean for them to. I didn't want to say that. At least, not in that way. I try to correct my tone. "I mean… look, Nico. I know he irritates you. It's obvious. But I just need to be sure, okay?" I search his eyes, hoping my words didn't hurt him.

"Asha, I know what I saw," he says. Clearly, he isn't going to let up until I cut Elias from the group, and that's not happening without proof. He seems to only have one thing on his mind, and it isn't my feelings on the matter.

"Elias is part of our journey. It's non-negotiable." My tone shows no qualms about the fact that I am mad at him for tossing my feelings aside for his own. "Just forget it. I need to talk to Lavinia." I turn to leave but he grabs my arm. I glare at him but the softness in his eyes makes me pause.

"Asha," he says, "my priority is yours and Lili's safety. That's all."

I sigh heavily. "Your support means the world, Nico, but I need you to trust me." His smile is a small, genuine curve of the lips that lifts some of the heaviness from my heart.

"Alright, Asha. You and Lili... you're important to me. I will trust your decision." He runs his hand down my arm and takes my hand in his. My heart races under his touch, but I gently pull away. I can feel my cheeks flushing as I glance towards the door.

"We should go," I say in a low voice. As much as I want to hold his hand, to feel something other than this inner turmoil, I can't. I need to focus. Why is that so hard for me to do when he's around? "Let's go," I say, moving past him. I just… I need to focus.

Approaching the ancient tree I feel enveloped by its mystique. The air around it seems to be whispering secrets only Lavinia can hear. She's sitting at the base of the tree, deep in meditation. I wonder what a tree's whisper sounds like. She turns toward us with a smile.

She welcomes us as she gets to her feet. "You seek understanding of Velloria."

"How do you always know?" I ask. I already know the answer, but I'm hoping she would reveal more about how it works.

"The trees whisper to me," she says with a smile, and I'm slightly disappointed. "The information of Velloria lies within the Arcane Archives. Come." She leads us to the Anything and Everything Door. With a simple gesture, she opens it to reveal a large, mystical chamber.

Stepping through, we find ourselves in a sanctum filled with the scent of ancient parchment. The chamber is lined with shelves piled high with scrolls and books. At the heart of this sanctuary is a table illuminated by floating crystals, casting a gentle glow on the papers scattered atop it. Seraphina and Alaric, the great mages from the Concord, greet us.

Seraphina's voice fills the chamber. "Welcome to the arcane archives," she says. "The archives hold the knowledge of Velloria. These mysteries have been entrusted to us since its fall." She steps forward to take my hands. "We have kept watch through countless eras for you."

Nico interrupts, "Wait… so how long have you been waiting exactly?" His question, though unexpected, elicits a gentle laugh from her.

"In the realm of the Arcane, time weaves a different pattern. Suffice it to say, we've been stewards of these secrets for more lifetimes than you have known." Refocusing on me, she adds, "Within these scrolls," she motions towards the extensive collection filling the room, "you will find the keys you need to fulfill your destiny."

"By 'keys', do you mean the shards of the Vellorian sword?" I ask. Alaric, who had remained silent, now speaks up.

"This repository emerges as a sanctum of knowledge. Enclosed within its sacred bounds are the sagas of conflicts ancient and forgotten, scrolls revealing mysteries and routes ensconced in darkness, alongside volumes of mystical forces that erstwhile fortified the bulwarks of the citadel."

"I'm sorry. I feel like you are speaking in riddles." My words come out slightly rigid, but his way of speaking is hard to follow and it's making me frustrated. "What exactly is my destiny? What is this mark on my forehead? What am I even supposed to do with the shards if I find them?" My questions flow out in a mess as I turn to Lavinia, looking for direct answers.

She stands at the doorway, the room's dim light casting over her face. "The quest to restore Velloria transcends the mere recovery of a blade's fragments," she says as she steps from the doorway. "It's about mending our entire realm."

"Why me?" I ask. "Why am I the one chosen for this?"

She seems to catch the storm of emotions brewing in me. "Asha," she continues softly, "your heritage isn't merely a lineage of rulers or warriors. The Vellorian Soulweavers were extraordinary entities, gifted with immense strength and ability. As the darkness encroached during the Darkest Battle, threatening all with oblivion, they foresaw their earthly end. It was inevitable. Faced with the enemy's insurmountable force, they made a choice."

"Soulweavers?"

"Yes, Asha," she replies. "The Soulweavers were guardians of the life force itself, entrusted with the balance of nature. As Velloria faced its darkest hour, they enacted a spell of profound sacrifice. They interlaced their essence into the continuum of time, embedding their spirits within the very DNA of life. It lay dormant across many generations, awaiting the strands to be reunited in the emergence of one, destined to continue their legacy. That person is you, Asha. You embody the collective DNA of the Vellorian Soulweavers."

I close my mouth before it can gape any further. The idea that I represent the convergence of countless lifelines instills in me a sense of purpose that starts to overshadow my prior irritation.

"But what exactly is a Soulweaver?" Nico interrupts my thoughts. His question hangs between us.

"Soulweavers," Seraphina chimes in, "were the keepers of the force that shape our world. They could command the elements, speak to the wind, summon rain, or calm storms. They were healers, capable of mending not just bodily afflictions but the very earth itself, healing wounds inflicted by time and turmoil." She continues to paint a picture of their vast capabilities.

"Some had the power of Soulbinding, allowing them to interact with spirits, seeking guidance from ancestors or containing malevolent entities. Some were able to manipulate time, hastening or decelerating its flow, occasionally reversing it to avert impending calamities." My mind flashes back to memories of the explosion in Elias's house, and the crimson lightning strike.

"I think I experienced that," I say. "There were times when I almost died. But time slowed down and I was able to escape." I looked back and forth between them, but they don't seem fazed by it.

Alaric finally breaks the silence. "The mastery of time's weave, indeed. Slumbering abilities may stir to life by thine instinct for battle or escape," he says. "In instances when thou art gripped by the ancient imperative to retreat, such powers may awaken, bestowing upon thee a significant mastery o'er events as they unfold. This art, with diligence and training, canst thou learn to wield at thy behest."

"Does he always speak in riddles?" I ask, turning to Seraphina hoping she will translate what exactly he has said.

"Alaric is, well, quite old and still retains his ancient way of speaking. For nearly six hundred years, in fact." She smiles.

"Six hundred years?" Nico exclaims. She smiles then continues her story of the Soulweavers.

"There was one Soulweaver, who was said to hold the power of Veilwalking. It enabled him to traverse the boundaries between realms. Between the seen and unseen. The mortal and the eternal. It granted him insight into the mysteries of existence beyond ordinary comprehension. Though, he refused to entwine his powers with the rest. He wished to die with his power than to die without it." Her words stir up a whirlwind of emotions in me.

"The very essence of your DNA is the Soulweavers' legacy. The natural world around you, every gust of wind, each stone, and leaf, vibrates with the same energy that resides in you. This connection to the ancient magics of your forebears is not learned but an intrinsic part of who you are."

As I absorb the magnitude of her words, Lavinia elegantly connects this storied past to my current quest. "The Soulweaver's Blade, the hallowed Blade of Velloria, transcends its physical form. It is a conduit for awakening and enhancing the latent powers of its rightful bearer. The shards you seek are not mere pieces of metal but are suffused with Velloria's spirit—each a part of a larger entity that, when combined, will unlock the full potential of your lineage. Each and every power of the collective Soulweavers." Her eyes lock onto mine. The room itself seems to listen, every book and scroll holding its breath along with me as my mind tries to comprehend everything I have just heard.

The quest for the shards has just morphed into something far greater than the simple search I had originally planned. It has become a quest to fulfill my destiny as Velloria's chosen and expel the darkness for good. I feel lightheaded. I grab hold of the table to steady myself.

"Are you alright?" Nico asks. He places a hand on my shoulder, but I shrug it away gently. I honestly don't know the answer to that. Looking up, I find his eyes deeply gazing into mine. I nod, but I'm not sure I am okay. It's so much to take in at once, and it seems like the more I venture down this road, the more I am piled full of new information.

"This is all just a bit overwhelming," I say.

"Undoubtedly," Alaric says as he begins to rummage through a collection of scrolls. "Verily, thou art the singular spirit to possess the might of every Soulweaver throughout the annals of time."

"Literally not helping," I say, annoyed at his confusing way of talking. "What am I supposed to even do with this information? Where do I even begin?"

With deliberate care, he lays out two scrolls on the table. "Thy journey commences hence. Behold, these be the charts of Velloria," he says, pointing at the scrolls, which look to be maps of the city layout. I look at Seraphina, and to my relief, she finishes explaining.

"They depict the city in its entirety — not only the visible structures but its underbelly. Velloria is a city built in layers." She points to a marking that seems almost to fade into the parchment.

"Here," she says, "is a passage hidden to most. Your instincts will guide you to it."

I hover over the maps, letting my fingers lightly brush over the ancient pathways. The hidden passageway and secret chambers of Velloria do spark an adventurous spirit within me, but they also haunt me. Velloria, in all its forgotten grandeur and shadowed corners, feels like a complex mystery to unravel. Buried somewhere in its heart, is the shard of the Soulweaver's blade. The first piece in uncovering my true power. Supposedly. Gently, I roll up the scrolls, securing them with a leather strap Alaric hands me.

"Thank you," I say. Holding the scrolls feels like gripping a piece of Velloria itself. Both Seraphina and Alaric approach me.

"Our blessings go with you," Seraphina says, resting her hand briefly on my shoulder. I feel a sudden surge of connection and warmth from her touch and somehow the pieces of the puzzle don't feel so jumbled in my brain anymore. I smile at her.

"Let the sagacity of the Soulweavers illuminate thy path, Asha," Alaric says. "In thee, the ember of Velloria's destiny is ignited anew, and our realm shall witness its rebirth." His words are now hurting my head, but I know he means well, and I can tell he is excited by it all. I politely give him a smile and thank him.

With their blessings, Lavinia guides us back to the forest, the door to the Archives closing behind us. The forest's embrace is immediately refreshing. I take a deep breath, allowing the air to fill my lungs completely. Then Nico's voice pierces my peace.

"So. This is pretty exciting."

"I suppose," I reply heavily.

"What's wrong?"

"It's just a lot to take in all at once," I say. "It's a bit overwhelming. And Alaric..." He looks at me with a smile.

"Yeah, I'm not sure I understood a word he said either, honestly." We both laugh. "We'll figure this all out together. But, given we're yet to secure any shards, perhaps arming ourselves would be wise," he proposes. His eyes sweep the surrounding woods as if something is lurking. I do agree with him. Without the power of the Soulweaver's Blade at my disposal, our vulnerability is obvious, and arming ourselves could very well tilt the scales in our favor.

Lavinia, a few steps ahead, pauses and turns toward us. "Indeed, Nico, your caution is warranted. As Asha's abilities continue to surface, physical armaments will undoubtedly offer you an extra measure of safety." She offers me a look of comforting assurance. "Regroup with the others and convene back here in the hour's half," she directs. I exchange glances with Nico, who now has a grin on his face.

"Let's go get the others," I say.

Stepping into Thaddeus's home, the usual lively chatter and laughter are replaced by the only the ambient sound of small gears turning inside a nearby clock. The room, with its vibrant collection of artifacts and contraptions, stands unusually still.

Nico surveys Thaddeus's eclectic hoard with a hint of amusement. "Has he even once thought about throwing some stuff away?" As he muses, he is gingerly lifting a device that looks like a mix between a clock and a teapot. His touch sets off a barrage of whistles and clanking gears. "Yikes," he says with a laugh, quickly setting the now-protesting contraption back as it huffs a puff of steam smelling like chamomile.

The silence that follows is abruptly cut short with Thaddeus's dynamic entrance. He's holding a large sack and followed closely by the rest of the group, each bearing wide grins.

"Nico, must you always be terrorizing my things?" Thaddeus teases.

"Thaddeus, do you ever think that maybe it's time to get rid of some of this junk?" Nico asks.

"Nonsense! The only junk in here is… well… nothing!" He laughs, setting the wriggling sack down on the floor. "Besides, while you were trying to get rid of my treasures, we've been out adding to the collection!" He reveals from the sack a creature so fantastical it seems to have leapt out of a storybook. Resembling a rabbit but with fur that changes colors like a kaleidoscope, and ears that flutter like leaves, I can't help but to laugh. The absurd looking creature is now eyeing me.

"Thaddeus, what on earth is that?" I ask.

"It's obviously a magical marvel," Thaddeus says with pride. "It's a Prismhare, a very rare find." He tenderly pets it, prompting its coat to shift from green to a vibrant yellow. The Prismhare, basking in the admiration, leaps onto the table. An array of hues display delightfully through its fur, before it exhales softly, releasing a glittering dust that floats in the air.

"It's the most magnificent!" Thaddeus's eyes are twinkling as he watches the Prismhare. Its tone shifts to a dark red as Nico takes a step towards it. "Be wary, Nico. Its fur not only mirrors mood but amplifies it. We wouldn't fancy an overabundance of drama from our inanimate friends, now would we?"

"Absolutely not. It's time I resign my curiosity in this treasure trove," Nico says. The Prismhare curls up in a patch of sunlight on the table, its fur morphing into a calm blue.

Skylar plants herself next to me. "Asha, you should have seen the place we went today. It was dreamy! Well, it was until Elias tried to hold my hand." She casts a look of disgust in Elias's direction. She covers her mouth to cough.

"The cold still hasn't went away, huh?" I ask. Although I'm more curious about why she didn't let Elias hold her hand. She shakes her head then continues talking as if I already asked her about Elias.

"He just… I don't know. He's cute, and funny, and sometimes…quite often now that I think of it, annoying." I notice Elias is glancing over grinning and she quickly looks at me with a terrified look and blurts out, "I just hate it!" A laugh escapes my lips and I cover my mouth.

"I'm sorry, what?" I ask, trying to hold my composure. "What do you hate? I thought you liked him." She starts to fidget with her hair.

"I do. But I can never tell if he likes me or not. He's always joking around. And that's fine, but it's also very confusing for me." She sighs.

"But, he tried to hold your hand. So that's a hint right?"

"I don't know, but it was only *after* he wrestled that thing into the bag. Gross." She rolls her eyes and I nod in full understanding now.

"Well, maybe you should ask him to wash his hands then?" Another eye roll tells me I apparently wasn't in full understanding. *I really hope I never have boy problems like this,* I think to myself.

"Don't worry. If he likes you he will eventually tell you," I tell her. Although I'm not convinced myself. Elias, as loud and obnoxious as he can be at times, isn't one to express his feelings. She nods with a smile. I need to step away before she continues. Talking about boys is not on my list of priorities right now. I give her a quick hug, then step into the middle of the room where Lili is now playing with the new creature.

"So, how was the adventure?" I ask her, kneeling down beside her. Her eyes light up.

"It was so much fun, Asha! I just want to live here forever. I wish mother was here to see this place. She would love it." Her words tear at my heart. I lean over and kiss her forehead.

"I know, Lili. I wish she were too." It's not a complete lie. I do wish she were here, though I don't wish it before knowing what she's truly involved in after having seen her signature on that paper. "She will come when she's done helping in Emberwyn, I'm sure. In the meantime, I have an announcement." Her eyes light up again.

"Alright, everyone," I say aloud, capturing everyone's attention, "tomorrow, we will be setting out for Velloria." The announcement isn't what Lili was hoping for and she grumbles to herself. "But, before we leave," I continue, "Lavinia is preparing some gifts for each of us, and we need to meet her in a few minutes."

Skylar momentarily diverts her attention from the Prismhare, and her boy problems. "Gifts, huh? I wonder what she has in store," she muses.

"No offense to Thad," Elias chimes in, "but hopefully it's something useful." Thaddeus looks shocked for a moment, then quickly regains his composure.

"My dear Beanpole," he replies, "there is not one thing in this house that does not have a use. If you weren't so tall, perhaps you could see it."

"Plus, you need to wash your hands," Skylar blurts out to Elias. Everyone in the room stops to look at her. She shrugs and quickly heads out the door. Elias looks at me and I shrug too. That wasn't quite how I had envisioned her telling him.

"Well, I guess we're off then," I say with a smirk and follow her out the door.

When we reach the Anything and Everything Door, Lavinia is waiting for us. Thaddeus, with Geraldine in her pouch, has decided to tag along. Lavinia greets us with a smile and a nod. Then, with grace, she opens the door to reveal a cozy, lantern-lit room that none of us has seen before. The warm light casts dancing shadows around the room, centering on an oak table that holds our attention with its carefully arranged parcels.

"As you stand on the edge of your journey toward Velloria," Lavinia says, entering the room, "understand that your readiness must encompass more than just intellect and courage. The road ahead will challenge you in ways you cannot yet imagine." She gestures towards the parcels with a welcoming hand. "Each of these gifts has been chosen with purpose, tailored to meet the demands of your journey and the trials you may face," she explains.

The room seems to hold its breath as we enter, and stand by our respective parcel with our name on it. Lili delicately opens her parcel first. Her fingers, quivering with excitement, reveal a gleaming amulet on a silver chain. The Amulet scatters rainbow hues across her face.

"Wow," Lili's hushed voice fills the quiet room as she gazes at the amulet with fascination.

Kneeling to Lili's level, Lavinia smiles. "This is a special gift for you, Lili," she says softly. "It is a protection amulet, designed to keep you safe from harm. It will be your guardian if ever you are in need of one." Lili's eyes sparkle. Holding the amulet close, she looks up at Lavinia.

"Thank you. I promise I will take good care of it."

Skylar's gift is even more intriguing. She brings out a satchel of exquisite craftsmanship from her parcel.

"Skylar," Lavinia says, "this satchel is a marvel of our ancient magics. It possesses the capacity to transcend the limitations of physical space. It will conjure whatever you require, precisely when you need it, from nourishment to medicines, to shelter against the elements."

Holding the satchel closer, Skylar lets out an uncontrolled cough, covering her mouth quickly. "Sorry," she apologizes, "I'm grateful, Lavinia. This is so beautiful." She reaches into the small satchel, her arm seemingly devoured by it, and withdraws holding a small book in her hand.

"It's the poetry book I lost when we came here." Her voice is softly shaking with surprise.

"Out of all things you could pull from that satchel," Elias says. She glares at him and he holds up his hands, not daring to say another word. Her eyes return to the book and carefully scan the pages as if each word was a precious gem. She stops at a page and reads it out loud:

"Whispers of the wind, dance through the leaves,

A tale of the moon, sewn into the eaves.

Stars twinkle in the sky, a guide through the night,

Guiding lost souls, with their gentle light."

She sighs heavily, a smile spreading across her face. Her eyes are moist with tears. It was a delicate melody that seemed to transport her to a different time, a different place, where pain is just a shadow, and joy fills the spaces in between.

"That was beautiful, Skylar," I say.

Elias, tired of waiting, starts unwrapping his gift. The room falls quiet as he unties the string around his parcel, revealing a bow of exquisite craftsmanship. The wood gleams with an inner light, the intricate carvings along its length seemingly alive. He lifts it and traces the pattern with his fingers. As he draws the bowstring to test its tension, a soft hum fills the air.

"It will never miss when shot with true intent," Lavinia's says. A spark of understanding lights up his eyes. He nods slowly, and for once, his usual jesting air is replaced by seriousness. With a slight smile, he looks up from the bow, meeting each of our gazes in turn.

"Guess I've got no excuse for missing now, huh?" he quips, looking at me.

"You still better be careful where you aim it," I say.

Nico starts to look inside his parcel now. I watch closely as he peels back the layers of cloth to uncover a short sword. The blade gleams with a subtle light. He lifts it, turning it in his hands. The blade seems lightweight but durable. It's perfectly suited for him. As he swings it gently through the air, a faint glow emanates from the metal.

"It alerts to unseen dangers," Lavinia explains. Nico's eyes meet mine. I know what he's thinking. If the sword lights up around Elias then I would have no choice but to change my mind. But it won't. And I won't. At least, I hope not.

I break his gaze and look down at my own parcel. It is wrapped in old, seemingly ancient fabric that is falling apart. I gently unravel the cloth to reveal a dagger with a blade as dark as the night sky. Made from a single piece of obsidian it is adorned with intricate silver filigree that shimmers in the dim light. The hilt, wrapped in straps of worn leather, pulse with faint blue veins.

As I touch it, the dagger suddenly changes shape in front of me. Its metal begins flowing like liquid, around my fingers and up my hand, before transforming into a leather bracer that fits itself around my wrist perfectly. It's new form, merging obsidian with leather, features complex blue designs that cling to my skin like tendrils, glowing softly. A unified gasp of awe sweeps through the room.

Lavinia locks eyes with me. "Asha," she says, "this is the Soulweavers' unmatched craftsmanship."

"It's stunning," I whisper, looking down at the bracer that feels both alien and perfectly suited to me.

"That bracer is more than just an ornament," Lavinia says. "It's your protector, your ally, and your guide. It will change, adapting to your heart's needs, when you need it.

It connects with your DNA, Asha, to the very core of who you are."

I watch the bracer's veins pulse, their light syncing with my heartbeat as I turn my wrist over to inspect it. I wonder if it could also transform into a sword. I feel a sudden warmth spread from within me that flows to the tendrils now linked to my skin. Everyone's attention is on me as the room's ambiance shifts.

"Wow," I say, barely above a whisper, as the bracer begins to shimmer, its glow intensifying. Within moments, it extends, morphing seamlessly into a radiant sword of pure light, its blade casting brilliant reflections around the room. The sword feels as natural in my hand as my own palm.

"It's magical," Skylar breathes, clasping her hands together.

"It's incredible," I marvel.

Thaddeus steps closer. "How does it feel?"

"It's very light, as if it's almost made of nothing," I say, moving it through the air. The sword leaves a trail of light, mesmerizing me.

"That sword is a manifestation of your intention, Asha." Lavinia says. I give the sword a final twirl before it shifts on its own. The transformation is smooth, the light retracting and coiling around my wrist, settling back into the familiar shape of the bracer. Skylar finally breaks the silence, a grin spreading across her face.

"Well, I guess we won't be needing torches where we're going. Asha can just cut through the darkness. Literally."

I chuckle, feeling a surge of confidence.

Lavinia places a hand on my shoulder. "Remember, the bracer is a tool. Your heart and mind are the true sources of power. Trust in them, and you will find your way."

"What about Geraldine?" Thaddeus asks. By his sly grin I can tell he's only partially joking. Lavinia's smile does not waver.

"Indeed, a gift has been arranged, though not for Geraldine." A hush falls over us. Our glances flick between Lavinia, Thaddeus, and his frog. "The real gift, Thaddeus, is that it is high time you took a vacation. You will journey with them to Velloria." The announcement sparks a range of reactions.

Lili's expression lights up with sheer delight, unable to contain her happiness. "Thaddeus is coming with us? Yes! That means Geraldine is coming too!"

Elias lets out an exaggerated sigh in feigned annoyance. "Great," he says with a mock groan.

"Quiet, Beanpole!" he retorts. "My tales enchant you, admit it. As for Geraldine… You two will be thick as thieves before this is over. Mark my words." Right on cue, Geraldine voices her approval with a croak.

"I highly doubt I will become best friends with a toad."

"Frog! And yes, you will. You'll see. It's your destiny." Thaddeus grins and I laugh much louder than I intended, but the thought of Elias having a frog as a best friend is extremely amusing to me.

Echoes of Velloria

"Rise and shine, you hibernating Manticores!" Thaddeus's voice booms through the silence, ripping us out of our sleep. Elias groans, clamping his pillow over his face. "The path to Velloria waits for none, and we are the bold few who dare to walk it!" His walking stick thuds against the floor for emphasis.

Elias, half-rising, retorts, "Have you ever thought of being a rooster?"

"Nonsense, Beanpole! Do I look like someone who would look good in feathers?"

Lili springs from her bed, now bursting with energy. "What will we find? Will there be more creatures?" she asks.

Climbing onto the end of her bed to meet her gaze directly, Thaddeus leans in. "Who knows? Perhaps dancing trolls or singing harpies." But his fanciful tale is cut short as he jumps down, commanding, "Forward!" and disappears out the door, leaving a trail of bewilderment in his wake.

"That little man has no sense of peace," Elias says, hopping out of bed. "Speaking of peace… seems it's time for breakfast."

Skylar, already getting dressed, shoots him a look. "That doesn't even make any sense. Besides, how are you always thinking about food?" she teases.

"It makes perfect sense! And I always think about food, even in dreams."

"Of course you do. Where does it even go?" She looks his slender body up and down. She does have a point. As much as he always finds himself snacking, it doesn't show.

"It all goes directly to my head. Fuel for my jests," he replies, tapping his head with his boot before putting it on. Skylar rolls her eyes and walks out the door without a word. As the others mingle towards the door, I linger back with Elias as he finishes lacing his boots.

"Elias," I say cautiously, preparing to finally ask him about the vial. But then he looks at me with a grin, and I hesitate.

"What is it, Asha?"

"I…" How do I even start this conversation? *Why did you try to kill us?* No. I can't bring myself to do it. Instead, I blurt out, "I just wanted to tell you that Skylar really likes you." By the fates, why did I say that of all things? I feel my cheeks flush. She's going to kill me if he tells her.

"I know," he grins. Then he sighs. "I like her too, but I'm a bit afraid to tell her. She can be quite scary sometimes. You know what I mean, right?"

"I'm not sure I do." I laugh. "Maybe you're overreacting. Sure, she's a bit… eccentric. But she's sweet and caring. You should just tell her, Elias." Suddenly, I'm mad at myself for playing matchmaker when I should be talking to him about the vial.

"I will. Eventually." He smiles and then walks away towards the dining hall. My shoulders sag in defeat. That was not the conversation I wanted to have. Although I'm slightly relieved, I'm a bit afraid what his answer would have been if I had asked him. What if he admitted to it? I would lose a friend and gain an enemy. After wrestling with this dilemma for a bit longer, I decide it's best just to wait it out and see how it unfolds. I finish dressing and head to the dining hall for a quick meal.

The hall, bustling with the morning's energy, greets me with the comforting aroma of freshly baked bread and the earthy scent of brewed tea. Around me, the others exchange stories and plans for the day against the clatter of utensils. I find a spot at a corner table, savoring the simplicity of the meal while my thoughts wander to Velloria. The anticipation stirs a mix of excitement and nerves within me. What would we find there? As I eat and ponder, Nico joins me, holding out a loaf of bread with a playful grin.

"Well, this definitely isn't Mrs. Dahlia's honey loaf," he declares, tearing off a piece and giving it a critical look before tasting it. His comment draws a laugh from me.

"You know," I respond, still chuckling, "I think Ms. Dahlia's cooking has completely spoiled your standards."

With a smirk, he meets my gaze. "Maybe so. But is that really such a bad thing?" I shake my head, unable to disagree, and focus on finishing my meal.

The meal concludes all too quickly and together, we collect our belongings and head to Thaddeus's hut. As we approach, we are greeted by the familiar sounds of Thaddeus's morning chaos. I swing the door open to reveal him, amidst a whirlwind of activity, rummaging through a collection of curiosities that would perplex even the most eclectic of collectors.

"What are you on about this time, Thad?" Elias asks.

"I'm in pursuit of my sanity, Beanpole! Seen it? It's about as tall as you, slim, and incredibly slippery."

"Can't say I have, but I'm also in the market for some. I think I misplaced mine when you began collecting Prismhares."

Finally, Thaddeus's hand finds its target. He triumphantly extracts a small, wrapped parcel from beneath a chaotic heap of magical charts and a partially consumed sandwich. Silence envelops us, our gazes locked on Thaddeus as he solemnly opens the package. He reveals a small leather outfit, tailor-made for a frog, complete with a tiny hat and vest.

"I should have seen that coming," Elias says, rolling his eyes.

"This is no ordinary attire! It is the pinnacle of amphibian exploration gear, featuring a waterproof finish and a magical compartment for, naturally, frog necessities."

"Frog necessities?" Nico says. "And what might that be? A tiny map to the nearest pond?"

"Nonsense! This pocket is meant for her treasured, flawlessly round stone she's taken a liking to." He fits Geraldine into her new outfit. The scene is delightfully bizarre. Geraldine, now wearing her exploratory gear, leaps onto the tabletop with a sense of pride, drawing admiring sighs from Lili and intrigued looks from the rest of us.

"Only you would dress a frog for an adventure," Skylar says with a laugh.

"Preparation is key, my friends! Besides, who's to say Geraldine won't be crucial to our quest? She may need to pull Beanpole over here out of a dragon's den."

"Dragons don't even live in dens," Elias says. "They live in—"

"Nonsense! Everyone knows dragons don't exist." Thaddeus bangs his cane on the ground as if that settles the matter.

"You're the one who just said—"

"I said no such thing, Beanpole. Besides, you wouldn't fit in a dragon's den if you curled into a ball, so there's no need to worry." Another tap of his stick and he turns to leave, but is halted as Lavinia steps into the room.

"It's time we discuss your passage to Velloria," she states. She pauses, glancing at the frog on the countertop. She smiles very subtly, then turns her attention back to us in a more serious tone. "The land route is treacherous. So, you will be taking a more… safe means of travel."

"What's the safer method?" Nico asks, leaning in with keen interest. In response, Lavinia, with a graceful flourish, retrieves a small, ornately carved whistle from her cloak.

"This," she reveals, holding it up, "is the Whistle of the windways. A single blow will summon the Zephyr Birds. They will swiftly and securely transport you to Velloria."

"Zephyr Birds?" Skylar's voice echoes softly. "I've only read of them in tales; they're considered mythical."

"They are mythical beings indeed." Lavinia smiles.

"Are we actually going to fly on them?" Lili asks.

"Yes, Lili, you will truly fly," Lavinia assures her. "Aerial journeys carry their own perils. But the Zephyr Birds will navigate the safest routes. Come now. It is time."

We follow Lavinia outside, down a small trail through the trees, and into a wide clearing. Lavinia positions herself, the whistle poised delicately in her grasp. Casting a reassuring look our way, she lifts the instrument to her lips and releases a single, resonant note into the quiet of the morning. Time seems to stretch as we wait… and wait.

"Well, I suppose we're walking then?" Elias finally asks, but suddenly, a shadow flickers across the earth and we all look up into the sky.

Their arrival is nothing short of majestic, their forms grander than any bird I've ever seen before. They are enormous, with wings vast enough to momentarily dim the sunlight. The Zephyr Birds' plumage, a tapestry of silver and turquoise, catches the light in a mesmerizing display of colors as they descend. With a grace that seems impossible for their size, the Zephyr Birds land in the field before us, every motion precise.

"They're so beautiful," Lili marvels, her hand hesitantly stretching towards one of the birds.

"Aren't they? I have only read stories of them," Skylar says, now walking towards the birds. I can only stand there, awestruck by the magnificence of these beings.

With a gentle wave of her hand, Lavinia invokes another marvel. From the ethereal folds of the morning light, something extraordinary begins to materialize upon the backs of the Zephyr Birds. They are saddles, but unlike any I have seen before. Each saddle is more akin to a capsule or a cocoon, crafted from a material that shimmers like the morning dew, reflecting the hues of dawn in its weave. As if summoned by the same silent command, ladders unfurl from the sides of these magical capsules, cascading towards the earth. Each ladder is made from ropes that glow softly. Lili's laughter fills the air as she bounds towards the nearest ladder.

"It's like a dream," she exclaims.

"Please be careful, Lili," I call to her. Lavinia smiles with a look of satisfaction on her face as she observes our reactions.

"The Zephyr Birds are no ordinary creatures," she explains, "and these capsules will keep you safe and comfortable during your journey." She then hands me the whistle and I secure it in my breast pocket.

The ladder feels solid and reassuring under my grasp as I climb to the top. The capsule is open with Lili already inside, brimming with excitement. As I settle into the seat, and put her on my lap, the material molds to our form, enveloping us in a snug embrace. With a final look at Lavinia, who nods encouragement, the capsule closes, sealing us inside. Through its translucent walls, I can see the top of the trees, the clearing, and my friends, now each encased in their own bubble of magic.

The Zephyr Birds unfurl their wings and their surge of energy lifts us skyward. Below, a mosaic of greens and browns unfolds. The sky splits open as the ground had when we fell into the abyss to get here. We glide through the vast opening, entering the surface world above. The dense, Whispering Forest canopy transitions into a broad, barren field, its early frost glinting in the sunlight like a field of glistening gems.

As I peer down from the heights, Velloria begins to materialize in the distance, shrouded in a dense cloud of fog. From this height, Velloria seems like a dream half-remembered with its details obscured.

Before I know it, the Zephyr Birds begin their graceful descent. They land softly in a field just outside of the city and the capsules open, welcoming us back to the surface world. As I step out, the icy morning breeze greets my skin. Lili slides off my lap and follows me down the ladder to the ground, her small feet leaving delicate impressions on the frost-kissed grass. Across the field, the city of Velloria looms through the fog, its spires piercing the blanket of mist like the crowns of the dead trees back in the Stygian Hollows.

"We're here," I whisper, mostly to myself, as Lili and the others step onto the frosty earth beside me.

"Are you sure?" Elias attempts to jest, but is rewarded only by silence because I'm too busy soaking in the moment.

"We should check the maps before heading in," Nico suggests. I nod, delving into my pouch to retrieve the maps. We huddle together on the frosty earth. Kneeling, I lay out the two maps Alaric entrusted to me.

"This first map is the surface. A layout of the city," I explain. "This second one is a map of the chambers and tunnels underneath the surface."

"There are so many," Skylar whispers.

"Yes, and we have no idea where the shard even is in there, but I think it's here." I point to a central chamber that seems different from the rest. Then I rub my hands together. The chill in the air is seeping into my hands and ears now.

"It's freezing out here," Elias grumbles, wrapping his arms around himself in an attempt to ward off the cold.

"Oh, would you prefer a heated chamber, perhaps with a view? You're not on holiday anymore, Beanpole," Thaddeus quips back.

Elias rolls his eyes. "Fine," he says. "I'll get some wood for a fire. At least we can have a bit of warmth while we pore over these maps."

Before Elias can take a step, Skylar, with a smirk, places her satchel on the ground. I watch in curiosity as she reaches into it, her arm disappearing up to the elbow into what seems like an impossible depth. With a triumphant smile, she pulls out a lit fire, complete in a small, contained pit, casting a warm glow on the astonished faces around her.

"You have got to be kidding me," Elias says.

"There," she says with a grin, placing the small fire in the center of our circle. "No need to chop wood when you have a magical satchel."

"That's absolute madness. But, I won't complain," Elias concedes, sitting down and rubbing his hands in front of the fire.

"That's actually very impressive, Skylar," I say. "Just out of curiosity, you wouldn't happen to have the shard to the sword in there, would you?" I am only joking, but Thaddeus answers.

"Ha! The shard isn't even in this realm, so it's impossible." He suddenly looks at me, seemingly as shocked at his words as the rest of us.

"Wait. What are you talking about?" I ask.

"Well, it's—"

"It's what? Not in Velloria?" Nico cuts him off.

"Perfect." Elias throws his hands up in a defeated manner.

"No, no, it is. Well, sort of." Thaddeus is now struggling with his words. I sigh and speak more softly.

"Thaddeus, tell me what you mean. If it's not in this realm then where is it?"

"It was hidden in another realm for protection long ago. According to what I've studied, it can only be reclaimed by completing a trial of sorts," he explains. With a reassuring smile, he adds, "No cause for concern. I'm sure we'll find out soon enough. Now, let's examine those maps."

"Trial? Why didn't Lavinia tell me about a trial?" I can't help be both concerned and irritated now.

"Yes, it's quite simple, I'm sure. She most likely didn't want you to worry more."

I am more worried now, but I turn back to the maps. Either way we are already here and if this is the only place we can release the shard from, then there's no choice but to continue. Nico's forehead creases in concentration as Skylar's enchanted flames throw light across the maps.

"This could be concealed anywhere in the city. We could be searching every dark nook for weeks," he says.

"He's right," I say. "Thaddeus, do you know exactly where the shard is? The place we need to go so we can unlock it, or whatever."

"It's in the underbelly, of course!" He laughs, then immediately stops when he notices me frowning at him.

"That doesn't help us. We need to find—" My words trail off as a sudden movement from my bracer catches my attention. The metal twists and reshapes, morphing into a looking glass with a glowing red lens laced with gold filigree. Amazed, I lift it and peer through the lens at the map.

"What's happening?" Lili whispers.

As I sweep my gaze across the parchment, a specific location begins to glow, marking the central underground chamber with the seal of Velloria. I lower the looking glass, stunned.

"It's pointing us to the shard," I assert, my finger landing on the central chamber once more. The looking glass transforms into a liquid that melds its way back around my wrist into the bracer. I glance at it, now still, its task completed.

"That's incredible," Nico murmurs, leaning closer.

"It's brilliant!" Skylar exclaims, clasping her hands together. "So where did it show you?" I glance over at Thaddeus who now has a smirk on his face.

"The underbelly!" he exclaims, chuckling.

"Fine, you're right," I concede. "Our goal is to get here." I pull out the surface map and gesture towards a large building. "Seraphina mentioned this spot as an access point to the underbelly."

"That's the Grand Palace," Thaddeus says.

"That's deep in the city," Elias mumbles.

"Don't be afraid, Beanpole! Geraldine will protect you."

"Just what I've always wanted. A guardian toad."

"Frog! Don't you dare hurt her feelings."

"Okay boys," I interrupt, stowing the maps back in my pouch. "Let's get moving. I would like to find this palace before nightfall."

"Boys," Skylar mutters, rolling her eyes and following me away from the fire.

Approaching closer, the city slowly reveals itself, materializing from the dense fog. Before us stands a towering wall of obsidian, reminiscent of Emberwyn's rim, though parts of it lie in ruins, giant pieces crumbled as if struck down by an unimaginable force. This sight sends shivers down my spine, prompting me to wonder what kind of power could break such a formidable barrier. The fog seems to whisper the answer just beyond comprehension. The remnants of the wall, once topped with menacing spikes, now lie partially sunken in the earth like silent watchers. Through the vast breach in the wall, the city of Velloria reveals itself. Its structures slowly take shape through the misty air.

"Well, here goes nothing. Lili stay close to me." I clasp her hand in mine. Carefully stepping across the scattered obsidian debris, the scope of the devastation becomes clearer. This place, once a pinnacle of civilization and strength, now rests in eerie silence, its tales and mysteries ensnared by the wake of war. Lili tightens her grip on my hand.

"What happened here?" she murmurs.

"It was the Darkest Battle," I reply, my eyes scanning the city before us.

Moving deeper into the city, the fog's density seems to eat the sound of our footsteps against the ancient cobblestones. Around us, the remnants of an ancient civilization peek from the fog. Buildings, that once must have been majestic in their prime, now stand as empty shells, their facades marred by the scars of neglect. Gaping holes puncture the exteriors, while their broken windows stare back, lifeless and hollow.

The roofs, or what remains of them, are sagging or caved in, succumbing to the relentless advance of decay. Others have vanished altogether, leaving the insides exposed to the whims of nature. Storefronts have their windows smashed and doors hanging open. Nature's fingers of moss and vine advance across the walls, wrapping around the skeletal structures in a tight embrace. Occasionally, a less ravaged building emerges from the mist, its shadowed windows appear to watch us indifferently as we stroll past.

Our wary passage through the fog-bound ruins is disrupted by the sound of metal clashing against stone.

Lili's scream cuts the air, her body quivering as she grips my side. I look around quickly at the others before breathing a heavy sigh of relief. Elias, his attention apparently lost to the enveloping fog, has collided with a heap of rubble and tripped.

"Stop disturbing the dead, Elias," Thaddeus says. The tightness in his voice echoes my own unease stirred by the noise. Skylar, coughing softly, looks less entertained and more worried. She casts a reproving look at Thaddeus.

"This is no time for jokes," she scolds sharply. "We shouldn't attract whatever lurks in this fog."

Turning to Nico, I see he's unsheathed his sword, yet its dormant state reassures me there's no imminent danger. In silence, I mentally thank Lavinia for such a gift, then my gaze shifts back to Elias.

"Be more cautious, please," I whisper.

"Sorry," he mutters, looking at the ground.

Moving forward slowly, my boot strikes something hard, sending an unexpected shock up my spine. I stop immediately. The group behind me freezes in response. Crouching down, I sweep aside a blanket of moss and accumulated debris, revealing the cool, fragmented remains of a ceramic pot, likely once a valued item in a merchant's collection. Looking up, I realize we're standing in the remnants of what used to be a vibrant marketplace, but is now a silent field of abandoned carts and broken pottery. Gently picking up the pot, a sense of nostalgia washes over me, conjuring up echoes in my mind of traders from faraway lands. Their carts were probably heavy with the scents of exotic spices and the vibrant colors of silks and rare goods, while their voices mingled with the lively din of bargaining.

My journey through the moment is abruptly interrupted by a harsh, guttural growl that pierces the quiet. Its primal ferocity sends involuntary shivers across my skin. The sound echoes off the crumbling walls of abandoned shops that line the square, their faded signs swinging in the wind.

"We're not alone," Thaddeus murmurs.

"What gave it away?" Elias shoots back in a harsh whisper.

"Shhh," I urge. My bracer suddenly glows and morphs into the red lens again. I lift it to my eye, scanning the thick fog. At first, nothing appears, but then, the lens uncovers large shadows that are gliding towards us with a slow, menacingly fluid motion.

"There," I point, trying to keep my voice calm despite my racing heart. Through the lens, I see three figures, each dwarfing any dog, their outlines fuzzy yet undeniably ominous.

"Where? There's nothing there," Nico says, his sword now emitting a red glow. The growling grows louder. My heart pounds against my ribs. Elias takes hold of his bow, readying an arrow.

"What is it, Asha?" Lili whispers, clinging to me. I find it hard to answer her as I edge backwards.

"Stay behind me," I whisper.

"Guys, we need to find shelter, and fast," Elias says. I quickly glance around. My lens catches a seemingly intact building through the fog nearly two corners away.

"There," I point, quickly looking back. Lili's scream pierces the air as a beast bursts through the fog towards us, filling my vision.

It's a nightmarish blend of scales and rough fur, its eyes bottomless, glowing pits. Its body is covered with twisted spikes, and a menacing, hissing liquid oozes from its gaping maw. I pull Lili close with one arm and shield my face with the other. The red spyglass flares to life and transforms into an energy shield before me. The beast slams into it, the shockwave trembling beneath our feet. The force knocks me backward, nearly toppling over Lili. The creature stumbles back, its pain-filled howl slicing the silence, offering us a brief moment to flee.

"Run!" I cry out, grabbing Lili's hand and sprinting towards the structure I'd noticed earlier. Behind us, the growls of monsters cut through the fog. The city turns into a perilous labyrinth as we dodge its ruins.

We burst through the door, and Elias quickly slams it shut behind us, throwing the iron lock into place. Our panting breaks the quiet, only to be shattered by the door trembling from the beasts' attempts to breach it. Their persistent battering chips away at my hope. The room feels like a trap, with no visible escape. Panic rises within me. *Think, Asha*, I silently urge myself, scanning the room for any alternative exits. But there are none. We're trapped. Elias, against the door, meets my gaze with an urgent look.

"It won't hold," he yells.

Panic grips me as I desperately search the dim room for anything to reinforce the door, to delay our inevitable confrontation. An instinctual urge suddenly propels me towards the door, but before I can reach it, it explodes into shards, hurling Elias and Nico to the ground. Three monstrous figures burst in, a whirlwind of snarling jaws and venom. Lili's and Skylar's screams pierce the chaos. In that frenzied moment, my bracer responds to the surge of adrenaline, transforming into a sword ablaze with an otherworldly glow. Time suddenly slows, and without a second thought, I rush at the intruders, sword in hand.

The first creature emerges from the pile of scrambling beasts like a wraith, its jaws wide in a grotesque imitation of a smile, its teeth glinting in the dim light. As it lunges at me, I drop to the ground. My feet skid across the debris-littered floor, kicking up a cloud of dust as I slide forward. My blade traces an arc of pure energy upward, cleaving through the dark air to meet the creature's descending jaw. The contact is silent; a whisper of death in a crimson spray of blood as it splits its head in two. The creature's form buckles, sprawling to the ground behind me as the second creature, driven by immense rage, lashes out with a guttural roar that reverberates off the walls.

I meet its fury with defiance, propelling my body into an aerial maneuver as it lunges. I soar over it, and the creature's momentum carries it forward, its massive form skidding across the cobblestone. But it is too slow; too bound by its own ferocity. I descend on it, letting gravity lend weight to my strike. The blade finds its mark, sinking deep into the creature's skull. The force of the impact ripples through the room, sending clouds of dust swirling around me. Silence envelops the room in the wake of the clash, yet one beast remains.

I whirl around, my blade slicing through the air in a wide arc aimed at the third creature, but its body twists in an almost serpentine motion to avoid my blade. Its eyes suddenly fix upon Lili as it lands, and launches itself at her with a ferocity that sends a spike of ice through my veins. Time stretches even more thin now, nearly to a halt, as the world around me narrows to the small space between predator and prey like a heartbeat suspended in the fog of war.

In this infinitesimal pause, my body responds with a grace of desperation. I hurl my sword. It is a throw born of a silent plea to the universe to intervene and protect my sister. It becomes a streak of light, like a comet arcing through the room.

The creature, so assured in its impending triumph, finds its advance immediately halted by the relentless force of the sword as it strikes with the sound of a storm breaking. Its tip drives deep into the creature's body and pins it against the wall with a finality that echoes in the sudden stillness. Just inches from Lili, the creature's form shudders against the blade. Its howl of thwarted rage and agony fills the room as it writhes in pain. Then it is quickly silenced as the sword's energy devours the creature's final breath, leaving it slumped in a shadow of splattered blood in the settling dust.

In the ensuing silence, I take a deep breath, the heritage of my ancestors wrapping around me like an ethereal shroud. I reach out my hand, summoning the sword back to me, and the creature collapses to the ground with a heavy thud.

LITTLE GUARDIAN IN THE NIGHT

"Wow," Nico breathes out, his whisper slicing through the quiet. "How did you manage that? Those techniques, your skill with the sword..."

I can only respond with a bewildered shake of my head. The adrenaline from the fight is still pulsing through me as I answer him.

"I think it's the DNA. It's nothing I've learned. It felt like... it just took over me."

"Looks like we've found our expert for chopping vegetables at lightning speed." Elias's chuckle draws a laugh from me. Thaddeus, examining the broken door, turns with feigned gravity.

"And if your words had the weight of a hammer, we'd have this door back on its hinges in no time," he declares.

Elias takes a breath, ready to retort, but I interrupt, mindful of dwindling time. Velloria, with its deepening shadows, waits for no one.

"That's enough, both of you," I say lightly. "We need to reach the palace before dusk." I lay out the map on the ground, the light from the broken door casting across it. I point to a small building on the map, close to the town center. "Here's where we are. We could backtrack to the square and follow the main road to the palace, or possibly take this alley here." My finger traces the route toward a narrow path nearby. I glance around, inviting input from the group. Nico leans in, studying the map with a thoughtful frown.

"The main road might be more direct, but it's probably crawling with more monsters. After what we've just faced, attracting more attention doesn't seem like a good idea."

Elias, however, seems less convinced, his gaze flitting between Nico and the map. "But that alley could be a trap. It's narrow, probably dark, and perfect for an ambush. The main street is open and we can see threats coming, especially with Asha's lens."

"And what? March into the open and announce our presence to every lurking enemy? Stealth over strength, Elias. We're not exactly an army."

"And sneaking through alleys isn't exactly heroic, Nico. Sometimes, visibility is safety. At least we can see what's ahead and not be funneled into oblivion."

The tension between them escalates, their voices rising just enough to echo off the stone walls surrounding us.

Attempting to mediate, Skylar chimes in with a hopeful note. "Both paths have their risks and advantages. Maybe there's a way to—"

"Enough!" I snap, my voice cutting through the tension like a blade. Everyone falls silent as they turn their attention to me.

"We don't have time for this," I continue, my tone firm yet weary from their bickering. "Both paths have their dangers, but we need to move now. The alleyway offers us cover and is less exposed. That's the path we're taking." I can see the reluctance in Elias's eyes as I roll the map and place it back in my pouch. "My decision is final," I say. He nods in reluctant agreement.

I take the lead, and we exit the dimly lit room, stepping carefully over the debris of the shattered door, to emerge in the fog-drenched street. With quick, yet soft steps, we cross the street, my eyes darting through the shadows for any hint of movement. The obsidian buildings lining the alley seem to devour any surrounding light.

The closer we get to the alley, the tighter the knot of dread gets in my stomach. It's a narrow passage, a dark crease flanked by towering structures of polished black stone that stretch skyward, almost touching at their peaks and throwing the alley into constant shadow. A thick fog from the street creeps in, alive and curling around us, intensifying the chill and dampness that seems to press against my skin with unsettling eagerness. A shiver races down my spine unbidden. Doubt gnaws at me – was choosing this path a mistake? Yet, second-guessing now might shake the trust my friends have placed in my ability to lead them. I steal a glance at the group. They trust me, follow me without question, believing in a strength I don't fully understand myself.

"We'll get through this," I murmur, more to reassure myself than anyone else. My words, soft and faint, manage to pierce the heavy quiet, drawing assenting nods from the group. I lead the way into the alley, and they trail behind, merging into the shadows alongside me.

As we venture deeper, the fog thickens, as though sensing our presence, wrapping tighter with each step I take. A rat scurries across the path, its tiny claws skittering on the damp cobblestone. From somewhere in the distance, a faint clatter of metal is a muffled echo through the fog, sending chills up my spine. Then a different sound softly emerges. I pause, my heart catching as it grows a bit clearer—a melodic hum or whisper, weaving through the fog.

"What is that?" Skylar whispers. I shake my head.

"Keep your senses sharp and your weapons ready," I say. "But be careful. This space is too small for swinging weapons around. Let's spread out a bit."

As I tread carefully ahead, the whispering hum begins to crystallize into a woman's voice, both melodic and mournful, as if emerging directly from the heart of the fog.

"Lost... so deeply lost..." it laments, enveloping me in its age-old sorrow, its source still a mystery. Now unmistakably speaking to us, the voice carries a deep, poignant curiosity.

"Few dare to tread the paths that shadows keep." A soft luminance begins to slice through the fog ahead.

"My name is Asha," I say, "and we are looking for the shard of the Soulweaver's blade." The air feels thick as I wait on a response.

"Your quest is noble, but be warned," she intones, her voice dropping to a whisper.

"One among you holds the heart of a betrayer. Tread carefully, for one may surely lead to your demise." Abruptly, the light vanishes, plunging us into a chilling darkness.

"Blasted old coot," Thaddeus mutters.

We exchange uneasy looks. My eyes settle on Elias, recalling the Concord and his vial—an oversight until now. Nico's gaze meets mine in a wordless exchange. Yet, Elias is my friend. I can't leave him alone in the shadowed expanse of this city. That's not an option for me. Confronting him will come, but not here, not in the confines of this alley. With a weight in my chest, I decide to retreat.

"We must turn back," I announce. "The main road will have to do."

Turning to exit the alley, I catch a glimpse of a vast shadowy shape gliding across the distant entrance, barely discernible in the weak light. As it moves past the entrance, it lets out a scream, resonating powerfully against the narrow alley's confines.

"Curse the fates," I mutter under my breath.

"We can't go back," Skylar says.

"And we can't go forward," Nico adds.

Our group shares uneasy glances. With the main route blocked and this alleyway shrouded in potential peril, our choices seem to dwindle.

"I don't want to go back," Lili says, her voice quivering. I draw her in for a reassuring embrace, and I set our course.

"We have to press on," I say. Casting a backward glance, the alley's path stretches into the unknown. The chill deepens, my breath becoming a misty exhalation.

As we advance, subtle luminescence of runes emits from the walls, casting eerie, shifting lights through the mist. What was once merely a path, now seems to transform into an entity with its own intent, as if to challenge my decision to continue. My pulse quickens.

"Fates be with us," I murmur, leading our group further into the unknown.

A subtle vibration starts under my feet, quickly intensifying into a thunderous cacophony as ancient stones grind together. The walls begin to move, creeping ominously closer, sparking a surge of panic as the way forward narrows into a suffocating corridor of darkness. Dust swirls in the thickening air, and the haunting voice returns, louder amidst the chaos.

"Turn back lest the path consume you!" But retreating isn't an option; the entrance has been swallowed by darkness and is no longer visible.

"Faster!" I yell, though my voice is nearly swallowed by the noise of shifting walls. We run, our steps a frantic rhythm on the stone as the voice's admonitions echo.

"Turn back, turn back!"

Its warnings fade against the backdrop of my racing heart and the grim thought that I might have just led us all to our end. As the walls seem poised to capture us, a flicker of hope emerges: an ancient, solid door set into the wall, groaning under the alley's metamorphosis. I throw myself against it but it refuses to yield. Skylar quickly steps forward without hesitation.

"Stand back," she commands, her voice cutting through the panic. With haste, she reaches into her satchel and pulls out an axe. With a cry, she swings it at the door causing splinters of wood to fly. Another swing and its ancient wood begins to buckle under the force, until at last, it gives way, breaking open to reveal the darkness beyond. We throw ourselves through the threshold, tumbling into the unknown as the walls behind us meet with a deafening crash, sealing the door with the finality of a tomb.

A beam from a lantern slices through the darkness, revealing Skylar, who has now traded her axe for a lantern. The glow bathes her in a welcoming warmth and my gaze lingers on her. The slight disarray of her brown hair, beads of sweat tracing paths down her face and over her lips, coupled with the sparkle in her brown eyes under the lantern's glow, unexpectedly casts a subtle allure.

"Skylar," I whisper, placing a gentle hand on her arm, "Thank you." She smiles softly in response.

Elias, catching his breath, leans against the wall, the light from Skylar's lantern casting shadows across his face. He looks at Skylar, then at the rest of us.

"I never thought..." he begins, his voice trailing off as he shakes his head. "Skylar, that was... you just saved us."

She places the lantern down, illuminating the small space we've found refuge in and wipes the sweat from her brow with the back of her hand.

"Oh don't make a fuss about it," she says, turning to look around the room.

The sight before me strikes a balance between the mundane and the unsettling. Shadows reveal the interior of a house long neglected, its surfaces cloaked in dust and draped with spiderwebs that resemble ancient curtains. The air is heavy, tinged with the scent of decay. My movement kicks up dust clouds that dance like spirits in the beam of the lantern.

"Let's have a look, I suppose. Couldn't hurt anything," Thaddeus remarks, a note of amusement in his voice. Exploring further, whispers of past lives seem to drift through the ruins around us. A dining table, its porcelain now tarnished and cracked, silently speaks of past gatherings. The chairs are arrayed as if in anticipation of guests who, I understand with a pang of melancholy, will never arrive. Beneath the table lies a faded rug, its once vibrant colors muted by layers of dust, and nearby, a bookshelf leans precariously, its books faded and titles lost to time. In a quiet corner, a grand piano stands, its keys cloaked in dust, amidst a scatter of music sheets, all waiting in hushed anticipation for a touch that never comes.

Adjusting to the dimness, a harsh reality sets in: our sanctuary is sealed, devoid of any exits, windows, or doors, save for the one through which we entered, now obstructed by the solid wall of the alley.

"We're completely doomed," Elias declares.

"That's just you, Beanpole," Thaddeus chuckles, "I, for one, appreciate a place with a 'needs love' atmosphere. It adds to its charm, don't you agree?" With that, he confidently approaches the old, dust-coated table. "Beanpole, would you care for a taste of the finest dust Velloria has to offer?" He motions to the ancient tea set.

Elias carefully lowers his tall figure into a chair opposite Thaddeus, engaging in a theatrical tea cup pour and toast. However, the chair, as if protesting Elias's size, groans and collapses dramatically beneath him. Surprised, he frantically reaches for the tablecloth in a bid for balance, but instead drags it down, unleashing a flurry of dust and the chaotic remnants of their tea party. Laughter bursts from the others, mixed with sneezes as dust fills the air. I, however, find little humor in it, feeling it's a slight to the echoes of past lives here. Amid the wreckage of his chair, Elias hurries to get to his feet.

"Alright," I say, with a hint of irritation, "let's make the most of our situation and look for another way out. There's got to be an exit somewhere." Skylar rests against a dust-laden counter and suddenly bursts into a fit of coughing. I look over at her in concern.

"Are you alright?" I ask, offering a comforting rub on her back. After a moment, she manages to catch her breath and offers me a weak smile in response.

"I'm fine, just allergic to the 'needs love' I suppose."

"Nonsense!" Thaddeus exclaims. "How can you be allergic to such a magnificent place?"

"Everyone, come see this," Nico calls out.

We gather around him. There, on the bottom of the tabletop, hidden from view until Elias's accidental upheaval, is a meticulously carved map that details the layout of the house with remarkable precision.

"This has to be significant," Nico says, pointing to a symbol carved near a wall on the map. Then, Thaddeus stumbles upon a breakthrough that pivots our fate. Hidden within the spine of an ancient, dust-covered tome, he finds a slender, metallic key. This discovery sends another wave of excitement through me.

"Aha!" he exclaims, holding the key as high as he can for all to see, which is not very high at all. A symbol on it glints in the lantern's light. He quickly brings it over to the map and it matches perfectly to the one etched into the table. It's a specific spot in the room—a seemingly unimportant section of the wall, hidden behind one of the larger tapestries. I walk over to the tapestry and move it aside, revealing a keyhole. The symbol is there, carved above the hole, mirroring the one on the key. Elias briskly takes the key from Thaddeus and inserts it into the lock.

"Sure, Beanpole. No matter if you do," Thaddeus mutters sarcastically.

"You couldn't reach the lock anyways," he retorts with a chuckle.

"I'll have you know—" His words are cut off by a loud clank of unlocking through the room. Holding his breath, Elias pushes the door open. We're greeted by the cool, open air of the main street outside and Thaddeus lets out a laugh.

"The irony," he says through chuckles.

"That was some shortcut, huh? What a strange little house," Elias replies.

"If I would have known, I would have just taken the main street to begin with," I say with a sigh. Night has fallen over Velloria now. The moon hangs low in the sky, casting its silver light over the deserted streets as we step out into the night.

"How is it dark already?" Lili asks.

"I don't know," I say, "we weren't in there that long."

The house, with all its mysteries, lies behind us, but the quiet of the streets offers little peace. Velloria at night is a different beast. Shadows seem to move in the corners of my eyes constantly but when I turn, nothing is there. I turn to Skylar, a sense of urgency tightening my voice.

"Let's turn off the lantern," I whisper. "We can't afford to draw any unwanted attention." Understanding flickers in her eyes, and with a soft click, the comforting light is extinguished, plunging us into near darkness.

"Stay close," I instruct, focusing my will on the bracer wrapped tightly around my wrist. In moments, the bracer morphs, its metal cooling and contracting into the form of the red lens. The darkness of the night begins to peel away as I look through the lens, revealing a world unseen by the naked eye. The shadows and fog are gone. In their place, a surreal landscape bathed in the ethereal red glow unfolds. Each broken column and crumbled facade is outlined with an otherworldly clarity. The sight is hauntingly beautiful, yet profoundly sad—a city lost, its heartbeat silent under the watchful gaze of a blood moon.

As we weave our way through the devastated streets, large bones against the ruin hint at creatures that once roamed the outskirts, now reduced to mere echoes of their former existence. Nearby, a child's toy peeks out from under the debris. Old books with torn and weathered pages lay scattered, their stories forever silenced. An overturned horse carriage, its wheels pointing at the sky as if cursing the gods, speaks of a desperate and thwarted attempt to flee. The collective remnants stir a deep sorrow in me for the life that once filled these streets, suffocated by the weight of war. Amidst this landscape of despair, Skylar's voice, tinged with fear, cuts through the night in a whisper.

"I'm scared," she confesses.

"Me too," Lili echoes softly. In that moment, the lens reveals a fleeting wisp of bright red light weaving through the desolation. I halt.

"Wait," I whisper. "I see something." The singular wisp of light flickers and flits like a lone firefly dancing in the rubble. Then, more lights begin to appear, blossoming from the shadows, their numbers growing, converging into forms that are both mesmerizing and unnerving.

"What's happening? What do you see?" Nico asks.

"I… I'm not sure," I say. Then a different red glow shines from behind me. I turn and my heart sinks. Nico's sword is glowing. I quickly turn back and watch as the lights begin to take on more distinct shapes. My heart starts pounding furiously. The ethereal beauty of the wisps were only a facade. A chill of fear washes over me as I understand the true nature of what I had mistaken for simple lights. Far from being harbingers of hope, these are foreboding watchers—either spirits or beings concealed by the shroud of night. Yet, they stay just beyond reach like silent guardians watching our every move.

"We need to keep going," I whisper.

"What's out there?" Elias asks, and I remember only I can see the revelations of the lens.

"There are… entities or beings all around us, just by the buildings, watching."

"This better not be a jest, Asha." His voice shakes slightly.

"I'm serious," I assure him sternly. "We need to keep moving. The palace is just ahead."

After a moment, I lean in to whisper specifically to Skylar, "If I tell you to run, ignite the lantern at once. We cannot be left in darkness. Keep tight and follow my steps." I pause for some moments. "On second thought, let's light the lantern now. They already know we're here and I'd rather everyone see where they're stepping." The light from Skylar's lantern sends a small wave of relief through me, though it doesn't illuminate the entities. They are only visible through my lens.

As we continue walking, the silent watch of these ethereal onlookers heightens my alertness. What should be a short journey to the palace feels infinitely longer. The deep quiet of the night is broken only by the gentle echo of our footsteps against the cobblestones and the occasional, far-off howl that raises the hair on the back of my neck.

As we near the palace's courtyard gate, the spectral forms that have kept their distance now edge closer, yet remain just beyond Skylar's lantern light. Through my lens, they begin to transform from mere silhouettes into tangible forms. The observers of the night materialize before me.

Their forms are gaunt and stretched, a disgusting blend of bone and flesh that contorts unnaturally. Their skin is pulled taut over their emaciated bodies. Each one features a gaping maw filled with razor-sharp teeth. From their backs spring bizarre appendages, like the gnarled branches of dead trees, moving as if alive. The sight of appendages emerging from their backs is horrifyingly surreal, turning my stomach with a desire to turn my eyes away from the abomination. They trail us, a mute convoy of the vile, keeping pace but never venturing into the lantern's sanctuary. The moment we pass through the Palace gates, Skylar stumbles and the lantern falls from her grip, shattering on the pavement. The protective light vanishes instantly, and chaos erupts.

A unified shriek from the creatures pierces the air, a sound so intense it seems to vibrate the ground. Lili screams, clenching to me with all her strength. Blinded and thrown into disarray, we frantically seek each other in the consuming blackness.

"Asha!" Skylar's scream is quickly drowned out by the shrieks of the entities, morphing into a grotesque cacophony of chattering and hissing, that echoes off the ancient walls of the palace. The sounds of their scurrying grows louder as they stir into a frenzy. I'm scrambling to find her in the dark. The sound of claws scraping against stone is a disorienting barrage that leaves me spinning, unsure of where to turn or run.

Lili's grip tightens further, her small body trembling against mine. I can hear Elias's strained breathing somewhere to my left. Nico lets out a grunt of a shout.

"Light a lantern!" My scream tears through the night, yet it's devoured by the suffocating doom that envelops us. Something cold and slimy grazes my skin. I recoil as a shiver crawls down my spine. A deep, menacing growl vibrates ominously close, more threatening than anything we've encountered before. My breathing comes in ragged, desperate gasps.

Just as the tension reaches its peak, a luminous sphere explodes into existence, enveloping us in a shield of light. The encroaching creatures are hurled back, ripped into pieces by the sphere's power. Searching for the source of our salvation, I spot Lili at the epicenter of this luminous haven, her small frame aglow, gripping her guardian pendant with white knuckles as she cowers on the ground, eyes shut tight in terror. I rush to her side and scoop her into my arms.

"Inside, now!" I yell, dashing toward the palace. The sphere of light around us keeps the creatures at bay. As soon as we're over the threshold, the darkness falls back, and their sinister cries fade into the night. Skylar swiftly digs into her satchel, pulling out additional lanterns, illuminating the palace's shadow-filled entrance hall. Clutching Lili, I gently pry her little fingers from the pendant.

"It's alright, Lili," I reassure her. "They're gone now." Her eyes slowly open, and she relaxes her grip. The protective light retracts into the pendant. Holding her close, I murmur thanks to Lavinia for her gift.

"You were so brave," I whisper, tears breaking from my eyes. Her heartbeat has started to become calm and steady.

"Asha!" Elias shouts. I quickly turn my head and my heart drops. Nico is sitting against a pillar, clutching his leg. I leave Lili with Skylar and quickly rush over to him.

"Nico," my voice comes out in a rasp. His trousers, beneath the knee, are torn to shreds and soaked in blood.

"I'm fine," he says, grunting slightly.

"Don't be a fool. You're not fine. Let me have a look," I say sharply. He removes his hands. The gashes from a creature's claws have cut deep, but not deep enough to reach the bone.

"It hasn't reached the bone, or cut into your veins. That's a good sign." I sigh with relief. "I'll have to wrap it."

"Can't you just use one of your powers and heal it?" he asks.

"I don't know how. Maybe once we find the shard. For now, we just need to bandage it and keep it clean." Skylar hands me a water pouch. "This will probably hurt, Elias find me something to bandage it with." I pour the water over the gaping wounds. Nico clenches his teeth and groans, but bears through it.

"Here, this should work," Elias says, handing me an extra shirt he has brought.

"Thanks." I tear it into strips and begin to wrap the wound.

"Thank you, Asha," Nico murmurs. I offer him a smile as I secure the final strip.

"Can you manage to stand on it?"

"I think so." He leverages himself up from the ground and starts to cautiously move, grimacing a bit with each step. He looks over at me, smiling through the discomfort.

"Ha!" Thaddeus bursts out. "I can finally walk faster than you!"

"In your dreams," Nico retorts, chuckling. "You'd still need to run to catch up with me with your small legs." The light-hearted banter lifts my worries slightly. Thaddeus stands up straighter, now with a mock-serious glint in his eyes.

"A race it shall be!" he declares,

"Let's not," I say quickly. "There's no need to put more strain on it. You need to rest it, Nico."

"Oh yes," Thaddeus says with a grin. "My apologies! What was I thinking?"

I help Nico settle back down against the pillar, making sure he's comfortable, before turning my attention to the task of preparing a sleeping spot for Lili and myself. Amidst the comforting circle of lanterns I lay out our makeshift bedding. The light creates an island of warmth in the darkness.

Once everything is in place, I coax Lili to lie down, wrapping an arm around her to provide both warmth and reassurance. The gentle rhythm of her breathing soon syncs with mine as we settle down, the lanterns' flickering light lulling us into a peaceful slumber.

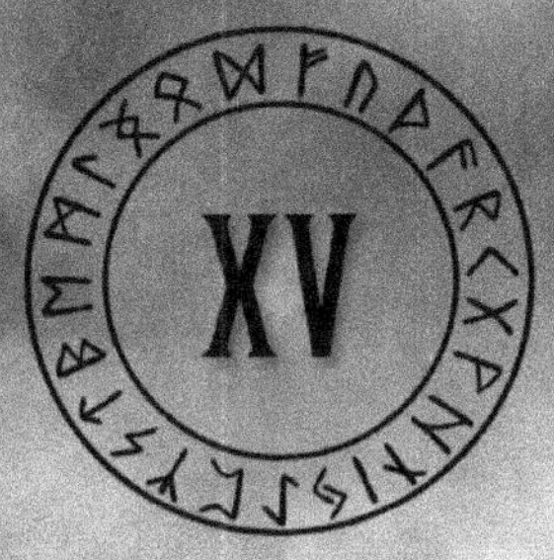

SECRETS IN THE GRAND PALACE

As the first light of dawn softly seeps through the grand arched windows of the palace entrance, it nudges me awake from a restless sleep. Every muscle aches as I rise silently, taking in the makeshift camp we've established here. The others remain in the grip of sleep, cocooned in an assortment of makeshift blankets and cloaks they've scavenged. The lanterns, their light waning in the dawn, have fulfilled their role of shielding us from the darkness.

The palace around me unfolds a tale of beauty marred by decay. Sunlight streams in, making dust motes pirouette in the air, illuminating both the remnants of its splendor and the silence of its decline. The idea that these corridors once thrummed with the pulse of bustling life now seems like a whisper from another era, almost too ethereal to grasp.

"Why didn't Thaddeus wake us up with his rooster crowing?" Elias mumbles, sitting up now and looking around the room. Thaddeus quickly perks up.

"Figured I'd spare you the wake-up call, Beanpole. You seem to need all the beauty sleep you can get." He chuckles as Elias gears up for a comeback.

Before he can fire back, a loud, distinct rumble interrupts—coming from Nico, who, with a sheepish grin, is holding his stomach.

"I couldn't agree more," Elias says, "Skylar, got anything edible in that enchanted bag of yours?"

Skylar, now awake but still cocooned in blankets, rolls her eyes mildly. Her arm is the only thing that protrudes from the blanket as she delves into her satchel, miraculously producing an array of food. She lays out bread, cheese, dried fruit, and a jar of honey, transforming the palace's cold floor into a makeshift dining hall. Elias briefly sets aside his banter with Thaddeus, his attention captured by the food. He theatrically pulls a fork from his satchel and Skylar gives him a sly look.

"You really brought a fork with you?" she asks.

"Why not? I knew it would come in handy," he replies, waving the fork triumphantly. "Let's eat, shall we?"

Lili now sits up, rubbing her eyes and we all gather around Skylar's spontaneous breakfast, our laughter and casual chatter echoing off the walls. The simple meal, that would have been mundane under different circumstances, takes on the quality of a feast as we share it. For these fleeting moments we are not just weary travelers, but a family of sorts.

After the final crumbs disappear and the last drops of water are consumed, a wave of satisfaction sweeps through us all. Yet, the burden of the shard quickly seizes me again. I spread the map on the ground, its aged parchment whispering beneath my touch. As we are gathered around the old document, I realize the symbol spans the entire structure on the map, indicating that the entrance to the depths could be hidden anywhere within the vast expanse of the palace.

"Well, it looks like we'll have to find the entrance ourselves," I say.

"We should split up into teams," Nico suggests, scanning the map and then the expanse of shadowy halls that branch off in all directions. "We can cover more ground that way."

Before the words are fully out of his mouth, Thaddeus pipes up with a tap of his walking stick on the floor. "I'm with Skylar and Beanpole!" His declaration is swift, leaving no room for debate.

Elias releases a heavy sigh. "Thaddeus, why do you insist on torturing me?" Though, the faint smile tugging at the corner of his mouth betrays his fondness for the torture.

"It's all part of my grand plan for you to become best friends with Geraldine," he exclaims, glancing at the frog who regards the scene with what one might interpret as a skeptical eye. "I promised her you two would be best pals before we return home. You understand, don't you? It's a matter of honor. I can't go back on my word."

I can't help but laugh at his earnest explanation. Geraldine, for her part, seems to puff up slightly at the mention of her importance in Thaddeus's grand scheme, though whether she's pleased or simply tolerating the attention is anyone's guess. With the teams decided we quickly outline a plan. Each team will take a different section of the palace, reconvening at the entrance hall in one hour, regardless of what we find—or don't find.

We set out our different ways. Lili, Nico, and I tread carefully through the shadowed hallways. The air is thick with antiquity and decline.

"How is your leg?" I ask, my eyes dropping briefly to the bandages. He pauses, assessing his response as he shifts his weight slightly.

"It's holding up," he replies after a moment. "Thanks to you." He smiles and I nod in return, relieved but still cautious.

"And Elias," I say, noting the shirt he provided to wrap it. His expression hardens slightly.

"I'm sure we would have managed without it."

"Nico, why do you despise him so much? What has he done to you?" He glances around as if searching for a reason. I scoff slightly. "You don't even have a reason, do you?" I am more frustrated for his refusal to look me in the eye than to actually answer my question. It's no use. "Just make sure you're not overdoing it. We need you in one piece," I add sharply. Why does he persist in acting so childishly towards Elias? I'm aware he's upset over the incident with the vial. Doesn't he believe I'll handle it? Irritated, I shift my focus, turning away to resume my search.

Winding through several convoluted passageways, we come across a magnificent door, its frame detailed with elaborate carvings. With effort, I open it to discover a museum filled with ancient artifacts and weaponry that belonged to both the heroes and villains of Velloria's rich history. Armor sets dimmed by layers of dust, yet still showcasing remarkable craftsmanship, stand on display near the walls. Tapestries that chronicle epic battles adorn the walls behind them, their colors faded.

"Wow, this place is amazing," Nico murmurs softly. I remain silent. The sting of my irritation with him lingers, and I'm not ready to let him off the hook just yet.

I delve deeper into the museum and my eyes catch sight of a display case with its glass shattered, revealing something that sends a shiver down my spine—an enormous claw, larger than anything I've ever seen. Its immense size, coupled with the dark marks tarnishing its pointed tip, tells tales of a creature both mighty and terrifying. I lean closer, trying to imagine the beast this claw once belonged to. I reach out to let my fingers brush over it. The moment my finger grazes its surface, the air around me shifts, and I am thrust into a vision of the Darkest Battle.

I am standing amidst a battlefield vast and chaotic, the ground beneath my feet quaking with the fury of the clash. The air is thick with the smell of iron and fire, a pungent mixture that stings my nostrils and coats my tongue. Ash rains from the sky like a snowfall, settling on my hair and eyelashes, blurring my vision. The sounds of the ancient battle envelop me in an orchestra of clashing steel and cries of the fallen. The sound is overwhelming. I can hear the whistle of arrows as they arc through the smog-laden air, the thunderous impact of siege weapons unleashing their deadly cargo, and the guttural chants of the Eyeless armies as they surge forward, relentless and unyielding.

The sky above roils with dark clouds. And then, amidst the chaos, the night is pierced by a terrifying roar as a white dragon emerges from the sky in wisps of clouds and smoke. *Astralith.* Its scales shimmer against the darkened sky. The dragon's roar shakes the very air with a sound so powerful it resonates within my chest. As it swoops down to engage the Eyeless, its massive form blots out the sky. Its movements are both graceful and devastating, each beat of its wings sending storms of ash swirling around the battlefield.

Amid its wild ballet, the dragon engages in a fierce battle with a swarm of the Eyeless, which burst forth from the earth and grasp onto its massive feet, desperately trying to ascend. Astralith lets out a heart-wrenching shriek and I cover my ears. A claw, severed by the Eyeless, falls to the earth. As quickly as it came, the vision fades, leaving me back in the quiet museum, heart pounding, with the echo of the dragon's cry still ringing in my ears.

"Dragon claw," Nico states from beside me, pulling my attention away from the display and towards him.

"This one belonged to Astralith," I say softly. He looks at me slightly puzzled. "I had a vision when I touched it." His eyes widen slightly.

"A vision of Astralith? But I thought that Astralith was just a myth."

I shake my head. "No, I was there. Well, sort of. It lost this claw fighting the Eyeless in the Darkest Battle."

"Wow," is all he can manage. I pick up the enormous claw in both of my hands.

"I want to take this. No one will miss it here anyways," I say. "I'll see if Skylar can fit it into her satchel until we get back." He agrees with a nod, and Lili's laughter draws my attention. She's captivated by a collection of fine figurines, her touch just brushing against the glass that shelters them. I move closer to join her.

"Pick one," I encourage with a smile, opening the case for her tiny hands to slip through. Her eyes, brimming with wonder and a dash of playfulness, lock with mine, silently asking for approval.

"For me?" she whispers, her voice a feather. I nod, feeling a warmth spread through me at her delight.

"Yes, go ahead." I laugh softly. With a brief pause, she gently selects a figurine, a dainty fairy whose wings glisten like fresh dew on a spiderweb at dawn. It seems just right for her tender heart and inquisitive mind.

"This one," she announces, her eyes sparkling. "It's so pretty." I secure the case and gently take the fairy from her to admire it.

"She's beautiful, Lili. Just like you," I say, returning it to her. She holds the fairy tenderly in her palms.

"I'll call her Ellia," she declares.

"That's the perfect name," I agree.

"Asha, can we talk for a moment?" Nico whispers from behind me. I sigh.

"Are you going to tell me what you have against Elias?" I ask stubbornly, rising to meet his gaze. Behind me, Lili twirls through the room, her fairy figurine swirling in the air. Nico takes a deep breath, his gaze moving from the ground to lock with mine.

"I guess… I don't know. I got jealous." His words shock me. Nico, jealous? Of Elias? The thought nearly makes me laugh but I hold it in. "Recently, I've been thinking…" he continues, his fingers tracing the contours of the display case, seemingly grounding himself within a whirlpool of thoughts. "…about us—about you, Lili, and me." My pulse quickens, and I struggle to maintain eye contact, my gaze drifting to the space behind him as he talks. "These last few days have thrown more at us than our whole lives combined, and it has led me to question our future, about our place once the dust of this journey settles." His words stir a storm of emotions inside me, scattering my thoughts as I scramble for a response. How do I even respond to that?

"Nico," I murmur, my eyes dropping to my feet, then flicking to his bandage, then everywhere in between. The notion of 'us' is genuinely intimidating. I've barely had a moment to entertain any thought of what might linger on the horizon. Yet, here he is, forcing me to confront these thoughts. A fleeting wave of irritation sweeps through me.

"Being with you, Asha," sincerity resonates in his tone as he continues, "means more to me than anything I've ever known. And it terrifies me because I dare to hope for a future for us... for something beyond this friendship." Internally, I'm moved, yet torn, navigating the perilous waters of our current reality and the possibility of a future together.

"Nico, I..." The words jam in my throat. I want to share that I've considered 'us,' yet a paralyzing fear clutches at me, dragging those thoughts to a place deep and dark, leaving me gasping for air. I lift my eyes to meet his. By the fates, those eyes…

"Nico," I manage to say, "to be utterly truthful, I'm afraid to dream about what comes after. I can't afford distractions for either of us while we're in the midst of all this." His expression dims at my words. I reach out, placing my hand on his, stopping its restless movement on the display case. "I don't want to cause you pain, Nico," I say softly. He offers a faint smile.

"I get it," he replies. "The future is a blank page. But, it was important for me to share my feelings, to let you know that you mean more to me than just a friend in this adventure." At his words, my heart fills with a bittersweet warmth. Here we stand, on the edge of untold tomorrows, tied together by the very quest that keeps us apart. A deep silence surrounds me, heavy with the weight of decisions. Decisions I don't want to think about right now.

"I will give it some thought, Nico. When all this is over," I whisper. My pause is short before my hand reaches for the warmth of his face, which seems to transfer some of his unease to me with the touch.

The air between us thickens. His arms wrap around me, and as I lean into his hold, the steady beat of his heart offers a momentary escape. I allow myself a brief indulgence in imagining our existence beyond the here and now. Visions of the future blossom in my thoughts, tender and full of promise, each one a fragile sketch of potential realities. Is there a place for us in that undetermined landscape? Caught in a dance of hope and uncertainty, my thoughts craft a fine mosaic of what might be, until Lili's lively shout pierces our quietude.

"Asha, Nico, are you coming? There's so much more to explore!" Her call acts as a soft pull back to the present. Reluctantly, I step out of our embrace, the enchantment of the moment ebbing but still leaving behind a lingering warmth. Our eyes lock briefly before I take a step back.

"We should get going," I suggest. He gives a nod, and as I turn away, I steal a final glance at the historical backdrop that cradled our fleeting connection, before making my way back to Lili.

Leaving the museum behind, we navigate deeper into the serpentine corridors of the palace, discovering rooms rich with the echoes of long-forgotten lore. The palace, for all its bewitching charm, clings tightly to its mysteries, offering no clues to the entrance of its underbelly. Our wandering eventually leads us to the entrance of an age-old library. With a collective push, we open the doors and enter a sanctuary of forgotten wisdom and are greeted by the scent of old paper and leather. Immense shelves, burdened with ancient volumes, stretch up to the high ceiling. The other group is already absorbed in their search, surrounded by heaps of old manuscripts and parchments laid out around them. The air is thick with the dust kicked up by their determined search.

"Any luck?" I ask, approaching the large table where they're gathered. Elias looks up from a thick tome.

"Just dust and more questions," he jests, then his eyes widen. "Hey, is that a claw?"

"It is. We stumbled upon a museum," I answer. "Skylar, can you fit this in your satchel? I'd like to bring it back." She walks over holding her satchel open, wearing a playful smile.

"Of course!" she assures. "This bag is practically a magic portal. Well, almost." I laugh as I carefully place the claw inside, which just manages to squeeze through the opening. It disappears as if into a void, and she snaps the bag shut with a satisfied pat.

"Told you," she beams. "There's also a wealth of history about dragons here," she mentions, diving back into her exploration.

"Skylar, look!" Lili rushes up to her, showing off her figurine. Their lighthearted chatter about fairies fades into the background as they explore together, and I immerse myself in the sea of books and scrolls. The library becomes a realm of focused inquiry, the silence broken only by occasional sighs of exasperation, or the soft thud of another book added to our hopeful pile. Then, Nico calls us over, waving an ancient-looking map with excitement.

"Look at this," he declares, unfolding the map for us all to see and pointing to a distinctive mark not found on any of my other maps. "I think this is it."

"Well done, Nico," I commend, drawing closer to examine the detail. I momentarily lose myself in the closeness, his shoulder brushing against mine.

"Let's see where it leads," I suggest, swiftly grabbing the map and pivoting in a flutter of awkwardness. The group tails me as we venture through the palace's intricate maze of passageways, guided by the map's directions.

Finally, we arrive at a nondescript door, its wood warped by time, yet remarkably intact. I push the door open. The bedroom that lies beyond is a capsule of time. Dust motes float lazily in the beams of light that fight their way through the grimy windows, illuminating a space that seems to have been forgotten by the world outside.

The bed, a large canopy structure, still bears drapes, though they are now faded and threadbare. A thick layer of dust covers every surface, softening the outlines of the furniture and giving the room a surreal, dreamlike quality. Beside the bed, a nightstand holds the remnants of a last, lonely evening: a candlestick with a candle melted down to a stub, and an open book, its pages yellowed and curling at the edges. Across the room, a vanity sits against the wall, its mirror dulled and speckled with age, reflecting a fragmented world back at itself.

Despite the decay, there's a beauty to the room. It's a personal chamber, a sanctuary that had once been someone's world, now sitting quietly, preserved by the years. I stand at the threshold, hesitant to disturb the solemn tranquility of the space, yet compelled to explore further.

"There's a story here," I murmur to myself, stepping into the room, the others following suit. Our presence, the first in hundreds of years perhaps, is an intrusion into the silent reverie of the past.

In the hushed stillness of the bedroom my gaze is drawn to the vanity. An anomaly catches my attention—an old, child's drawing etched in charcoal upon the wooden surface near the mirror. The simplicity of the sketch, a house flanked by trees and a smiling sun overhead, captures a sense of peace. My fingers reach out, almost of their own accord, to trace the lines of the drawing. The dust, undisturbed for centuries, piles against my finger.

A mixture of wonder, sadness, and an overwhelming sense of connection swirl inside me. Here, in this corner of a forgotten room, a child once played, dreamed, and lived. Who was she? Or he. What was the child like? Enchanting like Lili? The moment passes, but the emotions it has stirred retain the depth and complexity of the human experience. A drawing waiting in the silence for someone to remember, to feel, and to understand. *I am here.* The words flow through my mind as if sending a message of reassurance that this child is not forgotten in the dust.

Lost in the drawing, I barely register the shift in the atmosphere until Elias's laughter breaks through the solemnity like a clash of cymbals. Startled from my reverie, I turn to witness a scene that clashes violently with the mood that had enveloped me. There stands Elias, perched precariously on the ancient bed that had likely once cradled generations of dreams. Atop his head sits an old, dust-covered hat, its grandeur faded with time but now serving as a prop in his impromptu performance. In his hand, he wields an old wooden cane, not as a support, but as a sword, directing playful jabs in Thaddeus's direction, who, for his part, seems caught between amusement and concern.

"Are you serious, Elias!" I raise my voice in anger. "How could you?" He freezes, his amused look fading instantly. "This place, this whole palace, was someone's home," I insist, my voice shaking slightly. "And here you are, mocking their memory? What's wrong with you?"

The room is deathly silent now and Elias's expression shifts from confusion to remorse, the cane no longer a prop but a burden in his hand. He steps down from the bed and places the hat and cane back where he'd found them. The tension that had erupted so suddenly begins to ebb as he speaks, his voice low and sincere.

"I'm sorry, Asha. I didn't think—"

"Just be more respectful," I cut him off sternly, frustrated at his insensitivity. The undeniable history of this room demands a reverence he genuinely seems incapable of. Shaking my head, I turn away, allowing my words to hang in the air as I redirect my focus back to my search. The hidden entrance to Velloria's underbelly is a mystery that has eluded us this far, but its entrance must be here somewhere.

As I scan the room, the tension from our exchange begins to dissipate. Each artifact, each dusty tome, feels like a potential key, silently waiting to reveal its secrets. The room seems to watch us. I move slowly, my eyes sweeping over the ancient furniture and faded paintings, searching for any sign, any anomaly that might hint at the passage. The silence that envelopes us is suddenly broken by Skylar's voice.

"I found something!" she calls out, pointing at a small, framed painting hanging on the wall. Drawn towards the decor, I approach the painting, and my heart suddenly drops. The image before me captures a scene eerily familiar to me: a brown and black raven sitting on a skull in a desert. The raven, its eyes almost lifelike, seems to be watching me, pulling up memories of Elias on the black throne. My mind is trying to find a connection to this city and my vision but it's no use.

"That's creepy," Lili murmurs next to me.

"Do you think it means something?" Nico asks. I nod, unable to tear my gaze away from the painting.

"I've seen this before, in a vision," I confess, the words spilling out of me before I can stop them. I don't want to tell them about what I saw in my vision. The silence that follows is heavy. Finally, Elias relieves the tension.

"And how exactly is a gloomy picture going to help us, Skylar?"

"No, not the picture. Look," she insists, stepping closer and pointing to a detail we'd all overlooked. Carved into the wooden frame is a symbol, intricate and familiar—the seal of the Vellorian Soulweavers.

I move closer. The moment my fingers settle on it, the carving begins to glow, a soft light emanating from the lines as if they were smoldering embers about to ignite. A surge of warmth and light spreads through my fingertips. It flows through my veins, up my arm, and across my forehead, resonating with the seal of Velloria.

Then, as quickly as it had begun, the glow ceases, replaced by the sound of a mechanism clicking into place—or out of place. With startling suddenness, the top of the frame pops off the wall, revealing itself to be more than just a piece of art. It's a key, activating a door that had remained hidden in plain sight.

We stand in stunned silence, watching as the wall beside the painting shifts, a portion receding to reveal a narrow passageway that had been concealed behind the veneer. The passageway revealed by the displaced painting is unlike any part of the palace we have traversed thus far. Narrow and steeped in shadows, it descends downward sharply with a set of stone stairs, its walls made from the very bedrock upon which the palace is built. The air is cool and damp, carrying the scent of earth and stone long untouched by the sun.

Skylar pulls a couple lanterns from her satchel, and we make our way inside. The descent is gradual but relentless, leading us further into the heart of the earth. The sound of our footsteps echoes back at us. The further we go, the more the passage seems to constrict, the ceiling lowering and the walls drawing in, as if the very earth is pressing close, eager to reclaim this intrusion into its domain.

The steep pathway ends into a flat slab of walkway, leading into a passage that opens into a chamber. The chamber stretches out before us, vast and cavernous, its boundaries lost to the gloom. A faint, eerie light emanates from luminescent moss clinging to the walls, casting everything in a ghostly green hue that does little to dispel the darkness. It feels as if we have stepped into another realm, one where the rules of the living no longer apply.

The moment I step into the chamber, a chill creeps down my spine. The air is oppressive, like a heavy cloak that smothers sound. My own breathing sounds too loud, echoing back at me.

At the center of the chamber, an obsidian dais stands. Above, a fissure allows a sliver of light to pierce the darkness, spotlighting the dais in an almost mocking imitation of sanctity. We tread carefully around bones that protrude from the mossy ground. But it's not the bones that unsettle me, it's the shadows. They seem to move independently of any light source, forming shapes and patterns that seem almost sentient. I can feel their eyes upon me like a weight of malevolent attention that seeks to pierce through to my very soul. I approach the dais cautiously. On its surface are etchings in a language I don't recognize.

"Can anyone make this out?" I ask, though I already suspect the answer. The script is unlike anything I've seen before. The moment the words leave my mouth, my bracer transforms into the lens.

"That will never not be incredible," Skylar whispers.

I hold it up to the inscriptions on the dais. Through the lens, the mysterious characters shift, reshaping themselves into words I can understand. I voice the inscription aloud.

"Unto those who quest for the shard: The way that stretches before thee is shrouded not in the night of the world, but in the night of the soul. This trial requires one alone to delve into the depths of their own night. Only he who faces and conquers his paramount fear may lay claim to the prize. With a single drop of crimson, the covenant is forged, and the Trial of Shadows shall be set in motion."

A chill runs across my skin and I turn to face my companions, lowering the lens slowly from my eye. The understanding that the trial will involve shadows lurking in our own depths is a daunting realization.

"Well," I say, my voice echoing slightly in the cold stone chamber, "The inscription is clear. We must choose one." Elias is the first to break the silence that follows.

"It's obvious that you should do this," he says, looking directly at me. "Not that it doesn't sound like a lot of fun, or anything. But you're the best person for it." Of course he would be the first to back down. I roll my eyes.

"Sometimes the most obvious answer isn't always the best one," I counter. "Everyone here has a deepest fear. Ideally, the one with the smallest fear should go." The words hang between us.

A curious phenomenon then unfolds. As I try to identify my deepest fear, to articulate the shadow that might hinder me in the trial, I find myself at a loss. It's as if the chamber itself has cast a veil over my memories, obscuring the very fears that define me.

"I... I can't seem to pinpoint mine," Skylar says faintly, leaning warily on the dais. One by one, each of us echoes their sentiment. Our fears, so personal and defined in the light of day, now elude our grasp, hidden by the chamber's mysterious influence. The realization that we must choose without truly knowing what our fears are adds a layer of complexity, and the discussion circles back to me.

"Regardless, Asha has the greatest chance," Nico finally says. "Her connection to the Soulweavers is stronger than any of us have." He looks at me now. "Whatever this trial is, I know you will beat it. There's much depending on you. No pressure, I mean."

I absorb his words with appreciation, though it does nothing to ease my doubts. The enormity of what might lie ahead presses upon me with a crushing force. To step forward into the trial feels like I will have to grapple with unknown specters that define the deepest parts of my being, and I don't even know what those are. Yet, they are right. I most likely am more equipped to face whatever this trial is than any of them, and with luck, I will come out with the shard.

"Okay," I concede, "I'll do it." The moment I speak the words, a light emanates from the dais. I walk over, and new words begin to appear. I hold up the lens and read aloud. "With a drop of crimson, the trial shall be set in motion." My heart thuds heavily in my chest, the reality of what I am about to do setting in.

"Guys…" Skylar's faint voice cuts through the silence. As I turn around, her knees give way, and she crumbles to the ground.

"Skylar!" Elias yells and we rush to her side. He gently cradles her head in his lap.

"What's happening to her?" I question, noting her skin's chill and dampness.

"Perhaps hypothermia, worsened by falling into the freezing water days ago," Nico suggests. Skylar's eyes flutter open, offering a weak smile.

"Skylar, can you hear me?" I inquire as I feel her forehead that's now dotted with sweat. "By the fates, you're feverish."

"I just need some water," she finally manages to say. "The chill from our journey is catching up with me I'm afraid." Elias's worried gaze meets mine. Retrieving a water flask, I tilt it to her lips, watching as she drinks eagerly. After finishing, she uses her sleeve to dry her face, and manages to sit up as a subtle hint of color returns to her cheeks.

"There," she announces softly, followed by a fit of coughing, "much better. You should do the trial, Asha," she finally says.

"Alright," I murmur more to myself than her. I stand and take a place in front of the dais. As I retrieve my father's blade from my boot, the sharp, broken metal glints in the dim light of the chamber. With a deep breath, I place the blade against my finger. Its cold steel seems to suck the warmth from my skin.

A sense of anticipation fills the air as I press the blade down onto the tip of my finger, breaking skin with a small but decisive action. A single drop of blood wells up, pressing against my skin. Time slows, stretching seconds into an infinite expanse. This drop, vibrant crimson against my pale skin, quivers slightly, hesitant to part from its origin. It glistens under the chamber's dim light, transforming into a ruby beacon amidst shadows. My world narrows, focusing intently on this drop of blood, the pivot on which my fate will turn.

With a slow, deliberate movement, I tilt my finger. The drop, now loosed from its constraints, begins its descent towards the dais. Time seems to slow even further, to a near halt, allowing each microsecond of the drop's journey to be observed with excruciating clarity. The air seems to thicken, creating an invisible cushion that cradles the drop as it falls, its surface tension holding it together in a perfect sphere.

Light refracts through the droplet, casting fleeting prismatic shadows on the stone below. It spins gently, rotating in the air as it bridges the short distance between my finger and the dais. Each rotation reveals a new facet of its surface in a mesmerizing dance.

Then, with a sound no louder than a sigh, the droplet contacts the cold, unyielding surface of the ancient stone. The impact, though gentle, sends ripples across the droplet, momentarily distorting its perfect form before it spreads into a splatter. This finality snaps time back to its natural flow, and I watch as the droplet's crimson hue seeps into the stone.

We wait in anticipation, expecting the chamber to react, for the ground to tremble, for hidden doors to swing open, or for some sign that the trial has been accepted. But the moments stretch on, and the chamber remains as still and silent as it has been for centuries. No rumbling of stone, no shifting of the earth—nothing happens.

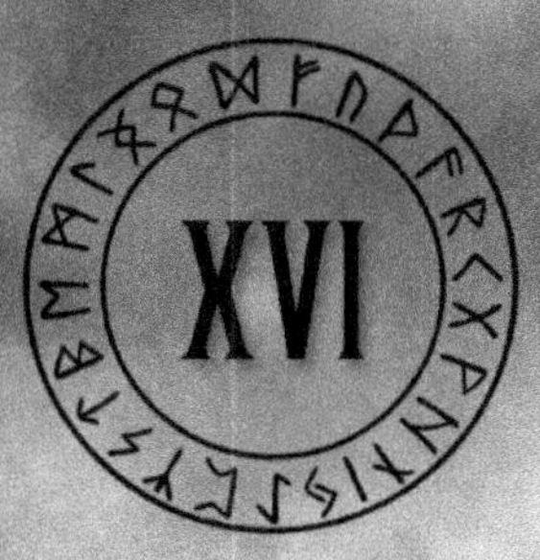

Trial of Shadows

The stillness that wraps around us is more oppressive than the stone walls encircling us. My heart drops as the reality of our predicament dawns on me. I've adhered to the directions given to me, yet find myself seemingly at an impasse. My frustration morphs into a smoldering anger.

"What kind of stupid trial is this?" I glance toward Thaddeus, who merely offers a noncommittal shrug in response.

"Maybe it's more metaphorical?" Skylar's suggestion floats through the air. Her skin is fully back to its usual glowing self now. The idea that I might have misunderstood the instructions adds another layer frustration. Am I missing something obvious, or have I taken the wrong approach entirely? Crimson must mean blood, right?

"Well, we've come this far. We can't give up now," Thaddeus says. I know his words are meant to inspire, yet they only serve to highlight the gravity of my predicament. The chamber, with its ancient secrets and silent judgments, seems to watch me struggle, indifferent to the desperation that claws at me. I feel so close yet so far from the shard. With a deep breath, I look at my friends, their faces now turned to me, waiting for a sign of what to do next.

"What am I supposed to do? We've hit a dead end," I say.

"We need to keep looking," Nico says. "There has to be a way forward. We just haven't found it yet." The already tense atmosphere thickens further as Elias lets slip a comment under his breath. I know it was intended to be inaudible, yet snippets of it have reached me, kindling a surge of irritation I've never directed at anyone. "Repeat that," I insist sharply, my voice slicing the quiet. Taken aback by my confrontation, he pauses, his eyes wavering before aligning with mine.

"I said, I wonder if you're truly the heir of Velloria," he declares, his tone now firm. His words strike me like an assault on my personal heritage.

"By the fates, Elias, why would you doubt that?" I press.

"Consider this, Asha," he begins, "your lineage hasn't really proven itself in the ways the legends suggest it should. The dais remained silent, too. And every threat we've encountered, every creature that has pursued us, seems magnetically drawn to you. If you were truly the heir of Velloria, wouldn't there be some form of safeguard, some hint of direction? Instead, we're just wandering aimlessly. It just seems like you're the magnet for all our misfortunes."

His critique strikes deep and the atmosphere grows tense, charged with my own unvoiced resentments and the sting of perceived betrayal. It's Nico who intervenes, his voice striving to mediate the escalating tension. Which surprises me, given his jealousy of Elias.

"Let's just pause for a second," he suggests, but the breach has already widened, the rift between Elias and me now starkly evident.

"No. It's not okay, Nico," I retort. My response, charged with a torrent of pent-up frustrations, now spills out unrestrained. "He's been recklessly indifferent all along." My tone is laced with bitterness as I recount my grievances. Turning to Elias, I continue, "You triggered the Valthorix at the Concord by tampering with that vial, endangering all of us, especially Lili! And your willingness to leave her behind when she was most vulnerable…How can you sit here and tell me I'm just a nobody, when you've been sneaking around undermining everything we've been working towards?"

I pace back and forth now. Lili is watching me with anxious eyes but I'm too angry to stop. "Throughout our travels, you've consistently ignored the repercussions of your actions and words. It's not merely the thoughtless remarks or the flippant attitude; it's the decisions you make, selfishly and without regard for anyone but yourself. Not to mention you tried to kill me with that arrow in the forest."

"What?" he exclaims. "I did not! I told you I was aiming for that creature and missed. You know I'm a horrible shot!" But his words trickle in through one ear and out the other. I don't care what he says now.

"How are we to continue together when you seem to challenge the very ideals we strive for?" My stern look bores into him now, silently demanding he acknowledge the validity of my accusations or provide some justification for his conduct. However, his response is not of defiance like I was expecting, and almost hoping for.

He averts his gaze, visibly contending with a maelstrom of emotions. When he finally speaks, his voice is laden with an earnestness that resonates throughout the space. "I wish..." he begins, the weight of his impending admission apparent in his pause.

Skylar reaches out, touching his cheek gently, her voice a whisper. "Elias, please."

The moment stretches, filled with a tension that is almost tangible, until Elias, breaking away from Skylar's comforting touch to look past her at me, finds the words that had been eluding him. "I wish you had never crossed paths with my grandmother. That our paths had never crossed." Skylar covers her face with her hands, turning away in tears.

His declaration strikes with force, its reverberations slicing through the veil of my anger and frustration, exposing a vulnerable chasm inside. The thought that our having met could be regarded with such regret by him jars me profoundly.

I lean against the stone wall. This place feels oppressive; suffocating. Within me, a storm of emotions rages. The blame for our perils, the threats we've encountered, and the strife that has crept into our ranks burdens my soul. Could I be the source of their anguish? Is my lineage and the quest I am so devoted to, a harbinger of misfortune rather than hope? The thought of that reality is devastating. Elias's voice shatters the silence again as he continues relentlessly.

"You're going to get us all killed, Asha," he declares, his tone icy as he edges closer. "Do you really believe you have the strength to alter the course of the world, to shoulder this burden? You don't. Your inability to face reality is dragging those you love down a path that leads only to their destruction. You'll get us all killed, or worse. At this rate, we're just going to abandon you like your father did."

With a cry that is part roar, part sob, I explode in a violent rage, my hands finding the fabric of his shirt. I slam him against the cold, stone wall with all the force my body can muster. The impact of his back against the ancient wall of the chamber is a physical manifestation of the turmoil within me. The stone cracks under the unexpected force, spiderwebs of fractures spreading out from where he is pinned. The sound of crumbling stone echoes through the chamber. The screams from my friends are too muffled to make out through the pressure in my ears.

Elias's face, just inches from mine, is a canvas of shock and realization. A single drop of sweat trails down his temple. My fists clench tighter on his shirt as I bore into him with a gaze filled with undiluted hatred.

"How dare you use my father to torment me!" I scream. My breath, hot and ragged, stirs the wisps of short white hairs on his head.

In the charged silence that follows my outburst, Elias's expression shifts subtly. The intensity of our confrontation seems to crystallize into a moment of clarity for him, and when he speaks, his voice is low, infused with a resignation.

"You're right," he begins, "I did steal the vial. I did summon the beast at the Concord. You nearly got us killed twice, Asha, and I was afraid you would eventually succeed. I wanted to stop you before anyone got hurt." The admission hangs in the air between us as his gaze locks with mine. "Decide my fate, Asha."

For a moment, I'm unable to think. The acknowledgment of his actions and their consequences is devoid of defiance; instead, it is an acceptance of the judgment that awaits him, and it only fuels my rage.

"Fight back you coward!" I scream through my tears, slamming him against the wall again.

"I'm not going to fight you, Asha. I accept whatever you decide. If my actions have endangered us, if they've brought us to this brink, then I will bear the responsibility."

With a scream I loosen my grip and take a step back. Elias, once a friend, has just become my enemy. I turn around, wiping tears to clear my vision. I can't allow him to come with us. Right now, I don't even care if he lives, but I can't kill him. I can't. I need to breathe, step away and calm myself. I turn back to face him.

"Leave. Go home, before I change my mind." My voice trembles. Tears overflow from my eyes as the pain wrenches my heart. How has it come to this? The last thing I ever wanted was to hurt anyone; to cause anyone pain. But he has chosen this fate himself. His eyes glance at the floor as he turns to head out of the chamber.

"Asha, please!" Skylar pleads through choked sobs. But I can't go back on my word. Once spoken, it must be final. I turn to Skylar who is a sobbing wreck. She loves him deeply and my heart genuinely aches for her.

"I'm sorry," I say softly. "But you heard his confession. I can't let him stay." A sudden outburst from Nico shatters the dense air that has settled over me.

"That's all?" he seethes. "Elias just gets to walk after putting everyone's lives in danger?"

"Yes," I say sternly. "What else am I supposed to do? He can't stay here." Elias has now paused in the doorway.

"I told her," Nico shouts at Elias while pointing toward me, "and she still gave you the benefit of the doubt and brought you along!"

"Nico stop," I say.

Instead of stopping, he launches himself at Elias, his fists finding their mark on his jaw. Elias struggles to defend himself, but the onslaught is relentless. I stand frozen, the shock of Elias's confession still reverberating through me, rendering me incapable of intervening. Or, perhaps, I simply don't want to. He does deserve it after what he's done. Around me, Skylar screams for me to do something, Lili's sobbing, and Thaddeus is shouting. But it all seems distant, muffled by the tunnel of focus that has narrowed my perception to Nico and Elias.

Then Nico, in a moment of unchecked rage, draws his sword. The air in the chamber thickens with the gravity of what is about to happen. In that heartbeat of a moment, before I can interject, Nico's blade slices through the air, destined for Elias as he now lies helplessly on the ground. I can't let him kill Elias.

My ancient DNA surges to life, commanding the flow of time to slow. My senses heighten, every detail magnified—the slight tremor in Nico's arm, the sharp inhale of breath from Elias, the electric tension that fills the chamber. I rear my arm and my bracer ignites in a blazing fury of electrical current. The bright and intense light coalesces into form and substance, morphing into a blade of pure energy. The air around me crackles with sparks. With a force driven by necessity to protect a life, I let the sword fly forward.

Nico's blade, in its deadly trajectory, is an inch away from Elias's face. Yet, my blade is faster. I watch as it cuts through the air, parting the very atmospheric particles around it. My blade crashes into Nico's with a sound that resonates like thunder. A shockwave of energy emanates from the collision. Nico's sword, unable to withstand the power of my anciently forged weapon, is sliced cleanly in two, the pieces clattering harmlessly to the stone floor as my sword sticks into the stone wall between them.

Time snaps back to its rightful pace. The chamber, once on the verge of witnessing a fatal strike, now bears witness to the thwarted attempt, the air still humming with remnants of the unleashed power. Nico stands frozen, his eyes wide in disbelief at the intervention that has spared Elias's life.

"Are you serious, Asha!" he raises his voice at me, and surprisingly it hurts.

"Yes, I'm serious, and don't you dare raise your voice to me like that," I say sharply. "Regardless of what he's done, his life is not yours to take."

In the heavy silence that follows, all eyes are on me, and I'm caught between emotions. I am more than upset at Elias for betraying me, for betraying all of us. I never wanted to lose him as a friend, but I don't really want him dead either. Then, I'm disappointed in Nico for attempting to kill him. I look around and my gaze settles on Nico's broken blade. The blade his father gave him for his name day.

"This," I say, gesturing to the scattered remnants of the sword, "cannot be what defines us. We have to be better. This journey is about more than just the shard. Do you think I want to put anyone in danger? Or to watch us kill each other off? I don't. You are all my friends."

I meet Nico's gaze, and then the eyes of each of my friends in turn. "Today, we are faced with a choice between life and death, and by the grace of the fates that watch over us, we are given a chance to choose again." Nico's eyes slowly soften and I walk over to him, placing my hand on his arm. "Nico," I say, now speaking directly to him, "I don't want you to have to live with the guilt of killing and losing a friend. As much as I know you dislike him, I also know you. This isn't what I want for you." His eyes find mine.

"I'm sorry," he whispers. "I don't— I don't really want to kill anyone." I look at Elias. Skylar is now tending to his wounds as he sits against the wall and I sit beside them.

"Elias, I understand your fear," I begin, my voice soft yet firm. "I understand why you made those choices. This hasn't been easy for any of us, and the things we've faced would make anyone question the course I've chosen. But know this—I will not lead us to our death. Forgive me for any doubts my actions may have caused, that led you to take the measures you did. We can do better. I can do better."

Elias, looking back at me, seems to search my face for the conviction behind my words. After a moment, a subtle change comes over him, a softening in his eyes that signals the beginning of understanding, of reconciliation.

"It's alright," he replies, a small smile edging his lips. "I should have trusted you."

Suddenly the room whirls and I find myself standing back at the dais, staring at the splatter of blood as if taken back in time. I look up. My friends are all standing next to me, still staring at the drop in anticipation. My mind reels. Then, the sound of gears grinding, a locking mechanism engaging deep within the walls of the chamber, draws my attention. We all turn in unison towards the source of the sound to see a door, previously concealed within the ancient stonework, slowly swinging open.

"Well, that was easy," Elias quips, breaking the stunned silence, a wry smile touching his lips as he leaves the dais and takes a step towards the door. As he moves towards the newly revealed doorway, Nico's attention shifts to me as he steps closer.

"Well done, Asha." He smiles, then noticing my eyes brimming with tears, stops. "Are you alright?"

"I—" my words catch in my throat. The question is simple, yet so profound. I can't speak. My mind is racing. I glance at Elias who is ruffling Lili's hair while Thaddeus dances around them holding his frog. I take a deep breath and wipe my tears.

"I think so," I reply, managing a small smile that seeks to reassure both Nico and myself. He smiles back, seeming to understand the words I can't bring myself to say.

None of it had been real. It had all been the trial to face my fear of losing someone I care about. Elias hadn't nearly died. But that means he also hasn't confessed to treachery either. I won't ever be able to bring myself to talk to him about the vial after what just happened. I'm afraid the next time that reaction will be real and not imagined. With a deep sigh, I reach into my satchel to retrieve the map of the underbelly and spread it out on the dais. I can't afford to waste time. The longer we're down here, the more danger I'm putting everyone in.

"We're here," I point to the chamber on the map and trace the line that leads away from it. "According to this, we don't have much farther to go. The main chamber should be just beyond this passage." The group gathers around, peering over my shoulder at the map.

"So, the main chamber is where the shard should be then?" Skylar asks.

"Fates willing," I say, folding the map carefully and tucking it back into my satchel. "How are you feeling Skylar?"

"Still a bit clammy, but better. Don't worry about me," she replies with a gentle smile. I smile back, then pick up my lantern and lead them through the passage entrance.

As we venture deeper, guided only by the dim light of our lanterns, the labyrinth seems to swallow the sound of our footsteps in the chilly, dense air around us. The passage leads us to an imposing doorway that opens into a massive chamber. Hesitation grips me at the threshold. Before us lies a vast expanse of polished obsidian. The chamber's sheer size and the darkness of the obsidian gives it an air of foreboding.

"It's too quiet," Skylar murmurs, her voice barely above a whisper. "Do you think it's safe?"

"Nothing about this place is safe," Elias replies with a chuckle.

"Give him your frog, it will help," Lili says to Thaddeus, stifling a chuckle with her hand.

"Absolutely not," Elias retorts.

"You're always so dramatic, Beanpole!" Thaddeus's voice echoes across the polished obsidian room and reverberates off the walls. Skylar laughs at his remark, nodding to herself in agreement.

"I guess we just need to keep going and find out," I say, taking a step from the corridor. Our footsteps echo off the walls as we walk deeper into the silent expanse of the chamber. My eyes are suddenly drawn to a singular point of interest: another dais situated at the far end of the room, bathed in a shaft of light that seems to pierce the gloom from nowhere. The very sight of it sends a ripple of unease through me. *Please don't let it be another trial,* I think. I can't handle it. With cautious steps, we approach the dais and I expel a breath of relief.

Resting on its surface is a small wooden box, its surface adorned with the intricate seal of Velloria.

"This is it!" I say excitedly.

I step forward, my hand trembling slightly as I reach for the box. The seal of Velloria feels cold under my fingertips. With a deep breath, I lift the lid, and a hollow void greets me where the shard of the Soulweaver's blade should have lain. The realization strikes a chord of disbelief and confusion. It's a momentary pause that quickly shatters as the floor beneath us begins to tremble. Cracks web across the obsidian surface, racing towards the chamber's edges as sections of the floor start to crumble away, falling into an abyss below.

Panic surges through me as we scramble to the remaining solid ground, finding ourselves huddled together on a tiny island of safety with the dais. A narrow, treacherous path shoots out over an open void of infinite depth. The path, barely wide enough for one person, spans the chasm like a lifeline. The way we had come from has fallen into the abyss.

Elias lets out a strained chuckle. "Well, it appears this chamber is more dramatic than me."

Thaddeus wriggles, trying to maintain his footing while clutching to the dais. "Drama? If I wanted drama, I'd be among the bards, not a band of adventurers teetering on the edge of an abyss!" He is clearly upset at the circumstances.

"We have no choice," I say. We have journeyed so far, only to find ourselves in a precarious trap dangling thousands of feet above nothingness, without the shard in hand. "We must keep going. Stay in a single file and move slowly," I instruct.

Taking the first step, I feel the stone beneath my boot. It seems solid. My heart hammers against my ribs. Lili's small hand finds mine with a firm grip. I squeeze back, hoping to convey reassurance.

I move with a slow precision. Behind me, Lili's breaths are fast and shallow as she clings to me. The chasm seems like a relentless beast, whispering promises of despair with every gust of wind. Suddenly, the path shudders beneath our feet. The sinister rumble sends stones skittering into the abyss. I halt as a section of the pathway ahead crumbles and falls away, leaving a gap that seems too wide to cross.

"Alright, this is manageable," I murmur to myself. Despite the intimidating expanse before us, it's not beyond our capabilities. "We have to jump," I announce. Positioning myself at the precipice, I survey the abyss stretching beneath us. It is an endless pit of foggy darkness. I inhale deeply, envisioning the trajectory and the beckoning landing area, before propelling myself across. Suspended in that brief eternity, my heart races until, at last, I land. Steadying myself I turn around.

"Alright, Lili. Are you ready?" I call out. "Just keep your eyes on me. Nico will give you a hoist." Nico steps up, cradling Lili with ease.

"You set?" he asks. She nods, bracing herself for the jump. With a confident motion, he sends her sailing over the gap, her slight figure slicing through the still air with a scream of fear and excitement. I extend my arms. My heart jumps to my throat as I catch her, and her weight nearly knocks me backwards. For an instant, the void seems to yearn for us, yet we remain unclaimed.

"That wasn't so bad." Lili grins. Nico then takes his turn, bridging the divide with a determined leap. He lands firmly on the narrow stone. Elias steps up next and Thaddeus shouts from the back.

"What are you dallying about? One step and you're across!" He laughs, but Elias doesn't respond. He jumps, clearing the gap with minimal effort. Skylar follows suit. When she lands she nearly loses her balance and Elias quickly reaches out and grabs her swinging satchel, pulling her in. My focus now shifts to Thaddeus, standing solitary on the opposite edge, his demeanor shadowed by concern. He starts pacing.

"It's impossible," he projects in defeat. "And even if I somehow manage, Skylar's grip won't suffice against my weight." A heavy silence falls over us.

"We didn't come all this way to leave you behind, Thaddeus," I shout. "We'll find a way." I exchange looks with the others.

Thaddeus chuckles. "Perhaps, Beanpole could lie down and make a bridge!"

"Hilarious," Elias shouts back.

"How about a rope?" Skylar suggests, already rummaging through her satchel. With a flourish she produces a sturdy rope and begins swinging it in a wide arc before letting it swoop underneath the floating walkway and wrap back around. Elias catches the end and hands it back to her. She ties it into a secure knot, testing its strength with a sharp tug before tossing the other end across the chasm to Thaddeus. He catches it with a smile and ties the rope around his waist. With a moment's hesitation to make sure Geraldine is secure in her little pouch, he takes a few steps back.

"Here goes nothing," he mutters, more to himself than to us I think, and then he runs and leaps into the gap between us. He soars for a moment with a look of terror on his face before falling through the gap. The rope goes taut as it holds him, and Skylar, with Elias's help, starts hoisting him up.

"Ha! See, Beanpole. All your fussing for scant!" he shouts up.

As Thaddeus dangles precariously over the abyss laughing, a sudden, ear-piercing screech echoes from the depths of the darkness below. I exchange a quick, alarmed glance with Nico, the urgency of the situation escalating exponentially.

BLACK RIVER, BLACK RIVER

Thaddeus, his small frame suspended above the void, starts to wriggle frantically. "Pull me up! Pull me up! Pull me up!" he yells. The fear in his cry spurs us into action, and Skylar, with Elias's help, begins to hoist the rope urgently.

Emerging from the chasm's depths, three grotesque figures with wings unfurl, their silhouettes sharply outlined by the minimal light that manages to pierce their realm. The sound of their wings, a harsh cacophony in the quiet, raises hairs on the back of my neck. They ascend with startling velocity, their cries melding into a harrowing din that claws at my ears.

As these nightmares emerge from the abyss, their screams cutting through the silence, a chilling truth settles over me: these flesh and blood predators have emerged with a singular purpose—Thaddeus, who has become dangling bait. My pulse races to mirror the wild beating of their wings. The lead creature, a nightmarish blend of serrated talons and a twisted visage, targets Thaddeus with its claws poised to strike.

Out of instinct, I retreat a step, my focus sharp on the imminent threat. Drawing in a deep breath, I launch myself from the bridge and into the abyss. My bracer ignites, wreathing my arm in a glow that coalesces into a blade of incandescent light.

I dive toward the beast and throw my blade at another. It cuts through the air in a blinding light, hitting its mark and completely severing a wing from its body. With a shriek of agony, the creature falls into the abyss from where it came. I land on the back of the second beast instantly, seizing a momentary advantage in this aerial battle. My hand slips on its slimy skin, struggling for purchase before finally finding a hold in a gill on the side of its neck. It shoots upward, but under my control it becomes just a mount in the open sky.

My sword, returning to my hand, vibrates with readiness. I place it under the neck of the creature and with a quick motion, behead it in a spray of bloody mist. I push off the now falling creature, diving toward the bridge. *I'm not going to make it. It's too far.* Then, as I fall, my sword transforms into a spear. Instinctively, I hurl the spear toward the bridge. It embeds in the stone with an explosion, forming a tether that connects to my wrist. I grasp the tether and arc beneath the bridge. Just as I emerge, the third beast flies in front of me. Our clash is a storm of energy as my body slams into it with immense force. The sound of its bones shattering echoes through the expanse before it hurls away into the abyss. The momentum from the impact swings me upward and I land back on the bridge. The tethered spear retracts, its job done, leaving me to catch my breath in the aftermath of the chaos.

"A little help wouldn't hurt." Thaddeus is still hanging from the rope. Skylar and Elias, momentarily stunned by my actions, snap to attention, and quickly haul Thaddeus up to safety. The moment Thaddeus's feet touch solid ground, we all let out a shared sigh of relief.

"Why thank you kind gent, and lass," Thaddeus says, brushing himself off.

"Don't thank us," Elias shoots back, glancing my way. "I was too busy watching Asha's bracer at work."

"Guilty too," Skylar adds, her light laughter mingling in the air. I smile in response, the corners of my mouth lifting despite the confusion swirling within me. How or why my DNA seems to wield such control over me, guiding my actions with an unseen hand, remains a mystery that eludes my grasp.

"Let's get off this bridge," I say.

With cautious steps, we move forward. As we near the end of the bridge, an otherworldly scene unfolds before us, taking my breath away. We stand before a realm of absolute darkness, a landscape seemingly formed from shadows. The ground beneath us is covered in black sand that stretches to the horizon, dotted with dark vegetation that moves without the wind's touch. Jagged stones of deep black are scattered throughout, their edges capturing stray light, creating a haunting luminescence in this realm of dusk. The entire world seems dipped in the darkest hue, under a sky of royal blue.

"This place..." Skylar's voice barely rises above a whisper, "feels like a dream. It's breathtaking."

"A desert underground. Fascinating," Elias says. His eyes roam cautiously.

Stepping onto the chill black sand, I feel its cold seep through my boots. It's a mesmerizing yet eerie sensation.

"We need to be careful," I say looking back at them. "This place is filled with a raw, ancient magic. I can feel it. We need to stick together and keep our eyes open." I check the old map for the underbelly and furrow my brows.

"This isn't right," I say.

"What is it?" Skylar asks, stepping in to peer at the map. I lay it down on the black sand, resting my finger on what I believe is the bridge we just left.

"If this is the bridge we came from, then this is where we should be now," I point to a room, depicted much smaller than the vast desert we stand in. Elias nudges next to Skylar.

"Well, I can't say I'm surprised," he says, "this place seems to have a mind of its own." I sigh, realizing this map isn't going to be of use in this desert. I place it back in my satchel and look into the distance for a landmark or anything, yet to no avail.

"Well, we can't go back so I suppose we keep going and hope we come across something. It's underground, how far can it possibly go?" Elias says. *Forever...* My mind echoes back.

The sands whisper beneath my boots, and the dark flora moves with an eerie grace, as though stirred by an invisible wind, their sway almost spellbinding. The obsidian stones seem to subtly shift as we progress, arranging themselves into forms that seem anything but natural. Or is it just my imagination? It's been nearly an hour since we left the bridge and we haven't discovered anything significant.

"This is fun," Elias says sarcastically.

"Hush, Beanpole! I'm trying to concentrate," Thaddeus retorts.

"Concentrate on what? There's nothing to concentrate on but sand!"

"I'm trying to comfort Geraldine here. She's upset." I snort, trying to stifle my laughter.

"Oh, my deepest apologies," Elias retorts, his voice dripping with mock concern. "Do tell. Why is your frog mad?"

"Because she wants to ride atop your head for a better view." Suddenly, he throws the frog into the air towards Elias's head with a laugh. Elias's eyes widen in surprise as Geraldine sails through the air. In a move that surprises everyone, including himself, he catches Geraldine gently, holding her aloft like a crown jewel.

"Ha! I knew you two would be friends!" Thaddeus exclaims. He does a little jig in the sand while twirling his walking stick. Then he stops when Elias, holding Geraldine by a leg in disgust, hands her back.

"That's not nice of you, Beanpole. I promised her." He gently takes the frog back and tucks her into her pouch.

"You shouldn't make promises you can't keep. I'm not going to be friends with a frog," Elias says. Skylar and Lili are now chuckling.

"But Elias, frogs are wonderful," Lili says.

"The only wonderful thing here is finding a way out of this forsaken place," he grumbles.

Just then shapes emerge against the low light ahead of us. They're large in the distance and I can't exactly make them out, other than rough outlines. *Mountains maybe?*

"Look," I say, pointing towards them.

"What is it?" Lili asks.

"I can't say for certain, perhaps a structure or mountains, but we should check it out." As we draw nearer, the shapes grow more mysterious, yet enchanting. It seems we've stumbled upon an extensive garden of obsidian sculptures.

"Have you ever seen anything like this?" Skylar whispers, her voice barely rising above the soft murmur of the sudden breeze that begins to blow between the stones.

"No, I haven't, but it's utterly captivating," I reply.

As I step into the garden, my feet sink slightly into the black sand that covers the ground like a shadowy sponge. The stones, dark and polished, are meticulously arranged in spirals and patterns, their surfaces so reflective that they seem to hold a piece of the sky captured within their depths. My own image greets me from every angle, multiplied in the mirror-like facets of the garden's design. The towering spires and looping arches craft impossible geometries that challenge my sense of reality. The air is thick with a magic that whispers over my skin, making the hairs on the back of my neck stand on end. It's as if the garden itself is alive, breathing a slow, rhythmic pulse of energy that vibrates through the ground and into my bones.

"I vote we send in the frog first," Elias says, glancing back at Thaddeus who cups both hands over Geraldine as if trying to hide her.

"Not a chance, Beanpole," he snaps.

"We should investigate. No sense in lingering around here," I say and begin to walk among the spiral sculptures, the others following behind.

Shadows dance and play along the black sand, animated by a sourceless light that wanders through a light haze that trickles across the ground. With each turn, the paths wind further into the garden, leading us through archways that frame the twilight sky. We reach what appears to be the heart of the garden, where a grand sculpture looms, an obsidian monolith that spirals towards the sky. The closer I get to it, the more I feel a sense of deep, enveloping peace wash over me.

"It's like the one in Emberwyn," Skylar says, reaching out and touching the surface.

"It's near identical," I admit.

Thaddeus, craning his neck to take in the entire height of the monolith, whistles softly. "Finally, something taller than Beanpole." We all laugh as Elias turns to give him a look of disapproval.

Near the monolith's base, a glint captures my attention. I walk over and pick up from the sand an ancient golden compass. Its dial is whirling uncontrollably.

"What's that?" Nico asks.

"It looks to be a broken compass." I hold it out to him. He takes it, stares at it with a furrowed brow, then gives it a shake.

"What a useless hunk of junk," he states, rattling it around.

"You just need to know how to use it," Elias replies briskly. Nico holds out the compass, silently urging him to show him how it's done. He takes the compass, giving it a shake similar to Nico's earlier attempt, a playful smirk crossing his face. Nico rolls his eyes in response, clearly unimpressed.

"Okay, give it back," he says, his patience wearing thin. But Elias, caught up in his own theory, isn't done yet, and continues to rattle the compass, as if willing it to reveal its secrets. In a swift motion Nico reaches out to snatch the compass back. The action is too sudden, and the compass slips from Elias's grasp, flying through the air before clattering against the base of the monolith. I hold my breath, half-expecting the ancient compass to shatter upon impact. Instead, it comes to a rest at the monolith's base, miraculously intact. The needle, which had been spinning erratically, now points steadily in a specific direction. Elias can't contain a triumphant grin.

"See, it just needed a little shaking, like I said," he declares. Nico, picking up the compass, lets out a reluctant chuckle.

"Looks like it's pointing us... that way," he says, gesturing towards a path I hadn't noticed before, hidden by the garden's twisting sculptures and shadows.

"Well, then, I guess we're venturing further into this obsidian garden," I say. "Nico, you're in charge of the compass. Let's keep going. The sooner we find the shard, the sooner we can get out of here." With one last look at the monolith, we set off in the direction the compass points.

Eventually we leave the enigmatic beauty of the obsidian garden behind, the black sand now crunching softly beneath our feet. The garden seems to bid us farewell with a whispering sigh, its obsidian sculptures fading into the background as we venture forward. The landscape before us gradually opens up, leading our gaze towards the horizon where another garden, strikingly similar to the one we have just left, stands solemnly against the sky's muted canvas. As we approach, an unsettling sense of Déjà Vu washes over me. This new garden and monolith seem to be an exact replica of the last. My steps quicken, but it is Elias who first notices the footprints in the sand.

"Someone's been here," he murmurs. We exchange uneasy glances. The realization that we might not be alone in this labyrinth setting adds a tense edge to my nerves. With cautious steps, we follow the trail of footprints, leading us directly to the center of the structure.

"Well, I hate to say it, but I feel like we just went in circles," Elias says.

"Nico," Thaddeus says, "lend me that compass for a moment." Nico seems glad to give it up. Thaddeus kneels down near the base of the monolith, and that's when I see it: the unmistakable round shape imprinted in the sand.

A heavy silence falls among us as the implication of the discovery sinks in. We are stuck in a loop, the labyrinth's cunning design leading us back to where we started. Nico now kneels, tracing the outline of the compass imprint with a tentative finger.

"Well, then," he says, his voice barely above a whisper.

"So, we *are* walking circles." Skylar's voice tingles with both awe and frustration.

"If the labyrinth can loop us back to the beginning," Elias says, "then there has to be a way out. We're missing something, a clue or a key hidden in the loop itself." I take a deep breath, rallying my thoughts.

"Then we need to pay attention to every detail," I say. "Let's keep going and try to find a pattern. Nico, where is the compass pointing?"

"Further in the same direction."

"Then let's keep going. Maybe the next one will be different."

"Perhaps the compass isn't leading us out of here?" Thaddeus now says. "Who would leave a compass if it led them home?" I don't want to admit it out loud, but he does make a valid argument.

"I don't think we have many options, Thaddeus," I say. "Let's just keep going, and we'll reassess at the next garden."

"So, at this one then?" Elias grins. I'm not in the mood for his jests right now. I turn away and walk further into the garden. They follow and it's not long before we walk to the next, and then the next. As we stand before the monolith for a fourth time, frustration begins to show among us.

"I'm tired of walking," Lili grumbles. Nico examines the compass again, his brows furrowed.

"I don't get it," he mutters.

"These symbols have to mean something," Skylar mentions, looking at the runes on the monolith. "But it's like trying to read a language no one's ever heard."

"We're just not seeing it. We're missing a piece of this puzzle," Elias, leaning against a stone sculpture, chimes in. "What if we're supposed to follow the shadow of the monolith? Or wait for some celestial alignment?"

"I'm not hanging around here for a celestial alignment," I say, pacing back and forth while trying to piece together our observations. Thaddeus, who has been quietly following our conversation, clutches his head.

"This is making my head spin," he groans. The word 'spin' echoes in my mind, spinning around and around. *The compass*.

"Wait, spin! That's it!" I exclaim. "What if the compass wasn't broken? What if it was reacting to the strongest source of magic? We assumed it was trying to point us north, but perhaps it's been pointing us to the answer this entire time." Nico extends the compass outward, its needle pointing further into the horizon without even a subtle flicker.

"So, we backtrack to the first set of sculptures?" Nico asks, seeking confirmation for the new strategy.

"Yes!" I say excitedly. "The spinning could indicate we're close to the shard or some mechanism controlling the loop. It's the strongest magical presence that's causing the compass to react." Revitalized from the discovery, I call the group to action and we head back the way we came.

Reaching the initial garden, where the air is still laden with that raw, primeval energy, Nico raises the compass high. As we cross into the garden's domain, the needle resumes its slow frenetic dance, confirming my suspicions. Its behavior grows more erratic the closer we get to the monolith in the heart of the garden. Surrounded by the silent sentinels of obsidian, we congregate around it, watching the compass needle whirl in Nico's grasp. The monolith stands before us, its carved runes emitting a soft glow. I am still inexplicably drawn to it, its presence offering a strange peace. I extend a tentative hand towards the cool, polished surface.

At my touch, a deep resonance fills the space. The earth shudders beneath us, and the monolith begins to rotate, its structure spiraling in a slow, deliberate motion, as if unwinding from the labyrinth's embrace. We all take several steps back.

"What did you do?" Elias shouts over the rumbling.

"I just touched it!" I shout back.

"And you couldn't have touched it the first time we were here? Save us a bunch of time, you know?"

As the monolith completes its descent, it gracefully submerges into the black sands, which gracefully part, reminiscent of water yielding to a sinking stone. The structure's disappearance beneath the sand unveils a vast opening. The compass, still clutched by Nico, settles its wild gyrations, its needle now unwaveringly directed towards the chasm that the monolith's retreat has exposed.

The darkness below is a dense void that seems to engulf light, sound, and any assurance I have left. But, despite its daunting presence, it seems to extend an invite into its depths. It is Elias who pierces the quietude as he peers over the edge.

"Any guesses on how deep this is?" His inquiry fades into the abyss, the lack of echo painting a vivid picture of his answer.

"Probably deep," Lili whispers and I chuckle. Elias looks at her and shakes his head before turning back. Skylar, delving into her magical satchel, retrieves a glowing white orb.

"Let's see," she announces, releasing the orb into the void. We track its descent, its luminescence gradually waning until it vanishes altogether, offering no clue about the depth or what awaits at the base.

"Fantastic," Elias mutters, leaning back against a nearby statue in resignation. Motionless, we form a semicircle at the precipice. The thought of plunging into the unknown abyss without any guarantee of safety is a paralyzing thought. Skylar begins distributing water and provisions from her satchel.

"We can't be at a dead end. There must be another way," she whispers, mostly to herself. She begins sifting through her satchel once again, her actions focused, as though commanding it to reveal a solution. Item by item, she lays out an array of random artifacts, each more curious than the last. First comes a pair of ancient, rune-etched boots.

"These could make us run fast," she exclaims. Her excitement is quickly tempered by Nico's skeptical glance.

"Right into the void? Maybe not," he counters with a dry tone. Unperturbed, she casually tosses the boots into the gaping abyss. Then, she retrieves a small, ornate bottle.

"This could help us sneak past... whatever's down there. It's an invisibility potion," she suggests, her voice tinged with hope. Elias raises an eyebrow in response.

"And how would being invisible help us not fall to our deaths?" he questions. With a shrug, she drops the bottle into the void, watching it disappear without a trace.

The procession of discarded items continues—a magical lasso, a shield too heavy to carry, and a set of wings that are, regrettably, only decorative. Each item is scrutinized, deemed impractical for our needs, and subsequently tossed into the abyss.

"Skylar," Elias implores, "what are you thinking, pulling out all these items?" He watches, captivated yet bewildered, as she sifts through her curious assortments. With a nonchalant shrug and a cryptic smile, she casually tosses a charmingly odd violet hat with a vibrant green feather into the abyss.

Feeling a mix of frustration and the need for clarity, I excuse myself, stepping away from the group to wander the labyrinth's daunting expanse, hoping to clear my head and maybe stumble upon some inspiration.

My mind whirls with thoughts, searching for any solution we might have overlooked. As I walk, lost in thought, my attention is ripped away by a pile—a pile of stuff Skylar has thrown into the void. My mind isn't quite understanding what I'm looking at, or *how* I'm seeing it here when it was thrown into the pit. I glance up at the deep blue sky. It is quite an odd color of blue for a sky, now that I think about it.

"Skylar," I call out, looking back at her from afar. "Throw something else down there." Intrigued by my sudden urgency, she quickly rummages through her satchel once more and pulls out something. With a puzzled look, she tosses it into the void as I requested. We all watch intently as the object seems to disappear into the darkness. I glance up just in time to see an object falling from the sky and take a step back as it lands with a thud near the pile. It is a hefty, rune-inscribed stone. "The sky," I mumble to myself, starting to put the pieces together. *But it isn't a sky at all, is it?* The implications of this discovery send a wave of realization crashing over me. I run back to them, nearly tripping in the sand.

"It's not a bottomless pit!" I announce. "It's something else—a black hole of sorts, but not one that leads to destruction. At least, I don't think it does. It leads there." I point above us at the deep blue sky. After a long pause of everyone looking up at the sky, Elias looks back at me.

"You have officially lost your mind," he says, shaking his head.

"I'm serious!" I nearly shout. "Go look for yourself. Every single thing that's been thrown down that hole is in a pile over there." I point in the direction of the pile. "It's not a sky."

"So, if we jump in, we'll fall to our death over there?" Elias points in the direction of the pile. "Sounds like a great plan. I'll have to pass on that one." I forgot

I'm talking to someone who has no imagination. It's like trying to convince a rock to dream. Without waiting for another word, driven by a blend of frustration, I walk into the void despite everyone yelling for me to stop.

The sensation is disorienting, a momentary feeling of being turned inside out, and then— I am standing on blue sand, under the ground, the world as I know it literally turned upside down. The sky above me is a cavernous ceiling, the familiar black sand now the sky. The transition was seamless, surreal, and utterly astonishing.

"You have to see this!" I shout, my voice echoing strangely in this inverted world. They don't respond and I realize they can't hear me. I walk back into the void, the world spins, and I emerge next to everyone's startled faces. "Hey," I say again with a huge grin, "you must see this." One by one, with varying degrees of hesitation, the rest of the group follows. As each of them experiences the disorienting flip, their expressions morph into ones of wonder and disbelief.

This new realm breathes surreal beauty. The sand beneath our feet glows with a soft, otherworldly light, casting everything in a tranquil azure hue. It feels like stepping into a dreamscape, where the rules of the world above no longer apply. The 'sky' overhead is a vast expanse of deep, impenetrable black, yet it doesn't feel oppressive. Instead, it frames the landscape in mesmerizing contrast, enhancing the ethereal quality of the light.

"This... this changes everything," Skylar breathes, her gaze sweeping across the inverted vista.

Elias, who has stumbled to the ground with a grunt upon entering, picks himself up, dusting off the blue sand. "I think I'm going to be sick now." He bends over, clutching his knees.

"So," I say, "if space is folded, then maybe the shard isn't 'above' or 'below' in a traditional sense. Maybe it's 'across,' in a direction we can't even properly conceive."

Thaddeus claps his hands together, a grin spreading across his face. "Well, that makes my noggin whirl. Let's start conceiving! Beanpole!" he shouts at Elias. "Pull yourself together. We've got a whole new world to explore down here!"

"Look, over there," I say, my eyes suddenly catching a strange sight far off in the distance. *Trees?*

"One way to find out," Thaddeus says cheerfully, followed by Geraldine's confirming croak.

"Can I carry Geraldine for a while?" Lili asks. Thaddeus turns to her with reluctant eyes. After a pause, he smiles and takes the pouch from his shoulder with the frog inside. Her eyes dance with excitement as he puts the pouch over her shoulder.

"There. But mind you don't trip and fall. Oh," he adds, "and don't mind her foul breath. I forgot to pack her tooth stick in that pouch of hers."

"You have got to be joking," Elias says, now fully recovered from his motion sickness.

"Shush, Beanpole! I never joke!"

"What are you talking about? You're always joking!"

"More lies!" Thaddeus exclaims, waving his walking stick as he turns to head toward the distant trees, followed by Lili and her new travel partner. Elias looks at me and I shrug.

"We all know he's a bit... strange," I say with a laugh.

"That little man is going to be the death of me if this place doesn't kill me first," Elias retorts.

"Oh, come now Elias." Skylar leans in with a smile and links her arm through his. I watch them head off and notice Elias's cheeks turn rosy red through his grin.

"Shall we, then?" Nico asks, then follows them. I feel a slight tinge of disappointment that he didn't offer me his arm. I had told him I would think about us. I suppose I can't be upset that he's giving me the space to do so. Although, I am slightly upset, I sigh and brush it off, following them across the blue sand.

After a while, the open expanse of glowing sand gives way to a dense thicket of trees. Each tree radiates an ethereal glow, bathed in a phosphorescent blue that paints the world in hues of twilight. Their foliage, a rich collage of midnight blue, seems to swallow the ambient light, casting our surroundings in a dreamlike veil.

"I could live here," Skylar says, gently caressing the blue leaves of a nearby bush as she twirls around.

"And me too," Lili adds with enthusiasm.

Navigating the thick underbrush, I am suddenly lured by the melody of water. A river, as dark as the void, meanders through the heart of the woodland. Its currents are slow like molasses creeping through the twilight. It converses in a chorus of bubbles and murmurs. The inky waters capture the faint glow of the environment, twisting it into kaleidoscopic reflections that dance and distort on its surface. From the river's depths, small plumes of vapor, or perhaps smoke, ascend with each bubble's burst, adding to the ambiance of this otherworldly domain.

"Would you look at that," Elias says, stepping closer to the riverbank. "A river of liquid night. Do you think it's safe to touch? I mean, we have to cross somehow, right?"

Before anyone can stop him, Thaddeus dips a finger into the river then quickly pulls it back with a grimace.

"Feels like chilled nectar," he reports, wiping his hand on his pants. "Tastes terrible, too, I bet. Not that I'll be fancying a taste. Geraldine?" He holds his black, goo-tipped finger up and the frog croaks in a manner I can only think is disgust, as she hunkers down in an act of defiance.

Skylar chuckles, pulling out a vial from her satchel. "Let's just take a sample. Who knows? It might come in handy." She crouches by the riverbank, her attention riveted on collecting a sample of the dark liquid. "You could probably use it in potions, Thaddeus. It would be—"

The serene air of her venture violently erupts, and her words are cut short as a shadowy tendril surges from the river's depths. She screams as the barbed appendage ensnares her in its grasp. Before I can even process the danger, it drags her into the river with alarming swiftness. Her startled cry is abruptly silenced as she vanishes beneath the surface. The river closes over her, leaving no trace.

"Skylar!" I cry out, bolting towards the water's edge, sword drawn. But it's too late. Elias plunges his hands into the murky depths, frantic to clutch at anything that might return her to us. Yet, the river betrays no sign of disturbance. It's as calm as if the abduction had been an illusion.

"Step back!" I command, yanking Elias from the brink, my heart torn between the impulse to save him and the terror of losing Skylar.

"We have to go after her," Nico insists urgently, but I'm frozen in place. I don't know what to do. I glance at him, terrified.

"Asha, do something!" Elias's demand cuts through the tumult in a raw blend of desperation and fear. Suddenly, the dormant force within me stirs to life, its power surging through my veins with the untamed might of a contained tempest. My hands, quivering under the surge of this strange new sensation, reach towards the inscrutable river. The murky and inscrutable river starts to react, yielding to the influence. The thick, shadowy waters begin to part slowly. This division of the waters, though gradual, is purposeful, uncovering not just the riverbed but a concealed domain beneath—the gateway to a world turned sideways, hidden beneath the river's deceptive guise. The waters recede, forming liquid barriers, revealing a path that leads directly down to the river's depths.

"Asha," Elias breathes. "How—"

"I don't know," I cut him off, "but we need to act—immediately."

I quickly walk to the edge of the gaping hole between parted waters and peer down the wall that houses the river. It has a stone pathway running straight down the wall. Instantly I know what to do.

"Follow me, quickly," I say. Then I run, the world turning sideways as I begin sprinting down the path that was just a moment ago, the wall. The others follow behind as the otherworldly terrain of the sideways realm unfurls around us.

The terrain underfoot is unfamiliar yet firm, made of compressed stone that glistens with a moist luster under the subdued illumination seeping through the immense water walls. These walls of dark water hum with the river's vitality, with misty bubbles bursting and murmuring. The atmosphere is laden with the scent of mud and the sharpness of minerals from the plumes of expelled vapor. Further on, the trail tightens, guiding us toward a distinct focal point—a door embedded in the riverbed's mucky floor. Its facade is sleek, lacking any knob or apparent way to open it.

"This has to be it," I say through gasps of breath, my hand hovering just inches from its surface. I push the door and it swings silently on hinges buried in the muck, revealing a room carved entirely from black obsidian. The air inside is cool and still, charged with an energy that sends shivers down my spine. In the center of the room, illuminated by a source of light is a concrete slab. And there, lying motionless upon it, is Skylar. My heart drops and a gasp escapes us in unison. The door swings shut behind us with a soft click that echoes like a final note in a joyless melody.

"Skylar," Elias whispers, breaking the silence. His voice is barely audible as he approaches the slab. I follow, my heart pounding in my chest, fear knotting my stomach. The closer we get, the more details become visible. Skylar lies still, covered in black filth from the river. Her chest is unmoving with gaping gashes where the monster's barbs have torn through her flesh, leaving trails of blood down the side of the slab.

"Is she..." Thaddeus's voice trails off, unable to complete his thought. I reach out, my hand trembling as I touch Skylar's cheek. It's cold. Icy cold. Tears blur my vision.

Elias, consumed by a torment that transcends words, becomes the embodiment of our collective anguish as he lets out a heart-wrenching scream. He falls to his knees beside Skylar, his hands shaking as he clutches at her lifeless form, his voice tearing through the oppressive silence of the obsidian chamber.

"Why!" he cries out, his plea directed at the gods, at the universe, at any force that would listen. I stand, remembering what Lavinia had told me. That one of the Soulweavers had the ability to heal. I place my hands on her, but the power inside me refuses to wake.

"Come on!" I scream, my voice breaking with a mix of tears and rage. "Come on!" Yet my call is answered only by a void that confirms what I've already known: the power to heal is beyond my command.

"Fix her, Asha! You have to fix her!" Elias's voice is a jagged blade, tearing at the fragile fabric of my hope, exposing the reality that lies beneath—some losses are irrevocable.

"I'm so sorry. I…" I stammer, tears streaming down my cheeks as I take a step back.

The room quietly observes as it holds Skylar in its indifferent grip, unmoved by our cries and blind to our profound sorrow. My grief becomes an almost physical, looming presence ready to consume me, pulling me towards the depths of hopelessness. I find myself on the cold ground, clutching a weeping Lili close. Amidst the crushing shadow of inescapable despair surrounding me, Elias's final words echo endlessly in my heart.

"I never got to tell her I loved her."

XVIII

WORDS LEFT UNSPOKEN

Time becomes a silent thief, stealing away the moments as we sit in the dimly lit obsidian chamber, my grief a heavy shroud that neither light nor darkness can penetrate. I sit there, numb and exhausted, the echoes of our cries and pleas fading into the oppressive silence that surrounds us. My head throbs with a dull ache. Each breath feels thick and suffocating. The others are shadows of themselves, their forms slumped in various states of despair around the room. Elias, a soul-tormented wreck, has quieted, his earlier outbursts of grief and rage giving way to a hollow silence that is perhaps more alarming than his screams had been. Thaddeus sits with his head bowed, his usual humor extinguished, replaced by a somber reflection of the pain we all feel. Nico stares blankly at the opposite wall, his gaze fixed on some unseen point, lost in thoughts I can only imagine.

The air in the room feels stale. Elias's words from my trial echo through my mind, carving a new cut deeper into my heart. *You're going to get us all killed!* Eventually, the silence becomes a presence too vast to ignore. We can't stay here.

"We... we need to keep moving," I say, the words feeling like betrayal even as they leave my lips. "We have to find a way out of here." Elias lifts his head, his white hair now ensnared in a vile tapestry of black ooze and blood.

"Leave me here," he says, turning back to lay his head on Skylar's arm. The pain is too much for him. Not even a month ago, he had lost his grandmother, Amara, Emberwyn's storyteller. Now, in this nightmare, he has lost the girl he loved, yet never mustered the courage to tell. His words, a whispered plea to remain in this tomb of obsidian and sorrow, cut through me sharper than any blade. His loss seems a wound too deep for words to heal.

"Elias," I whisper, "we need you."

"Just go. Leave me here." His voice breaks like the shattered pieces of his heart that lay scattered around us. I wipe my tears away, drawing in a deep, steadying breath, my voice barely above a whisper as I address him.

"Elias," I say again, "we need you." My voice is firmer this time. "You are part of us. Skylar... she wouldn't want you to give up. Leaving you behind would be leaving a part of her, too."

He remains motionless for a time, his head resting on her arm in a final, intimate moment of farewell. Then, slowly, as if each movement costs him a piece of his soul, he begins to rise. He stands there, a figure sculpted from the depths of despair. Turning to face Skylar for one last time, his voice emerges in a fragile whisper.

"Farewell, Skylar," he murmurs. "You were the light in the darkest of places. I wish I had told you... everything. I hope you knew. I hope you felt it, even if I never found the courage to say it." He pauses, then adds, "By the way, your poetry was as lovely as you." With a final, lingering look, he turns away. He faces me and I'm uncertain how to interpret his gaze. Was he angry at me for not saving her? For bringing them here and getting her killed? I can't bear the thought. Tears well in my eyes again but his small flicker of a smile is reassuring, even if it doesn't quell the pain I feel.

Lili moves forward, her movements echoing the tender sorrow of an angel in grief, as she tenderly tucks her fairy figurine into Skylar's unmoving embrace. Then, with a soft touch, she lays a small hand on her cheek in a gentle goodbye. "I will miss you forever," she whispers, brushing away her tears. I lower myself, opening my arms wide, and Lili rushes into them, crying.

"She walks with the spirits now, Lili," I whisper.

"We go forward," Elias says, his voice steady and commanding even in its softness. I rise, gently placing my hand on his shoulder.

"We'll return for her," I assure. He gives a nod, and together, we head towards an opening set into the wall.

As we trudge through the long, dusty corridor, Thaddeus glances towards Elias, a mischievous twinkle lighting up his eyes. He gently takes Geraldine from Lili.

"Beanpole," he begins, his voice tinged with a playful seriousness, "in these trying times, it's important to remember what we still have. For instance, Geraldine here has been feeling particularly neglected."

With a grand gesture, Thaddeus reveals the frog, perched contentedly in his palm. The sight of the small creature, so out of place in the moment, yet somehow right at home with our motley crew, draws a collective pause from the group.

"How about a hold, huh?" Thaddeus continues, stepping forward and offering the frog to Elias with an exaggerated bow. The absurdity of the situation strikes a chord. The corners of Elias's mouth twitch. It's a small victory, a tiny crack in the wall of sorrow that has enclosed him, but it's enough. Taking Geraldine gently into his hands, Elias looks down at the frog.

"Don't think this means we're best friends," he says. Geraldine, for her part, seems entirely at ease. For a brief moment, the dusty corridor feels a little less oppressive, and the weight on my shoulders a bit lighter.

At the end of the corridor, the dust and shadows give way to another door, this one appearing as unassuming as the many we have passed through. With a sense of anticipation, I push the door open, bracing myself for what lies beyond. The transition is abrupt. Light floods in, so bright and overwhelming that I instinctively raise my hands to shield my eyes. I stumble slightly as I cross the threshold. The air is fresh and filled with the scent of earth and greenery. As my eyes adjust to the brilliance, the blur of colors before me begins to take shape, coalescing into a scene that is at once familiar and utterly unexpected. There, standing majestically before us, is the ancient tree in the Whispering Forest.

The moment shatters abruptly as Elias's gaze sweeps over the landscape, his eyes widening as a realization hits him like a physical blow. The color drains from his face, leaving him pale and stricken under the dappled light filtering through the leaves. His hands, clutching Geraldine, tremble, and the frog, sensing his distress, lets out a soft, uneasy croak. Suddenly, Elias's legs give way beneath him, and he collapses to his knees on the soft, leaf-littered ground. A gut-wrenching scream tears from his throat with a torment that transcends words.

"We were so close!" he wails. The anguish in his cry pierces the tranquil ambiance of the forest, sending birds fluttering from their perches in startled flight. His body shakes with sobs. The revelation that Skylar, the one he had cherished in secret, had been taken from us just as salvation was within reach, is a cruelty no soul should have to face. Thaddeus approaches Elias and places a tentative hand on his shoulder, and gently takes Geraldine.

"I'm so sorry, Elias," I say, my voice a mere whisper, barely audible above the whispering leaves. The words feel inadequate, a paltry response to the magnitude of his pain, yet they are all I have to offer. "We are all here with you. You're not alone."

Lavinia suddenly comes rushing from the forest to us. Her usually serene face is etched with worry, her robes whispering against the underbrush. The sight of a familiar face makes me choke up even more. Elias, his sobs subsiding into shuddering breaths, looks up with tear-streaked eyes.

"Lavinia," I call out, stepping forward and embracing her, my own sobs now burrowing into her shoulder. Her gaze sweeps over us, taking in the scene of our anguish with a depth of understanding that only heightens her concern. When her eyes land on Elias, still kneeling on the forest floor, a look of compassion softens her features.

"What has happened here?" she asks softly. I step back and wipe my face. Elias struggles to find his voice, the words catching in his throat as he attempts to articulate the depth of our loss.

"Skylar," he manages to choke out, "she was so close... she almost made it." Lavinia's expression shifts with the gravity of our situation. She kneels beside Elias, offering a silent strength that seems to anchor him amidst the storm of his grief.

"The Whispering Forest grieves with you," she whispers softly, her hand reaching out to gently touch his shoulder. "But remember, in this place, not all is as it seems. The forest listens, and sometimes, it answers. For now, Thaddeus will brew you up a potion to help ease the soul's pain, and then I want you to rest." Thaddeus, without hesitation, grabs Elias gently by the arm and tugs.

"Come, Beanpole, I'll brew you up something nice and strong." Elias slowly rises, and with a slumping form, follows Thaddeus into his hut.

"I want to go with them," Lili whispers. I kneel down and hug her tightly. If it had been her that was dragged into the river, lying dead on that cold slab, I would never heal. I give her a long kiss on her forehead and usher her off to go with them. Turning to face me and Nico, Lavinia's gaze holds an undefinable spark.

"Come," she urges, standing once more, "we must talk." Then, with a grace that seems to command the very essence of the forest around us, she pushes open the door we just came from to reveal a cozy room. It's bathed in a soft, ambient light from luminescent flowers. The air carries the scent of moss and the subtle sweetness of blooms, crafting an atmosphere that momentarily eases the sharp edges of my grief. Lavinia settles herself gracefully into a chair. She gestures for us to join her, and her voice when she speaks, is gentle. "Tell me of your journey," she urges, "did you find what you sought? The shard?"

Lavinia's question pierces me. I look into her eyes, finding an ocean of understanding and compassion that beckons me to speak my truth. Taking a deep breath, I try to steady my voice, though it quivers with the effort to contain the emotions that threaten to spill over.

"We didn't find the shard." I shake my head in a confession of failure. "The only thing I managed to do was get Skylar killed." The words, once spoken, threaten to consume me. Nico reaches out and takes my hand in his. The room's nurturing glow wraps us in a gentle embrace, acknowledging the weight of my words without judgment. Lavinia's voice, soft and filled with sorrow for our loss, somehow warms the entire space.

"I am deeply sorry. Though, your journey has not been in vain. Remember, no journey lacks meaning, and every sacrifice holds its value. Skylar's spirit stays with you," she assures me. "Though the shard remains elusive, there is always a way forward, even when hope seems lost." As Lavinia's words offer me a fragile peace, her demeanor subtly changes, signaling a shift in the atmosphere from calm to one of pressing urgency. She leans forward, illuminated by the dancing shadows cast by luminescent flowers.

"I'm afraid the stakes are higher than we realized," she starts. "Beyond the labyrinth's confines, the world has not stood still. The Legion of Embers is rallying their Eyeless army on the outskirts of the Frozen Plains."

Her words cut through me. The Legion of Embers has always been a distant menace, haunting my every step.

"They draw nearer, and I fear war might soon be coming," she warns.

The room grows colder. The thought of impending war, a battle against an Eyeless army, is a heavy weight that seems to crush me further. As Lavinia begins to speak of unity and preparation, her words fade into the background as my thoughts take the fore. One daunting question looms above others in my mind.

"Lavinia," I start, my voice cutting through hers, "how can we even hope to win without the three shards and the sword? Our quest in the labyrinth was to retrieve only the first. But we have nothing."

She pauses, gathering her thoughts before responding. "The shards and the sword are indeed powerful artifacts, and their absence is felt deeply, not just by us but by the very fabric of this realm." Her gaze sweeps across the room to include both of us in her address. "However, we do not have the luxury of obtaining them before they attack, I fear. We will have to make do with what we have. I'm afraid there's no time to go back into the underbelly and search." I don't even consider that an option right now. I can't go back there.

"Lavinia," I whisper, "Skylar's…" I can't bring myself to finish telling her that we left her body behind. But I don't need to. She knows.

"I will send some Guardians to retrieve her. She will not be left there." She pauses for a moment. "Your hearts are heavy," she finally says, "it is enough for now. Rest, both of you. Tomorrow, we will talk more of plans and preparations." She rises, moving with purpose toward the door. "I will fetch Lili and bring her to sleep as well. You all need the comfort of companionship tonight. Let the worries of the world wait until morning. Tonight, you are under the protection of the Whispering Forest, and nothing shall disturb your rest."

Her words are like a small melody of hope I've been longing for. *Undisturbed rest.* Nico and I walk through the door, straight into a bedroom, and crawl instantly into our own beds. In the cozy room, we are surrounded by the soft glow of the luminescent flowers on vines creeping up the wall, and the earthy scent of the forest. A sense of peace begins to settle over me, though thoughts of Skylar still fight their way to the surface.

"Asha," Nico finally breaks the silence, "are you alright?" His question hangs in the air. I turn to face him, seeing the flicker of flower light reflected in his eyes.

"I don't know," I admit, my voice barely a whisper. "Everything feels so... overwhelming. We lost Skylar, and now, with the Legion... and without a shard…" My voice trails off, the lump in my throat making it hard to continue. Nico nods.

"I know. It feels impossible. Although, so has everything, lately, and somehow we're still here."

"Skylar's not," I snap, choking on my words.

"I know, that's not what I meant. I just mean—"

"It's okay," I cut him off, "I know that's not what you meant. I just… I don't know."

"We will figure it out together," he tries to assure me.

I let out a shaky breath. "How do you do it, Nico? Stay so strong in the face of all this?" He's quiet for a moment, considering my question.

"I'm not always strong," he confesses, "but when I see you, Lili, and even Thaddeus and Elias pushing forward, it gives me hope. We've faced darkness before, Asha. We'll face this together, too. I believe in you." His words are meant to comfort me, but I find myself resenting them. I don't even believe in myself. I couldn't save Skylar. I can't control my powers. I feel like a pawn in some sick game, a mere plaything tossed in the turbulent seas of fate.

Lavinia returns, leading Lili by the hand. A sleepy smile spreads across Lili's face as she greets me.

"Hi, little one," I say, opening my arms to her. She curls up beside me, her small frame fitting perfectly against mine. The room fills with the soft sounds of our breathing as the light from the flowers dims.

Lavinia watches over us for a moment before speaking softly, "Sleep well, my brave ones. Let the forest watch over you tonight." With a final nod, she turns and leaves, closing the door gently behind her.

In the hush that follows, sleep comes more easily than expected, a gift from the Whispering Forest itself. As I drift off, with Lili's steady breathing beside me and the presence of Nico near me, I feel, for the first time in a long while... nothing. But that peace that envelops me, the deep sleep I have been granted, is abruptly shattered. My eyes flutter open to the sight of Lavinia standing over me, her expression grave in the dim moonlight that filters through the room.

"Asha," she whispers, her voice barely above a breath yet carrying a weight that pulls me instantly to alertness. "Come with me, quietly." The urgency in her tone is alarming. Something is wrong. I glance briefly at Lili, still sleeping soundly beside me, and Nico in the embrace of slumber.

Nodding silently, I rise, taking care not to disturb them. I follow her out of the room, my feet barely making a sound on the soft, moss-covered floor. The moon hangs low in the sky, casting a silvered light over the forest that transforms it into a landscape of shadows. Yet, the magic of the scene is lost on me, overshadowed by the apprehension tightening in my chest. Lavinia stops and faces me. Her eyes reflect the moon's glow.

"The Legion of Embers has moved faster than we anticipated," she begins, her voice steady. "A few of their scouts have been spotted on the surface not far from here."

The news hits me like a physical blow, the breath hitching in my throat. The war looming on the horizon is no longer a distant possibility. It's here, at our doorstep.

"What can I do?" I ask, my voice firm despite the fear clawing at my insides.

"I need you to take on a critical task," she replies. "We need to know how many scouts there are, and how close they are to discovering our whereabouts. I need you to go to the surface and bring back any information you can. There's a small farm where we believe they are holed up. Go there. Any scouts from the Legion of Embers you encounter... we cannot allow them to report back on our defenses or the location of the Whispering Forest." My eyebrows arch. She wants me to kill them.

I've never killed a person before, only creatures of the night. The thought of venturing out, of facing the enemy in such a direct manner, sends a jolt of adrenaline through me. Before I can respond, a slight noise from behind catches my attention. I turn to see Elias, his face appearing from the doorway of Thaddeus's hut, where he evidently was listening.

"I'd like to go with her," he states, stepping forward into the moonlight. It slightly unnerves me. I'm still uncertain if he harbors hard feelings about Skylar's death towards me. I remember I still haven't spoken to him about the vial. Now is definitely not the time, and I don't think I want him to come. Although perhaps it would be good to get his mind off Skylar. Before I can form a solid opinion, Lavinia settles it for me.

"That's an excellent Idea," she concedes. If the trees had whispered to her my conflicts, and she approves of him coming, then perhaps I need not worry. "But you must be swift. The scouts of the Legion are not to be underestimated. Guard each other."

Without another word, she turns and leads us through a winding path in the forest. We arrive at a clearing where the air feels charged. In the center stands an elegant stone door, an anomaly like the Anything and Everything door, standing on its own with no walls to support it.

"This door," Lavinia begins, "leads to the surface, directly to the outskirts of the Frozen Plains, close to where the scouts have been sighted. It is bound by ancient magic, a passage between spaces that the Legion cannot perceive. It should put you right inside the forest, out of sight, but stay cautious." She steps closer to the door. "Once you have completed your task, you need only walk back through it to return here." Elias and I exchange a look. With a nod to Lavinia, we both step forward. Elias reaches out, his hand finding the door's handle, and with a deep breath, he pushes it open. A rush of cooler air greets us, a sign that we are indeed stepping into the frosty surface, away from the protective embrace of the Whispering Forest.

We step out at the forest's brink, where trees stand like quiet sentinels, their limbs creaking under the nocturnal breeze. The terrain beyond stretches into a broad expanse, dotted with rolling hills and the remains of homes, either forsaken or ravaged. The air, sharp with pine's essence, bears a subtle trace of smoke from far-off flames. Elias and I move with utmost stealth, silent as shadows, wary of any scouts hidden in our path.

As we move forward, the dense protection of the forest begins to wane, revealing a landscape scarred by conflict. Fields that were probably once lush with crops now stretch empty and unyielding before us. The land now presents a scene of stark emptiness. Yet, even in this wasteland, life clings with stubborn resilience. A deer, taken aback by our presence, swiftly vanishes into the underbrush, the nocturnal air hums with the chorus of insects, and the lone call of an owl echoes in the distance.

"Elias, wait," I murmur, gently gripping his arm. My breath turns to vapor in the chill of the night. "Are you okay? Can you handle this?" My question is laden with concern and a whisper of my own uncertainties. He halts and faces me, his features divided by moonlight and darkness. He appears to grapple with his response briefly before exhaling and speaking.

"There were so many things I wanted to tell Skylar," he admits, his gaze drifting past me, absorbing the vast darkness that envelops us. "I needed her to know... she was everything to me, more than she could possibly imagine." He pauses, allowing the silence to grow between us as the depth of his confession hangs in the chilly air, its sharpness tugging at my heartstrings.

"She really fancied you, you know?" I murmur. He remains silent, lost in his thoughts, a shadow of contemplation cast across his face.

"I know," he finally utters, "I was still afraid to tell her. But dwelling on the unspoken, on what I didn't do, it won't undo the past. I need to clear my head, Asha. I need to... find my balance again, aim for a future where sorrow doesn't shadow every step. There has to be a future like that, right?" He looks at me with hope in his eyes.

"I would like to believe so," I say softly.

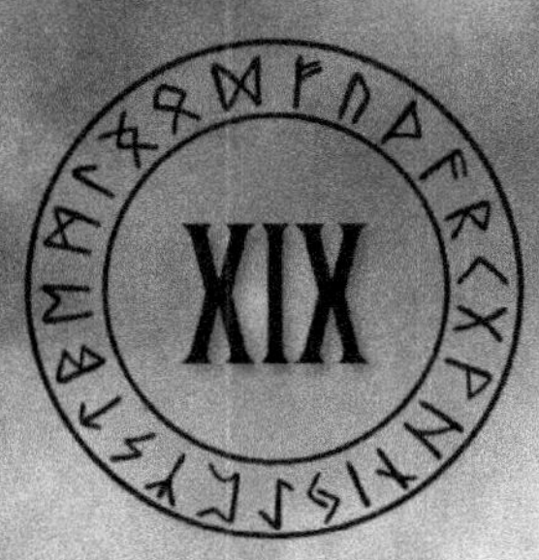

A Thousand Cages

Elias and I meld with the shadows at the forest's edge, becoming one with the cool, welcoming soil beneath us. The ground, a tapestry of moss and fallen leaves, welcomes us with its cool, forgiving embrace. The landscape is peaceful, yet our intrusion stirs the serene night air. My senses stay sharp, vigilant for any hint of the Legion's scouts, though all remains undisturbed, save for the occasional leaf fluttering in the gentle night wind. My gaze then catches a dim glow in the distance, breaking the endless sea of darkness. A solitary farmhouse cuts through the darkness. Its lone illuminated window shines like a solitary star in the void.

"Elias," my whisper cuts through the silence, directing his attention to the faint glow in the distance, "There." His eyes settle on the farmhouse.

"Might be scouts," he contemplates.

"Right. Approaching will likely lead to a confrontation, but it's vital we gather intelligence on the Legion's activities. We need a strategy."

"I could create a diversion at the front, drawing them out. That would give you a chance to enter from the back unnoticed," he proposes.

"That's a good idea," I say.

Like ghosts weaving through the night we part without a word. The chill air bites into my skin. The ground, hardened by frost, plays a crunching melody beneath our feet. A shadow flickers across the window. We quickly hide behind the meager refuge of a dilapidated farm wagon's carcass. This thin veil hides us from watchful eyes, barely sufficient but enough. As the shadow vanishes, our gazes lock. Being seen could spell disaster. As the shadow passes, we continue. Our footsteps, light against the frosty ground, seem to taunt us with the risk of detection. I press my back against the farmhouse's rough exterior, stealing a fleeting glance at him.

"I'll hold for your signal," I whisper. "And Elias, please be careful." He acknowledges with a nod, disappearing into the shadows with ease. Alone, I edge along the wall, every sense heightened. As I reach the corner, a pause grips me, my eyes sweeping over the window before I proceed toward the back door. The gentle light of a lantern spills out, casting a warm, flickering glow through the glass, painting shadows that dance with an almost mocking liveliness.

I dart a swift glance through the door's window. Shapes morph silently among hushed whispers of men, their outlines blurred by the frosty glass. A soft rustling nearby, perhaps a small creature navigating the dark, heightens my alertness. With a determined breath, I extend my hand, calling forth my sword. It emerges not as a bright energy but as darkness incarnate. Its surface, a deep matte black, absorbs the surrounding shadows, melding seamlessly into the enveloping night.

As I await Elias's signal, my gaze inadvertently drifts to the distant Celestara mountain range, outlined against the dark sky. Thoughts of Astralith, the legendary white dragon, infiltrate my mind. Could she have endured through the centuries? The notion seems nearly impossible. The mountains, stoic and towering, appear to conceal the truth in their silent vigil.

Abruptly, my reflections break by a clatter from the front of the farmhouse. I take a deep breath then advance, the door giving way under my gentle push, opening with merely a soft squeak that's lost in the noise of Elias's diversion. Stepping into the gloomy interior, I'm immediately shrouded in darkness. The lantern's gentle light spills deep shadows down the hallway, concealing my presence. My movements are deliberate and soundless, propelling me deeper into the house. The scouts, distracted by the commotion at the front, remain oblivious to my infiltration. As I navigate the corridor, my heart keeps a steady beat. This night, I move as a shadow among shadows.

As I blend into the shadows, the room's heavy air assaults my senses, filled with the unmistakable odor of leather, unwashed and soaked in the metallic smell of blood. The table that stands between us bears not only a dimly lit lantern and a map, but also raw chunks of meat from a deer they've recently killed. Its head, complete with a majestic set of antlers, dangles off the edge of the table, its eyes now vacant, staring into nothingness. This grim trophy, juxtaposed against the tactical map, paints a chilling picture of the scouts' callousness. A surge of anger wells up within me.

Clad in battle-worn leather, four scouts by the windows seem giants among the shadows, their tangled hair and weather-beaten skin marking them as veterans of countless skirmishes. The room is thick with the odors of decay and the unmistakable, raw scent of deer meat, casting a grim atmosphere of survival and conquest. It's a place where the untamed wild's primal instincts clash with the hunter's cold, calculated brutality. Tonight, however, the tables have turned—they have become the hunted, with me as their predator.

In a furious burst of energy, I attack the space between us, kicking the table with all my might. It skids across the floor, transforming into a barricade that crashes into two of the scouts, pinning them with thunderous impact against the window. The lantern tumbles to the ground. Caught off guard, they find themselves momentarily ensnared.

The other two scouts whirl around, their hands automatically reaching for their swords. Yet, their reflexes lag just a moment too long. I exploit their delay, moving with the swiftness of a storm, my approach almost blurring. I leap like a shadow taking flight, and collide with the nearest scout, my boots driving into him with relentless force. The collision sends us tumbling, but not before my shadowy blade arcs through the air, striking his nearby companion with lethal precision in our descent. Our collision echoes solidly through the space as we crash to the ground, my weight pressing down on him.

The remaining duo swiftly frees from the wreckage of the table. One brandishes his sword, aiming for a lethal blow. I spring from the scout beneath me, the force of my departure crushing his ribs and burying them into his lungs. This act of defiance propels me backward. A whirlwind of shadowy steel lashes out, severing the swordsman's arm. I find myself squarely between the last two foes now—one gripping an axe, the other hollering while nursing his severed limb in excruciating pain.

With a quick sweep of my leg, the axeman is sent sprawling. To the unarmed man, my hand extends, unleashing a torrent of energy so potent it seems to split the very atmosphere. His body hurls through the farmhouse wall in a cloud of splinters, scattering them into the air as he disappears into the icy night beyond. For a moment I stand there in shock at the raw power that has just come from my hand. The axeman now attempts to regain his footing, drawing me back into the fight, but nothing will save him from his fate. I turn and my blade sweeps down, slicing through the air. As it connects with his skull, he crumples, his body folding onto the ground with a dull thud as he's laid to rest among the others.

My breath, still quick from the exertion, mixes with the quiet of the aftermath. The abrupt sound of footsteps at the entrance heralds Elias's arrival. He crosses the threshold into the dimly illuminated space, his eyes rapidly scanning the aftermath. A soft whistle slips from his lips as he surveys the scene. His gaze shifts from the motionless scouts to me.

"Nicely done, Asha," he says. His lips quiver with an amused smile. I return the gesture with a sarcastic bow, a light-hearted acceptance of his commendation.

"Thank you, kind sir," I reply, rising with a small smile. "And thank you for the diversion. It played out just as we planned."

"Anytime." He steps further into the room. "Though, I must admit, I didn't expect to come back to... quite this. Couldn't you have just sung them to sleep instead of throwing them through the wall?" I just chuckle, glancing around the room at the bodies lying in pools of blood. A part of me thrives on the rush of adrenaline that still surges through me.

"Where's the fun in that?" I ask, then feel a tinge of regret. I just killed four men, and I'm laughing about it being fun? I shake my head, trying to dispel the unease inside. I don't want to enjoy killing people. Yet, part of me does and it terrifies me.

"That's a fair argument, I suppose." He nudges one of the scouts with his boot. My thoughts subside as my gaze sweeps the room and catches on the map under the lantern's flickering light. Drawing closer I pick it up and wipe the splatters of blood with my sleeve. The map's details are still visible. The Whispering Forest's location is emphatically circled. I lift the map and turn to Elias.

"Look at this. They are aware of the Whispering Forest." He leans over, his brow knitting together. After a pause, he looks up.

"They may know its rough location, but accessing it is another matter. Besides, this information might not have reached the Legion yet."

"You're right," I acknowledge, holding the map carefully. "Also, the forest is shielded by enchantments. Knowing its location isn't enough; they'd need to breach its magic." Lavinia's urgent plea for me to find the scouts haunts me. If she's concerned, maybe the forest isn't as impregnable as we believe. The weight of the map's implications press on me. "With the Legion setting their sights on the forest, we can't afford to let them find an entry. Let's search the place before we go."

We begin our meticulous search of the farmhouse, sifting through every nook and cranny for clues or resources to take back with us. The burden of our circumstances bears down on me as I search. Ever since we left Emberwyn, the ceaseless struggle against the Legion and its darkness has kept me perpetually on edge. A part of me, fatigued and worn, can't help but yearn for a life that might have been, had I embraced the role of the High Priestess, leaving behind the thirst for answers to age-old mysteries.

My attention is drawn to the deer lying on the table. I approach slowly, a pang of sorrow threading through me for the innocent creature caught in the Legion's death grip. Kneeling beside the table, I extend a hand to gently touch the deer's face. Flies buzz around it, their persistent hum blending with the silence of the room. The fur feels coarse under my fingertips. I notice an unusual patch of white fur, stark against its otherwise deep brown coat, shaped almost like a crescent moon right above its eye.

"Rest now, creature of the forest," I whisper. "May your spirit find the ancient paths to the realms beyond. Your journey here concludes, but the dance of the wild endures. Farewell." The moment the words leave my lips, a subtle, thin strand of golden magic begins to unravel from its body. It weaves through the air, its luminescent thread encircling me in a silent goodbye before drifting through the gaping hole in the wall, returning to the wilderness from whence it came. A deep, resonant calm settles over me.

I rise from my kneeling position beside the deer and continue the search. Yet, our thorough search yields nothing noteworthy until we examine the fallen scouts. The task of going through the deceased's effects is grim, yet necessity compels me. Among personal items and weaponry, something unexpected emerges from one of the scouts—a cold iron key.

"I doubt this key fits any lock here; it looks far too large," I muse aloud, turning the cold iron key over in my hand. Elias, peering over my shoulder, concurs with a nod.

"Perhaps it unlocks the barn," he suggests thoughtfully.

We leave the house behind and draw nearer to the barn, its form casting a sharp shadow against the night. Towering before us, the barn is worn by time and elements, its timbers creaking softly with each gust of wind. The doors, warped by years without care, are ajar, their groans seemingly beckoning us into its depths. Stepping inside, the aroma of old hay and the earthy tang of moist ground surround me. The air feels cool and slightly musty, hinting at the presence of animals long gone. Venturing further, my foot stumbles upon something hidden beneath the hay's surface.

"Over here," I gesture. Clearing the hay reveals a door, hidden from casual view, and firmly locked. When I insert the key, the door reveals a ladder descending into darkness. A foul smell wafts up, causing us to grimace in unison.

"Remarkable," he coughs, "there goes my appetite. What could possibly smell so bad?"

"We're about to find out," I say, my voice steady despite my unease.

He hesitates. "Maybe we should fetch some guardians for this?"

"There's no time," I insist. "A quick look, that's all." He sighs, but nods, and we begin our descent. The world above fades, darkness enveloping us. The air grows colder, damper. Our steps on the wooden rungs echo like a haunting melody against unseen walls.

Reaching the bottom, I pause, allowing my eyes to adjust to the profound darkness, to no avail. I summon the lens from my bracer and peer through it. It cuts through the darkness with a blood-red light, revealing the cavern's secrets.

"It's a cavern. Stick by me," I caution, delving deeper into the earth's depths. The air grows heavier, our steps cautious, accompanied by the solitary sounds of our movement and the steady drip of water echoing off the stone walls.

Suddenly, immense wooden doors infused with iron emerge before me. A chilling sight halts me—a sea of towering cages stretching into the darkness, each one cradling an Eyeless. Silent and motionless, they seem to slumber, as if awaiting a cue to awaken. The air is thick with a stomach-wrenching scent, causing Elias to nearly gag.

"Countless," I whisper, my voice a mere breath.

"Countless what?" he asks.

"Eyeless. Confined in cages," I reply.

Approaching the cages, I become engulfed by the endless sea of slumbering shadows encased in iron. I edge nearer to one of the cages. The Eyeless giant remains motionless, except for its vast chest rising and falling in measured breaths. Its skin is stretched taut over its skeletal frame, and its wide mouth, a cavern filled with sharp teeth, slowly leaks a dark, thick substance. Its long arms dangle with clawed fingers just touching the cage's floor. A shiver of cold dread runs through me.

"They appear to be in a sort of hibernation," I whisper softly. The realization that we are standing in the midst of an impending disaster, with each creature a potential harbinger of destruction, instills in me an intense need for action.

"We need to figure out who's orchestrating this and how to put a stop to it," I say. The discovery of the Eyeless horde signals a pivotal moment, one that could determine the fate of our struggle against the encroaching shadows that menace our realm.

"But… I really don't want to," Elias murmurs, his fingers now clutching at my cloak for assurance. I understand the critical nature of our predicament; our moments in these shadowed depths are dwindling. Elias seems on the brink of panic if we don't make our exit swiftly. At that moment, the darkness is pierced by the flicker of a lantern between the cages. A figure, cloaked in a hood, steps into the corridor. My heart sinks—the same figure from the Emberwyn ruins is here before us once more. The lantern sways gently in its grasp, throwing moving shadows against the dungeon walls and over the motionless, eyeless watchers.

I stand frozen, breath stolen by a deep-seated fear that anchors me to the stone beneath my feet. The emergence of this hooded specter deep within the cavern intertwines the fate of the attack on Emberwyn with the slumbering army at our doorstep. The figure proceeds with a grave stride, its lantern shedding an eerie luminance upon the path. Sensing our presence, it pauses. A heavy silence blankets us, only disturbed by the far-off sound of water droplets. Slowly, turning towards us, the figure raises the lantern, dispelling the long shadow between us. Even from this distance, the weight of its gaze pierces the darkness, as if reaching out to ensnare our souls. Realizing we've been spotted, that our presence is no longer a secret, ignites a rush of adrenaline within me. In that stretched moment of silent standoff with the hooded figure, the stillness is violently shattered as it releases the lantern. It crashes, the sound piercing the quiet, sending a cold shiver cascading through me. Darkness swallows us again, the brief interlude of light snuffed out.

Suddenly, the cavern echoes with a sound indescribable—the clatter of a thousand iron locks disengaging. It's a sound that sears itself into my senses, a cacophony that edges every nerve towards panic. My heart pounds against my ribs, dread swelling as the truth of our situation unfolds. The Eyeless are now unleashed.

"Run, now!" The command tears from my throat, urgency propelling my words into action. Without hesitation, I grab Elias's arm and sprint back the way we came. Our flight is a blind, frenzied dash through the oppressive black, the sound of the awakening Eyeless a growing storm at our backs. The clamor of chains clanging, gates groaning, and the ominous sound of countless beings descending upon the ground fuels a terror-driven surge of speed. A ghostly breath caresses my neck sending me into a panic. Their snarls and whispers weave a chilling chorus that seems to animate the very darkness, hungering for our fear.

Each stride is a risk, navigating the cavern's precarious terrain, where each step might be our last. The ladder, our only hope of escape, emerges ahead. The threat of the Eyeless shifts from a distant echo to a palpable, encroaching atmosphere, intent on ensnaring us.

Clambering up the ladder, I emerge into the safety of the barn and whirl around to aid Elias. But in a flash, disaster strikes—an eyeless beast ensnares Elias, dragging him back into the abyss below. My hands close on nothing but air as he's torn from my grasp with a scream, devoured by the darkness I've barely escaped.

"Elias!" My shout reverberates off the barn walls. Collapsed by the ladder, I stare into the void, desperate for any sign of him. Then, shadows begin to stir, and the Eyeless ascend the ladder with unnerving speed. Adrenaline surges, spurring my frantic defense. A kick sends the first tumbling back into the darkness.

Immediately, I slam the door shut and lock it. But the click of the lock brings me little comfort. My heart pounds in a rhythm that mirrors the chaos that brews just beneath me. As I pivot to make my escape, the sound of wood being torn asunder sends a jolt of cold fear through me. The door to the ladder shaft explodes open, and the Eyeless' haunting cries flood the barn.

Panic propels me toward the exit that leads to the Whispering Forest. The night blurs around me as their pursuit grows ever closer. I reach the door, my trembling hands struggling with the handle. With a forceful push, I hurl myself into the sanctuary of the Whispering Forest, the magical barrier sealing shut with an ominous finality.

I lie there, desperate for a fragment of tranquility, yet the forest's quiet grants no relief, compelling me to rise. My journey through its tangled underbrush becomes a laborious trudge, and all the while, visions of Elias and Skylar gnash their teeth at my sanity. The weight of those I couldn't shield becomes unbearable. Tears stream down my face, the grief and memories melding into a tide of despair that threatens to drag me under. Defeated, I crumble to the forest floor. The burden of pressing onward feels insurmountable. How can I stand against the darkness when it has already claimed so much? How can I lead when each choice seems to lead to death?

Alone in the Whispering Forest, my resolve crumbles. The temptation to abandon my role as Soulweaver, to escape a life overshadowed by darkness, is overpowering. I long for a simpler time in Emberwyn, before the burden of destiny was mine to bear, before I knew of eyeless hordes and the sting of loss. To be just a girl again, free from prophecies and the endless conflict that seems only to promise further sorrow.

Tears flow freely as I grapple with the prospect of moving forward without Elias and Skylar, of confronting future terrors without their friendship. The road ahead appears devoid of hope. The idea of retreat tempts me; the urge to abandon our mission and all it represents is beckoning. In the depths of my despair, the thought of surrender offers a twisted solace, a means to evade the ceaseless wave of grief ready to engulf me. Suddenly a subtle crack of a twig disrupts the quiet.

A stag steps out from the shadows of the forest, its presence commanding yet gentle, as if drawn by my despair. It approaches, its majestic form bathed in the dim light, and I can't help but notice the distinctive white crescent moon marking above its eye—the same mark as on the deer I found lifeless in the cabin.

"How are you here?" I whisper, but my mind is too numb, too fragmented to make any sense of it and my thoughts drift back to the plea of surrender. As I teeter on the brink of giving up, a gentle voice breaks through the silence.

"Don't surrender yet, my daughter." This voice, both unexpected and achingly familiar, pierces me. Lifting my gaze, I find myself confronted by my father.

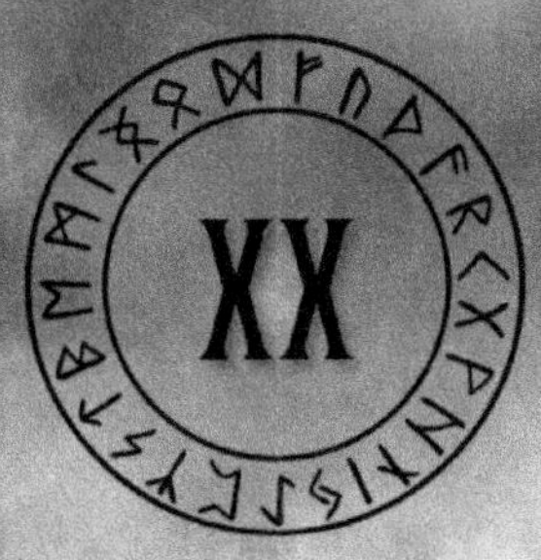

The Heart of Darkness

The sudden presence of my father in the soft light of the Whispering Forest strikes me with a mix of shock and disbelief. For a moment, my senses seem to deceive me. The grief and despair from recent events twists my perception into something almost dreamlike. His figure embodies raw strength, yet is softened by the passage of time. Silver braids cascade past his shoulders, and ancient tattoos mark his weathered face, narrating stories of a life immersed in battle. His eyes, a vivid grey-blue, possess a depth akin to a misty ocean. Dressed in leather, he exudes the wild essence of the forest. Yet, when he opens his arms, the unmistakable warmth of his embrace engulfs me, dissolving the fortress of emotion I've been sheltering behind.

I collapse into his arms, my sobs wracking my body. The weight of leadership with the shock of reuniting with my long-lost father sends me into a torrent of sorrow and relief.

"How… I thought… but you were gone," I manage to choke out through tears, my voice muffled against him.

He tightens his embrace. "Not gone, child," he says.

In his arms, I revert to the child I was before the world demanded my strength; before the scars of duty had formed on my skin. The resilience and resolve that had driven me forward wane, revealing the raw vulnerability of someone who has faced too much, lost too much.

"I can't do this anymore," I confess, overwhelmed by a tide of despair. "I can't lose anyone else. I'm terrified of moving forward, only to encounter more shadows, more pain. I just can't bear it, father." He pulls back just enough to look into my eyes, his gaze steady.

"Asha, my courageous daughter," he says softly, cupping my face in his large, rough hands. His thumbs wipe the tears from my cheeks. "You bare a unique gift, unasked for, yet bestowed upon you alone. Heed my words, daughter. You are more than sufficient."

His words cut through my heart. I missed him so much. Yet, hearing his words, the shadow of doubt lingers stubbornly within me.

"How can I be enough?" I whisper. "How can I hope to stand against a force that seems so vast, so unstoppable? That keeps killing my—" My words choke in my throat.

He cradles my face in his hands. "Because you hold what the darkness cannot fathom—the might of heart and hope. These are not frailties, daughter. They are the strongest of virtues. You fight not for power like they, but for the vision of a hopeful morrow."

His belief in me slowly cuts through the haze. Taking a deep breath, I find my footing, clearing the tears that obscure my view.

"I miss them so much," I admit, giving voice to the sorrow that will forever accompany me.

"Not gone, daughter," he says, placing a hand over my heart. I let myself hold him for a while in silence, before finally speaking again.

"Father," I ask through quiet tears, "what happened to you at the Rim? You were just gone. I looked for you." The forest around us seems to hold its breath as my father starts to unravel the tale of his disappearance. His voice, steady and solemn, paints a picture of a past that I had never known.

"When you were born," he starts, his eyes wandering through memories of ages past, "there was something in you – a light that no one could explain. As you grew, it was clear you were unlike others, special in ways beyond the simple." He tells of years spent searching through old scrolls and tales, trying to trace the lineage of the Soulweavers, a family line thought lost to history. "During my searches, in the hidden places of the world, I found what I sought. You were bound to the bloodline of the ancient ones." He pauses, looking deeply into my eyes before continuing. "Such power is often feared, not understood by the leaders of our lands. When I shared my findings with the council, it birthed fear in their souls. They wished to control or destroy anything they could not understand. They saw you, my daughter, not as the hope I did, but as a threat to their rule, to the order they wanted to keep. They wished to destroy you."

"They wanted to kill me?" I ask. The council's readiness to end my life as an infant, to extinguish the chance for good, sheds a new darkness on fellow villagers whom I had once trusted.

"Rather than letting fear decide your destiny," he continues, his voice strong with a decision made long ago, "I offered them an oath. For your safety, for a promise that no harm would come to you, I agreed to leave Emberwyn and never return. You would be raised in ignorance, but alive. My disappearance was the price for your protection, a sacrifice I made willingly to see you grow. However, they had not honored their word, and the men they sent to escort me, turned on me. I did what I had to do."

My heart sinks lower than before. The weight of his sacrifice, the years of separation and silence, are a testament to his love for me, and the lengths he would go to protect me.

"Father," I whisper, "how did you know I'd find my way here?" He smiles. His eyes seem filled with both sadness and pride.

"The heart knows, daughter. I've watched over you in ways you might not grasp. Deep in my heart, I knew you would find your way, that the light within you would lead you through darkest nights. This is one reason I left my blade; a sign. I had faith that you would not rest until you uncovered truths." I draw his blade from my boot with a newfound respect.

"I've always felt drawn to it," I confess. He nods, his eyes mirroring the flickering forest light.

"You were drawn by the desire to find me. Yet, that blade was handed down through many generations of my bloodline, and it is more than steel and craftsmanship. It was destined for you, to guide you, shield you, and, when the moment is right, to bring you home. One day, you will understand."

"But, I don't understand, and everyone expects so much from me. I'm not a leader, father. How can I be what everyone expects me to be?"

"Asha." He reaches out to place a reassuring hand on my shoulder. "You have overcome trials that would have broken the many. Your destiny is not about being who others expect you to be; it is about being true to your soul, knowing you are sufficient. That is your power, and it will guide you through the darkest times."

In his presence, I feel a grounding force, a reminder of the love and strength that have always been a part of me, even when I felt most alone. The conversation shifts, the night around us seeming to lean in, as if the forest itself is listening. He looks at me, his eyes searching mine.

"Daughter, search within you now. What are you afraid of?" The question pierces through the layers I had built around myself. In the quiet of the forest, with my father's gaze holding mine, the walls I had constructed to keep my fears at bay begin to crumble.

"I'm afraid of failing," I whisper, the admission feeling like a confession. "Not just failing in my quest, but failing those who have placed their trust in me, those who have sacrificed so much. I'm terrified of letting anyone down, of not being strong enough to protect them, to lead them. Especially after failing them already." His expression softens.

"Strength is not just about wielding power or leading battles. It is found in your moments of doubt, in the willingness to be vulnerable, to acknowledge your fears and face them." As he takes my hand, I feel tangible warmth spreading from his grasp. "Fear is an important part of us, a reminder of what's at stake. But it does not define us. Your fear doesn't weaken you; it is your humanity."

The simplicity of his words flow over me like a refreshing river, easing the inner chaos.

"Thank you, father," I manage to say, my voice now slightly stronger. He smiles that same warm, reassuring smile that I had missed so much.

"You are never alone," he says. "Remember that."

Feeling a tremendous sense of relief, I wrap my arms tightly around him. The embrace bridges the years we've been apart. He still smells of forest and leather armor.

"Come. I want you to meet my friends, and Lili will be so glad to see you," I say. Grabbing his rough hand and moving to introduce him to the others, I feel a subtle, unmistakable resistance holding him in place. My steps falter, confusion filling my heart as I turn to him. A realization grows inside me.

"You aren't really here, are you?" I whisper, tears welling in my eyes again. His gaze meets mine. With a gentle nod, he acknowledges the truth I know but wish weren't so. The forest seems to exhale, mourning the transience of our meeting. He offers a tender, sorrowful smile that says so much.

"No, daughter," he answers, his voice carrying a resonance that seems to flow from the forest, "not as you wish. But not gone, child." I experience a pang of profound emptiness where I had hoped for a solid presence. Yet, as this realization dawns, so does an understanding, an acceptance. His form, even as it starts to vanish, emanates a warmth that penetrates my very being. "Remember, Asha, our bond is not confined by presence or absence. It is interwoven into who you are."

As his image fades into the night air, leaving me alone among the ancient trees of the forest, a profound sense of peace wraps around me. Although the physical presence I long for is out of reach, the essence of our bond, the love and wisdom he shared, will stay. With a deep, steadying breath, I turn back towards the forest path. The night doesn't feel as dark anymore nor does the path seem as intimidating.

Stepping back into the clearing, seeing the ancient tree and Thaddeus's hut under the moon's gentle glow strikes a chord of both welcome and sorrow. The quiet of the night surrounds me. There, at the clearing's edge, stands Thaddeus, illuminated in silver light, clutching Geraldine close. His eyes, laden with hope and fear, scan the shadows I emerged from, searching for the companion I've left behind. The sight of him, hopeful yet braced for grief, splits my heart in two.

"Beanpole?" His whisper breaks the silence.

The word hangs between us like a delicate bridge over the abyss of loss that yawns at our feet. I wish I could rewind time, and come back with Elias at my side, saving Thaddeus from the harsh truth pressing against my lips. *Your jesting partner is not coming back.*

I inhale deeply, the night's chill sharp in my lungs, and meet Thaddeus's searching eyes. My silence conveys the dreaded answer he never wanted to hear. The light of hope in his eyes fades, replaced by the slow, painful acknowledgment of loss, reflecting my own sorrow.

"I... I couldn't save him," I whisper, a tear falling from my cheek. The words, though faint, are thunderous in the clearing's stillness. "I tried, Thaddeus. I really tried."

He tightens his hold on Geraldine, as if the tiny creature could anchor him against the coming storm of grief. For a long stretch, we remain silent. Geraldine emits a soft croak.

"Beanpole," Thaddeus says again, the name now a parting word, a goodbye. He looks at me, his eyes tearful yet resilient, embodying the spirit Elias always showed. Then he turns and walks slowly into his hut, closing the door behind him.

As he vanishes into the solitude of his hut, the first hints of dawn begin to color the sky, the night's darkness softly giving way to morning's gentle light. The ancient trees of the Whispering Forest, their leaves rustling in the early breeze, seem to lean in, sharing our sorrow.

In this moment of transition, from night to dawn, Lavinia approaches. Her presence is like the dawn itself, a beacon of hope amid the shadows of mourning. Without a word, she envelops me in an embrace. I lean into her, allowing myself this moment of vulnerability.

"I know, dear," she whispers, "the forest has told me." I dry my tears, stepping back to meet Lavinia's gaze. "Come, tell me what you've found above," she prompts, signaling for the story of our recent ordeal. We sit at the foot of the ancient tree, where sunlight sifts through the leaves, casting mottled shadows around us.

"There was a farmhouse," I begin, the memories returning with sharp clarity, "seemingly deserted, but with a light burning." Lavinia listens closely, her serene presence urging me to unfold the story further. "Scouts from the Legion were there," I add. "We had to stop them. It was the only way to ensure they couldn't warn the others." She nods solemnly.

"They also had a map," I continue, "with the location of the Whispering Forest circled. But that isn't the worst part. We found a key that opened a trapdoor in the barn, leading down into an underground cavern."

"And what did you find beneath the surface?" Lavinia's voice gently nudges me on.

"It seemed to be a breeding ground for the eyeless. Rows of them, dormant in iron cages. It was horrifying. There was also a figure," I tell her, a chill tracing my spine at the memory. "A hooded figure. I've seen this figure before, in my village, in Emberwyn when it was destroyed. It let them out, Lavinia. All of the Eyeless are out of their cages and on the surface."

Lavinia places her hand on my shoulder. "This is indeed grave news, Asha. The Legion's reach and preparations are much more extensive than we anticipated. We must act quickly."

"What can we do?" I ask.

"Go, Asha," Lavinia urges, "gather Nico and meet me in the archives. I will call upon Seraphina and Alaric, and tell Thaddeus to care for Lili. We have a lot to do and scant time to do it. Go." She quickly rushes off, leaving me alone.

Waking Nico weighs on me as I head to the small, cozy bedroom. The first sunlight streams through the window, spreading a soft, golden glow across the room. I pause at the doorway, drawing a deep breath to steady myself. The news of Elias is a burden too heavy to share just yet. I gently approach Nico's bedside and touch his shoulder.

"Nico," I whisper. His eyes flutter open, confusion giving way to concern as he sees my face. "We need you," I manage to say. But the truth is I need him. He nods and gets dressed in silence. After he's ready, I open the bedroom door and step directly into the Arcane Archives. Stepping into the ancient building, the air carries the distinct smell of parchment intertwined with a hint of magic. Lavinia is there waiting, and beside her stand Seraphina and Alaric. They greet us with a nod.

"I thank you all for meeting here," she says. "The Legion is positioning their forces just across the plains as we speak so there isn't much time. Everyone, follow me." Following Lavinia's lantern glow, we exit the archives and step outside. Our footsteps echo softly against the forest floor, a somber cadence under the night's quiet.

Lavinia breaks the silence. "We're heading to the surface. The Guardians are fortifying positions surrounding the chasm."

Nico, silent until now, glances at me, confusion flitting across his face.

"Did I miss something?" he murmurs.

Drawing in a deep breath, I muster the courage to speak. "It's about Elias," I begin, my words a mere whisper in the silence. Each syllable is like salt on an open wound. "He... he accompanied me on a mission to scout the Legion. He—" My voice falters, but I catch the dawning realization in his eyes before the sentence is complete. "He's gone, Nico." He halts in his tracks, turning to face me.

"I see," he says quietly. I thought he would be more upset, cry, or show emotions; something. But he doesn't even offer comfort, just turns quietly and continues walking. I inhale sharply, the silence stretching between us like a chasm.

"Nico?" My voice carries a mix of confusion and a plea for... anything. Yet, he keeps moving forward, his steps measured, his back to me. "Why aren't you saying anything?" The question spills out, tinted with desperation. I'm seeking a crack in his composure, a sign that this news shatters him as it does me. He pauses, turning his head slightly.

"I just... I need to process everything," he finally says. I nod, acknowledging his need. Understanding it, even though I often find myself struggling to process my own whirlwind of emotions. Without another word, we resume our journey and eventually break free from the forest into an open field where four Zephyr Birds wait. Their feathers shimmer like morning dew. Their calmness makes me feel somewhat relaxed.

We mount the Zephyr Birds, and I quickly find harmony with the beat of their wings. The climb from the forest's underground sanctuary to the surface world marks a shift from the forest's lush air to the sharp chill of the open land. Below, frost blankets the fields, with the dark outline of the forbidden forest at the horizon.

We quietly approach the encampments, set up around the edge of the chasm. The wings beat loudly as we land, kicking up wisps of frosty air beneath them. The forest's Guardians, deep in battle preparations, hardly glance our way. As we dismount, the ground crunches with frost. The horizon, marked by the scattered lights of the Legion's campfires, hints at the size of the enemy force.

"The Legion encircles us," Alaric says in his usual, ancient way of talking. "Their numbers greatly surpass our own."

"We've reinforced our defenses with all known spells and tactics," Seraphina says, indicating the barely visible magical dome barrier shimmering in the morning light. I nod subtly then glance around. The encampments are alive with preparations. Smoke from the Legion's camps blurs the horizon, a clear sign of the enemy's proximity and our precarious position.Nico and I stand, watching over the encampment, our breaths painting the cold air. A Guardian, his armor a tapestry of leather and metal etched with symbols of valor, approaches with a determined pace.

"Come," he commands without stopping, "our spies bring urgent tidings." Without awaiting our acknowledgment, he strides toward a tent that stands as a bastion of command for the Guardians. This fabric fortress, resilient against the elements, embraces the warmth of a central fire within its confines. The space is a repository of martial prowess, adorned with artifacts of battle, strategic maps, and scrolls laid across tables.

He leads us to the core of the tent, where a table burdened with maps beckons. As he draws us near, his fingers dance over the terrain depicted on parchment, outlining the invisible lines where friend and foe will likely meet. He then points to a location on the map.

"Here lie the means from which the Eyeless draw their vile strength," he reveals. "The Shadow's Heart, a nexus of dark energy that sustains their legions, lies concealed within a chest." His finger pauses over a mark dark as night. "Enshrouded by potent magics, and zealously guarded by legions and monsters most foul."

"The Shadow's heart?" I ask, my eyes meeting Nico's in mutual surprise. Despite our extensive travels, the thought of it had slipped my mind. "Just days ago, it was inside the monolith in my village," I say, looking up at the Guardian. His brows draw together, clearly intrigued by what I've said.

"Well," he responds, leaning in, "they must have taken it. Our spies have reported seeing it here."

Nico shifts next to me. "If this is where they draw their power, then securing it would turn the tide of this war." His fingers trace possible paths to the enemy camp's core on the map. The Guardian nods in response.

"Exactly. But to reach it, especially with its protection spell in place, will demand a plan," he says.

"Then let's devise a plan," I say. "One that catches them off guard. We have the element of surprise on our side. They won't expect us to strike at the heart of their power."

The tent suddenly becomes a hive of activity, with Guardians and strategists gathering around the table, pouring over the map and discussing various tactics. Nico and I join the discussion, offering insights from our own experiences and knowledge. I can't help but feel a surge of hope. The Shadow's Heart, a source of such devastation and power, now represents a chance for a victory, which is more than I've had since I've left Emberwyn. The planning goes deep into the day, with every detail scrutinized and every possibility considered. Yet, a solid agreement seems to elude us and tensions start to flare.

"I told you," I say sternly, "we need a small, highly skilled team. Stealth will be our ally. A direct assault would be met with overwhelming resistance, but a covert approach could get us within striking distance of the Shadow's Heart."

"No, no. You don't know the ways of war!" the Guardian retorts. "Sneaking into a camp is not a plan at all. That's a death wish!"

"And your idea of storming the front is surely not?" I let out an exasperated sigh, pinching the bridge of my nose. "You're making my head hurt."

"See," he exclaims, "you complain about a headache but think you can handle sneaking into a camp? Preposterous!" He laughs. I've finally reached my limit with this madness. I slam my fist down on the table, seething as I glare into his eyes. A fierce wind gusts through the tent, sending parchments flying and nearly snuffing out the fire in the hearth.

Seraphina quickly leans in and grabs my arm and I look at her. She shakes her head subtly. I slowly relax under her grip and the wind dies down and the tent grows silent. The Guardian stares at me with wide eyes that echo how shocked I am myself about what just happened, though I don't show it.

"Fine," he finally says reluctantly. "Have it your way. But don't come back complaining when you're dead." He picks up the old map from the floor and places it on the table before storming out. I glance at Seraphina, and she smiles slightly. I turn back to the others in the tent.

"We do this my way. Does anyone else have an issue with that?" I look around the room and no one speaks up. "Good, then let's continue. We will have a small team go in, and if that fails, then by all means, wage war. But," I say sternly, "if we are not discovered then there will be no troop movements. If they think we are attacking then they will be on high alert, and we will most likely be discovered. Are we clear?" My tone brooks no argument, and everyone nods quietly.

"We need to bypass their outer defenses undetected. That means avoiding patrols and any magical enchantments they've set up around the perimeter." I continue, "Once inside, we will need to deal with the protection spell surrounding the Shadow's Heart. That will require a powerful counter-spell, something that can break through their dark magic without alerting the entire camp to our presence."

"Exactly. And that's where we come in," Seraphina says. "We have been studying the Legion's magic for decades, looking for weaknesses. We believe we've found a way to temporarily disrupt the protection spell, giving us a window to destroy the Heart."

"The success of this plan hinges on precision timing, unparalleled stealth, and the strength of that counter-spell," I say. "Once the Heart is destroyed, we need an immediate extraction. The moment that Heart goes dark, the Legion will know. We'll have to move quickly to avoid being overrun."

"We'll have Zephyr Birds on standby," Nico suggests. "They can get us out fast, and their speed is unmatched."

"Excellent idea, Nico." I smile at him. The plan is bold, its execution dangerous, but it instills a hope in me. This could actually work. As the plan finally solidifies, the responsibility of assigning roles falls upon me. I'm almost certain the other Guardians in the tent understand that my small team will not include them, but I speak it regardless, making sure there is no confusion.

"Nico and I will lead this mission," I say, feeling the weight of every gaze upon me. "Joining us will be Alaric and Seraphina. Their knowledge of the Legion's dark magic and their prowess in counter magic is crucial. We'll depart as night falls with the Zephyr Birds taking us swiftly and silently behind enemy lines, landing us within distance of the camp but far enough to remain undetected. Once on the ground, we'll rely on stealth to bypass the outer defenses. With Seraphina's cloaking spells, we should make our way to the tent undetected." I can see Nico nodding out of the corner of my eye. Alaric and Seraphina exchange a look with a smile.

"The moment the protection falls, and I destroy the Heart," I reach into my pocket, producing a small, intricately carved whistle, "we call the Zephyr Birds for extraction." The room goes silent, every member of our team absorbing the details of the plan. I look around at the Guardians still lingering, their gazes fixed on me.

"The moment you see our birds approaching, strike with all the force you have. They will be weak and vulnerable. If we can hit them with enough force, and fast, they may at the very least withdraw. We have one shot at this." I conclude, meeting the gaze of each person in the room. "We can do this. I believe in us." Nods of agreement and murmurs of assent fill the room.

VALLEY OF THE SHADOW OF DEATH

I lean against a rough wooden post, silently watching the enemy camps across the horizon. The sun hangs low, its golden light stretching shadows across the ground. The air smells of pine and distant smoke of a simmering war. The wind whispers through the tents, and the occasional clink of armor breaks the quiet.

Memories of Elias and Skylar flood my mind as I stand there. I close my eyes, taking a deep breath, and let their laughter envelop me. Their presence feels so tangible in this quiet moment. I remember the way Elias would throw his head back when he laughed, his eyes sparkling, and Skylar's gentle chuckles, always more reserved but equally heartfelt as she pretended not to care for his jokes. Losing them cuts deep, reminding me of life's fragility.

As the sun sets, painting the sky in oranges and pinks, I breathe in the cold air and open my eyes. The enemy camps, with their dark tents and small fires, seem less threatening now, an illusion of weakness in the fading light. For a moment, I let myself imagine a world beyond this conflict, where peace has returned, and the scars of war have begun to heal. Holding onto that vision, I steel myself for what's to come. The night may be closing in, but our fight is far from over. With a final glance at the dimming horizon, I turn back to the camp and see Nico approaching.

His mere presence offers a quiet comfort as the sky darkens around us. Without speaking, he wraps me in an embrace. I lean into him, finding a sense of peace in his warmth. The smell of his clothing, a blend of pine from the nearby woods and a soft note of smoke from the campfires, fills my senses, anchoring me firmly.

"I'm afraid to lose you." The words escape me with an openness I hadn't really meant to share. His embrace becomes firmer in a nonverbal comfort that speaks louder than words.

"You won't lose me," he says, his voice steady, "no matter what unfolds tonight, you won't lose me."

This simple yet profound promise, delivered with such unwavering conviction, kindles a small flame of hope within me. In this instant, as the scents of pine and smoke wrap around us and the distant enemy encampments become less defined in the twilight, the shadows cast by my fears begin to recede. I turn my gaze away from the darkening horizon, seeking refuge in the comfort of his embrace, allowing his steady heartbeat and the solid reality of his presence to dispel the last vestiges of my apprehension.

Under the cloak of the evening, with the world around us a blur of shadows and the last light, our shared solitude against the backdrop of an impending challenge becomes a crucible for something more profound. The remembrance of my promise to him, the words I had whispered about thinking of 'us' after the dust settled.

I lift my gaze to meet his, and the world pauses. The distant noise of the camp and the whispers of the wind through the trees fade into silence. In his eyes, I see a reflection of the turmoil and hope that brought us to this moment, like a mirror to my own soul. The promise of tomorrow, of a future uncertain, hangs in the cool evening air. It's a moment suspended in time, a breath held tight, as the weight of what lies ahead presses close.

Then, I bridge the gap between us. My lips find his in a tender touch that seals my vow to him in a whisper of hope amidst the storm. It's soft, fleeting, yet it holds the entirety of our journey within the touch of our lips. I linger for a moment, not wanting it to end. As we pull away, our gazes remain intertwined, capturing a myriad of unspoken emotions. The world around us starts to come back to life, but for a moment longer, we remain anchored in the bubble of our connection, a haven from the chaos. Our fingers intertwine, silently promising that no matter what the future holds, we will face it together.

Alaric and Seraphina suddenly approach us, their robes whispering against the grass, breaking the spell of the moment Nico and I are sharing. I sigh lightly. The evening light casts long shadows from their forms, giving them an ethereal appearance as they join us. Alaric, with his sharp eyes and an aura of intense concentration, nods in greeting. Seraphina offers us a gentle smile.

"We're here to discuss the cloaking spell," Seraphina starts, her voice as soothing as the breeze that dances through the encampment. "It's essential you understand how it works before we embark on our mission. This crystal" — she holds up a clear gem that emits a very subtle glow — "is the key to our cloaking spell. Rather than bending light or creating a spectacle, it works by harmonizing our energy with the natural world around us, making us virtually undetectable."

With calm, she begins to whisper incantations under her breath. I watch, fascinated, as the air around them starts to shimmer subtly, like heat rising off the ground on a summer's day. As the incantation continues, the shimmer becomes more pronounced, blurring their outlines until they seem to merge with the air itself. It's as if the space they occupy simply becomes an extension of the environment, their presence fading until they are no longer visible to the naked eye.

"Verily, motion and whisperings hold sway." Alaric's voice emanates from the void. "This spell shrouds us not in total absence from sight but grants us a semblance most elusive, should our steps be soft and our sounds but a murmur." With another quick chant, Seraphina and Alaric reappear, their forms gradually taking shape from the air itself. The crystal, now resting gently in Seraphina's palm, returns to its initial subtle glow.

"The crystal will extend its protection to all of us," Seraphina adds, closing her hand around the gem. "But we must remain close, and our minds focused. Distractions could weaken the spell, making us visible." Somehow, I feel she's speaking directly to me about distractions. I nod, impressed by the elegance and efficiency of their magic.

"Thank you," I say. As we huddle, finalizing our plans under the dimming sky, an unexpected yet familiar figure emerges from the shadows, cutting through the tension. Thaddeus guides Lili by the hand to our circle with Geraldine riding in her little pouch on Lili's shoulder

"I thought a touch of light might lift your spirits before you embark," Thaddeus says with a grand gesture of his walking stick.

"Thaddeus, Lili," I call out, my spirits buoyed by their presence. Bending down, I envelop Lili in a warm embrace.

"Are you going to war?" Lili asks softly.

"No, my little one," I lie, and I hate myself for it. "We're going on a small adventure, and we'll be back in a few hours." Geraldine croaks and Lili pats her on the head.

"Promise?" Her eyes long for reassurance as much as her heart does. I hug her, squeezing her tight.

"I promise. We will be back soon, don't you worry."

Thaddeus laughter, rich and heartfelt, scatters the gathering gloom if only for a moment. "Come now, Lili. We have creatures to catch and potions to brew!" he says, casting a fond glance at Lili, who now clings to him, her trust evident in her tight grasp. "And fear not, for we shall keep the hearth warm, awaiting your triumphant return." Alaric and Seraphina, seemingly touched by the show of unity, nod their respect. Nico crouches, offering Lili a playful ruffle of her hair.

"Keep an eye on Thaddeus for us, will you? You know he has a knack for finding trouble," he teases, earning a smile and a chuckle from her in return.

"Nonsense! I never caused a lick of trouble in my long life," Thaddeus retorts. I laugh and let the warmth of his returning personality soak in.

"It's crucial," I stress, eyes on both Lili and Thaddeus, "that you remain safe while we're gone. Thaddeus, her safety is in your hands."

"Without question," he assures, "we'll manage. Isn't that right, Lili?" Her nod is firm and resolute.

"We'll be here," she says with a smile, "and Geraldine too." Our farewell is marked by embraces, whispered words of encouragement, and a few croaks from Geraldine.

The moment is here at last, a threshold between hope and the daunting task ahead. As I move towards the Zephyr Birds, each step feels like a declaration, my heart syncing with the gravity of our mission. The evening air, crisp and cool, brushes against my skin. My footsteps thud softly on the ground. Around us, the camp falls into a hushed anticipation, as if the very earth and sky are holding their breath, waiting for the outcome of our endeavor. The Zephyr Birds, majestic creatures of the air, await us with quiet dignity, their large, luminous eyes reflecting the rising moon.

Approaching one of the birds, I pause, allowing myself a moment to connect with the creature that will carry us through the night sky. The wind, a whispering companion, caresses my cheek, carrying with it scents of pine and earth. I reach out my hand, brushing my fingers against the bird's feathers, marveling at the softness and the strength within each plume. The bird shifts slightly under my touch.

Closing my eyes, I take a deep breath. The weight of our task lies heavy on my shoulders, yet in this moment, there's also a sense of liberation, of stepping into the role fate has carved out for me. I am a Soulweaver, a protector of the Whispering Forest, and the last Heir of Velloria.

Opening my eyes, I meet Nico's gaze, finding in it a reflection of my own determination. Alaric and Seraphina stand ready, their expressions set with the calm of seasoned mages and warriors. Together, we are a force to be reckoned with. I smile at them, and with a final glance back at Thaddeus and Lili, I climb the ladder and seat myself in the capsule on my Zephyr Bird. The creature beneath me stirs, ready to take to the skies, its powerful wings unfurling with magnificent grace as the seat forms to my body.

Once we are all ready, the Zephyr Birds take flight, ascending into the night, their powerful wings cutting through the air with precision. As we climb higher into the sky, the world below stretches out in a breathtaking panorama, a mosaic of peace and turmoil seamlessly intertwined. The encampments sprawl below us, alive and pulsing against the frost-kissed landscape, their existence marked by the gentle dance of campfires. To one side, the Stygian Hollows stands as a bastion of the wild, its dense, shadow-laden canopy in sharp relief against the exposed vulnerability of the plains.Below, ethereal barriers glisten, creating glowing shields swirling with radiant energy that beats in harmony with the earth. The horizon melds into a dusky blur where the enemy masses like a smudge of darkness under the fading light. Smoke columns twist into the cooling air, their sources obscured. The enormity of the enemy, a tide of ill intent, looms vast, threatening to extinguish every glimmer of hope.

Drawing closer to hostile lands, the landscape transforms. Deep crimson barriers encircle enemy grounds, snaking through the terrain like arteries of fire.

These menacing veils, alive with a predatory glow, mark a frontier of evil. Our Zephyr Birds, attuned to the looming threat, alter their path, their wings beating faster as they soar above the shields. As the barriers draw nearer, their sinister hue bathes the ground below in an otherworldly light, casting long, twisted shadows as we arrive behind their lines.

In a display of elegance, our mounts adjust their descent, wings angling to moderate our speed. The drumming of their wings transitions into deliberate, measured strokes, steering us with precision through the twilight. Suspended in this moment of descent, the earth rushes up to greet us, the impact of our landing a definitive note in the quiet of the evening. The birds, having fulfilled their charge, tuck their wings, settling into the landscape as if whispering secrets to the soil beneath. This touch to earth marks not just the end of our flight but a return to the tactile reality of our mission.

I climb down the ladder, the crunch of frost beneath me breaking the night's stillness. The chill bites through my boots. The night wraps around us in a symphony of the unseen—owls call from a nearby tree, leaves whisper secrets on the wind, and in the distance, the low thrum of enemy activity murmurs like an ominous heartbeat.

The barriers, glowing with a deep, blood-red light, stretch into the night, their towering forms casting elongated shadows that dance at our feet. Here, in the heart of enemy territory, the weight of our quest presses down on me with tangible gravity. Isolation clings to me like a cold mist, even as we gather into a tight knot of resolve behind a concealing mound of earth. The barrier's ominous presence is a mere stone's throw away, its vibrant energy humming a warning. Nico, hunkering down beside me, eyes the barrier with wary intensity.

"How do we breach this?" he murmurs. "Can our veil of invisibility even blind such magic?"

"It must," I whisper back, meeting his gaze. "Seraphina and Alaric assured us the crystal's veil would shield us from their sorcery." I look over at Alaric and he confirms with a nod, and his usual ancient words.

"This barrier searches for breath and purpose. A frontal attack would lay us bare, yet our mantle conceals both essence and will, rendering us unseen to its questing gaze. Place thy trust in the rites we have wrought." Me and Elias glance at each other, seeming to share the same feeling of confusion at his words. I shrug and shake my head. I don't know what he said, but I trust them. Seraphina, eyes sharp and assessing, scrutinizes the barrier's pulse.

"Speed is our ally. Lingering here heightens the danger of discovery," she says. I inhale deeply, my resolve crystallizing.

"Then let's not wait around," I say, slowly standing, but keeping low. Stealthily, we advance together towards the mystical barrier of writhing arcane power that guards the encampment like a looming sentinel.

Drawing closer, the barrier reveals its intricate nature as a labyrinth of crimson tendrils, alive with the pulse of dark magic, coiling and uncoiling in a macabre dance. These magical strands, glowing with an infernal light, weave through the air, their movement reminiscent of serpents in a ritual dance, casting unsettling patterns on the ground. The very atmosphere vibrates with their power, a humming that resonates deep in my bones, while the earth beneath seems to thrum in echo to the barrier's sinister rhythm. Its vines, charged with malevolent energy, respond to our approach, their movement growing more agitated, as if aware of our trespass. The sensation sends a shiver down my spine.

In this eerie glow, barely a breath from the enemy's vigilant gaze, Seraphina and Alaric step forth, their expressions carved from stone with concentration. Seraphina, with a knowing glance, draws forth the crystal, cradling it gently in her hands. The crescendo of their hushed voices summons forth a gentle, nearly invisible energy from the crystal, enveloping us in a cloak so subtle it's nearly imperceptible. This magical veil bathes me in a warmth that feels like the brush of dawn. As the spell takes hold, our figures blend seamlessly with the shadowed air. My fingers stretch out, barely grazing the vibrant haze of the crimson barrier, half-expecting a jolt of arcane force to repel my touch. Yet, there's merely air, the barrier's foreboding glow offering no resistance. We step forward, the formidable barrier dissolving before us as though it were merely a wisp of fog.

"We've breached it," escapes my lips in an excited whisper. The once menacing luminescence of the barrier dims into obscurity behind us.

Veiled in our enchanted camouflage, we tread silently, delving deeper into the enemy's stronghold. The once invigorating night air now thickens with vile odors— a sickening brew of perspiration, decay, and the acrid scent of spilled blood suffusing the air, giving a tangible smell and taste to the desolation that permeates this place. I grimace, repelled by the noxious stench. Trying to quell the rising bile, I focus my attention on the encampment.

An array of tents sprawls before me, a chaotic labyrinth of fabric and rope. Erratic torchlight flickers, casting ghostly illuminations over the faces of patrolling soldiers. Their voices, a blend of murmurs and orders, weave a deceptively mundane soundscape, masking the grim purpose of their assembly.

My attention shifts beyond this immediate disarray to a more distant, chilling sight near the front barrier, in which rows of towering cages stand sentinel. The mere sight sends an icy dread coursing through me, recalling the unspeakable horrors from the caverns' depths. Yet, here on the surface, the Eyeless have been locked back in their cages, ready for war. The evil here feels as thick as the air I breathe.

A soldier's loud laughter breaks the quiet around us, too close for comfort, slicing through the silence like a sudden storm. For a moment, our magic protection wavers. It's a brief slip, but enough for the soldier to stop laughing and look our way, his eyes searching the darkness with the focus of a predator. The air feels charged, time seems to freeze. My heart races, fear and anticipation pound loudly in my ears. The soldier's cautious breathing and the distant sound of campfires add to the tension. I'm about to summon my weapon when Alaric stops me with a firm hand on my wrist, silently telling me to stay quiet and still.

In that moment, I'm hit with everything at once—the cool night air brushing against my face, the rough dirt under my boots, and a mix of smoke, blood and metal tainting the air. But it's the fear that really gets me. It's this deep, gnawing feeling of getting caught and what it would mean not just for me, but for my friends and our mission. Then, just like that, the soldier shakes it off, laughing to himself as if he's just thought he's seen a shadow or imagined us. He stumbles a bit and moves on, and the threat of being found disappears as quickly as it came. We all breathe out a silent, collective sigh of relief into the night. The near encounter was a sharp reminder of how thin a line we're walking, and how easily our magical disguise could fail us. We look at each other, and without words, agree to be even more focused from now on.

Moving closer to our goal, just a few tents away now, the air between us is thick with tension. Every move we make is careful, silent, always on the lookout for danger. Then we see something that makes us all stop. Tied to a post with a heavy iron chain is a beast of nightmares.

This creature, a product of dark magic, is massive, its huge body straining against the chain. It walks on its hind legs, resembling a wild wolf, but much more menacing. Its fur-less skin is a leathery black, muscles moving under it as it paces, restless. Its eyes, glowing with a dangerous light, scan the surroundings non-stop. What is really eerie, though, is the silence around it. In the middle of the noisy camp, there's a quiet bubble around this beast, as if even the air is too scared to get close.

Seraphina's voice is so quiet I have to strain to catch her words. "Nightmarrow," she barely breathes out. "They act as living alarms, attuned to any magic disturbances around here. It won't see us because of our spell, but it can feel sudden magical shifts which means our sure focus is paramount."

Realizing this creature could detect us, despite our invisibility, adds a whole new level of risk. We're hidden from sight, but not from the Nightmarrow's magical senses. Any careless step could trigger it to alert the whole camp. With the Nightmarrow so near, we have to focus every move, every bit of magic, to avoid setting off its senses.

The moment we decide to press on, our invisibility spell suddenly starts to waver, then vanishes altogether, leaving us standing bare and exposed. Almost instantly the Nightmarrow responds to the disturbance, its body tensing as it senses our magic waning. Its head whirls around in our direction.

With a terrifying growl that seems to shake the very ground we stand on, it drops to all fours, its claws digging into the dirt, clawing and digging like a predator ready to pounce. The air fills with its enraged hisses and gnashing teeth. With a fluid motion, as natural to me as breathing, I extend my arm, calling forth the sword of shadows. The blade, instantly streaks through the air, meets the Nightmarrow's temple with precision. Its dark energy cuts through the beast as if it were nothing more than a whisper of smoke. The Nightmarrow's growls cease abruptly, its body collapsing to the ground in a heap. My blade returns, and realizing the urgency of our situation, we don't linger. The fall of the Nightmarrow has not gone unnoticed.

The encampment is awakened by the sudden disruption. We need cover, and fast. Nearby, an empty tent offers the refuge we desperately seek. In mere moments, we duck into the tent, the fabric flap falling shut behind us with a soft whisper. Inside, the tent is sparsely furnished, shadows clinging to the corners where the dim light can't reach. The air is stale, heavy with the scent of dust and old leather that tickles my nose. We crouch low, barely daring to breathe as we listen to the distant shouts of soldiers, the clanking of armor, and the more immediate patrols that begin to sweep the area for the cause of the alarm.

My heart is racing, beating in unison with the increasing tempo of activity outside. In the dim confines of the tent, time seems to stretch thin. We wait there until the commotion outside gradually begins to subside, the initial flurry of activity giving way to more methodical searching by the soldiers. Despite the decrease in noise, the tension within me is like a string wound too tight, ready to snap at the slightest provocation. We can't linger here.

With the noise dwindling outside, suggesting a temporary pause in the commotion, I muster the courage to move. Glancing through the tent's slit, I catch sight of guards clustered around the Nightmarrow's still figure, their attention locked on the fallen creature, murmuring in a blend of confusion and speculation. They haven't connected the dots to its fall, their understanding as veiled as the night shrouding us.

"We can't risk the front," I whisper, my voice a faint sound in the compact space. The others signal their agreement with silent nods, aware of the dangers awaiting us if we choose the path we entered by. I draw my father's blade, stepping cautiously towards the tent's rear. The fabric, thin yet significant, stands as the last barrier between us and our pursuers—a barrier I'm poised to cross. With careful movements, I cut a small opening in the material, just enough to peek outside. The view offers both relief and a new challenge. The tent, distinct in its appearance, is merely steps away from us. Its black canvas is marked by the bold red insignia of the Legion of Embers, its tassels fluttering gently in the night's breeze.

"Alright," I say softly, turning back to see my allies' determined faces under the faint light sneaking through our hideout's fabric. "I'll cut a slit and we make a break for the next tent—our goal."

Without waiting for their words, I slice through the fabric silently. The cut reveals the dark gap between our current hideout and where we need to be. I halt, ears straining for any hint of discovery, but the night remains quiet, disturbed only by the far-off, subdued noises of the camp.

I glance at Nico, Alaric, and Seraphina, giving a single nod to signal it's time to move. "Stay close," I breathe out, ensuring my voice remains a whisper. We each take our turn, slipping through the slit into the night, blending with the darkness like phantoms. Upon reaching the Legion's tent, I don't hesitate to repeat my earlier actions. I poke a hole and peer inside. *Thank the fates... it's empty.* My blade slices through effortlessly, carving a doorway into what we hope will dismantle the Legion's strength.

Crossing into the tent feels like entering a new domain. The air hangs heavy, charged with the remnants of spells. A soft, red light seeps through the fabric from the proximity of the forefront barrier, casting unsettling shadows that dance across the tent's interior and bathing it in a surreal glow. At the center lies an ornate chest on a pedestal, its carvings alive with a subtle, ominous power. Within this closed chest lies the Legion's might, the

Shadow's Heart. The same artifact of ancient power my mother once revealed to me in Emberwyn's darkened halls.

Nico, Alaric, and Seraphina step in behind me and survey the chamber. Without words, Alaric and Seraphina approach the chest, their fingers tracing the air with the complex motions needed to break the chest's enchantments. I watch from a slit in the tent's door, every sense on high alert for any hint of detection. Outside, the camp is unaware of our breach. Yet, a knot of tension remains within me, my pulse quickening with the realization of our delicate position.

Time stretches, each second pulling tighter, until a massive commotion suddenly erupts outside. Alaric and Seraphina momentarily pause at the dreadful sound, but I recognize it instantly, and my heart drops. It's the sound of thousands of iron cages swinging open.

"Hurry!" I urge in a loud whisper, turning back to the tent's entrance to peek outside.

Through the slit, the encampment before us morphs into a hive of heightened vigilance. The soldiers, rather than succumbing to fear, are mobilizing with precision, their gaze piercing through the darkness for any sign of threat, their bodies coiled in readiness. As the eyeless creatures emerge from their confinement, a silent order seems to sweep through them, directing their focus towards our concealed spot.The Eyeless, seem to be reacting to our efforts to dismantle their protections. They start to converge on our location, their approach steady and slow. The air feels electrified, laden with the magic that binds these beings to the Legion's command.

Seraphina turns to us, her face tense and frustrated "The black magic... it's too potent. We need more time." Her words land like a blow, the grim reality of our predicament settling in like a heavy stone.

"Forget it," I say decisively, the next step clear in my mind. "We need to leave, now." As we stand there, our strategy to remain unseen is overwhelmed by the clash of magical forces. The dark aura radiating from the chest is a tangible, dense fog that dulls the effectiveness of our invisibility charm. The crystal flickers weakly, like a star waning at the break of a shadow-filled dawn.

"We can't summon the birds, not with the hoard this close," Seraphina murmurs. It's obvious we need to put distance between ourselves and the source of this dark power, to find a spot where we can safely disappear from view. I quickly lead the way as we sneak out the tent's rear, melting into the camp's enveloping darkness. The night buzzes with activity—the calls of soldiers and the eerie screams of the Eyeless blending into a noisy veil that shields our escape. As we flee, the encampment transforms into a whirlwind of chaos. But with each step away from the dark heart of the camp, the idea of escape shifts from mere wishful thinking to a solid possibility. Our flight narrows the world to nothing but the beat of my heart and labored breathing. An earth-shattering growl suddenly rips through the night.

Out of the darkness between two tents, a Nightmarrow emerges, woven from the dark fabric of fear and aggression. Its scream, a sound that borders on the insane, signals imminent death. Yet, even as the monster advances, blotting out the stars with its bulk, a primal part of me refuses to succumb to terror. Time stretches, allowing me to take in every horrifying detail—the shine of saliva on its teeth, its muscles rippling beneath the skin, and the deep-seated malice in its gaze, reflecting a hellish origin.

When the Nightmarrow dives towards me, everything slows down to a near halt. My body moves with pure instinct, evading its massive form. The earth beneath me turns into a frigid cradle, its chill seeping into my spine in a transient embrace as I navigate the tightrope between life and death. Particles of dirt dance into the air, trailing behind as my boots etch their legacy into the ground in my sliding evasion.

In that moment, my blade awakens into a tempest of darkness, its form shrouded in a wrathful dance of smoke and shadow. Then, with the suddenness of a storm breaking the horizon, sparks of orange flicker into existence, crackling with a life of their own. My weapon transforms, no longer merely steel but that of infernal fire, a blaze that the depths of the netherworld can only envy. It carves through the air in an upward arc piercing the slow-motion fabric of the moment.

As my fiery blade intersects with the Nightmarrow, it tears through its underbelly. The beast's form, a mere shadow overhead, offers no more resistance than a whisper of despair being cleaved in two. Its blood, a sable torrent that mirrors the abyss itself, pours forth in an eerie silence, each droplet suspended in the air like dark, gleaming jewels against the backdrop of conflict. The fire from my blade, a ravenous entity all its own, licks hungrily at the wound, illuminating the night with a crimson glow that casts an otherworldly light upon the scene in a grim ballet of shadow and flame.

I land beyond the Nightmarrow's towering shape, rolling and rising in one smooth, continuous movement. As my feet find the ground, time snaps back into its rapid pace, the momentary lapse shattering around me. The Nightmarrow crashes to the ground with monumental force, its demise sending vibrations through the soil. In the beast's wake, a profound silence envelops us as my gaze lands on a glimmer in the disarray—a sparkle of shattered crystal. The pieces of Seraphina's invisibility crystal lie scattered, dropped in her moment of panic. But this quiet is quickly torn apart by a burst of activity as the Eyeless, those relentless hunters from my worst fears, unleash their attack. Their growls and screams slice through the calm, a wild orchestra of fury as they converge on us with the single, horrifying goal to kill.

"Run!" I scream. I don't look back to check on my friends; I just sprint, pushing myself toward the magical barrier we had crossed earlier. Our escape becomes a desperate dash for life against the enveloping shadows. The shield barrier now stands as our sole beacon of hope against the relentless nightmare on our heels. I don't know if we can penetrate it without the crystal, but we can't turn back. It's all or nothing. I say a silent prayer to the fates, and reach out instinctively.

A surge of power rises within me, converging into a luminous energy in my hand. With a shout, I launch it. Its path is a lethal dance, colliding with the barrier in an explosion of crimson sparks. These sparks scatter like newly formed stars, performing a complex dance of light close enough for me to witness. A gateway opens before us, the heat from the sparks caressing my skin as I dive through. The Zephyr Birds, amidst chaos, await with their plumage catching the dim light. I dash to them, mounting swiftly. As we ready ourselves to flee, the Eyeless assail us in a wild onslaught. My Zephyr Bird lets out distressed calls, its movements erratic, as it confronts the looming shadows. It battles bravely, beak striking and wings beating, in a desperate attempt to repel the looming threat.

Nico, caught in the heart of the maelstrom with his Zephyr Bird, faces a dire struggle. The bird's attempts to ascend are thwarted by the suffocating mass of the Eyeless, their numbers seemingly endless, each wave more determined than the last to pull us back into despair.

"Nico!" My voice shatters, tears streaming, yet it's lost amidst the eyeless's shrieks and the birds' cries. Then, in a burst of determination, my bird tears through the chaos. We explode off the ground and soar, the earth shrinking below as we climb higher. My relief is fleeting; dread chokes me as I see Nico's plight worsen.

His bird, despite its courage, is overwhelmed, engulfed by the dark tide of the Eyeless, snuffing out any chance of escape. The sight of Nico's bird, besieged by the unyielding attack, burns into my mind. My breath stalls, a scream trapped in my heart. In that instant of helpless watching, reality seems to skew, the sky and ground merging into a whirlwind of terror and loss as tears distort my vision. The Eyeless, that unstoppable force, has taken another, blind in their quest for ruin. All I can do is watch, drifting higher into the night, leaving a tableau of chaos behind.

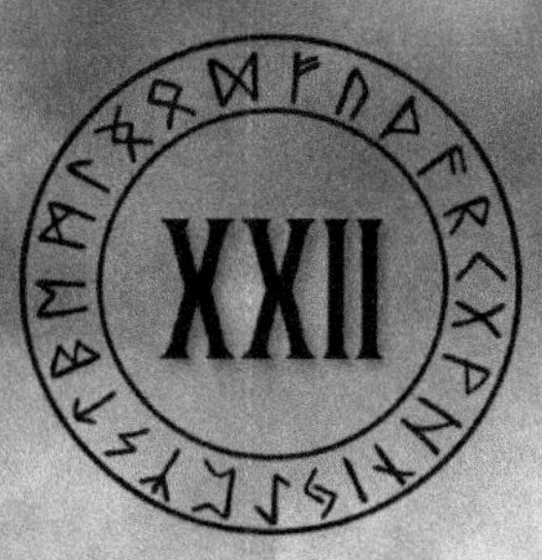

FRACTALS OF REALITY

As we ascend, the chaos below shrinks into a mosaic of shadows and flickering lights, with encampments blending into the landscape. The cold air lashes at my cheeks as my eyes scour the ground below, waiting and hoping for Nico's bird to explode from the darkness. But, it doesn't. The dark mass that swallowed him is now just a collection of moving shadows, indistinguishable from one another. Here, high above the ground, the world feels impossibly vast and lonely. Realizing Nico is no longer part of this world, my world, adds a weight that seems to drag at me from the skies.

I raise my face to the sky and let the wind sweep away the sound of my tormented soul's scream, scattering the echoes across the plains below. The horizon extends infinitely, with the moon throwing elongated shadows that blend into the dark outlines of the encampments. I angle my face towards the breeze, allowing it to evaporate the tears streaking my cheeks, the cold penetrating deep into my bones. Suddenly, a flash of red light cuts through the night. My gaze catches the sight just as my Zephyr bird, sensing the danger, banks sharply to the left.

An orb of red, electric magic, a comet of destruction, sails through the air with malevolent grace. It's a spectacle of terror and beauty and its trajectory is unwavering. *What have we done,* I think. As the Zephyr bird maneuvers to avoid it with precision, I hold tight, my eyes locked on the descent of the fiery sphere. With a sound like the world tearing apart, the ball of magic collides with the magical barrier protecting the Guardian's encampments. The explosion is a symphony of light and sound as the energies clash in a moment of apocalyptic fury. Red and white sparks erupt in a shower of fiery stars born from the violence of the impact. The barrier holds, but the force of the explosion sends ripples through the air, a shockwave of power that makes my bird falter in its flight. I watch, heart in my throat, as the red sparks dance wildly around the barrier.

As the tempest of red sparks continues its defiant ballet, I dare a glance back, hoping one last time that I will see Nico. Instead, my hope is rewarded with a terrifying sight. The frozen plains behind us are no longer empty but awash with a tide of darkness—a black sea of the Eyeless that surges forth in a flood of malice rolling across the earth. The barrier, a thin line of luminescence against the night, stands as the only thing between them and the Whispering Forest.

In that breathless moment, my bird plunges, its wings cutting desperately through the air to land with unexpected grace amidst our encampment. The instant its claws touch the earth, another orb of magic detonates upon the barrier with unmatched intensity. The noise sets my ears ringing as I quickly descend the ladder and find my footing on the ground. The barrier, sturdy yet quivering from the attack, flickers as though in agony. It remains intact, but the surrounding air trembles. It won't hold for much longer. The once freely spinning energy of the barrier now swirls in a fury, caught in a struggle between protection and destruction.

My bird emits a cry that slices through the din of battle as the Eyeless slam into the barrier in a tide of darkness and venom. Sightless yet driven by insatiable hunger, they start a wild climb, piling over each other. Their forms meld into a living wall of darkness creeping up the barrier, each entity scrambling blindly toward the top. As they ascend, another magic orb races towards the barrier and strikes with a thunderous impact. The barrier trembles. The Eyeless plummet, yet swiftly resume their ascent. It holds, but just barely, hanging on by a mere filament, a breath away from collapse. Lavinia's voice suddenly slices through the darkness, sharp as a knife, as she dashes by me.

"It's on the brink!" she shouts. I swiftly catch her arm, halting her movement.

"Where's Lili?" My voice struggles to pierce the tumult enveloping us.

"With Thaddeus, in safety. Find her immediately." With those words, I let go, and she resumes her urgent flight to escape.

Without a moment's delay, I pivot sharply and dash toward the war tent, the din of combat and the bellowing of the Eyeless swarm melding into a tumultuous roar that seems poised to engulf us entirely. Charging into the tent, my gaze instantly locates a brass horn placed on the central table. Seizing it, the metal feeling cool and solid in my hand, I hurry back outside. Taking a deep breath, I raise the horn to my lips and sound it. The sound that emerges is not a call to battle but a somber lament that reverberates across the valley. It soars over the clamor of the conflict, signaling our troops to retreat to the safety of the underground forest before it's too late.

Figures clad in the remnants of war turn, their actions a chaotic dance as they heed the call to retreat. As the last note of the horn fades into the din, I cast one final look at the barrier, its light dimming under the mass of the Eyeless that have climbed overhead and blotted out the sky. The moment hangs like a fragile pause in the chaos, until suddenly the barrier can withstand no more, and shatters in a final, devastating explosion. It bursts into a thousand shards of light, each piece a silent scream as it dissolves into the darkness. With its fall, the Eyeless begin to rain from the sky.

Panic surges through me. Around me, the world spirals into chaos, soldiers and sorcerers alike scattering in a frantic search for safety. The air grows heavy with the promise of death as the Eyeless descend, the impact of their bodies thundering like a thousand storms.

Without thought, my legs propel me forward, every sense heightened, every heartbeat a drum of war in my chest. The ground beneath my feet blurs, the screams of allies being devoured becoming distant echoes against the roar of my own survival. Bursts of magic tear through the night in a last stand by those still on their feet, battling towards any semblance of safety.

In the heart of this maelstrom, I summon the essence of my blade of fire from my bracer. A wave of heat surges through the air, mingling with the acrid smell of burning flesh as the blade meets the onslaught of the Eyeless. Their agonized hisses are abruptly silenced by the blistering inferno of my weapon. The heat from each clash floods across my face, intensifying the scalding spatter of the Eyeless' blood. The distinct crackle of fire joins the discordant symphony of battle—metal clashing, spells erupting, and the earth itself seeming to groan under the strain of conflict.

Ahead, I glance at the entrance to the Whispering Forest standing as a beacon of hope, its dark maw promising refuge from the unrelenting horror. Encircled by the pressing mass of the Eyeless horde, their bodies seemingly endless, I forge ahead. My fiery blade slices through them, casting arcs of light and leaving trails of ash in its wake. The overwhelming numbers of my foes become irrelevant in the face of my urgent need to reach Lili, to ensure her safety above all else. With every falling Eyeless, the entrance to the Whispering Forest grows closer.

The smell of charred flesh and the remnants of magic gag my senses as I finally reach the entrance and hurl myself in. The ground disappears beneath me as I plunge into the void. The fall is a moment of eerie silence before I crash into the river below. The cold embrace of the water shocks me. This river, the same one that greeted me on our first day here, serves as my savior once again as its currents sweep me away from the chaos that shatters the night. I gasp for breath as it threatens to pull me under. Around me, the Whispering Forest stands silent, witnessing my desperate flight.

I finally latch onto the bank, pulling myself from the river's grasp. With my heart pounding and limbs heavy with exhaustion, I push through the underbrush of the Whispering Forest. The river now betrays the presence of my pursuers with every loud splash echoing in the shadowy depths behind me. The Eyeless have breached the sanctuary of the forest.

My mind races, fragmented by adrenaline and the singular focus to reach Lili before the Eyeless can. As I weave through the dense foliage, the ominous sound of the river's disturbance seems to grow ever near. Then, beneath the ancient tree, I spot Lili. Her figure radiates the small grace of a guardian spirit, oblivious to the looming threat.

"Lili!" I scream. My voice comes out urgent and rough, piercing the heavy silence with a plea for her to hear, to flee, to survive as the Eyeless close in on me from behind. She whirls around, her face morphing from surprise to terror in seconds. Our gazes lock, and wordlessly, I scoop her up and make a mad dash towards the Anything and Everything door. Her little hands clench me tight as the sounds of pursuit from behind become a symphony of terror driving me forward. Their screams drive me even faster as the forest seems to close around us.

Arriving at the door feels akin to stepping from a nightmare into a realm of dreams. The knob is icy beneath my shaking hand. I quickly push the door open and step through, the Eyeless' screams intensifying behind us. In an instant, we transition from the forest's suffocating shadow into the welcoming familiarity of the bedroom. Slamming the door, I pause panting as I attempt to bridge the gap between our harrowing escape and the adrenaline still pulsing through me. The bedroom, with its plush linens and the moon's gentle illumination seeping through the curtains, is worlds apart from the world we've just evaded.

Though the shrieks of the Eyeless have faded, they still echo in my thoughts. We've managed to flee, but to what end? The lines between sanctuary and battlefield grow ever more indistinct with each moment.

"Lili," I whisper, my hands shaking, "where is Thaddeus?" Her eyes fill with tears and her words come out in sobs.

"He went in his house to bring the truffles we made for you." She grabs me and squeezes me tightly, her wet tears becoming one with my cloak.

"Lili, listen to me," I say, still holding her close, "I need you to stay here." She holds me even tighter in a plea for me not to leave. I don't want to leave her; I can't. She's all that remains. Nico, Elias, and Skylar are no more. A lump forms in my throat, tears welling in my eyes. Her grip strengthens. Her fear and plea are a tangible grip on my heart.

"Please, Asha, don't go," she murmurs, her voice cracking under the weight of her fear. "I need you here with me. Please!"

The room feels like it's closing in on me. Her words slice through the defenses around my heart. I pull her away gently and look into her eyes, our hands entwined.

"Lili, I need to find Thaddeus."

"But why you? Why does it always have to be you?" she barely breathes out.

"Because I can't just watch our world crumble. Because I need to know I did all I could. Thaddeus needs me right now and this room is safe. You will be safe here, I promise. You need to be strong now." My mind flashes back to the promise I made her only hours ago, telling her Nico and I would both come back. A promise I find myself unable to admit I've broken.

"You're safe here, Lili," I say steadily. "This room is protected from the Eyeless. Do not leave until I'm back. Promise me." I cup her face in my hands and wipe the tears from her cheeks. She nods slowly and reluctantly.

"I promise," she whispers. "Just... come back to me. Please, Asha."

"I will, as fast as I can," I say, planting a long kiss on her forehead. "And I will bring Thaddeus and Geraldine." After a final hug I rise and head towards the door. Each step from Lili seems like five steps, pulling me away from my core.

Stepping into the night, the moon drapes over the landscape in a silver glow. It's quiet. Too quiet. The way to Thaddeus's hut is clear in my memory. My steps quicken as the forest canopy murmurs overhead. The Whispering Forest, once a charming name, now echoes a dark forewarning. Every snap of a twig, every whisper among the leaves sends my nerves over the edge.

Suddenly, an Eyeless bursts from the shadows to my left. Instinct takes over, and I swerve, the world slowing to a dreamy crawl as I harness the energy coursing through me. As the creature lunges, my blade arcs downward through the air. For a moment, the creature is suspended in time. My blade cleaves it in half, black liquid erupting from its severed body before the halves fly past me on both sides. The black spray splatters my face in a burning sensation. I quickly wipe it off with my sleeve and silence descends once more.

My pulse races as I hasten towards Thaddeus's hut. When I arrive, the sight that greets me bypasses any need for formalities—no knocking required when the door lies in ruins, its pieces scattered like echoes of a foreboding welcome. A chill of apprehension sinks into my bones, burrowing deeper than I imagined possible. Sword in hand, I cross the shattered threshold.

"Thaddeus?" I call out in a whisper that barely disturbs the heavy air, only to be met with an oppressive silence. Stepping over the threshold, I enter the hut's eerie silence. The interior, once alive with laughter and magic, now lies in a chilling stillness. The air feels so vacant as if the very essence of the place has been hollowed out.

I move deeper inside, every sense alert for the slightest whisper of movement or sound, yet find only the distant, eerie calls of the Eyeless. A survey of the room makes the tangible absence weigh down heavily—the scattered tomes, their pages fluttering like wounded birds, and the shattered remnants of potions and vials bleeding into the floorboards.

Amid the rubble and clutter, a sound catches my attention. It's a weak creaking sound, yet persistent, slicing through the silence. I follow the sound, moving aside piles of books and scattered papers, until I find the source.

Geraldine, Thaddeus's frog, is pinned under a fallen shelf, her eyes wide with distress. Gently, I lift the debris, freeing her. As I pick her up, her small body trembles in my hands, and she lets out a series of small, plaintive croaks.

"Where is Thaddeus, little one?" I ask softly. Holding Geraldine close, I survey the room once more, hoping for any clue, any sign that might indicate where Thaddeus has gone or what has befallen him. Not seeing any blood is a relief, but beyond that relief, the hut offers no answers, only the remnants of a struggle and the heavy absence of its owner. Thaddeus is gone, vanished without a trace, leaving behind only questions and a sense of foreboding that tightens around my chest. Geraldine's presence, however, is a small comforting reminder that not everything has been lost to the chaos.

I safely nestle her in the warmth of my coat and step back into the night. With her soft croaks a constant undercurrent to my racing thoughts, I begin to make my way back to Lili. She is the only one I trust to care for this small beacon of hope in our unraveling world. The only one left who can.

The return to the bedroom is swift, but as I push open the door, the scene that unfolds before me is one I had not prepared for. The room is empty, devoid of the comforting presence of my little sister. Lili is gone. Panic takes root, spreading its icy fingers through my heart as I shout out her name. My voice echoes against the walls, but is met only with silence. I search the room desperately, the fear of losing her, my precious little sister, clawing at my chest. The bed is neatly made, untouched since my hurried departure earlier. There is no sign of struggle, nothing to indicate what has happened to her. If she had opened the door, it could have taken her anywhere and I will never be able to find her.

In that moment, the weight of everything, every loss and every battle fought in the shadow of creeping despair, comes crashing down upon me. I scream the anguish from my soul as my knees buckle, and I find myself on the floor. The cold, hard reality crushes me from all sides. *You're going to get us all killed!* Elias's voice screams in my mind. Tears breach the walls of vulnerability I can no longer contain. Geraldine offers a series of soft, comforting croaks. But there is no solace that can reach the depths of my despair. I had promised to protect Lili, to keep her safe, and I have failed her. I have failed everyone I loved. Just as the weight of my sorrow threatens to consume me whole, the door opens. I whip around, wiping the tears from my cheeks, my heart caught between hope and dread.

"Lili?" My voice carries into the silence, expecting her response. Yet, it isn't Lili who appears. Instead, my mother stands framed by the doorway. The world stands still, holding its breath as our eyes meet. The flood of emotions surging through me is overwhelming—anger, confusion, pain, all mingling with a thousand unasked questions. How is she here? Why? Then I notice, in her hands, the Shadow's Heart.

A torrent of memories floods back, each one a piece in the puzzle of betrayal and truths long buried. My mother, whom I had once believed to be a victim of the darkness encroaching upon our world, was actually its architect. And she has brought the Heart here, to raise her army of Eyeless, and destroy everything. The realization hits me like a physical blow, a betrayal that cuts deeper than any blade could.

With every fiber of my being screaming for retribution, I stand, summoning the sword of black shadow, its form a fitting reflection of her darkness that has seeped into the very marrow of my life. I step forward, sword raised, ready to bring an end to the architect of my suffering. My mother's face, a mask of calm, watches me approach. Suddenly I halt, stunned into disbelief. I can only stare as a smile, unsettling and out of place, plays across my mother's lips. The sight of it, so out of place with the gravity of the situation, sparks a fury within me that I struggle to contain.

"Where is my sister," I demand.

"Have you learned nothing since you've been here?" she replies, her words slithering through the air like a snake. But I don't care what she says, unless it is to tell me where Lili is.

With a scream that tears from the depths of my being, I lunge forward, my blade slicing through the air. My mother's smile fades instantly, and her face now bears the imprint of my fury. Her eyes then narrow with an emotion I can't read. Her hands rise in a swift, deliberate motion and hold up the Shadow's Heart. From the Heart, an explosion of energy unfurls like a tempest born from the ether, its force a visible shockwave that ripples through the air.

Time, obedient to the chaos of my heart, slows to a crawl, stretching the moment into an eternity. The scene before me unfolds with haunting grace, as waves of red energy, birthed from my mother's defiance, ripple through the space between us. These undulations move with a deliberate slowness, distorting the air, warping the very fabric of reality around them. Each wave shimmers with a red so deep it borders on the edge of the visible spectrum. The smoke trailing from my blade swirls in complex patterns, dancing like dark spirits as they react to the red energy in the air. The moment my blade meets the first undulating wave of this energy, my resolve is crushed, and the world's suspended breath is released.

Time lurches forward with a violence I've never felt before. The collision is cataclysmic, sending me hurtling backwards. My breath is ripped from my lungs in a desperate, silent gasp as the room blurs into a whirlwind of colors and shapes. I slam against something solid. The impact resonates through my bones and darkness encroaches as stars dance at the edge of my vision. I collapse, gasping for breath. And then, abruptly, the pain vanishes. My body's agony fades, and the throbbing in my head ceases.

Gradually, I muster the courage to open my eyes, discovering the familiar confines of the room replaced by an expansive snowy forest where trees stand as silent guardians amidst the overwhelming quiet. Snowflakes meander from a clouded sky, each making a whisper in this tranquil, icy realm. Leaning against a tree, its bark rough against my back, I feel the cold seep through my clothing and embrace my skin. Despite its mysteriousness, this place is peaceful, and thoughts seem to evade me here. For a fleeting moment, I wonder if this could be the spirit realm. Have I died?

Rising to my feet, the snow under my hands is shockingly cold yet oddly comforting. Despite my unsteady legs, they support me as I take in the forest's vastness. Its silence is profound, punctuated only by an occasional branch creaking or the gentle descent of snow. The forest darkens into a dense maze of white and gray, presenting a landscape that is both mesmerizing and ominous.

I begin to tread forward with steps silent upon the thick snow, leaving a lone path of footprints in my wake. The chill nips at my cheeks and my breath forms fleeting clouds in the frigid air. The world feels as if it's suspended, caught in a breath held just for me. Yet, there's a lingering feeling in the back of my mind. *I am not alone.* A shiver, borne not from the cold but from the sensation that unseen eyes are following my progress, runs through me.

"Who's there?" I call out, my voice resonating stronger than anticipated, cutting through the silence before being softly swallowed by the snow and trees. There's no answer. Yet, despite the absence of a response, the sensation of being watched intensifies. In the haunting silence of the forest, every step feels like an intrusion.

A sudden snap behind me—a twig breaking under an unseen weight—sends a surge of panic through my veins. The towering trees, their branches like twisted arms, seem to sway, casting fleeting shadows that dance at the edge of my vision. I begin to move faster, urging my legs into a desperate shuffle through the snow-blanketed underbrush.

The trees suddenly seem to animate with malevolent intent. Branches twist and reach for me, their wooden fingers grasping at my cloak, tugging at my hair. I dodge and weave, a primal fear lending speed to my steps. Just when I think the forest will consume me, I burst into a clearing and stumble upon a camp that appears as if conjured from thin air. The aggressive pursuit by the trees halts abruptly at the camp's boundary, leaving me panting. Tents, scattered haphazardly, flap wildly in the wind, their shadows dancing on the snow-covered ground. Flurries of snow spiral around, caught in the glow of a fire hidden from view, casting a warm, inviting light that flickers and dances behind the canvas shelters.

The camp's eerie stillness is shattered by a sudden, deep roar, sending a wave of alarm rippling through the air.

This ferocious bellow vibrates with a terrifying force. Accompanying it, the ominous clink of heavy chains grows steadily louder. I venture cautiously past the canvas shelters that dot the encampment, and find myself drawn to a clearing bathed in the ethereal glow of a campfire. The atmosphere here feels charged with a static tension that tugs at the edges of my awareness.

In the center of the clearing, an enormous beast, reminiscent of a black wolf, rears against the constraints of its bondage. Its fur is a dark abyss that seems to swallow the light around it. Dragon-like spikes, cruel and jagged, adorn its head, casting sinister shadows that dance on the ground. Despite its enormity, a sense of hopeful longing seems to radiate from it. The creature's eyes, a fierce and defiant blaze, meet mine, transmitting a silent plea. Thick iron chains anchor this magnificent beast to the earth. Each link resonates with the sound of struggle. The ground around it is scarred from its relentless fight for freedom. Witnessing this, a profound sorrow grips me, stirring a deep, inherent need to liberate this noble creature from its unjust confinement.

I step forward cautiously, feeling an undeniable connection to the chained beast before me. My heart synchronizes with its labored breathing. As I move closer, the atmosphere thickens, and the creature's aggressive growls fade to quiet breaths.

Our eyes meet, and its fierce gaze softens into a silent recognition of my approach. The spikes on its head, once menacing, now retract into its thick fur. Tentatively, I touch the creature's head, surprised by the icy coolness of its fur. Under my touch, the beast calms further, permitting me to rest my head against it. A deep purr emanates from its frame.

"I will set you free," I whisper. Yet, my intentions crumble when my mother emerges from the slender space between the tents.

She is accompanied by two Eyeless creatures, their claws scraping against the snow-dusted ground. Memories flood my mind – the bedroom, the Shadow's Heart, Lili – all coming back in a vivid rush. I instinctively retreat from the beast, which now snarls at my mother, its spikes emerging menacingly from its fur. The Eyeless creatures draw near and skillfully tighten the beast's chains, securing it even closer to the ground. Their actions, precise and habitual, suggest they have repeated this ritual countless times. A question haunts me: how long has this creature been held in bondage here?

A wave of anger surges within me, my hands balling into fists at my sides. The blatant exertion of control and dominance over a being with its own sentient will ignites a deep-seated fury.

"Why?" the single query slips from me angrily, "why are you doing this?" Her eyes move from the beast to lock onto mine, her face betraying nothing.

"I am not doing this, Asha," she begins, her voice steady, "this creature, for all its grandeur, possesses powers that you cannot fathom."

"In other words, you're afraid it will wreak havoc on you and your creatures if let loose?" I scoff, my anger now surging through me.

"Asha, it's not that simple. There are reasons for everything—"

"Reasons? What reasons could possibly justify any of this? You've used the Shadow's Heart to unleash the Eyeless that killed my friends!" Pain cuts deep into my heart as the words leave my mouth.

"Asha, you need to listen to me now." Her words are firm.

"No!" I shout. The sound of twigs breaking behind me is barely perceptible, drowned by the forming pressure in my ears. "I'm done listening to you. You've been lying to me about everything my whole life. About father and about the Shadow's Heart. All you do is lie to me!" I wipe tears from my eyes to clear my vision.

"Asha, please. You need to listen. The Heart, the Eyeless, they're not what you think."

"Yes they are! Amara told me everything. I've seen the order with your signature. You concealed the truth from the world, and you brought this darkness upon me."

Suddenly my mother pulls out the Shadow's Heart from her cloak and holds it in front of her. Fear grips me as I recall the powerful blast of energy that plummeted me into this frozen wasteland. *Had she killed me? Is any of this real?* I reach down to summon my sword from my bracer, but a new fear grips me as my hand only finds my own flesh. I glance down and realize the bracer is gone, lost in the collision of power.

"Have you truly not learned anything? What have you been doing here?" she says. The tension between us is almost like a tangible force clawing at the edge of my sanity.

"What have I been— what are you talking about? Actually, I have learned something. I've learned that you are a pathetic excuse for a mother! You need your Eyeless creatures to do your bidding. What's the matter? You couldn't kill my friends on your own?" The words leave my mouth like shards of glass, cutting through my soul as they leave my body. The enormous beast seems to grow even more aggressive now as it struggles to break free.

"Oh, Asha. You don't understand. These are not my creatures," she says softly, her eyes now seem filled with sorrow, not anger or defiance. "They are yours."

Her words hit me like a physical blow, knocking the breath from my lungs. A twig breaks behind me and I turn around. The Eyeless have now completely encircled the camp, their silent, ominous figures sharply contrasting with the chaotic rage of the beast chained behind me. But its wild struggles and roars seem distant now, like I'm hearing them through water.

I try to process my mother's declaration, each word heavy with a dark, twisted irony. My gaze sweeps over the Eyeless, their clawed feet shuffling quietly in the snow, their faceless heads turned toward me in a grotesque semblance of loyalty. The beast's continued thrashing and snarling in the background becomes a muted soundtrack to my spiraling thoughts. I'm rooted to the spot, my heart pounding, as I try to understand the truth that is unfurling around me like a shadow across my soul. *They are yours.* No. She's just trying to manipulate me like always.

"What is this?" I ask abruptly, whirling back to face my mother. "What lies are you weaving now?" She begins to walk towards me, holding the Shadow's Heart out in front of her.

"Not a lie, Asha. You must face the truth. You cannot avoid it any longer. This artifact represents—"

"Enough!" I snap, fed up with hearing her speak. "I really wish you would just stop talking and do what you came here to do. You want me dead. So do it already." Tears begin to flow from my eyes now. "I have nothing left. Just take my life and go," I murmur, the words barely a whisper. She stares at me for a moment. Her form sinks as if a heavy weight has just landed on her shoulders.

"Then you have failed," she sighs softly.

"Thanks for telling me what I already know. I'm a failure. I have failed everyone I ever loved. Even you. Now stop talking and finish it so I can find peace." I sink to my knees in the snow, utterly defeated and ready for this to end. Without my bracer I have no fight. Even with it, I'm not sure I have any fight left in me. I glance up at the beast, chained to the earth, now lying there in defeat. Something has changed. It's as if this beast is a mirror of my own turmoil.

"If you truly don't see... so be it." My mother raises the Shadow's Heart and red electricity sparks to life across its surface. The air crackles with power. In this fleeting instant, a flood of memories surges through my mind. The echo of Skylar's mirth as she shares Emberwyn's latest tidbits with me. Elias's smile as he steals pieces of my honey loaf in the bakery. The image of Lili's radiant grin and laughter on Nico's shoulders, trying to catch fairies at the Concord. And then, there's Nico, whose kiss had lit up my soul, and his eyes… by the fates, those eyes... These are the moments I will take to the afterlife. The moments that have made me who I am.

Who I am, the words clink together in my mind, forming a moment of clarity that pierces the confusion clouding my mind, revealing a fundamental truth that alters my entire understanding.

My deepest fear was never losing someone I loved. Yes, I feared that, but deep down I feared losing what makes me who I am, amidst my relentless pursuit for the shard. I glance up at the Eyeless lurking around me. They seem more like creations of my own mind in this context, protective constructs designed to smother me; distract me from facing my fear. The more I fought them, the more they intensified. In my relentless crusade against the Eyeless, I inadvertently nourished them with fragments of my soul until they became an overwhelming force. Was it all a diversion? I chuckle softly at the idea, but it seems more real than anything else right now.

I glance up at the beast lying chained to the earth. Not a beast, I think, but a power lying dormant within myself, chained to the earth by the same constructs designed to enslave me. Suddenly, I realize. My mother was never the creator of this darkness. She had been right all along. I am its architect. I am the keeper of this dungeon of my own making, and its iron locks are enforced by the Eyeless.

Then, my mother releases a torrent of red energy from the Shadow's Heart, propelling the Eyeless into a fierce onslaught. The air shivers with the unleashed power, crackling around us in violent waves. Yet, I know now where we are. This is the realm of my soul, and it is not hers to command. Despite the chaos erupting, a profound calm settles within me, an unshakable certainty that this space, this moment, belongs to me.

Lifting my hand, time halts, stretching into an endless expanse where each second unfurls revelations with piercing clarity. I rise from the snow, its crystals glittering like diamonds under the pale moonlight.

Around me, the Eyeless now stand frozen like statues in a tableau of halted ferocity. I walk among these creatures of my own making. Their existence is nothing more than a manifestation of my psyche to hide my fear and enslave my power. *Enslave my power.* I glance up at the beast. The snow beneath my feet crunches softly, the sound oddly loud in the suspended silence.

As I approach the beast, its massive form looms larger, its fur a dark tapestry against the snow, each strand defined and still. The campfire nearby, its flames arrested in mid-dance, casts a warm, golden light, creating shadows that play across the creature's spikes. I can see the rise and fall of its chest, a slow, measured rhythm, the only movement in this paused world. Its eyes, wide and aware, meet mine. Here, in this moment frozen in time, I stand at the crossroads of my past and future, the world of fear I've known and the one of freedom I've yet to create.

"Forgive me," I whisper, my voice a gentle murmur against the backdrop of this silent, frozen world. I kneel down, my fingers gliding through its icy fur, each strand a cold whisper against my skin. "I'm sorry for not finding you sooner." The beast's eyes, deep pools of understanding, hold mine. In their depths, I see not just the beast, but the very essence of my soul, chained to the earth. "You never deserved this. Years of captivity, and it was by my own hand."

Glancing around, I see the Eyeless, frozen in time. My gaze shifts to my mother, the Shadow's Heart clutched in her hands, its crimson energy stilled in this timeless moment. Everything feels surreal, like a painting capturing a single, eternal second of revelation. I turn back to the beast, our eyes locking once more.

"Tonight, I set us free." My hand reaches out, fingers brushing against the cold, massive iron chains that bind the beast. At my touch, a subtle vibration begins — a hum of power that courses through the links. With a loud clink, the shackles unlock, and fall away with an echo that resonates through the halted moment. The sound is not just physical; it's symbolic, a release of the chains that have held me tethered within the realm of my own soul.

As the chains hit the ground, the beast rises, its movements no longer hindered. I feel a surge of power as I stand up, my head barely reaching its shoulder blade. In this moment, the connection between the beast and me is complete, our fates intertwined, our souls no longer chained but soaring free. It is a uniting of power that I have taken far too long to understand. But I am here, and I understand now.

We begin to walk through the suspended time, between the Eyeless. New, radiant white strands of energy begin seeping from around my mother's eyes and the hollows where the Eyeless should see. They have siphoned enough from me—my essence, my soul. Now, it is time to reclaim what is rightfully mine.

I extend my hand before me. These soul-strands drift in the air, ready to be rewoven into the essence of my being. My movements are measured as I walk, each gesture threading the scattered pieces of my spirit back together, breathing life into every strand. The fragmented parts of my essence intertwine, intensifying with every weave. The fear of losing myself, the fear of darkness, even the fear of death, fades in the brilliance. I am Asha, a weaver of souls, and I am no longer afraid.

The white energy performs a ballet in the ether before it seeks out the mark on my forehead, merging with me. The moment the last soul-strand enters me, the beast beside me lets out a roar so profound that it causes reality to shatter around us, breaking into splinters of light. The snowy forest, my mother, and the Eyeless dissolve, merging into a tapestry where the tale of the Soulweaver is written—a story where internal darkness is faced and overpowered by an everlasting, indomitable light.

At that moment, a lone sliver of light, mirroring my own reflection, drifts through the air, carried as effortlessly as a leaf on a gentle breeze. Drawn to it, I extend my hand toward the meandering splinter. The air around it vibrates softly. The moment my fingertip brushes against the shard of light, a sensation unlike any I have felt before courses through me. It is not merely a touch; it is a connection, a communion with the very fractals of reality. But with the wonder comes a sharp sting, a prick on my finger where the light made contact. I pull back reflexively, a drop of blood welling up at the point of contact against the ethereal glow of the shard.

With a slow, deliberate movement, I tilt my finger. The drop, now loosed from its constraints, begins its descent. The slowed time allows each microsecond of the drop's journey to be observed with excruciating clarity. The air seems to thicken, creating an invisible cushion that cradles the drop as it falls, its surface tension holding it together in a perfect sphere.

A strong scent of moss and damp stone reaches my nostrils as the shards of light around me begin to form a new reality. The drop spins gently, rotating in the air as it navigates downward. Each rotation reveals a new facet of its surface in a mesmerizing dance of light and shadow.

And then, with a sound barely louder than a sigh, the droplet makes contact with the cold, unyielding surface of an ancient stone dais. I watch as the dais erupts in a brief, brilliant flare of light the moment the drop meets its surface. As quickly as it blazes to life, the illumination wanes, leaving in its wake the gleaming shard of the Soulweaver's Blade.

"Well, that was easy," Elias quips, breaking the stunned silence, a wry smile touching his lips.

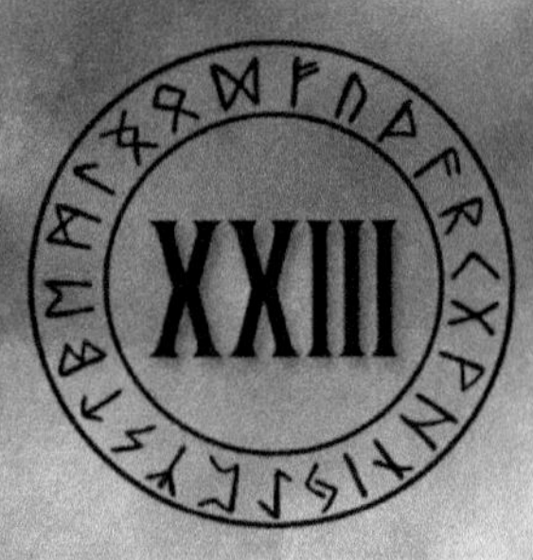

Storm on the Horizon

The full weight of my circumstances crash over me with staggering intensity. This was more than a mere trial; it was a voyage into the realm of my soul to find my fear and liberate myself from its grasp. The ordeal began with a trivial wound, a mere prick on my finger, and concluded in the brief span before a single drop of blood could even begin its descent. I glance up.

Around me, the vibrant, living faces of friends I've mourned, whose loss has haunted my very being, surround me. The realization that their deaths, the relentless chase by the Eyeless, and the grueling journey I've survived were all facets of an intense journey through my soul's realm leaves me breathless. Beneath the surface, a profound anger brews over the manipulation I've endured and the fate that deemed such a trial necessary.

A cry escapes my lips, echoing off the ancient stones, laden with pain, anger, relief, and sheer exhaustion from an ordeal that has challenged every facet of my emotions. My knees buckle and I fall to the ground. I extend my hands, desperate for the physical confirmation of their reality, needing to feel the solidity of those around me, to affirm that they are, against all conceivable odds, alive.

Amidst their urgent pleas to understand what is wrong, in their touch, I find the anchor I have been desperately seeking. I cling to Lili and my friends tightly, the physical connection grounding me until the waves of grief finally begin to subside. Then, amidst the silence that follows the storm of my sobs, a laugh bubbles up from within me. I lift my face to look at them, a smile breaking through my tears.

"We did it," I manage to say between laughs and tears. Their looks of concern now turn into wide grins, and even though I know they don't understand what transpired in that split second, I smile back and wipe the tears from my eyes.

"You should have the honors," Skylar says, looking up at the shard.

The gleaming shard on the dais, a symbol of my triumph and the trials I have endured, catches the light in a way that seems almost alive. I stand, steadying myself with a deep breath. Extending my hand, it lingers above the shard, the surrounding air vibrating with energy. The moment my fingers brush against its surface, a warmth spreads through me. It's as if the shard recognizes me, acknowledges me as its wielder, and in that recognition, I feel a surge of strength. Holding the shard aloft, its light casting radiant patterns on the ancient walls, I turn to my companions.

"We did it!" I declare, my voice resonating across the chamber. Their voices fill the space with celebratory shouts. Even Geraldine, nestled in Thaddeus's embrace, joins in with eager croaks. Thaddeus begins to swing her around in a dance. As the laughter and celebration begins to settle, a sense of completion washes over me.

"Let's go home," I say with a smile. The thought of rest and the comfort of familiar surroundings beckons me. Elias, his arm thrown around Lili's shoulders, nods in agreement.

"I've had enough adventure to last me a lifetime," he declares. *If he only knew*, I think to myself, a wry smile tugging at my lips. The road ahead is certain to be filled with more challenges that Elias would, no doubt, face with the same grumbling enthusiasm, and I find myself longing for it.

"Come now, Beanpole. You'll be begging for another adventure before the week is out. How else will you keep that sharp wit of yours honed?" Thaddeus says, banging his walking stick on Elias's shin.

"Ow, you crazy little old man!" Elias says, rubbing his shin. Thaddeus chuckles. I've missed them so much.

As we exit the chamber, the precious shard of the Soulweaver's blade safely in my possession, I can't help but pause in the doorway and marvel at my friends. The warmth in my heart bubbles over as I watch them proceed down the corridor, their figures illuminated by the dim light. Tears well in my eyes but I wipe them away. Nico lingers at the doorway, allowing the others to pass before turning to envelop me in a tight embrace.

"What happened back there?" His voice is soft. Drawing in a deep breath, I exhale slowly, searching for the words to say.

"Where do I even start?" I whisper. But deep inside, after facing the terrifying visions of his end during my trial, I know exactly where to begin. Rising myself on my toes, I erase the space between us with a kiss. Only this time, I stay a moment longer. As we eventually separate, his smile spreads contagiously, igniting a burst of laughter from within me.

"Come on. Let's catch up with the others," I say with a smile, linking my arm with his as we navigate the musky corridor towards the dusty bedroom. Skylar's reaction upon seeing us arm in arm is instantaneous—a mixture of glee and romantic fervor that manifests in her bouncing on the spot, barely containing her eagerness. She's so overjoyed it sends her into a coughing fit.

"What's gotten into her?" Elias inquires, his curiosity piqued by her animated display. His gaze shifts to us, a knowing smile spreading across his face. "Ah..." he comments, though his expression reveals a flicker of disappointment before he offers a smile. I briefly furrow my brows in response, then let it go. Whatever it is, it can wait.

Lili's small hand finds Nico's in a simple gesture that seems to fill the room with a sense of completeness. Our laughter and light-hearted exchanges create a harmonious melody as we make our way to the palace's main hall. Yet, just before stepping out into the crisp morning air, I hesitate.

"Nico, just a moment," I murmur. I approach Elias, who stands a short distance from Skylar. "Can we talk?" I ask. He agrees, following me to a secluded spot away from prying ears.

"Asha, I..."

"Elias, whatever it is, we can talk about it later," I begin, "I need to get something off my chest. Right after I pricked my finger, the trial started instantly." His gaze, intense and searching, seeks clarity in my statement. "For me, the trial spanned three days." His eyes widen now, a mix of shock and dawning comprehension etching his features. "I... I lost everyone. Skylar was the first," I continue, my voice faltering as the echoes of past screams haunt my mind. "What I'm trying to say is... tell her, Elias."

The shock in his eyes is replaced by understanding. Following my gaze, he turns to Skylar, who stands dreamily gazing out into the mist-shrouded streets of Velloria, leaning against the ancient door frame. When he looks back at me, his smile is tinged with gratitude.

"Thank you, Asha," he says, embracing me briefly.

"But I need to ask, " I say, "why did you summon the Valthorix at the Concord?" The question has haunted me, demanding answers I'm not sure I'm ready to hear. His confusion is immediate.

"What? I didn't," he says, visibly taken aback by my accusation.

"But you told me—" My voice breaks off as the realization hits me like lightning. The confession I remember so vividly never happened; it was a fabrication of my trial. My mind swirls, trying to decipher what is real and what was an illusion. The air thickens with awkward silence and it's Elias who finally shatters it, his voice soft.

"Asha... Skylar is dying." The words slice through my soul. What is he saying? "You remember that sickness she had as a child? It was never a sickness. She was cursed by the Eyeless commander, Bhailer, and it's been eating her from the inside out ever since."

My gaze flickers to Skylar, leaning against the door frame, her body wracked with another fit of coughing, and my heart splinters for her, for Elias, for all of us. This nightmare isn't a trial. This one is real. My mind races back to all the moments of her coughing fits, the fainting, all played off as aftereffects from the cold.

Elias's gaze bores into me as he continues, "The vial I took... it wasn't to summon the Valthorix," he reveals, now whispering, "it was for summoning Bhailar. Thaddeus suggested it was the best chance we had, but Lavinia... she wouldn't allow it. She feared what calling Bhailar might bring upon us. But I had to try. So, Thaddeus gave me permission to 'steal' it."

Elias's confession shatters the last of my doubts, leaving in their wake a resolve as sharp as a blade. He isn't the betrayer I had thought, but a guardian navigating the treacherous divide between light and darkness for the sake of love.

"I couldn't tell anyone, not even you, Asha," he admits. "The risk was too great."

I remember my father once telling me as a child about curses not just binding the soul but entwining it with the fabric of the dark magic that sustains creatures like the Eyeless. If Skylar is truly cursed, it is more than her life at stake; it is her very essence.

"What happened when you met with Bhailar?" My voice cuts through the tension.

He hesitates. His conflict is not just evident in the storm raging in his eyes but also in the way his hands tremble, barely noticeable at first but growing more pronounced as he struggles with his words.

"He refused," he manages to say, his voice breaking under the strain. "Refused, unless..." His voice trails off, faltering as if the very act of voicing his fear is a betrayal in itself, his hands clench into fists at his sides as if to physically hold back the truth.

"Unless what, Elias?" I urge, my heart racing, watching as he seems to fold in on himself, the burden of his next words almost too heavy to bear. Taking a deep breath that does little to steady his shaking frame, he faces me, his confession barely louder than a whisper, as if carried away by the wind.

"Unless I give him the shards." His eyes, wide and tormented, refuse to meet mine, staring at a point just over my shoulder as if the admission is causing him physical pain.

"The shards?" My voice echoes my disbelief, fear, and a new subtle hint of betrayal vying for dominance, while Elias looks as though he's been struck, the color draining from his face.

"I couldn't," he rushes to explain, his voice choked with emotion, tears now freely streaming down his cheeks, tracing lines of raw anguish. "I would never agree to it, Asha." His hands, previously balled into fists, now open in a gesture of helpless desperation, trembling visibly as he reaches towards me but stops short, as if unsure of his right to seek comfort. "I tried to find another way, but Asha... he's merciless. I don't know what to do." His voice cracks on the words, the last vestiges of his composure shattering as he stands broken before me, his spirit shattered by the weight of his choices.

"We'll find another way, Elias. If he won't lift the curse, then we will figure it out."

"I don't think you understand," he says, shaking his head.

"Then tell me, Elias. What don't I understand?" I ask firmly. His eyes shift back and forth at mine.

"I… You will never forgive me for not telling you sooner." He stalls and my frustration grows.

"Elias," I say firmly. He looks at me and rummages through his pockets, eventually pulling out the note Amara had left him. He hands it to me, and I begin to read it silently.

Elias,

There is not much time so I must be swift. Emberwyn has been the home of two ancient lineages. By now, you must already know of the Soulweavers. The second is the Nethyllian Lineage. The hierarchy that controls the Legion. I have gone to much length and trouble, yet have finally uncovered the one within our walls. It is imperative that you protect Asha at all cost. Promise my spirit now, Elias. The name of the one who has infilt—

Suddenly, the ground beneath us shifts and I glance up as a sinister mix of crimson energy and smoke cleaves a vertical line through the air, leaving a rift pulsating with malevolent energy in the center of the room. From this chasm, a figure slowly emerges, its form seeming to form from the world's darkest recesses. Red and black energy swirls and solidifies into a cloak that devours what little light the windows dare to shed. He stands, an entity so vile and feared by the natural world that even the air seems to recoil from his touch.

This is the specter of my vigilance, the hooded figure that has haunted my steps. Bhailar, the Eyeless commander, stands before us, a defiance to the world's order. A primal dread whispers in my soul, evoking tales of Bhailar, whose very name is a curse capable of tearing open the fabric of one's being into a void devoid of light. The air itself seems to bow, the darkness around him writhing in either reverence or terror. Where a face should be, there lies only an abyss, a void as deep and unfathomable as the night sky, yet his unseen gaze bores into us with a weight unbearable, slicing through flesh and spirit without hindrance.

Before we have a chance to respond, his attention sharply turns to Skylar. Out of nowhere, an invisible power ensnares her, yanking her down to the ground. She fights back fiercely, her fingers digging into the earth, trying in vain to resist the force that is hauling her towards the rift. Her scream pierces the air as she's pulled into the void.

"No!" I scream, collapsing to my knees. The hold on Amara's unfinished note slackens, causing it to drift to the ground. Bhailer whirls around, his voice a chilling whisper that winds its way through the air.

"The girl's freedom has expired," he declares, his words a slithering poison. Then he turns, his gaze momentarily landing on Nico before he walks back into the rift, disappearing in the smoke. The silence lingers, the rift remaining ominously open. I consider diving in after her, but then hesitate. No, that must be what he anticipates, the very reason he's left it gaping. A heavy step echoes on the stone, drawing my gaze. Nico walks over to stand beside the open rift, gazing intently into it.

"Nico, no! We don't know what's in there!" I shout. But my fear is turned to confusion as he speaks.

"Well," he mumbles, "that is unfortunate." He turns toward me. My mind reels in a fury of questions, confusion and anger. I jump to my feet, a rage starting to boil inside me as he speaks.

" I have to admit, I don't know how you didn't see this coming. I suppose your quest for the shard blinded you. Which is what I had hoped for, so, well done." He claps his hands slowly then continues, "Here's the truth, Asha. You have your lineage, and I have mine. It's in my blood and there's no escaping it." He now looks at Elias. "Skylar's curse granted her only fifteen years of freedom and her time is up. Time really does fly." I can physically feel the new hatred I have for him festering beneath my skin.

With a scream of rage, Elias rushes forward. Nico raises his hand and a powerful red bolt of energy emits from his palm, slamming into Elias's chest and hurling him into the wall.

"Stop!" I scream, rushing over to Elias. He's alive, but in pain. I stand swiftly and glare at Nico from across the room ready to fight, but my mind flashes to his eyes, his kiss, his touch. I hesitate.

"Unfortunately, Amara," he continues, "she found out about me and my father and threatened to tell your mother. I couldn't let that happen and, well, you know the rest of that story. Which brings me to you, Asha. I knew you were the only one who could unlock the shard in Velloria. I knew I had to push you to it. It wasn't hard, actually. You were always uncertain of what road to take, so reeling you in was easy."

"You killed Amara?" I shout.

"That old hag?" he scoffs. "Before your initiation. It was painless, I promise." He ponders his words for a moment then continues, "So now, unless the three shards are surrendered, Skylar will die, and Emberwyn with everyone in it will remain under Legion control. Which means, it is in your best interest that you relinquish it and bring me the other two before it's too late." He pauses and his gaze softens. "Despite your hatred for me, my love for you remains," he says. But hatred barely scratches the surface of my feelings towards him, and his pathetic attempt at expressing love only stirs a nauseating urge within me.

"How could you betray us like this! Turn against your own home? Against Skylar! How could you betray me, Nico? Me! You love no one but yourself!" I cry out. He takes a step closer with a smugness that makes my skin crawl.

"Look, Asha. You have no idea about my lineage, where I come from, and why I can't afford to care."

"So all of that... your feelings for me... it was all a lie?" My voice quivers, tears now running down my cheeks. How could he do this? He sighs heavily.

"No, not all of it was a lie. I do care about you, about Lili."

"Don't you dare speak her name. You betrayed her. You betrayed me." I glance at Lili, now huddled tightly to Thaddeus, crying. My anger surges and I look back at him, wiping my own tears to clear my vision. I will never forgive him for this.

"Asha, I would love to stay and talk about it, but there's a storm brewing on the horizon, and I need to make my way back to prepare. Let's skip the theatrics. Hand over the shard so I can be on my way."

My pain and hatred begins to crystallize within the depths of my soul, morphing into a formidable beast clawing fervently for release. I draw in a deep, steadying breath, poised to unleash this tempestuous force.

"Actually," I counter, "I have a far more appealing proposition." I thrust my hand forward and the fabric of time doesn't just halt—it trembles, buckling under the force of my command. With a single, decisive gesture, I rend the very fabric of reality beside me, cleaving open a portal of my own, directly to the depths of my soul's domain. Snow erupts from the breach, its whirlwind tossing my braids and spreading an icy chill through the air. From the open rift, the beast I had untethered in the trial steps forward.

Its presence commands the room as it unleashes a roar so powerful that the air warps in submission, sending a cascade of shivers racing down my spine. Nico, suddenly gripped by terror, whirls to flee into the rift at his back. But his efforts are futile, for I am master over time, and the space that stretches between us belongs to me. The atmosphere trembles as I compress the gap between us, yanking him back towards me. I lash out and grab him by the throat.

"Allow me the honor of introducing you to the beast of my soul," I say, "Valkrathos. Valk, to my friends. But to you, know this: her disdain for you is as boundless as the skies." I run my fingers through her icy fur and a small smile plays across my lips as her spikes protrude and she gnashes her teeth near Nico's face. She would claim his head in one snap if I command it.

"Please. Please, Asha—"

"Stifle your speech, traitor!" I thunder, pulling him closer. I now bore into him with relentless fury. "Grovel back to your vile masters bearing my decree. Should I find that their shadows have suffocated my people, and laid chains upon the land that birthed me, then there is no dark crevice in any realm where they can hide that I will not ferret them out. No refuge will spare them from my wrath. I am the tempest who will ravage their shores, and vows to annihilate all traces of their existence. Including yours. You've mistaken me as the last Soulweaver, so let me correct you—I'm the first of my breed." I push him away, and with every ounce of fury coursing through my veins, I unleash a final, defiant surge of energy that culminates in a devastating kick aimed directly at his breastbone. The sound of impact is a sickening crack that echoes through the palace like a thunderclap as my boot connects with an explosion of force. The power behind the blow is so immense that the very air around us vibrates with the echo of fracturing bone. His body hurtles backward into the rift, and as it snaps shut with a sound like the world itself is tearing apart, I catch a brief glimpse of something in his eyes: A flicker of terror and understanding— I am the storm on the horizon.

TO BE CONTINUED...